'From the first page to the precious flicker of the last, *Remember, Remember* is an exquisite read. Meticulously rendered, deeply felt and full of fury, beautiful, tender, and ruthless. Elle Machray has created a novel steeped in history and the depths that love can go to. Machray is going to be a force to be reckoned with' **HANNAH KANER, #1 internationally bestselling author of** *Godkiller*

'Unforgettable ... Will stay with you long after you've finished reading' **STACEY THOMAS, author of** *The Revels*

'*Remember, Remember* weaves together a masterful tapestry of resilience, love, and the pursuit of freedom. It's a novel steeped in so much heartbreak yet so much beauty; a novel so compulsive in its plot yet so meticulous in its exploration of its characters' emotional landscape' **ELVIN MENSAH, author of** *Small Joys*

'Deliciously evocative and atmospheric ... Reminiscent of *The Confessions of Frannie Langton* and *Pandora*, *Remember, Remember* is immaculately researched and powerfully executed; a rousing war cry for justice from the past that feels every bit as urgent today. Machray expertly intertwines the high-stakes history of the era with compelling fiction and a rebellious heroine who gives a voice to the voiceless. The pace is cinematic and the characters pull you into their world with a breathless urgency. It's punctuated with twists you don't see coming; I was utterly gripped until the final explosive page!' **HAYLEY NOLAN, historian and #1 bestselling author of** *Anne Boleyn: 500 Years of Lies*

'*Remember, Remember* is a book we undoubtedly need right now – a rallying call to join the movement of contemplation, compassion, and action. With a setting both luscious and raw, and a defiant female lead, Machray reminds us all of the power we have within' **BRONWYN ELEY, author of the 'Relic' trilogy**

Remember, Remember

Remember, Remember

ELLE MACHRAY

Harper North

HarperNorth
Windmill Green
24 Mount Street
Manchester M2 3NX

A division of
HarperCollins*Publishers*
1 London Bridge Street
London SE1 9GF

www.harpercollins.co.uk

HarperCollins*Publishers*
Macken House, 39/40 Mayor Street Upper
Dublin 1, D01 C9W8

First published by HarperNorth in 2024

1 3 5 7 9 10 8 6 4 2

Copyright © Elle Machray 2024
Dinkus and part title page illustrations: Shutterstock

Elle Machray asserts the moral right to
be identified as the author of this work

A catalogue record for this book
is available from the British Library.

HB ISBN: 978-0-00-855953-3
TPB ISBN: 978-0-00-864110-8

Printed and bound in the UK using 100%
renewable electricity at CPI Group (UK) Ltd, Croydon

This novel is a work of fiction.
Some of the names, characters and incidents portrayed in
it are the work of the author's imagination.

All rights reserved. No part of this publication may be
reproduced, stored in a retrieval system, or transmitted
in any form or by any means, electronic, mechanical,
photocopying, recording or otherwise, without the prior
permission of the publishers.

This book contains FSC™ certified paper and other controlled
sources to ensure responsible forest management.

For more information visit: www.harpercollins.co.uk/green

*For my nan,
thank you*

Historical Note

Four generations after a failed attempt to destroy the British Parliament, an enslaved man, James Somerset, was to be transported from London to a Caribbean plantation.

He refused.

Somerset's case was brought to trial in a time of social unrest. A revolution was brewing in America. Britain was rapidly industrialising, and its streets were fraught with protests against government corruption and unfair working conditions.

He won.

Somerset's rebellion marked the beginning of the end of the transatlantic slave trade, altering the fates of approximately twenty thousand Black people living in Britain at the time and millions across the British Empire.

Though the events in this novel are fictionalised, and some alternative timelines have been used, *Remember, Remember* is inspired by his bravery and countless other tales of resistance.

Prologue

Ranelagh Pleasure Gardens, London, England
4th June 1766

Delphine emerges from the maze.

Thirty feet covered in an hour, the distance navigated in darkness, her thoughts scattered and uncountable as the stars.

She is free. She is tethered.

She escaped. She is devastated.

Delphine lifts her skirts and runs away from the orchestra's bright rhythm, from the masses celebrating the King's birthday, from the girl she left behind in those twisted hedges. Black grass slackens underfoot, now-stolen velvet slippers dampening and sliding on midnight dew.

A firework booms overhead, and she flinches, ducks beneath an exploding cartwheel of red and gold.

It is exactly as they'd planned, except Delphine is alone.

Aside from the two hundred boats crowding the Thames and the acrobats and the fire-breathers and the hot chestnut sellers, the wigged gentlemen dining in the rotunda, the harlots lining the balcony of the China House, the couples twirling between rows of lanterns to Mozart's latest composition. They're all out in celebration of His Royal Highness. Delphine hurries towards the boats, and a firework crackles again.

Though she should have expected it, the sound catches her off guard. Delphine stumbles. The violins quicken, and she glimpses His Majesty waving a stiff farewell to the crowd as she falls, bumping into the back of a woman in a most fashionably wide skirt. Yelping, the woman loses her balance and teeters into a nobleman, who collides into another, triggering a satin and lace-clad sequence of missteps. Delphine backs away as the French horns blare out four triumphant beats before the domino reaches the King.

All Delphine sees next is the tail of a ruby cloak falling into the murky water.

Submerged in glory, he emerges in a fury, shoving away helping hands from his amused wife and shocked King's Guard.

Delphine hastens again, slipping behind an ash tree on the riverbank before a regal roar freezes her in place, silencing the orchestra's crescendo. Dismissing his cooing entourage, His Majesty stamps a damp boot. Demands the event abruptly end. Decrees that no other carriages shall move until he has returned home and threatens to unleash a monarch's wrath on any person, creature or peasant that gets in his way.

An altogether measured response for ruining his birthday.

King George III rides from Ranelagh, and Delphine is trapped.

The waterways are closed, and she must cross the river. Two hundred boats, but none will disobey the King. Her stagecoach leaves in two hours, and the station is four miles from here. Four miles between her and her only ticket out of the city.

This obstacle is not the beginning she was expecting. Already, her bones are tired, weary from anticipation and loss. But she keeps moving, asking every stationary sedan driver and half-sober pedestrian if they know a quicker route. Delphine steels herself against pickpockets and other nefarious night-dwellers as she journeys across London. She will carry on until she's certain the coach has pulled away.

Delphine decided to leave the maze alone. Now, she chooses to race towards an uncertain future, to flee from her masters and inevitable heartbreak.

Part One

Liberty and Progress

Chapter One

Due to popular encouragement, V. 'Freedom Fighter' Mourière and D. 'Quickfoot' Turner will return to the theatre this evening to exhibit the 'Art of Boxing'. With both men's reputations on the circuit eclipsing the celebrity of boxers of yesteryear, the evening's entertainment promises to be the most exciting fight of the season.
—LONDON GAZETTE

Delphine

Theatre Royal, Covent Garden, London
6th May 1770
There are too many hats in Covent Garden. Too many tricornes tilted in the shadows, passing secrets to fluttering lace fans. Delphine hates the sconces, too. The whispers spread through their flames. *You're not welcome here,* they seem to hiss beneath the moonlight. Most evenings, she'd add an extra turn to her journey to avoid the place, but tonight... She traces her fingers over the ticket in her pocket – the smooth parchment and the promise she and her brother made long ago settles her thoughts.

'*Même bête, même lam,*' she whispers, the Patois falling from her tongue like a fading dream. *Same beast, same soul.* A vow to share each other's successes and lighten each other's burdens. Vincent didn't hesitate when he presented Delphine with a pit-entrance ticket for his final match. She had to be here.

But the more pressing question is: how to get in?

Two door bullies guard the Theatre Royal's grander entrance. The red-lipped ladies of the night and stiff-lipped ladies of society drape themselves on wealthy men's arms in near equal attendance. Head bowed, Delphine skirts past them and their jasmine perfumes. The sweet scent is swiftly replaced by sour ale as she glances around the corner, where poorly-tailored shopboys and off-duty traders stagger towards an alleyway.

The passage to the pit?

She turns back to the door bullies and begins asking if this is the correct entrance when a group of gentlemen barge into her, piling silk coats and nivernois in her arms before she can finish her question. It's her own fault, of course. She shouldn't be lingering by the front door if she didn't want to be mistaken for a servant. Now, there are four options. First, Delphine could interrupt their passionate discussion about some radical MP's release from prison and inform the men that she does not work here. They would probably ignore her and carry on their conversation.

Secondly, she could run off with their possessions — the silk is soft as a newborn's skin, the floral embossments rather lovely — and sell them to the nearest peddler. She'd make a few coins, certainly, but would also risk hanging. Not preferable.

Or she could chuck the items on the ground. This would probably get their attention, but then the door bullies would deny her entry for such improper behaviour.

With a resigned purse of the lips, Delphine chooses to say nothing. She wipes her feet before following them into the theatre's glimmering lobby. Passing between two of the four Palladian columns, she cranes her neck over the pile to glimpse golden chandeliers raining light on the gentlemen's coiffed white wigs. Ahead, muscular statues of men she's probably never heard of flank a staircase that flows like a marble waterfall into a pool of ivory tiles.

The men saunter past the stairs towards the bar, another servant deftly scrubbing the muddy trail left behind them. Delphine veers off to the right, briefly admiring a life-size painting of white women dancing unashamedly in a forest and another of two pale red-coated men with long swords drawn, before she reaches the oak-panelled cloakroom. Once her assigned role of portable coat rack has been fulfilled, she'll find a shadow to retreat into, a Black woman invisible once more.

'Odds are on the Freedom Fighter,' one of the cloakroom attendants says as Delphine drops the belongings on the desk, a queue of bored footmen and assistants tapping their boots behind her.

'He's getting on, though,' the older attendant chirps, not looking at her as he dusts off the hats, plucking stray hairs from each one. 'Quickfoot's undefeated this season.'

'Mourière has more to lose – you ever seen him fight when he's down? It's that Carib hoodoodoo, I swear, possesses him. I seen it me self.'

As the younger one hands over the cloakroom stub, Delphine summons all the *hoodoodoo* she has to keep her face blank. Along with invisibility, restrained compliance is another power Delphine's acquired over her one-and-twenty years. Both have been vital for avoiding capture since she escaped enslavement. A stark contrast to her brother, whose boxing prowess has made him one of the most famous Negroes in London.

After discarding the cloakroom stub behind a potted fern, Delphine swipes a tray of champagne flutes from the bar as recompense for her earlier humiliation. If anyone asks, she'll say she's delivering it to her master and his guests. But the barman is disinterested; she points vaguely at some spectators milling past, he nods, and she slips away with her drinks, between rustling skirts and cackling laughter, back through the packed lobby.

She's gambling with her freedom by coming here tonight. If one of Lord Harvey's acquaintances recognises her, they could force her to return to 20 St James's Square. It's not happened so far – her master's guests rarely paid Delphine much attention – but today could be the day. And it is reckless to risk being caught for something as frivolous as stealing champagne.

But these little rebellions, as her mother used to call them, the choices so small, so subversive, that others barely notice them – until it's too late – are everything to Delphine. The threat of the noose has always shadowed her, but she's learned to find light between its threads. These little rebellions are just enough to remind her she is more than her fear. Tray in hand, Delphine rounds the corner to a quiet hallway and lifts two glasses, leaving the rest on an abandoned table. With her back against the wall and a quick glance around, she drains the first glass, then the second, savouring the tartness of the bubbles before re-joining the crowd and heading towards the low hum of the pit.

Vincent

Vincent watches the seconds tick by in his dressing room. The problem with time, he thinks, is there are always too many seconds when you don't want them and never enough when you need them. His right leg bounces against the scratched bench he sits on. It stops. Then, the left leg begins again, repeating the cycle.

Impatient, he groans as he rises before striding to the mirror. Looping his arms behind his head, he mutters words of self-encouragement, hot breaths fogging up the frameless glass. As the mist fades, he says to his outline, 'One more fight.'

Truly, he didn't expect this day to come. Every bruise, broken nose, and coin Vincent has earned has been for this night – his emancipation. The excitement fizzes in his throat. He swallows it back down, afraid it might escape.

Of course, his master hadn't said it would be tonight, but Vincent's worked it all out: the odds, the scales, everything. It is better to arrange his future in advance than rely on Lord Harvey – with his shoddy calculations and tendency to add new conditions to unwritten promises. But there's no changing their contract. His master's terms are filed safely away, set and dried in ink: win your weight in coin, and you'll be free.

Vincent is nineteen pence short.

If he bests today's opponent, it will even give Lord Harvey some change.

He jabs in the air, waking the blood in his tired muscles. All he has to do now is win.

'You're on in two, Mourière,' the match announcer says through the door.

He breathes out, takes another lap around the windowless room, and sighs at the day's mint green livery suit and obnoxiously ruffled shirt hanging from the coat hook. After tonight, he'd like to throw every pastel garment into the Thames.

Although the building is but forty years standing, the Theatre Royal's back rooms have fallen into disrepair. The walls are yellowing and sweat-scented. A plant lies withered beyond recognition on his crooked dressing table, its leaves so curled and brown that he doubts even his herbalist sister could revive it. If he weren't so excited, the dreariness of the place might dampen his mood. It can be easy to let the decay seep into his thoughts when left alone. Often, the worst fights are with himself.

Tentatively, he tucks the ominous plant behind the dressing table mirror, then turns his attention to the floor below. He stoops down, the wood creaking beneath his weight, and lifts a poorly fitted board to reveal his stash: a small tin of lemon bonbons.

These are not just sweets. Delphine used to sneak him a few from Lady Harvey's crystal bowl each Christmas. He hasn't been brave enough to continue her tradition since she escaped. Still, he saved a penny or two from each boxing victory to purchase a tin from the wisteria-fronted confectioners in Berkley Square.

Vincent twists the tin open, releasing a flurry of white powder and a zesty aroma. He pries a sticky bonbon from the bottom and makes an invisible toast to Delphine as he pops it in his mouth, tartness drawing in his cheeks.

If Lord Harvey finds him eating them, he'll undoubtedly accuse him of theft and beat him with the pug-topped cane he clings to – a display of status rather than a necessary crutch.

The bonbons give Vincent courage; one final caning would be worth the risk. Of course, there are other things he could do to feel powerful, but he pushes away the thought – an idea too far beyond a little rebellion.

Delphine

Deep in the pit, Delphine dodges the pull of the spectators jostling their way to the stage. She hoists her skirts over her ankles and laments forgetting her nosegay as she sidesteps an acrid-smelling puddle of vomit and spilt ale. She misses the luxury of the lobby already.

As the wait before the match stretches out, Delphine twists and tears her ticket into a dozen anxious pieces, regretting her decision as they float down to the sticky floorboards. Vincent might have liked it as a keepsake.

Resolving to make up for it, she elbows through the crowd of drunken clerks, artisans, landladies and tradesmen to the bookmaker's table. She passes potters with clay-dusted boots and leather-faced tanners with their unyielding rotting iron odour on her way. Although Delphine doesn't belong to this burgeoning middle-class ensemble, they usually don't make life difficult for her. Only two men and one very tall woman push in front of her before she can hand over a ha'penny to the bookie in exchange for a betting slip and vague good-luck wishes.

A much better memento: the crinkled paper is lined with promise. Vincent has repeatedly said that promise fuels the ring's success. The kind that thousands buy into. Take a chance, fight the odds, wager it all, and maybe you'll find everything you ever hoped for. Which tonight, in Vincent's case, is his freedom.

Delphine's heart lightens when Vincent emerges from the plush crimson curtains on the stage's wings. Looking out to the crowd, he waves with the confidence he deserves but likely isn't feeling.

Clinging to the betting slip in her hands, Delphine wills the four words on the paper to come true:

Vincent Mourière to win.

Vincent

Vincent leans on the wooden post at the edge of the ring and folds his arms over the thick braided rope. It's designed not to hold the fighters in but to keep rowdy onlookers out. The post is dented in the middle and streaked proudly with dried blood — a reminder of how much this could cost. Panic flutters and tight warmth rises in his chest.

'Gentlemen, take your seats,' the announcer calls from the centre of the ring. 'The match is about to commence.'

Vincent eyes up Quickfoot Turner, his opponent. He's much smaller than Vincent's carved, wide frame, but that doesn't make him weaker. Vincent's learned that from experience. The bell's metallic shrill echoes in the fallen silence, and he smiles — a once unreachable dream now within punching distance.

Turner bores straight in and darts across the mat towards him. Turner sweeps tufts of auburn hair off his face and makes the first move — what should be a sharp hit on Vincent's left side.

That's always his opening.

Vincent easily slides his torso away before he strikes back with a blow to Turner's gut. One punch down, he smirks; keep your breath steady.

A hiss escapes Turner's lips as he rebalances himself and slips like a shadow from side to side, as fast as his nickname suggests. When Vincent swings, Turner evades his outstretched arm and whacks the side of his head. It leaves Vincent's ear ringing like the match bell. Turner lunges once more, but Vincent's too slow to react as the redhead showers a burst of punches onto his unguarded chest.

The crowd roars their approval. Turner's been the favourite since the match announcement. Vincent tells himself the cheers are for him. In a rhythm now, Turner strikes again before Vincent can catch his breath. He wallops him in the jaw and jabs his fists into Vincent's cheek. Vincent sucks down the iron taste from his gums. His head fills with smoke, clouding his vision. Another blow, and he's down. Vincent staggers backwards.

'This can't be it,' he says aloud, spitting blood out of the ring.

He blinks away the perspiration burning between his eyelashes and refocuses on his target.

This won't be it.

He leaps forward and lands a hook on the underside of Turner's jaw.

His neck cracks as his head is flung backwards.

Vincent's knuckles glisten beneath the swinging oil lamps. He's still in this. He's going to win. He has to.

Flustered for barely a moment, Turner swipes again. Vincent blocks him with one arm, the other pounding into Turner's face. He strikes repeatedly until Turner gasps for air, and his knee sinks to the floor. Vincent thinks of his lemon bonbons, his little rebellions and Delphine. They power him through hit after hit until Quickfoot Turner collapses face-first into the mat. His body shudders against it as he claws his way back up. Sweat flies from Vincent's forehead as he throws one final blow to his opponent's neck.

He waits a moment, watches, hopes. Turner doesn't get up.

The audience cries for it; those about to lose their bets hurtle obscenities as the seconds trickle down. The announcer re-enters the ring – holds out his arms – and settles the yells from the crowd as he counts down. Ten, nine, eight ...

Nothing. Seven, six, five ... Nothing.

Four, three, two ...

Quickfoot Turner twitches and taps his hand on the mat to admit defeat.

'Mourière wins!'

Vincent's face breaks into an untempered smile, and he punches the air. The crowd roars. Winning a match is one thing, but this is much more. It is a new start.

He searches the pit for his sister, lost in the clamouring darkness. It's no surprise that he can't see her. This year is her fourth spent in hiding. His fourth of meeting her secretly in dark taverns and cemeteries so their master wouldn't discover her.

No longer. With these winnings, they can finally leave London. The next moments pass in flashes. Turner is aided out of the ring.

The theatre empties. Vincent's body cries for ice amid all the rapturous pats on the back from stagehands. Applause follows him to his dressing room, where his triumphant grin fades from his face.

'You are a liar, boy. And a cheat,' his master says. Lord Harvey seems to loom over Vincent despite being a head shorter than him. He uses the silver pug at the top of his cane to push back a few strands of grey-blonde hair that have fallen loose beneath his freshly powdered white wig. Two deep lines cast a shadow between his brows, permanently fixed in place by the lord's most common countenance: repulsion. The very expression he wears now.

'Master, I—'

Lord Harvey's open palm hits Vincent's cheek with a crack. Of all the blows he'd suffered tonight, he did not expect this one. It seems he is about to have his second fight of the night. He folds into himself, cheek burning, and lowers his eyes to the ground.

'A bet for your freedom, you say?' his master spits. 'How convenient.'

'There was a contra...' Vincent tries, but it's useless. The words curdle with nausea in his stomach.

'Indignant, disloyal wretch. You say I offered you freedom, but where is your proof?' Vincent staggers back as the lord thrusts his cane into his chest. 'You have none.' Lord Harvey hits him again. 'None.' And once more, this time landing on a freshly bloomed bruise.

Vincent winces and then forces his body to remain still. Submission is expected of him, but to show pain or discomfort – that is something neither he nor his master can tolerate.

Their eyes meet, any familiarity between them blinded by betrayal. 'I forbid you to speak of this again.'

But Vincent wants to. The sickness builds inside him, rising with something long suppressed: hot, simmering rage. It is always there; Vincent is ever mindful of it, so it doesn't boil over.

'After all I have done for you,' the lord scoffs in disbelief, 'saving you from a fate in the fields.' Harvey begins pacing, no longer looking in Vincent's direction, swinging his cane like a vindictive tutor admonishing a student. Silence lingers, and Vincent pushes down another terrible feeling. Like he is beginning to lose hope.

'I thought you were a breed apart from them, the common Negro. I allowed you to rise! An education, a christening – a future. Not just as some fool boxer to entertain the masses but to be above them. I see now that I was the fool.' He snarls. 'You truly are all the same.'

With cool precision, Harvey unbuttons the length of his navy jacket and removes his embroidered silk waistcoat. He folds them both neatly, methodically, before laying them on the dressing table.

'Here, boy,' he commands.

With clenched fists, Vincent obeys.

Lord Harvey flicks his eyes over to the wall and simply says, 'Hands.' Vincent flattens his palms against the wall, his knuckles bruised from the evening's sorry, hollow victory. He could fight back. He could easily overpower Lord Harvey, but to resist or strike his master would be to raise one man's fist against the Empire.

Vincent's eyes stay fixed on the wall, and he focuses on the small brown cracks in the plaster. The harder he stares, the easier it will be to brace for what's about to come. He's often felt like Sisyphus pushing a boulder up a hill. It is not the first time Lord Harvey has sent him rolling backwards. But it's the first time he truly believed he would reach the top.

The cane lifts from the floor.

'You are not worthy of freedom, beast.'

Vincent will not be crushed under that boulder's weight again. His fury erupts in a scream. He turns from the wall, and after a lifetime of being forced to slump, rises to his full height. At long last, he towers over his master, whose knees buckle at the unprecedented sight before him. Vincent strikes Lord Harvey, desperate and afraid. The blows land in the place you'd expect: his heart. The force sends the lord stumbling back towards the door.

Fire raging in his ears, Vincent charges and pushes the lord again, so hard that his master's head slams into a hook on the coat rack, sending his limp body and Vincent's livery coat to the ground with a calamitous thump.

'Let him go!' cries a voice — Delphine's — as his sister bursts into the room. Had she overheard him ruining their future? She must have thought his situation was dire — by revealing herself to their master, she is risking everything. Vincent sinks to the floor, his body a mass of trembling limbs and gasping breaths. The room seems to pull away from him. Though Delphine is speaking, perhaps taking in the truth of this tragic scene, Vincent cannot hear her. He's barely registering the opening and closing of her mouth. It's as if a swarm of locusts has flooded his ears, his thoughts, his vision.

Lord Harvey lies still on the floor, wigless and with a knot of bloody hair splayed over the hardwood, crimson pooling on a mint jacket. Delphine leans over their master; he thinks she's watching for the rise and fall of his chest.

'Oh no, oh no, oh no,' he cries. Is Harvey breathing? Vincent cannot tell. He is ready to be dragged down through the floorboards and meet his eternal damnation.

Then he feels Delphine heaving him to his feet, gripping his shoulders tighter and tighter until the sharpness of her touch commands his attention.

'He's still alive. We need to get out of here,' she says, and he senses the clarity of a plan behind her eyes.

Delphine holds out her hand, and he takes it. She says, 'We have to go. Now.'

And instead of walking into their freedom, they run for their lives.

Chapter Two

> I should have perceived that I had much more yet to suffer than I had before experienced, and that my troubles had as yet barely commenced.
> —UKAWSAW GRONNIOSAW
> *1705-1775, enslaved 1720-1747*

Delphine

There's a familiarity to fear. The way it spikes Delphine's blood and sharpens her senses. The way it carries her feet, leaving trails of silver footprints behind her.

To be on the run again. To flee through the same deserted alleyways and narrow yards. It triggers a darkness in Delphine that could easily swallow her whole.

So, she focuses on the plan. It is the same as always: to protect her brother. She cannot dwell, cannot think past the next few seconds — the best she can do is keep moving.

It'll be worse than Hell if they find him. He could be hanged.

Or transported back to the colonies.

Throughout their final months in St Lucia, Delphine and her family thought her brother would be sent to England alone. It wasn't until they were saying goodbye that Lord Harvey took Delphine, too. His daughter, an only child in London, was of similar age and would certainly appreciate the gift of a serving girl. He owned her. Delphine had no choice.

And neither did her parents.

But no matter how bitterly she'd wished to stay with them, her existence on the plantation could hardly be called a life. It'd be better if Vincent died on the passage than return.

She blinks away the memory as Vincent says, 'Where do we go now?'

'I've a room at the Temple of... at Marion's,' she pants and stops momentarily, hunching over while her heart slows.

'Is it safe?'

Delphine grimaces between gasps for air.

Months after Delphine's escape at Ranelagh, Marion found her half-starved in an alley and brought her to the Temple of Exoticies, a brothel at 35 Carnaby Street. The bawd gave Delphine new widehooped dresses, food and rest.

Then, she dusted her body with gold and said she'd be worshipped like a goddess with the other girls.

It wasn't long before men began spilling their complaints. They'd paid for wild and alluring, only to be met with Delphine's stiff limbs and absent gaze. The bawd would have kicked her out if Delphine didn't have other skills; she can brew protections and potions like her mother — a midwife and healer — taught her on the plantation. In exchange for ensuring Marion's coffers were full and the nursery empty, Delphine retained her place. The Temple's keeper of house and health. Twice Marion has saved Delphine's life — but the terms for the safety she offers are strange. The kind that only comes from a woman who sells other women's bodies. A balancing act of profit and care that traps the girls working for her in unending cycles of debt.

'It's safe... to start with,' Delphine says. Before long, nowhere in London will be safe for him. She squeezes Vincent's hand, and they are away again, running until they reach the Temple's doors ten minutes later. A redbricked, three-storey establishment in Soho opposite a bustling tavern.

Delphine twists her key in the lock. It isn't yet midnight, but most of the candles are out. A slow evening will not help their cause.

They linger momentarily in the coral-wallpapered hallway, fear leaving Delphine's chest as she breathes in the familiarity of home. In every room, from morning 'til night, they burn their house scent on tin plates: fragrant rose petals harvested from Delphine's window boxes mixed with sweet benzoin oil. It masks the odour from the market at the end of the road and any other foul smells penetrating the halls.

'You've brought a big 'un,' a wispy voice coos from the receiving room.

It's Charity, still dressed in her daywear, a lavish mauve gown that shines against her mahogany skin. The fuchsia ribbons of her corset sway along with her fresh shoulder-length twists as she saunters towards them.

'He's not a cull.' Delphine keeps her voice low. 'He's... my friend.'

'Oh?' Charity pouts. 'Marion won't like that.'

Charity raises an immaculately shaped eyebrow and steps away. Despite her breezy facade, Charity is always the first to sniff trouble and promptly walk in the opposite direction.

Delphine tilts her head in acknowledgement. 'Where is she?'

Charity points a braid towards the cellar.

I can do this, Delphine reminds herself as she crosses the hallway. She clenches and unclenches her jaw with each step to the top of the stairs and calls out, 'Madame? Are you down there?'

Marion bellows from below. 'Delphine, is that you?' The bawd's voice grows louder, her accent three continents whirling in a hurricane. 'It's nearly midnight. If you were any later, I'd have locked you out! Left you to sleep on the streets like a common rat. Get down here!'

'Sorry, madame,' Delphine says, unsure exactly what she's apologising for. She hurries down the uneven steps into the cellar, leaving the door open to retain a sliver of light. At the bottom, she ducks beneath a bowing support beam, her eyes adjusting to the darkness. Only a few tallow candles splutter light across the vast space. The sweet, damp smell from the moss-covered bricks mixes with dust and the woody scent of rum.

Below, she passes cement shelves lined with tankards and broken objects waiting to be fixed: a legless stool, abandoned shoe buckles, bones from old corsets, lidless travel cases, and baskets of kindling and coal.

Marion is mumbling something at the far side of the cellar in a ruby satin dress; a teardrop jewel dangles at the end of her necklace as she inspects the contents of a wooden crate. Half a dozen are piled on either side of her, and as Delphine approaches, she notices the door behind Marion — which leads to the tunnel — is open.

That door is usually locked tight. Tonight, there's a woman in the frame.

It wouldn't be the first time Marion has brought a potential harlot in via this tunnel — entered via the disused alley at Nailer's Yard — but she doesn't look like a typical recruit. With tawny skin and serious eyes, she leans assuredly on one hip.

'I didn't know we were expecting a new girl,' Delphine says as gently as she can. 'Did you need me to set up a room, madame?'

From the withering glance the woman tosses in Delphine's direction and Marion's tutting, she sees she's made a mistake.

'The next shipment'll be in a fortnight,' the woman says, ignoring Delphine. She pushes herself away from the door and adjusts her dark cloak. 'Anything you ken on Lord Blandford wouldnae go unthanked.'

'Of course,' Marion says cordially, bowing her head. Once the woman — clearly one of Marion's smuggling connections and not a prostitute — has disappeared down the tunnel, the bawd straightens.

'Take one of them boxes upstairs if yuh done playing a fool.'

Delphine does as she's told, easily lifting the first open crate from the pile. It's stuffed with rags to keep the contents secure — which could have been anything from stolen Worcester porcelain to cut-price tins of tea. One time, it was a packet of seeds for Delphine's rooftop garden; another time, just a sheet of parchment bearing a postal address. Tonight, it's fruit. A coconut's black eyes and mouth stare up at her, a hairy baby tucked in a dirty cot.

Delphine rarely sees the smuggling firsthand, but it's Marion's preferred method of acquiring and sometimes sending goods. The bawd is halfway up the stairs when an idea strikes Delphine.

'There's someone here to see you, madame.'

'Eh?'

'The boxer, Vincent Mourière.' Delphine conveniently leaves out the words, *my brother.*

Marion's intrigued *hmm* reverberates down the steps before she adds, 'Arrange the fruit then.'

When Delphine emerges from the cellar with the crate, Marion is shaking Vincent's hand in the hallway. 'Ah, Mister Mourière,' she says in a voice usually reserved for genteel company, 'an honour to meet the Freedom Fighter.'

Vincent appears to flinch from his assigned title as the bawd leads him away to the receiving room.

Delphine hastily positions two coconuts, a pineapple, some greenery and other less exotic fruit on the display table by the door. Contraband fruits are a fraction of the cost they'd be if Marion legally purchased them, but still expensive enough that their abundance varies in accordance with the house's footfall.

It has been a good year so far.

From the rainbow of drapes and soft furnishings in each room to bright island-palette outfits worn by the women, everything in the Temple of Exoticies has been carefully chosen to match its vibrant name. It's the only bawdy house in Britain where every harlot is darker than the rum.

Following them into the receiving room, Delphine sees Marion ushering Vincent into an armchair the colour of a perfectly ripe banana. 'Come now, Freedom Fighter.' Her voice takes on a clipped but soothing tone, like the end of a wave hitting the shore. 'You rest here by the fire, young man; we'll find a warm place for you to wet your wick.'

Delphine drags a stool over to join them, then mutters into her stays, 'He's not here for that, madame.'

'Well, whydya bring him here then?' Marion snaps. Vincent jolts back in his seat as the bawd throws herself into the one opposite. 'They outta canary in Kensington?'

Vincent keeps his head bowed as Delphine fills Marion in on the details of the evening. She'd only heard the tail end of his confrontation with Lord Harvey but remembers how tightly their master had always controlled Vincent's movements, much more than he had hers. Male Black servants are a more valuable possession than she could ever be. And Vincent's famous. Lord Harvey will advertise his escape in every newspaper from Hammersmith to Greenwich. If the cash reward for his apprehension isn't enough, he'll send thief-takers after Vincent, too. Lord Harvey won't stop. Every second her brother remains in London makes it less likely he'll make it out. Which brings Delphine to the idea she had in the cellar. And the favour she must ask of Marion.

By the time Delphine's finished, Vincent's hunched forward in his seat, elbows resting on his knees. His eyes are closed, his fingers interlocked as if in prayer. There hadn't been time to ask if this was what he wanted, but now they're here; it feels like the only way forward. They need Marion to convince the smugglers to get Vincent out of the city as soon as possible.

Marion says nothing for a moment and crosses her legs while she thinks. Then she smacks her lips. 'I ain't Queen Marion of the Maroons, girl. It ain't my burden to lead slaves to freedom.'

Vincent folds further into himself, not meeting Delphine's gaze. She should have pulled Marion aside in the cellar and asked then.

Now, her boss feels pressured. The open fire suddenly feels too hot, too close. Delphine angles herself away from it on her stool and leans towards Marion. 'Madame, Marion, please. You've helped people out of worse situations.'

Marion glares at Delphine. 'And they paid me back. You've got nothing but air in those pockets of yours.'

Delphine digs frantically in her pocket to grab the few pennies she won from Vincent's match. Her fingers brush the betting slip: she'll keep that safe and give it to Vincent later. 'It's not much, but take it,' she pleads, thrusting the coins into Marion's hands. 'Sell all my dresses, I'll lose my day off. You wanted to replace the cook? I'll do that too.

You wanted me to sell my potions? Fine. I'll work from dawn to dusk. Please, madame. Get him out.'

Vincent clears his throat. 'And I can work. I'm strong; got a head for numbers. Anything you need.' Though his words come out steady, Délphine sees the tightness in his jaw, the shimmer coating his eyes. They both stare at Marion, a woman who has survived the middle passage, a plantation and life beyond.

The bawd considers their offer while tapping her fingers on the arm of her chair. 'You know, Vincent,' she says after a long pause, 'you remin' me of me late husban'. He were a hardworking man, too.' This is a lie. The girls who knew Albert have often told Delphine that he was lecherous and lazy to his dying day. Marion's voice softens as she leans into her warped memory. 'He freed me, you know? Brought me to England on the right deck of the boat.' The bawd pauses again and thumbs the ruby at the end of her necklace. 'I understand what it mean to be free. If you're true to your word and Delphine do what she say, then I'll see what I can do.'

Vincent's shoulders fall like a cut thread. 'I won't let you down.'

Marion grins. 'Delphine, grab the rum.'

'Thank you,' Delphine says, her voice cracking. She springs up from the stool and lands unsteadily on her feet, momentarily unbalanced as her mountain of worry lifts. Crossing the room to the beetroot-dyed drinks cabinet, Delphine draws out a fingerprint-smeared bottle and three tumblers. As she pours, she tries to push away the feeling they've all but traded one master for another.

'It's a shame you nuh arrive an hour ago,' Marion says to Vincent as Delphine returns to the table, 'I could've sent you with the girl from the tunnels.'

Delphine pours each of them a drink and regrets that she didn't have that idea a few moments earlier.

'The tunnels?' Vincent asks.

'Ha!' Marion chuffs, 'I'd wager from that accent of yours you dun know nothing about real London.'

He shrugs in admission and remains silent. A wise move.

Marion sips her drink, prompting them both to do the same. 'Let me tell you something about this city and its secrets.'

Delphine wraps her feet around one of the stool's legs and leans forward. Marion's about to tell one of her stories, and the bawd's as famed for them as she is for seduction.

She begins slowly, her words soft and enticing like a feather gliding over skin. 'Dem say this city is thousands of years old. Conquered and damaged and rebuilt so many times, there must be hundreds of tunnels hidden beneath these streets — maybe thousands. But we forget, bury our past under bricks and mortar, and them tunnels go with it. Most we leave to the duppy. But some…' she says, her voice a shade above a whisper, '… we still use.'

'Oh?' Vincent says, masking his intrigue with another gulp of rum. '*Mmhm*,' Marion says, glossing her lips with her tongue. 'Some we use for running water, others for pleasure, streetwalking whores fucked against crumbling wet walls. However, there's also a more noble group.'

Marion flashes Vincent a coy smile like she shouldn't be telling him this, which only makes him draw closer.

It seems even the fire has ceased crackling to listen.

'Few know where they're based. Dem only trade with the ones dem think worthy.' She winks. 'With the rebels and rabble-rousers and with me, a foreign woman tryna make a name for herself. But they don't expect no coin in return.'

'A poor business endeavour,' Vincent chuckles.

'You're wrong about that,' Marion shakes her head. 'There's more to be earned in this city than money. Wealth can buy a tapestry, but power is choosing threads for the loom. Steal or swap one, and the whole picture changes.'

'So, these people. They smuggle goods in exchange for what?' Vincent asks, frowning. 'Surely you pay them with something?'

'With secrets, Freedom Fighter,' Marion says, tossing back the rest of her drink. 'Because a shilling will always be a shilling, but secrets you can weave into gold.'

'And what secret will you give them to help me?'

'If I tell you that,' Marion says, a flicker of amusement lighting up her eyes as she rises from her chair, 'it won't be much of a secret, will it?'

They all laugh then, even Delphine. The evening has turned out as well as it could have. Her brother is safe for now. The rum's dulled her fears; tomorrow, they'll figure out more of a plan.

With a yawn, Marion stretches out her arms and says, 'Delphine will prepare a cot for you in the cellar. Goodnight.'

As Marion treads up the stairs, they sit in contented silence. Delphine is grateful for this moment of peace with Vincent. Thankful she can take in the way the fire gently lights the side of his face. But the second they hear the bawd's chamber door shut upstairs, Vincent's foot starts to tap an anxious rhythm.

'What's wrong?' Delphine says.

'I can't ask you to do this,' Vincent says, bolting from the armchair. A weary shadow has formed over his eyes, and he envelops himself, crossing his arms over his chest. His words are muffled into his shirt sleeves, but Delphine hears them clearly: 'I can't stay.'

Chapter Three

I was born in slavery, but I received from nature the soul of a freeman.

—TOUSSAINT L'OUVERTURE
1743-1803, enslaved 1743-1776

Vincent
Harvey Plantation, St Lucia
Hurricane Season, 1757

Vincent leans against a palm tree. One hand is balanced on the trunk, the other held in a salute over his brow, shielding his eyes from the bright sun. He scans the beach, still damp from an earlier downpour, and sees no footprints. With no messages to deliver in town, he's been searching along the shore, his face wet from tears and sea spray.

It's been three nights since he last saw his mama. He hugged her goodbye near the waterfall and returned home to their cabin, but his mama didn't come back at all. Thinking about it makes his stomach ache like he's swallowed lousy water. He is asking himself for the hundredth time where she could be when a rustling noise pulls his attention away from the coastline. It might only be the wind, but he follows it, batting pink-fingered shrubs and yellow hibiscus from his path. He runs, the sand morphing into the forest floor beneath his feet. He jumps over bits of fallen branches and rocks, praying he's headed in the right direction. Then, a small something — a small someone — runs head to chest, straight into him.

'Watch where you headed,' Vincent says, shrugging the small thing off him. He's not normally so rude, but it's been a bad day. The girl flops to the ground with a dramatic thud, her basket of herbs tumbling into the grass.

'You daft fool,' she says with a scowl, sounding like she grown. She can't be more than seven or eight. It's her four braids that give her away, the cowrie shells threaded at the ends peeking out beneath a too-big straw hat. It's the same sun-bleached colour of her dress.

'Why get in the way like that?'

She swings her legs around, kneeling in the grass, and begins gathering the long green fronds and fire-coloured flowers that fell out of her basket.

'You the one in my way,' Vincent claps back. He glances behind her in case someone else is following her, in case it's his mama. When no one does come, the heaviness returns to his chest and disheartened; he slumps down beside her to help. 'What kinda pick'nee goes saying daft fool?'

'Someone with brains bigger than you,' she says, snatching a flower from Vincent's hands. He decides she's what his mama would call *upty*.

The girl cocks her head, her scowl fading as her eyes search his face.

'You Abigail's boy?' She asks like she's been reading his thoughts. Vincent stares at her.

Even though there aren't many kids on the plantation, he's not seen this girl around. The couple of kids he does know, he doesn't know well – they spend their days in the cutting or weed-pulling gangs. Vincent is a messenger instead.

When they ask him why he gets an easy job, he tells them it's only 'cause his mama's a free Carib. His daddy was a slave, and that makes Vincent a slave, too, but his mama says it won't always be that way. He doesn't tell the others that though, because he doesn't believe it.

Maybe the girl just want to hear that story. Or maybe she know where his mama is.

'Might be,' he says, cautiously replacing the last fronds in her basket. 'Who are you?'

'Name's Delphine. My mama sent me to find you.' She puts her hand over his, and before Vincent can ask why, she smiles and says in that odd grown way, 'Don't fret, boy, I'm here to help.'

Neither of them knows just how much he is going to need it.

The Temple Of Exoticies, Soho
6th May 1770

'What?' Delphine croaks.

In her eyes, Vincent sees the weight of the world reflected back at him. He knows all too well what his sister is feeling from her shoulders, held a fraction too stiff.

Pressure.

It's all he ever feels, too.

He wants to tell her he's grateful for all she's done. For helping him flee, for Marion, for the smugglers. For being his sister ever since his mother abandoned him.

It wasn't unusual for Abigail to spend the night away from Vincent. Until the night of the gathering, he'd sleep soundly while she was away, confident she'd return to make his runny eggs in the morning. She was always a loving mother and, though they had little, generous with her time and affection.

But in the weeks before she left, Abigail had been acting strangely, disappearing for longer during the day and lavishing her son with gifts on her return. She brought colourful beads for his cornrows, a new woollen blanket and hand-carved wooden toys. He never thought to ask where they were from. Now, he assumes they were to lighten her guilt at leaving him behind.

It was months before he gave up his search. Years before he stopped seeing his mother around every corner, in every dream, every shadow.

Their neighbours supposed that, since she was a free woman, she had simply had enough of living among slaves.

Vincent never blamed her for leaving. Evidently, she'd felt the pressure, too. And when Delphine's family took him in, he was too grief-stricken to thank them.

He wants to say all this to Delphine. But the words don't come up. They sit in shame, a heavy stone in the pit of his stomach. He unfolds his arms and paces between the chair and the fireplace. 'If I stay and they find us, you know what will happen.'

Every moment he spends here increases the risk they're both caught. If he's dragged to the gallows, he'll find a way to make peace with it, but he wouldn't forgive himself if they took her as well.

His mama was free, and it was his birth that trapped her on the plantation. He felt no guilt about this as a child, but he's old enough now. There's no way he can stay here and trap Delphine, too.

Delphine stares at him as if she can't believe he'd say that. 'I made my choice the second I entered that dressing room. And Marion knows what she's doing. Trust her.' She seems to mean, *trust me*.

Of course Vincent trusts his sister. But Marion? She is a stranger to him, and as much as he enjoyed her story, smugglers aren't like Robin Hood. What's to stop them arranging his passage one day and then selling his whereabouts the next?

'I know you both want to do the right thing,' he says, in case interested ears are still listening, 'but the safest option is for me to leave.'

'Then I'll come with you.'

'No. Delphine, you have a life here.'

Delphine scoffs. 'Some life.'

Vincent wants to deny it, but looking about the receiving room, he finds little evidence of a life Delphine would wish for. The thriving roses beneath the windows are his sister's handiwork, but the crudely painted urns? The gaudy furnishings? It's a caricature of how he imagines white men view the Caribbean – a place for pleasure and business but not a home.

Maybe if they leave now, it would be enough of a head start on the slavecatchers or whichever brutes come after him.

'You'd really come?' he asks, placing his hands on her shoulders.

They're trembling more than he'd realised.

She looks up at him sharply. 'That was always the plan. Tonight changes nothing for me.'

They could be in Somerset in a week if they make it out of the city. He's fantasised about living there since he accompanied Lord Harvey on a business trip to Bristol two years ago. When they passed through the county's sprawling orchards and meandering rivers, for the first time in ages, the storms of his mind settled, soothing him like petrichor: he was home. Yesterday, he was more than a hundred pounds richer in that dream. In tonight's version, he has a sweat-stained shirt and a target on his back. But at least there's still Delphine.

'Même bête, même pwel,' he says — same beast, same hair — his half of their promise.

He bows his forehead to Delphine's as she replies, 'Même bête, même lam.' They keep their heads pressed together for a moment before Delphine breaks away.

'Food.' She nods. 'We'll need food.' It's her turn to pace now. 'Also, water. Are you injured from the match?' Her eyes dart from his face to his shoulders to his fists. 'I've a yarrow-honey salve for cuts and arnica for bruises?'

'Yes to all of it, but quickly. I'll get some bread and a couple of flasks.'

'In the kitchen.' Delphine points to the hallway behind her. 'There's a bread box by the oven, flasks in the first drawer on your way in.' Vincent heads in that direction as Delphine turns for the stairs. 'I'll grab my trunk,' Delphine says. 'I know somewhere we can sell the dresses I've paid off. And if they fit, I'll grab a few seed packets, some candles, and maybe a blanket, some soap and my physick garden book, too.'

An odd assortment, he thinks, but then remembers Delphine has done this before — he was the one who bought the tickets for her escape.

'Five minutes,' he says. 'Can you manage that?'

'Easily.' Delphine's hand glides along the railings as she runs up the stairs. 'Go to the kitchen. I'll see you in two.'

Vincent follows Delphine's directions and quickly locates the bread bin. He is beginning to feel excited and hungry, too. He grabs a loaf of bread, and is picking up a second when a thunderous crash reverberates from the street outside, followed by a thud.

The front door has been kicked down. Somehow, he'd known this was coming.

'Mourière!' an unknown voice roars from the entrance as heavy footsteps file into the Temple. Is that four or five men? 'He's here, lads, I can feel it. Mourière, you dog, come out!'

Torn between finding some hiding place in the kitchen and facing his pursuers, Vincent realises he can do neither: his feet are stuck as if his boots are nailed to the stone floor. For now, he remains unseen – but there is only the receiving room and two doors between him and the intruders.

'What are you doing in my house?' Marion bellows from above. If she's afraid, there's no audible trace of it. 'I've paid my protection. Leave!'

'Don't move,' shouts one of the men, 'don't you bloody move!' And though the words sound no closer, Vincent hears something else, like rattling on a belt, something metal and lethal being unhooked. 'Where's the boxer?'

There's a smash of what sounds like breaking pottery, followed by a series of rolling thuds on the hallway floor.

Vincent winces. This is precisely what he'd feared.

He's caused enough trouble tonight. For Delphine, for Marion, for everyone. Continuing to hide will only make it worse.

'Through here!' he calls out, raising his hands behind his head. Better to alert them to his presence than risk surprising them. Time seems to skew as he urges himself forward, the future he envisaged rapidly fading with each slow step. 'I'm coming out.'

Before he reaches the door, there's a clatter of approaching shoes around the corner, and four Runners in navy uniform lunge into the kitchen. With the ferocity of wolves cornering their prey, they set upon him. Three have flintlock pistols dangling from their belts. The fourth's gun is drawn and aimed squarely at him.

'Not so strong are you now, eh, Freedom Fighter?' one spits as they force him to the ground. White heat burns beneath his armpits as they yank his arms behind his back, tying them together with fraying rope.

Keep it in, he tells himself as their nails dig into his underarms and drag him into the hallway, across the splintering hardwood.

'Stop!' Delphine shouts. Vincent looks up to see her running down the stairs and rushing towards the Runners. 'Stop! He's not resisting!'

Vincent opens his mouth to yell at her to *be still, please, there's a gun*. But one of the men knocks her out of the way, letting out a taunting laugh as she lands on the floor near the smashed fruit bowl. It seemed to take less strength than batting away a fly.

'Don't touch her!' Vincent yells, his eyes meeting Delphine's, bright with tears. 'It's me you're after. Leave everyone else.'

'A noble runaway, are ya?' the man chuckles, returning to loom over Vincent. 'Never heard the like. Not of a mind to hear it now neither.' He drives his boot into Vincent's side, and Vincent grunts. The blow landed on a bruise Turner had given him, and the pain is both sharp and lingering.

Despite the hurt, Vincent heard the man. He called him a runaway. Not assailant or violent criminal – just runaway. Did Lord Harvey not tell them of the assault? Will they take him to St James's Square then, not Tyburn? Vincent's unsure which fate is worse. He doesn't want to find out.

Vincent struggles as two men attempt to haul him to the doorway, thrashing his legs and ripping his elbows back, but they cling to him tighter. Their fingers drain the colour from his skin, bone white, then piercing red; soon, it'll be battered black. They only pause to make him watch as the others revel in destruction.

One by one, the brutes send those uncouth vases hurtling to the floor. Delphine wails, but Marion is motionless. Her expression, the cold, hard fury of someone resigned to their fate. A woman who knows she can only rebuild if she's still breathing. With a heave, the leader kicks the door open, and they drag him towards an open-backed cart — one used for transporting criminals. *Why didn't I fight harder against them?* he cries silently. The cobblestones feel like ice on his ankles. For almost twenty-six years, he has endured every insult and obeyed every command. For nearly twenty-six years, he has resisted the urge to rebel against his master. *Why did I ruin everything?*

But these questions are futile. The damage is done. There's only one way he can get out of this now. Only one way he can survive the lord's wrath. And it involves pinning his hopes on his master's nephew. 'Delphine!' he gasps again, stars fluttering across his vision.

The men are hoisting him onto the back of the cart; Delphine runs into the street after him. A whip cracks, and in the second before he's taken away, he meets his sister's terrified gaze. 'Get Nick!'

Chapter Four

TO BE SOLD
A pretty little Negro boy, about nine years old and well limb'd. If not disposed of, is to be sent to the West Indies in six days' time. He is to be seen at the Dolphin Tavern on Tower Street.
—DAILY ADVERTISER

Delphine
Get Nick.

Vincent's words repeat in Delphine's mind as she hurries towards New Palace Yard.

They were all she could think of last night as she swept up the broken pottery and scrubbed the bawdy house floor. She'd wanted to chase after the Runners or the Night's Watch, whichever louts Lord Harvey had sent after her brother, but Marion had pulled her back by the fichu, tearing the lace, and hissed at her to not be such a fool. Not until she'd cleaned up the carnage first and ensured the Temple was ready to open for worship.

It has been ten hours since then. The sun should be approaching its midday high, but the clouds hold its rays captive. The rest of London moves about its day with a steady hum: men carrying sedan chairs or rolling barrels without breaking a sweat, women chortling along the pavement with floppy-eared dogs. A skeletal boy in shorts that don't reach his knees searches the gutter for bits of food or coin. Delphine pushes the heel of bread Charity insisted she take with her into his hands. A morning without food is less likely to hurt her.

Passing under the chessboard tower as Charing Cross merges into Whitehall, Delphine slows her strides and sinks into the crowds, reminding herself for the thousandth time not to rush. Some well-meaning clerk will ask where she runs from. A good citizen will grab her arm, unbidden, and enquire where her master is. They will accuse her of fleeing when she tells them she has none. There may be thousands of Negroes in London, but barely any of those are free women. Then they will see her gold mantua, and although it is thirdhand and the fabric dulled, they will still accuse her of stealing – which is punishable by transportation. Or death. So, she carefully adjusts her pace to match the realities of her presence.

Get Nick, she thinks again as Parliament looms into view. Why Nick? Not Nicholas, or Mister Lyons or the master's nephew, but Nick. There's a familiarity between them Vincent has not shared with her. Doesn't he share everything with her?

The Nicholas she knew had been fond enough of her brother, but she wouldn't have called them close. He was rarely invited to St James's Square – allegedly, his mother disgraced the family name by marrying a commoner. As if to make up for the infrequency of his visits, Nicholas would hand Vincent whichever dull philosopher's work he was studying and demand Vincent read passages aloud. Then, after Nicholas graduated from Oxford and inherited his father's parliamentary seat as the Member for Kettering, he needed help organising the family's modest estate. In a rare act of civility, Lord Harvey loaned Vincent to him for a while. To Delphine, it seemed Nicholas had only been intrigued by the novelty of a literate Negro. Any praise he offered Vincent was functional as if he was reviewing a sheet of parchment's ability to absorb ink. Why on Earth does Vincent believe he'd help him now?

And why wouldn't he turn Delphine over to his uncle? The thought stills her on the pavestones. Attending the match was a calculated risk, but after last night, there is no way she'd be received with forgiveness. Vincent earned his freedom and was offered the cane – what's more, it had often seemed to Delphine that Lord Harvey *liked* her brother. The same could not be said for her. She raises a hand to her chest and takes two deep breaths. The man behind grumbles and pushes past her; the string of dead rabbits he's carrying grazes her elbow.

Vincent might not have had time to carefully consider his words, but there was only one Nick he could have been referring to. For now, she'll do as he asked. But she'll need to decide whether or not to trust Nicholas on her own.

On the corner where Parliament Street meets the bridge, Delphine passes the slaughterhouse, and her stomach turns. The reek of the carcasses rises with the warmth of the late-spring day. She fumbles in her pocket for something to mask the smell but finds only crumbs and the bit of cloth that had wrapped the bread. It will have to do in place of a nosegay.

Thankfully, the stench recedes as she makes it to New Palace Yard. One side is lined with carriages, another with traders hawking everything from hot baked apples and oysters at twelve pence a pot to bags of coal and matchboxes.

Delphine lingers near the river, taking in the looming Palace of Westminster: the dozens of statues carved into its towers, medieval windows lining its many halls, and the ivy neatly trained to run up the Privy Garden walls.

Then, the abbey bells ring midday, and the great doors of Westminster Hall swing open. A swarm of gentlemen exit, more closely resembling jostling schoolboys than respected dignitaries of the British Empire.

Other than slight variations in gait or tailcoat colour, they all look remarkably similar: wrinkled and rich, pale and pompous.

But Mister Lyons is among the easiest to spot, twenty years younger than most and wearing a sapphire jacket. He's pursuing a group of ministers who seem as eager to escape him as Delphine was to flee the slaughterhouse.

'Gentlemen,' Nicholas cries, frantically waving his hat after them. 'Gentlemen, I implore you to hear reason!' He almost stumbles over a box of timber as he follows the men towards their carriages.

'What I failed to explain in session...' he pants, his desperation evident. 'If you'd only consider...'

They're halfway across the yard now, and Delphine leaves her spot near the water to follow. She's almost right behind them when a pinch-faced minister turns and curses at Nicholas.

Mister Lyons stills like the statues on the tower, one arm frozen in the air.

Delphine stops, too, half concerned, half amused.

'Mister Lyons,' she says in her most demure voice. She walks over to him and politely folds her hands together in front of her.

Nicholas doesn't notice her. His gaze is fixed on the ministers laughing at him. They disappear into their carriages, and his spine slumps, defeated.

'Mister Lyons?' She tries speaking a little louder. Nothing.

'Nicholas!'

At last, he startles, and Delphine witnesses a transformational shift in his appearance. First, his furrowed brow relaxes into something that could only be described as befuddlement. Then, he replaces his hat, a wide grin drawing across his face.

'Delphine,' Nicholas says, coolly extending a hand as though she hadn't been missing for almost four years. 'I'd heard you were on a grand tour of the underworld.'

'Mister Lyons,' she says again, but nothing follows. The weight of the morning is suddenly closing in on her. Tears prick at her eyes, not only for Vincent and the fact he was supposed to start a new life today, but also for herself and Nicholas' indifference towards her alleged fate.

But she pulls herself together, not because she feels better but because she must.

For Vincent.

'As you see, sir, I am not dead,' she says, hoping the quiver in her voice is imperceptible. 'But if I may, I'd like to request your help with something.'

Nicholas' smile grows. 'Well, now! How may I assist you, most pleasant ghost?'

'It's Vincent,' she says, and Nicholas seems to pale. 'He may become one.'

Inside the packed coffee house, conversations bubble like water on a stove. Delphine catches snippets from where Nicholas has left her, a table wedged in a nook of the sconce-lit room. Balding white men are sitting spread-legged along their benches. The ceiling is streaked yellow from constant puffs of tobacco smoke, its earthiness swirling with the coffee's nutty, invigorating smell. Other men hunch over parchment in solitary booths, their white coffee cups interspersed between quills and ink pots. Having never set foot in such an establishment before — as much through lack of desire as lack of coin — Delphine watches the scene with fascination as Nicholas places their order.

'Just look at the front page of today's *Chronicle*,' says one of the men on the next table. 'It's flagrant. Those crooks the King entertains will attempt to remove any member of the Commons they dislike.'

'And to change our electoral rights without so much as a vote!' another says, wiping steam from his glasses. 'Abhorrent is the word the paper used, was it not?'

The first man passes him the broadsheet, and the second jabs at words on the page. 'Abhorrent... vice-ridden... impotent. I have a few more, but—'

'Mark me,' the first cuts in, 'we've not seen a season as discordant as this since the civil war. I'm loath to admit it, but Wilkes was right. We must seek reformation before they—'

'Gentlemen,' the third warns, cocking his head in Delphine's direction. 'Pray lower your voices.'

They huddle in closer so she can no longer overhear.

She leans back in her chair, marvelling at how they openly criticise the King and government and talk as though they can change things. Oh, to be a voting man. If she said the same, they'd call it treason. Though Delphine's yet to receive her coffee, she swallows a bitter taste.

When Nicholas returns to the table, he's followed by a server in white overalls, who throws Delphine a glance so frigid it could freeze the sun before laying down their cups.

'Am I even allowed to be here?' she asks Nicholas when the server has gone.

'Allowed? Of course!' he says, dropping three sugar lumps into his drink. 'There are no rules formally forbidding women from coffee houses. The question is, will you be welcomed here?' He pauses for a moment, stirring his drink with a rose-handled spoon. 'Let us say there is a difference between what is permissible and what is done.' He taps the spoon on the side of the cup with a *tink* before replacing it on the saucer, then winks. 'But so long as you behave yourself, you'll fare well enough.'

Delphine clenches her jaw. She won't rise to his distasteful jest, at least not if he can help her brother. She cuts straight to the point. 'And if Vincent were to call on his master's nephew for aid, would that be permissible?'

'Well, that would depend on a variety of factors,' Nicholas begins, but then his mouth snaps shut, and his eyes widen. 'His freedom!' he exclaims and beats his forehead with the base of his palm. Delphine shrinks back in her chair. 'God dammit.' His jaw tightens. 'His final match was supposed to be last night, wasn't it? What happened?'

Surprised, she asks, 'You know about the deal with Lord Harvey?'

'I do,' Nicholas says more calmly. 'A year or so ago, we met at a tavern, and he asked me for some advice about the contract.'

'What about the contract, exactly?'

'Put simply, the legality of it.' Nicholas wraps his hands around his coffee cup, drinks, and then replaces it on the saucer. 'I'm no expert on our country's slave laws, contradictory as they are, but I do know a thing or two about contracts.'

Delphine assumes that to be true. He studied law at Oxford, and Vincent once told her he'd been admitted to the bar two years earlier than the usual age.

Nicholas continues, counting each point on his fingers. 'I told him to keep track of the dates and times he received his winnings, the location they were stored, when and how much he gave to my uncle, as well as noting every farthing he was allowed to retain possession of.'

'And it was legal?' she asks.

The walnut wall clock behind them announces quarter to one, and many of the men rise from their tables with a grumble, presumably to return to their working days.

'As far as I'm aware, yes,' Nicholas says, raising his voice over the commotion. 'Against my better judgement, I did ask my uncle if I could view the terms, but he declined, and I didn't push.'

Delphine wants to press the issue, but Nicholas turns up his palms. 'It wasn't my place. I'm not Vincent's lawyer, and after all, he is a slave.' The way he says this is so matter-of-fact. Like there is nothing else Vincent could ever be. Unsure how to respond, Delphine takes her first sip of coffee, wondering if Nicholas ever considers its true cost.

'But last night,' he says again. 'What happened? Did he lose the match?' Delphine recounts the events of the last twelve hours, pausing every so often to check that none of the coffee house's other customers are listening in. For now, she omits the part where Vincent struck Lord Harvey. In her experience, men like Nicholas tend not to give people like her brother the benefit of the doubt.

When she's finished, Nicholas remains silent for a while. He tilts his head to the side like he's been offered tickets to a visiting circus and can't decide if he's curious enough to part with his coin. But if there's anything she remembers about Nicholas, he must always have a cause. She hopes that this one will tug at his heartstrings. His brows knit together like the tip of the circus tent from Delphine's imagination, and a few seconds later, he says:

'Well.'

Delphine is confused. 'Well?' she parrots.

'Well,' he says again, thumping his hands on the table so loudly it startles the server passing their table. 'There's only one thing for it. We'll have to pay a visit to St James's.'

Delphine is confused, and stunned.

'What?' Delphine says, more sharply than she'd intended. 'I can't go there.'

Now it's Nicholas' turn to look baffled. He digs around in his pocket before scattering a few coins on the table. 'Whyever not?'

She doesn't know where to begin with this man. It's not just because she's a runaway that she's spent four years avoiding the place. There are too many memories in that house she wants to forget. Because contrary to logic and reason, her most painful memories of 20 St James's Square are also the fondest. Of the girl who once made living there bearable, but who is now lost to her forever.

But if Nicholas knew about those, there is no chance he'd help her. So, instead, she states the obvious. 'Because, like Vincent,' she chokes out, 'I am a slave.'

Nicholas' mouth slackens. He blinks once, twice, three times before he speaks again. 'Delphine, do you remember what I said about the difference between what is permissible and what is done?'

'Yes,' she says, unsure where this is going.

Mister Lyons's next words come out slowly and cautiously. 'You sit before me, a runaway slave declared deceased. My uncle claimed your insurance almost four years ago. Did you know that?'

Delphine nods. Vincent had told her.

'Had that not happened, from a purely legal standpoint, I ought to have returned you to him. As I said, Britain's slavery laws are complicated — so much so that there's not even a committed agreement on whether slavery is enforceable on British shores, but that's an entirely different conversation. My point is that although they are complicated, they are clear on this. You cannot enslave the legally dead.'

Nicholas finishes his coffee, his eyebrows raising expectantly behind the cup's rim.

Delphine's mouth hangs open. Did she hear him correctly? Is he saying she's free? Could that possibly be true? All these years she's spent hiding in a brothel. She could have tried to build a life outside the shadows, become a nurse or an herbalist – maybe even allowed herself to fall in love again. She can't begin to imagine what it would have been like. To have had all this time without the constant fear of losing everything.

As if sensing that she is overwhelmed, Nicholas reaches a hand across the table, pushing the coins to one side. When she doesn't take it, he says, 'That's why I'm relatively certain he won't recapture you. If worst comes to worst, we can always threaten my uncle with insurance fraud charges.' He scoffs. 'He can pay off any fine, of course, but he'd do anything to avoid that. Nothing spooks Lord Reginald Harvey IV like embarrassment of the family name.'

All this time. Delphine is still shaking her head in disbelief. It is the best and worst news she has ever received.

'Why?' is the only thing she can think to say. 'Why do you want to go to St James's Square?'

'So I can explain to my uncle, nicely, that he is in breach of contract,' says Nicholas. 'He must release Vincent.'

'You think that will work?' Delphine can't see Lord Harvey changing course so easily. And even if he admitted Vincent was no longer his slave, what then? Might he change his mind, and turn Vincent in for assault instead?

'Like I said, pride is my uncle's fatal flaw,' says Nicholas. 'If what he is doing is illegal, which I believe it is, he won't want his friends at the House of Lords to find out. He won't like it, but if I promise my silence in exchange for Vincent's freedom, I think it might just work. He will keep his honour intact at all costs.'

Delphine considers her options. If Nicholas' theory is correct, Lord Harvey's vanity might just keep Vincent out of prison.

And even if it doesn't, a free man's sentence for Vincent's crime would be lighter than a slave's. It would be worth almost anything if Nicholas could persuade the lord to free Vincent.

She's tempted to agree to his plan.

But she's yet to ask him her most burning question.

'And why do you want to help Vincent? Why help either of us?'

Nicholas huffs out a laugh. 'Because Vincent is a good man. A rare friend who helped me through a great number of scrapes.' His voice wavers, but he seems to shake it off. 'And, to quote Montesquieu: *a truly virtuous man would come to the aid of the most distant stranger as quickly as to his own friend.* So what kind of man would I be if I did not at least attempt to help?' This is certainly not the same boy she knew growing up. Men like Nicholas are hard to measure – their words are often prettier than their actions – but she thinks she's beginning to see why Vincent asked her to find him.

'Thank you,' Delphine says. 'Thank you for saying that.'

'Your thanks is appreciated but not necessary.' Nicholas beams, rising from his seat and buttoning his waistcoat. 'Shall we?'

Despite the fluttering in her belly, Delphine decides: 'Yes.'

Chapter Five

> Constant experience shows us that every man invested with power is apt to abuse it and to carry his authority as far as it will go.
>
> —BARON DE MONTESQUIEU

How different Delphine's world is in one fall of the moon. She'd dreamed of spending today journeying towards the West Country meadows and woodlands with Vincent. Instead, she's walking beneath the trees of Mayfair with a man she scarcely knows en route to visiting the man she detests.

White gravel crunches underfoot as Nicholas leads them up the long diagonal path that cuts through St James's Park. The magnolias are in full bloom, spring's last pink blossoms curling on the branches. It is undeniably pleasant in Mayfair. At least for those who have the luxury of leisure time. Among the flirting swallows and courting couples on their chaperoned strolls, Delphine and Nicholas must seem an awkward pair. Silence stands like a stranger between them. After years of distance and a lifetime of difference, this is no surprise.

While Nicholas looks pleadingly to the clouds that drift overhead as if accusing them of carrying away all topics of conversation, Delphine considers the possible outcomes of their talk with Lord Harvey. For Vincent, it could be freedom, prison, or continued enslavement. And for Delphine? Nicholas was *reasonably* sure Lord Harvey would not be able to reclaim her. But *reasonably* would not suffice.

She could tell Nicholas she's changed her mind. Ask him to go in without her. But if she does that, how can she trust that he will report back faithfully on what was said? If Nicholas is Vincent's only hope, she needs to know if she can trust him. She needs to be in the room where the conversation happens.

'I have a plan,' she says abruptly, 'for what to do if things go wrong in there.'

Nicholas makes an appreciative *hmm* sound, and they step onto Pall Mall. They look up the bustling, broad street, then down, before crossing between the carriages. 'Most sensible. Do tell.'

'I know that house well enough to get out if I need to. All I need is to be closer to a door than he is.' *And to pray that his age and yesterday's fall have slowed Lord Harvey down enough that he can't catch me.*

Nicholas guffaws. 'That's hardly a plan!'

She wants to scowl at him; in fact, she is scowling, and he's just noticed. To Delphine's surprise, instead of reprimanding her, he looks chastened. 'That's not the whole plan,' she says.

'Apologies.' He clears his throat. 'Please go on.'

'If I cannot run away,' she says, 'or if someone catches me, then I shall strike a bargain with the lord instead.' She weighs up how much of this next part to reveal to Nicholas. 'My... employer provides services to people with secrets. Those secrets are more valuable than I am.'

As she speaks this last sentence, Nicholas makes a vaguely disapproving noise, but she ignores him. It is a simple fact. Regardless of whatever uncomfortable grimaces Mister Lyons makes, thousands of Negroes are sold every day for no more than the price of a plough horse. Delphine just hopes Marion's claim — *secrets you can weave into gold* — is also true.

'I know what I'm doing,' Delphine says, choosing not to expend her energy reassuring him. 'Vincent trusts in our abilities. Do you?'

'I...' He hesitates. 'I do. And if you *do* make a run for it, I shall try my utmost to aid your getaway. Perhaps I'll restrain my uncle, or trip him up, or distract him with an interesting piece of trivia.' Delphine cannot tell if he is joking, but then his tone becomes serious. 'I highly doubt it will come to that,' he says. 'Logic and the law are on our side.'

Delphine swallows, then reluctantly meets his gaze. 'And I can trust you?'

With not a hint of mockery, Nicholas places his hand on his heart. 'I would never lead you into harm's way.'

'Good.' Delphine sounds more assertive than she feels. Already, her knees are shaking — and the last time a member of the Harvey family said *that* to her, it turned out to be a lie.

They round a corner, and the iron-railed central garden of St James's Square comes into view. The square is almost exactly as she remembers. Two new houses have been erected, but other than that, it's as though no time has passed — like her life didn't irrevocably change here.

Blood thrums from her wrist to her temples as they approach the door to number twenty. The house stands proud like a Kingsman, with three stories, a white brick facade, and nine superciliously arched windows.

Stepping to the rapid rhythm of her pulse, Delphine tells herself *it is all right to be afraid*. Her fear is a warning, but she won't let it hold her back now. Not if doing this means she and her brother may be free of Lord Harvey once and for all.

'Pigging 'eck!'

Hetty, the Harveys's cook, stands in the doorway. Her rosy cheeks paled the instant she saw Delphine. 'Good god,' she cries, 'Not here, spirit, not today! I beg you!'

'Hetty,' Delphine tries to calm the woman, grabbing her wrinkled hands and pulling her closer. 'Hetty, mark me I am no spirit!' It's no use. The cook trembles, like flour shaking through a sieve. 'Hetty, please, it's me, little Delphine.'

But Hetty is still cowering, and Nicholas valiantly steps in.

'Come now, woman. Can a spirit touch you as if it were flesh?' He gestures to Delphine's hands on hers. 'Don't these feel warm and living? Not cold and dead?'

Hetty whimpers for a moment more before the terror recedes from her eyes, replaced by fury.

'How dare you show your face here again!' Hetty scolds, cheeks regaining their colour, sparse eyebrows raised. 'Four years I've mourned your loss. You run off like a scamp. Let everyone think you're dead. Then you suddenly reappear?' She flings her hands up, making them flash like fireworks. 'On the *front* doorstep, might I add! If you weren't so big, you'd be in for the hidin' of your life! And not just from the master.'

Despite the cook's rage, Delphine fights back a smile. This tirade is more or less the welcome she'd envisaged. When she worked under Hetty, the cook often threatened all sorts of punishments for her slightest of misdemeanours. But Delphine knew that no matter what she'd done, the cook would never whack her with her rolling pin. Hetty always had an eggshell temper but a melted butter heart.

She's wrong about one thing, though: Delphine never faked her death. The only fraudster here is Lord Harvey.

Delphine glances at Nicholas and catches his eye. He is covering his mouth with a closed fist and tapping his foot. She can't tell if he's impatient or amused.

'I'll tell you now, little D,' the cook says, pursing her lips and adjusting her flour-dusted apron. 'There's no job going if that's what you're after. But, but...' She deflates and pulls Delphine into a bone-crushing, soul-refilling hug. 'By Christ, I'm glad to see you.'

It unsettles her that Hetty used the word *job* as if Delphine had applied for the position of house slave – but Hetty works so many extra unpaid hours herself, she may well see it that way.

In any case, it's no exaggeration that Delphine would rather die than work here again.

Abruptly, Nicholas jostles past them into the hallway. 'That's enough for now, Hetty,' he says. 'We have important business to attend to with my uncle.'

Reluctantly breaking away from Hetty, Delphine resists the urge to scowl at Nicholas for a second time. She's grateful he's so eager to help Vincent, but you can tell a lot about a person by how they treat their staff.'

Hetty stands aside to let her pass, and now, Delphine swallows a dry crumb of nerves. The doorway is so wide it could fit a lady dressed in the most extravagant of hooped petticoats. Her foot hovers over the threshold before she takes her first step inside.

The interior is unchanged: the hallway is painted brilliant white, with matching wainscoting. It's thrice the size of her chambers at the Exoticies. The floor is still lined with swirling white and grey marble, which is so pristine that it reflects the heavenly fresco of dancing cherubs on the ceiling. The familiarity of it all sets Delphine's heart thumping again.

Hetty curtseys to Nicholas, although he's already halfway up the stairs and no longer looking at her. She pats Delphine gently on the arm and whispers, 'Be careful, little D.' Then, she disappears back towards the kitchen.

'Slow down!' Delphine calls out to Nicholas, running up the stairs until she has caught up with him. She clings to the banister as they approach Lord Harvey's study, bracing for her next challenge. Before reaching the office, they must climb another flight, but first, they'll pass through a corridor lined with six oil paintings. She thought she'd never see these artworks again and remembers one of them all too well. She's not sure she could face seeing it alone.

As they turn into the corridor, she focuses on placing one foot in front of the other. First, they pass a hilly landscape painting of the family's Malvern estate. The next four are austere portraits of each preceding Harvey generation: the lord's great-grandfather, a navy merchant; his grandfather, an admiral; his father, another admiral. Three steps later, the portrait-perfect lord himself appears. Delphine wavers as she passes it. Reaching the final painting, she forces herself to look up, to come face to face with a ghost.

The sixth piece depicts a girl captured at seventeen, posing with her hands folded across her ample middle in a salmon satin dress. Delphine remembers how violently the sitter hated the gown, clawing it off the moment her sitting ended. But instead of her discomfort, the painter had captured the softness in those heavy-lidded grey eyes and rosebud lips. The girl wears a necklace strung with the celestial gems she was named for: Pearl.

In another life, Delphine steadied those hands after Pearl ran tear-stricken to her bedroom. In another life, Delphine felt those tears become her own as their cheeks drew closer, then their lips. In another life, Delphine saw that same sincerity painted in Pearl's eyes when she stood before this very portrait and told Delphine that her father, Lord Harvey, had ordered her to marry. She begged Delphine to run away with her.

Then, at Ranelagh, Pearl decided love was no substitute for luxury and Delphine escaped alone. Their vows to each other were broken, and Pearl married a baron. As Delphine grieved the love she'd lost, word came she'd need to mourn Pearl's death, too.

'Are you quite well?' Nicholas calls down from the floor above. His mousy hair falls over his eyes as he leans over the railings.

Delphine blinks up at him. 'Many memories here.'

Nicholas nods once, and his hair bounces. 'It won't do to dwell,' he says and vanishes again.

She dashes up the final flight of stairs after him, and they remain silent until they reach the white double doors to the lord's study. 'You're certain?' Nicholas says, hands hovering over the brass handles.

'Yes,' Delphine says, her voice barely audible.

Nicholas pushes open the doors, revealing the room Delphine hates most in all of London. Previous generations used this grandiose space as a second drawing room, but the current master of the house prefers it for his sole use. The high, domed ceiling features a fresco depicting each of the four seasons, and the walls are papered in navy damask.

Lord Harvey sits at the far end, sealing letters behind a hulking mahogany desk. He seems to have recovered quickly from yesterday's events, but Delphine spies the outline of a bandage at the base of his neck. The dark circles beneath his eyes are evident even from across the room. The lord's mouth twitches as they enter, but he doesn't look up.

Be strong, she thinks. *He cannot keep you this time.* Nicholas clears his throat. 'Uncle?'

Lord Harvey doesn't react; calmly, he reaches for another letter to seal. 'My *lord*,' Nicholas tries again.

The lord clicks his tongue, blows on the hot wax, and sets the envelope aside. His eyes are still fixed on the desk.

'*Mister* Lyons,' he says without moving. Nicholas flinches at his condescending tone.

Delphine's chest tightens. She should open her mouth to speak, assert her place, try to break the tension building in the room, but she also knows that if she does, it might be the last thing she ever says. So, instead, she balls her fists and waits.

Having recomposed himself, Nicholas attempts conversation once more. 'Uncle, what is this I have heard about Vincent? Is he well? May I see him?'

The lord finally looks up. He notices Nicholas first. Then, his gaze settles on Delphine and flares with rage. He presses his lips into a thin line, considering his following words.

'You know,' Lord Harvey begins, his eyes boring into Delphine's as if Nicholas hadn't spoken, 'I received correspondence from an acquaintance in Jamaica not long ago. He told me of the most comedic method for punishing runaway slaves. I would try it now, girl, but alas, I have no limes to hand.'

Delphine opens her mouth to reply, but she can't. The menace in his words has turned every object in the room into a threat. She can feel it all: the sharp, red pain in her gut from the stab of a letter opener; the crunch of her windpipe beneath the clawed foot of the Chippendale sopha; her world turned black by the blunt weight of the bronze door stopper. The phantom blows build in her ribcage until she releases one frightened breath.

'Come now,' Nicholas cautions his uncle, moving into the space between him and Delphine. 'It is Vincent we are here to discuss. You and I both know he has earned his freedom and—'

'Let's not talk of Vincent, Nicholas.' Lord Harvey is playing with the candle he was using to heat his sealing wax, passing one finger back and forth through the orange flame. 'Not when more of my property has returned.'

'She is not your property,' Nicholas says crossly, 'not anymore. I am here with Miss...' he seems to search his mind for a surname he has never cared to learn, then powers on, 'Miss Delphine to act as Vincent's advocates. Now, if you'll just be reasonable—'

'Reasonable?' Lord Harvey slams his hand on the desk so violently the candle splutters out. The shock sends both Delphine and Nicholas staggering back.

'What would be reasonable, I wonder?' The lord turns to Delphine and smirks. 'To sell you at the merchant hall or trade you for some good quality Madeira? Then again,' he smiles wryly as he elevates himself from the seat, 'I doubt you'd be worth the seller's fees. I wasted enough coin in the week we spent searching for you.'

Delphine's mouth goes dry. Four years she'd been hiding, and he'd stopped looking after seven days. She knew the lord didn't think much of her, but never has he made her feel quite so pathetic.

'Vincent, on the other hand,' Lord Harvey says, casting his eyes towards one of the cabinets in the corner of the room, 'will fetch a fine price.'

Delphine grips her fists tighter, pulse throbbing in each knuckle. Of all the punishments she'd feared for Vincent, transportation was the worst.

'You can't be serious,' says Nicholas.

'Oh yes,' Lord Harvey says restlessly, 'I've grown tired of the boxing game. And you'd be surprised what plantation owners will pay for an athletic, young buck. Care to guess how much, Delphine?'

All she can manage is a shake of the head.

The lord strides towards her with a snarl, but Nicholas leaps between them again.

'That's far enough!' he cries, throwing out both arms as a human barricade. 'Bloody hellhounds, Uncle. I was hoping it wouldn't come to this. Just release Vincent to me immediately, or—'

'Or what?' Lord Harvey spits, slapping Nicholas' hand away. 'You'll take this to the courts? Ask them to release my property to *you?* A man with no title, barely a penny, and no claim. Never forget that I can make your life much harder, Lyons.'

Nicholas' arms drop to his sides. With his back turned to her, Delphine cannot see his expression.

'Vincent will be on the Atlantic before the week is out,' Lord Harvey hisses, close to Nicholas' face. 'Sooner, if you don't leave now.'

It's over, Delphine thinks, eyeing the door. What had she expected, coming here? That when Nicholas threatened his uncle, he wouldn't retaliate? A low-born lawyer cannot afford to make an enemy of a wealthy lord. Nicholas will back down now. She will run for her life again, and Vincent will be lost.

'No, Uncle.'

Delphine blinks. Cautiously, she drags her eyes away from her escape route to Nicholas.

'You cannot bully your way out of this. You may have ostracised my mother and hated my father. But you are not above the law. It is illegal to sell a slave on English shores.' Amazingly, Nicholas sounds like he believes it.

'Tell that to the African Company of Merchants!' Lord Harvey snorts. 'You are as delusional as your parents were. The realities of the world do not change simply because you stamp your foot, nephew.'

But there's a crack in Lord Harvey's porcelain veneer. It's clear that what Nicholas has just said — *it is illegal to sell a slave on English shores* — has caused the lord to doubt himself. She had never seen her master rattled before. Does that mean it's true?

Observing for the first time the twitch in Lord Harvey's creased temple, the preoccupation in his tired eyes, Delphine realises something. This man has become almost mythic in her mind. The inescapable antagonist of her nightmares.

And yet.

He is only a man.

And it is from this fragility that she draws strength. Nicholas stamping his foot may not change the world, but perhaps her words might. Delphine draws in a breath, preparing herself to do something she has never dared before: talk back.

'If you will not release Vincent.' She swallows. 'Then we will release the truth.'

Both men turn to her, open-mouthed.

'You filed an insurance claim knowing I was alive. That was fraud. And selling Vincent would be a crime, too.' Delphine rolls her shoulders back, a self-assured gesture she's borrowed from Marion. 'If this went to trial... You know what they'd say at Westminster.'

'You,' Lord Harvey growls, curling a finger at her, then at Nicholas. 'You think anyone will believe *you*? A runaway Negress and a galumphing blunderbuss from the *midlands*?' That sneer widens. 'Everyone will see you for what you are — a harlot — slippery as Eden's serpent.'

A harlot she might have been, once. But the lord can't know that, and she won't let him see his banal insult aimed true.

'And yet,' Delphine half-smiles, 'you are the one filled with venom.'

The lord looks like he might explode, and Delphine relishes in her candour.

Then Harvey opens his mouth, a torrent of abuse gushing forth. Words and phrases so vile that Nicholas backs away from his uncle towards her as if he can shield her from it. But Delphine has heard worse.

For a heartbeat, Delphine wishes she could kill Lord Harvey. Simply end her and Vincent's pain by ending his life.

But that impulse didn't serve her brother well.

And if what Nicholas says is true, there might be another way. 'We are going, Nicholas,' she says, cutting off the lord mid-sentence. There's no telling what Lord Harvey might do if they push him too far. 'I am walking out of this room, and so are you.' Her knees threaten to buckle beneath her skirts, but her voice is steady and clear. 'You have no power to stop us seeking justice. And believe us now, my lord. Heed us when we speak. You will not get away with this.'

Chapter Six

> A Negro serving girl who had been many years in her master's service has been resold into perpetual bondage and shipped to Jamaica for £80 colonial currency. It has been reported that 'when she put her feet into the fatal boat at Lamplighter's Hall, her tears ran down her face like rain'.
> —BRISTOL JOURNAL

'What do you mean we can't board?' Delphine taps her foot against the warehouse floor, disturbing the dust below. Her ears are flooded with the noise of the docks: the rhythmic sawing of wood, clatters of metal against stone, and haunting sea shanties from a nearby tavern.

Three days ago, Delphine's hunch that Vincent was being held on the *Ann and Mary* proved correct. Nicholas immediately filed two injunctions: the first to visit Vincent and the second to prohibit the ship from setting sail. Two days ago, both requests were granted. So, Delphine has been mentally preparing for a trip to the docks for the last day and a half. No small task, given that the *Ann and Mary* is the same vessel that brought her to this country. This place will only ever remind her of seasickness and longing for home.

'See here, August,' Nicholas says, digging around his jacket pocket for the court documents. 'I have permission from the High Court.'

August Grey, a broad man with a barnacle-grey beard, lifts a hand to draw an invisible circle around his rough-skinned face. 'Only authority here is the captain,' he says to Nicholas. 'And you'll win no friends here with that sort of informality, Mister Lyons.'

Outside, barrels thud as they roll over stone — heavy with cocoa, cane, or another ill-gotten good on its way to increase Lord Harvey's fortune. They'll be sold for six times the price Marion pays the smugglers.

'Apologies, Captain Grey,' Nicholas says, 'but as you know, my family owns this ship.' He stands a little straighter as though looking down on the man may encourage him to change his mind.

'Your *uncle* owns this ship,' Captain Grey corrects, without malice. 'And if you needed a bit of parchment from the court to let you on, I doubt he wants you here.'

'Please, Captain?' Delphine says, stepping into his eyeline with purpose. 'We'll be no trouble. We only wish to enquire after my brother's health.'

'Oh aye?' The captain smiles as though Delphine has said something amusing and pushes off the pile of cotton bales he was leaning against to face her. Grey takes a second to steady himself, as if unmoored on land after a lifetime at sea. *'No trouble,* she says. Only, the way I remember it, Trouble is your middle name.'

Trouble? Delphine peers closer at the man and his sun-weathered eyes. The beard, she now realises, is new. As is the title of Captain. But the way he calls her *Trouble,* with that teasing northern lilt, is the same as the day they met.

She was at Castries Harbour in St Lucia, eleven years old and distraught. Earlier that day, she'd been ripped from her father's arms as her mother fell to her knees, begging Lord Harvey not to take away her only daughter. The lord had looked on, indifferent, as her mother keened and keened.

It was Grey who tried to calm Delphine when they first threw her and Vincent on the ship. He introduced himself as Grool — an affectionate nickname the crew had constructed from *Grey* and *Liverpool* — and wrapped her in a rough blanket on a day far too hot to need one. Then he patted her on the shoulder, called her *Trouble,* and joked that she'd best quieten down lest one of the grumpier sailors throw her overboard.

'I remember,' Delphine says, willing herself back into the present.

Grey raises a bushy eyebrow. 'So don't think me unkind when I say I can't help you.'

It didn't feel like kindness at the time – not in the way Captain Grey seems to be remembering it.

But if he believes he helped her once…

'Can you not do me one more kindness, Captain Grool?'

He answers by shoving them out the door.

'Well, that's that then,' Nicholas huffs, kicking a stone towards the water. Delphine follows its path until it's lost beneath the two-dozen mud-flecked boots, trudging amid hooves and cartwheels along the narrow riverbank.

A fleet of dark clouds is sailing their way, threatening to dampen Delphine's mood further. With a well-practised effort, she locks away each intruding emotion. 'What can we do?'

'I'm thinking,' Nicholas says.

Delphine is, too. Thinking of how badly Harvey's men may have hurt Vincent. What will happen if his wounds are left to fester? What if he… What if they… What if, what if, what if? The only certainty is her fears won't abate by remaining still.

'We can't leave him on there,' she says. Without waiting for Nicholas, Delphine turns on her heels and heads for the ship.

She makes it three steps, before—

'Wait!' Nicholas yells, yanking her back the second before a canopied wagon hurtles past. Spinning her towards him, he places his hands on her shoulders. 'Just. Wait,' he insists. 'This is a legal matter. And though I'm hardly a model of impulse control, is there a need for such hysterics?'

Delphine says through her teeth, 'Does the captain truly have more authority than the court?'

'Laws between land and sea are complicated,' he says. 'But ultimately, yes. We're committing piracy if we board the *Ann and Mary* without the captain's permission. I'd quite like to keep my neck, wouldn't you?'

'Piracy?' Delphine regards the myriad ships bobbing along the dock with renewed interest – maybe a pirate could give her better advice than Nicholas. 'What is the value of a court order if the captain can overrule it?'

'As I say, the law is complicated.'

Delphine's temper rises like a flag on a mast. 'You keep saying that, yet you don't explain how.'

'Delphine, men who've studied law for years struggle with its complexity. Forgive me if I don't produce a chalkboard and write out the Responsible Shipowner's Act for you now.'

Usually, she tries harder to mask her discontent, but if Nicholas is truly her ally, maybe she shouldn't need to. 'Did you mean it when you said we are to address each other as friends?'

'You may speak plainly, yes,' Nicholas glances sideways at her, suspicious.

Delphine meets his glance with a glower. 'Then, Mister Lyons… If we don't stop thinking and do something in the next thirty seconds… I'm afraid I'll have no choice but to unleash the full extent of my *hysteria*.'

His eyebrows arch in surprise – she, too, is aware her current expression is rarely worn by a friend – but he seems to shrug it off. 'Please, do not scream,' he says. 'I only meant that recklessness gets people killed. Or transported across oceans with no way of getting them back.' He buries his hands in his pockets. 'As I said before, there is a difference between what is permissible and what is done. If the ship were to set sail, yes, they'd be breaking the law, but ultimately, the Crown isn't going to pursue a ship for the return of one slave.'

It was a depressing statement but one she could have predicted. 'So, what do we do?'

'We go through the justice system,' Nicholas says, his tone determined. 'Secure a writ of habeas corpus that forces Captain Grey and my uncle to surrender Vincent into court custody.'

'And then what?'

'And then, there will likely be a trial. Not only will I need to persuade the court Vincent cannot be transported from England, but I'll also do my best to convince them he should be freed. No doubt my uncle will play the wounded party, and it'll be for me to prove otherwise. This could be a landmark case.' His eyes widen, charged with intellectual zeal. 'How far can a master's authority go on English soil?' he murmurs, almost to himself. Then, his gaze shifts from Delphine into what seems like an explosion of thought.

To bring him back, Delphine asks, 'You'd do that for Vincent?'

Nicholas blinks, then nods. 'I'll do what is right.'

Delphine forces a smile. She wants to believe him. But faith in Nicholas alone won't save Vincent.

Can she believe in everything Nicholas is proposing, too? That the law can save her brother. That the ship won't set sail, that the courts will hear the case, that Nicholas can win, that Lord Harvey won't do something terrible to stop him. So many elements of his plan rely on things outside of her control.

But what is the alternative? To break Vincent out? Condemn him to a life on the run, like hers? Vincent doesn't want that. So she can't want it either.

Despite her every impulse not to, she chooses to believe. 'When do we start?'

Nicholas' eyes crease with gratitude, further fuelling Delphine's suspicion that people do not often agree with his plans. He pulls a palm-sized notebook, a tiny ink pot, and a quill from his coat pocket.

For the first time today, Delphine could laugh. Only *he* would carry around such things on his person.

'Come to my residence north of Clerkenwell in a fortnight, and I'll have made progress.' Holding the parchment to the nearest wall, he deftly balances the open pot of ink between two fingers, scrawls down his address, and hands it over. 'Until then – don't cause any trouble, *Trouble.*'

No trouble in a whole fortnight? For a clever man, Nicholas can be most naïve.

Chapter Seven

Did I consider myself an European, I might say my suffering were great: but when I compare my lot with that of most of my countrymen, I regard myself as a particular favourite of heaven.

—OLAUDAH EQUIANO
1745-1797, enslaved 1756-1766

Vincent

Trapped aboard the *Ann and Mary*, Vincent chokes on fetid air. With each gentle rock of the vessel, voyages-old urine drips down into his cell from the pissdale on deck. Every time the ship moves, ammonia catches in his throat. Every time the vessel steadies, his nostrils are filled with another browner smell – like curdled milk in bitter, over-stewed tea.

It has been several days since then.

He has not got used to it. He still dreams that he won't have to. But that dream drifts further away with each new tide.

It's not all bad, the kinder voice in his head tells him. At least they have given him a hammock, so he is raised above the splintered floor.

At least the hammock is sturdy, the tears competently patched over. There's a slitted window facing the dock, and a couple of rats he's grown to regard as pleasant company. He'd had a heated exchange with the large black one that bit him in the night, but now they all seem to have come to an amicable understanding.

How has it come to this? he laments in a darker moment, wincing as he throws his palms flat to the ship's wall. He pushes his forehead so hard into the wood he hopes to be able to emerge like a ghost on the other side. *How did I let it come to this?* It is all his fault. Perhaps they wouldn't have found him if he'd run when he could. Indeed, if he hadn't pushed his master, he wouldn't be here, on a shit-stinking ship bound for a life back in chains. That is where he'll be headed, they said – back to some plantation thousands of miles away.

Maybe he deserves it.

The transportation. The beatings. The rat-infested solitude. Maybe he deserves all of it – for dreaming he could ever be more.

For even thinking he could be anyone at all.

When the thugs dragged Vincent across the Carnaby Street cobbles, he expected to be taken straight back to St James's Square, not to some half-empty warehouse near the Tower of London. A room hastily set up with shackles around a chair and an open fire.

It could have been worse, he supposed. In the colonies, branding was the price for failing to escape, but no, to be bound and beaten was his punishment. He'd shouted and fought as best he could. The men passing on the dock below did not stop or come to his aid – either unaware of his cries or hardened against them.

Days later, his shoulder splits every time he lifts it.

But despite everything, Vincent tries to anchor himself to happier memories. Of dasheen and pork chops, of playing games with his mother before she left, of the first time he wrote his name, of winning his first boxing match, of the morning he learned Delphine had successfully escaped their master.

All is not lost. His sister will seek out Nick, and they'll find a way forward. And while he waits face down and corpse-still on the hammock to suppress the pain, Vincent clings to optimism like a life raft. He may not have chosen to be here, but above all else he will always choose hope.

The ship rocks, sending his bruises pulsing, and the dark thoughts threaten to return.

But at least he has a hammock.

Night has fallen outside the ship. The docks are quiet. So quiet that Vincent can hear the ripples lapping against his wooden prison, and the rhythm of the waves silences his thoughts. Until the melody is interrupted by a faint *clunk*.

'Vincent?' a distant voice says, followed by another clunk. 'Vincent? *Ès ou anba-a la?*' the voice says again. *Are you down there?* And though there's a tinge of a London accent, the voice's soul hails from the West Indies. Delphine. He knew she'd find him.

With a pained hiss, he hauls himself down from the hammock and over to the window.

'Delphine?'

'At last,' comes his sister's voice. 'I only had two rocks left.'

'How did you find me?'

'I got Nick.'

Thank God, Vincent thinks. His little sister is a brilliant woman. 'Is he with you?'

'No, I'm alone. I had to make sure you were still here.'

He has been here physically, but until now, Vincent hadn't realised how much of him was missing. The parts of himself that cannot be sold, the parts that make him a friend, a dreamer, a brother.

'I'm still here,' he says, shaking off that thought, 'but you shouldn't be.' He stands on tiptoe to try and see out the window, but despite his considerable height, he cannot reach. 'What if you're caught?'

'I'm not allowed to board the ship,' Delphine says, 'but no one said anything about not talking to it in the middle of the night.' After a pause, she adds, 'How bad is it?'

'Our parents dealt with worse.' He won't burden her with the full extent of his injuries. And it's true – his pain is nothing compared to the dangers of cane mills and sugar-boiling houses. 'I'll recover. So, what does Nick think? Am I doomed?'

'He thinks,' she says, 'Lord Harvey cannot do this. He says selling you would be illegal, and he's taking Lord Harvey to court. But first, we're trying to get you off this ship.'

If it weren't for his throbbing shoulder, Vincent would raise both hands to the ceiling and praise God. He tries to keep his voice calm, though he could weep with relief. 'That is good news.'

'We have reason to hope you might be freed,' Delphine continues, 'and in campaigning for your freedom, we might just help other people to be freed as well. I didn't understand it all when Nicholas explained it, but he said this trial, your trial, could change everything.'

'*Everything?*' As wonderful as that sounds, Vincent doesn't need to change everything right now. He just needs things to change for *him*. Nick tends to overcomplicate tasks by focusing too much on the principle and not enough on the results. Consequently, many of his grander projects go unfinished. 'Please tell him how appreciative I am.'

'And if we *don't* win the case,' Delphine continues, 'I'll grab the nearest chain breaker, and we'll run. For as long and as far as we need to.'

Vincent can tell she means it. He's always been able to rely on Delphine to help him out of trouble. Once at 20 St James's Square, he came to her in a panic because he'd broken Hetty's favourite serving dish. Some siblings would have ratted him out. Others might have taken the blame for him. But Delphine? She vanished for a few minutes, then returned with a pocketful of plump dates, two forks and a six-step plan for his acquittal. By the time they'd carried it out, the entire household staff was convinced the culprit had been a stray cat of Delphine's invention.

Vincent chuckles at the memory. His body shakes, and his cuts sting, but for once, it's worth it.

'There you are, brother,' Delphine says.

'Where else would I be?' he jokes, but what he truly means is, *thank you for bringing me back.*

A tumult of drunken laughter pierces through his window – too deep to belong to his sister. It sounds like it's closing time at the dockside inn.

'I have to go,' Delphine says as the men's caterwauling grows louder. 'I'll be back as soon as I can.'

Vincent smiles. 'Get home safe.'

'I'll be back just as soon as I possibly can.' she says again. 'Until then, *kontiné lèspiwasyon.*' *Keep breathing.*

'I will,' he whispers. 'Goodnight.'

As Vincent lies back on the hammock, he sends another thankful prayer, then shuts his eyes and dreams of eating a delightful pudding baked with plump dates and Somerset apples.

Chapter Eight

> Philosophy is best practised, I believe, by the easy and affluent.
>
> —IGNATIUS SANCHO

Delphine

Two weeks after Nicholas' invitation, Delphine stands further north in London than ever. On the corner of Cold Bath Square, she clutches her headwrap against her curls while huddling on the porch of a sandstone building. Behind her is the magnificent dome-topped bath house that lends the street its name. Behind it, the square opens onto verdant fields dotted with straw-topped farmhouses and smoking chimneys.

She secures her shawl with one hand and uses the other to pull Nicholas' address from her pocket. He's written *Cold Bath Street* in a spidery scrawl and sketched the design of the arched fanlight window above his door — what looks to be a flower trapped in a spider's web. Modern advances like house numbers have yet to make it as far north as Clerkenwell.

Braving the blustery wind, Delphine turns the corner and wanders twice up and down Nicholas' road, until she finds the corresponding fanlight of his apartment building. It's no grander than any other beige-fronted home on the street.

Delphine raps the knocker.

A prunish woman answers, her pit-like eyes roving over Delphine. With scrunched lips, she states she's the landlady and questions why Delphine is loitering on the doorstep. Does she not know there's an almshouse for her kind in Mile End?

Delphine bites her tongue to stay it and winces as she hands over the note where Nicholas scrawled his invitation.

Tutting and tsking, the landlady reluctantly allows Delphine inside, muttering that Mister Lyons said nothing about an unchaperoned Negress visiting.

The woman's body creaks in time with the floorboards as they climb two flights of stairs to Nicholas' apartment. She bangs on Nicholas' door with impressive force, then shuffles back the way she came with a final irritable huff.

Hearing Nicholas' muffled words, *Do come in, it's open*, Delphine enters and finds no one in the hallway. It's like so many she's seen in London — tired paintwork, no window, a faint smell of damp — except that the floor is littered with clothes.

'Nicholas?'

'Hullo!' His cheerful reply comes from the open door at the end of the hallway. When he doesn't come to greet her, Delphine picks her way through the discarded shoes and jackets to find him.

To her dismay, the trail continues in the next room — crumpled shirts and grimy breeches — as does the odour. Dirty plates are piled on the mantlepiece, and there are four concentric tea rings on the nearer of two low, sopha tables. Beneath that, an enormous map of the British Empire is spread out over a Persian rug. The tassels peek out inches from Delphine's toes, seemingly matted with dust, hair and unidentifiable crumbs. All this from a first glance.

'At last!' Nicholas catapults from his chair. 'I'm entirely glad you're here.'

Delphine accepts his extended hand, which he shakes so enthusiastically her whole upper body moves with it.

'It's... pleasant to see you too,' she replies, more accustomed to his landlady's style of hospitality. Though she could hardly call the chaos surrounding them pleasant. 'Is all quite well?'

'Oh,' Mister Lyons says, following her gaze to the thick milk skin formed on a half-eaten bowl of porridge beside his left foot. He laughs awkwardly as he slides it beneath the tea-ringed table, and the spoon clatters onto the floor. 'Mrs Cooper, my housekeeper, has quit. I'm afraid I'm quite hopeless alone.'

'It's not *that* bad,' she lies, licking her thumb to rub one of the rings away. 'I'll help while we talk.'

It isn't Delphine's job to replace Mrs Cooper, but she feels eminently calmer in tidy spaces – keeping clean is one of the few things she can usually control in her life.

'*Thank* you,' he says with a slight bow. Then he sniffs and dashes over to the bay window to let in some fresh air.

Delphine sidesteps the map and follows him. She uses the edge of her sleeve, which fortunately is already light grey in colour, to dust the bookshelves on either side of the window.

'How is Vincent?' Nicholas asks. 'Do not feel obliged to lie twice, for I knew you would not stay away from him.'

'He is well,' Delphine admits. 'Injured more than he would care to admit and lonelier. But he seems to be healing, and he says the captain sups with him. I don't know how Grey can act so friendly while forbidding our visits.'

'I suppose August is trying to ease his guilt while remaining in my uncle's employ. The *Ann and Mary* doesn't usually carry human cargo, after all.'

Except when said cargo is Vincent and me, Delphine thinks. Since meeting Grey again, she's often considered their horrendous crossing from St Lucia. So many tears slipped from her chin onto that wretched ship's decking, she was surprised it didn't sink. 'Must he stay aboard until the trial?'

'Fortunately, not,' he says. He bends and sets about retrieving pieces of clothing from the floor, folding them into a pile on the sopha. 'I convinced the courts he should be transferred to the King's Bench.'

'The prison?' Delphine asks. That's on the other side of the river. From what she's heard, the King's Bench doesn't have a stellar reputation for treating inmates fairly. 'When is he going there? Today?'

She should have asked Marion for the entire day off.

Nicholas retrieves a frock coat, which had been hanging over a handsomely painted globe beside the sopha. 'No, not as swiftly as that. My uncle has filed an appeal to overrule the transfer. While it's a blessing he's adhering to the rules, it means it may take another week or so of court dates before Vincent can be moved. I'm confident he will be, though.'

'That's wonderful news,' Delphine says. She could hug Nicholas. They will likely all sleep easier once Vincent's there. But instead of embracing him, Delphine shakes out her sleeve, coughs, and resumes dusting the shelves. In hindsight, she should have asked for a feather duster, though she doubts Nicholas would know where it's kept. 'And it's safe there, at the prison?'

'For those who can pay, yes,' Nicholas says. 'And on the subject of payment, I have more good news. I've been in touch with Vincent's godparents. They are both on our side.'

It is rare for masters to christen their slaves – Delphine herself has no godparents – but shortly after coming to England, Lord Harvey decided to make an exception for Vincent. If he was to be educated like a white man, he should be christened like one as well. So, Sir Christopher Wishaw and Mrs Eliza MacLeod were called upon.

Vincent hardly knows his godparents besides letters exchanged at Christmas and the occasional Church visit. Both are reclusive – the one a bookish aristocrat, the other a widow who reportedly spends most days seated at her pianoforte. It was Lady Katharine who selected them, and – since Lord Harvey's wife cared little for anything that couldn't be studded with jewels – Delphine suspects she arbitrarily chose two names off a guest list. It is fortunate then, that these lonely souls seem to genuinely care for Vincent's.

'They have each agreed to fund a retainer for the duration of the trial,' Nicholas continues. 'Put together, it should cover Vincent's living expenses at the prison with enough left over for me to acquire a legal assistant for his cause.'

Delphine makes a silent note to pray for Sir Wishaw and Mrs MacLeod every night for as long as she lives. 'That is generous indeed,' she says. 'And you have done well, Mister Lyons. Thank you.'

Nicholas shrugs from behind an armful of breeches and shirts. 'Frankly, due to the modesty of my income, I am very glad of the supplement. And call me Nick, please.'

With that, he flops onto the sopha, apparently fatigued from tidying, and begins rambling about various books he's reading on the topic of chattel slavery. As she listens, Delphine begins to declutter the sideboard, tucking Nick's overflowing papers into each of the four drawers. But when she makes to close one of his books, he stops her. She tries to close another; he stops her again.

'Are you also reading all of these?' Delphine gestures to the tomes splayed open over the arms of each velvet chair, the multitude of scrolls flung across the room's every surface.

'How could only one keep my attention?' He points to each volume in turn. 'There are entire continents to explore, histories to uncover, scientific breakthroughs to appreciate, philosophical ideas to ponder...' He shakes his head. *'I've never known any trouble that an hour's reading did not relieve.* There's some more Montesquieu for you...'

Delphine finds it hard to believe. It would take her a day to read a chapter, let alone several from different books. The only reason she can read at all is because in St Lucia, her mother could not complete all her work alone. The island's doctors needed assistance from a knowledgeable herbalist, and her mother was the very best.

So, as soon as Delphine was old enough to hold a quill steady, she too learned to read the names of medicinal plants, label the jars in the infirmary, and complete the annual *inventory of slaves*. She'd write down each slave's assigned name and age, any scars and injuries they had beneath a box marked *condition*, and the job they were designated. Then, the doctor would use the information to determine each person's value.

She learned the words *weak* and *strong* before she could read the days of the week, *invalid* and *able* before she could recite the alphabet.

'... Though of late,' Nick is now saying, 'I've been reading for Vincent's purpose, not for pleasure. I've acquired so many research materials, I had no choice but to buy a new bookcase, too.'

He sounds inconvenienced, but his grin tells her otherwise.

'And you've read all these?' she says, gesturing to the shelves of begilded spines lining every wall.

'Of course not, it would take a lifetime,' he says with a wistful chuckle, 'but I do worry that if I stop buying them, I'll eventually run out of things to read. Better to be safe and buy more than wait until I have finished them all. Depending on the author, I may buy another copy or two – just in case one is damaged.'

'Good sir, that sounds like an addiction.'

'Oh, indubitably.' She turns to him, and Nick rushes over to meet her, a burgundy, leather-bound book in hand.

'This one,' he says reverentially, 'is my current favourite.'

He hands it to her softly, like a baby, and she holds it with the same care.

'*Candide* by Monsieur Voltaire. Say what you will about the French, but they have produced some of the best thinkers of all time. Others may favour the Prussian philosophers – Leibniz, Wolff, and Kant. However,' he leaves a dramatic pause, 'I just *can't*.'

Delphine stares blankly.

'One day, someone will laugh at that,' he mutters, then says, 'I'm ashamed to say this edition is translated from the original. I suppose you read better in French than English?'

Delphine turns over the book to admire its intricately designed cover, stamped with a border of tumbling swirls and delicate fleur-de-lis. It's weighty, and when she opens it to look inside, running a finger gently down the crimson ribbon marker, the endpapers are decorated in feathered blue and gold.

'I can speak some French,' she says, doubtful she could carry a conversation. French Creole was her primary tongue until she was six, and Lord Harvey acquired the plantation. The French overseers were replaced with English ones, and it soon became evident a language barrier was no excuse for disobeying orders. She's been a quick study ever since. 'But I've never attempted to read it.'

Nick's cheeks flush. 'Of course, I should have realised.'

'I can read, though,' Delphine blurts, her own cheeks prickling from embarrassment. Not wanting to feel inadequate, she adds, 'If I may, I'd like to read this.'

'By all means.' Nick flourishes his upturned hand, welcoming her to begin this very moment.

Delphine turns to the opening page, unwilling to admit that the only book she's read in four years is the heavily illustrated *A Curious Herbal: A Physik's Guide to Medicinal Remedies*. The first word seems to repeat the title on the spine: CANDIDE.

The next word is easy – THE – but the final one she stumbles over before making it out to be OPTIMIST.

A word she is unfamiliar with, but she trusts herself to puzzle it out. She flicks to the first chapter, and reading the three opening paragraphs takes a few minutes. Increasingly aware of Nick's eyes on her, she shuts the book and asks, 'What's it about?'

'Oh, so many things!' he exclaims, grey eyes lighting up. 'It's a novel. About optimism and realism, about the folly in believing mankind has reached its peak when there is still so much needless suffering.' He throws his hands up in awe like he has just finished the story for the first time.

'A novel,' Delphine repeats, sliding the ribbon marker into place before handing the book back to him. 'So, it's a work of make-believe?'

'Exactly!' He takes it from her, apparently elated by the question. 'A work of make-believe, yes. For despite Monsieur Voltaire's ending, I think… No, I *believe* that with the right effort, we *will* craft a better world of our own.'

Ah, so that is the definition. Mister Lyons is undoubtedly an optimist, Delphine decides. She likes to think she is, too, but while her dreams of a better world are clouded by experience, Nick's are clear as the brightest day.

'On the subject of crafting a better world,' Nick says, 'let us discuss our next steps for Vincent.'

He invites her to sit in the armchair least encumbered by reading matter while he returns to the sopha and his haphazardly heaped wardrobe. 'I'd hoped to have secured offices by now, but I've not found a respectable building owner who would lease to me for our cause. So for the time being, I shall remain in my drawbrary.'

'Draw-berry?' It takes her a moment to understand him. But when she looks around her again, it seems obvious. Instead of a desk and wooden chairs as you'd find in a library, here there are ink-stained tables beside plush green velvet sophas, cushions and candle sticks scattered between piles of books. Where there'd be portraits on a drawing room's walls, here are bookcases. 'This is your drawing room *and* library?'

'Drawing room library, indeed! You are quick, Delphine!' Nick runs a hand hastily through his blond hair. 'Not that I ever thought otherwise.' He clears his throat. 'A much more economical use of space to combine both. Don't you agree?'

At a loss for reasons to disagree, she murmurs in the affirmative. 'Though the more I think on it,' Nick goes on, 'I see that Parliament would be our best base going forward. Ah!' He stands abruptly. 'Forgive me. I haven't offered you anything to drink!'

'There's no need,' Delphine assures him — his erratic movements are hard to keep up with, and frankly, she would rather be thirsty than dizzy. But Nick has already marched to the far corner of the room, where one rogue shirt remains strewn over an amply stocked drinks cart.

He plucks the shirt from the cart, revealing four crystal decanters — one spherical, two conical, one rectangular — and flings the white shirt over his shoulder like a cook with a dishcloth. 'As I was saying...' There's a *pop* as he pulls the cork from the spherical one. 'If we base ourselves in Parliament, we'll have access to the libraries *and* be much closer to Vincent.' He places the cork between his lips while he retrieves two stemless glasses and pours the plum-coloured wine. The next words come out muffled on account of the cork. 'Woul hu'orrow soo? Or woul hu ar-ha higin on Munhay nex?'

Delphine suppresses a laugh. 'I'm afraid I don't follow.'

He removes the cork from his mouth and drops it onto the cart instead of resealing the bottle. The action seems so routine it makes Delphine fear the quality of the wine.

'I said,' he says, returning with a glass in each hand, 'Would tomorrow suit to commence preparations? Or would you rather Monday next?'

Even without the cork, his thoughts are a struggle to detangle. 'For...?'

'I beg your pardon.' He offers her the glass and sits back down. 'I have been presumptuous. Do you not wish to be my assistant in preparation for the trial? I'm sure I can find a willing aide elsewhere, somehow...'

Nick, Delphine is coming to understand, is a man of perpetually perplexing ideas. Can he really be suggesting she can work in Parliament as a lawyer's assistant? And even if she could, what would they say about her status? Her education? He's just witnessed how rusty her reading skills are — he must be struggling to find someone more qualified.

But Vincent needs her. And if this is how she can help him, she must rise to the challenge. 'I would be honoured,' she says. 'Only... there's my accommodation to consider. I lodge with my employer, and I fear she will ask me to leave if I quit my position.'

Nick only shrugs in response. 'We shall come to a suitable arrangement, I'm sure. We can pay your rent out of the stipend.'

That sounds like an attractive deal for Marion. But she hasn't yet told Nick of Marion's primary means of income. Will he agree to spend Vincent's godparents' money at a brothel?

'That might work,' Delphine says. Still slightly afeared the wine has spoiled, she takes her first hesitant drink, and is surprised to find that it goes down smoothly. 'But there's something you should know about where I live. It's a... a...'

'Temple of Exoticies?'

Delphine gawps at him. 'How did you know?'

'I may have made an assumption based on where the Runners picked up Vincent. Given the circumstances, it's rather ideal.' He wiggles his eyebrows. 'Because surely, it follows that your employer is adept at trading women's time for money?'

'That she is,' Delphine replies, then takes a long second gulp of wine. As far as she can tell, there was no judgement in Nick's voice, but warning bells toll in Delphine's mind. Nick once said he'd not put her in harm's way, but she can't help but wonder: is he really a progressive optimist, or just ignorant of her vulnerabilities?

'Perfect!' he exclaims. 'Then let your mistress fix a price, and we shall pay it. What Vincent's godparents don't know won't ruffle their feathers.' He smiles triumphantly. 'Now, one more thing...'

Mister Lyons leaps to his feet again and invites Delphine to look at the scroll on the tea table closest to the window. It's held down at the corners by heavy Moroccan-style paperweights, and he crouches to better make out the lettering.

Delphine remains upright.

While Nick consistently surpasses her expectations of most men, he probably has the mind of one, and kneeling next to him would feel too intimate for her liking.

With a quick look up at her, he continues unperturbed. 'Going forward, most of our time will be consumed with plans for Vincent's trial. But I've also taken the liberty of beginning preparations for his life thereafter.'

She leans forward to peer closer at the scroll and sees the outline of a county drawn in black ink. In bold letters at the top of the page is the word SOMERSET.

Vincent has often joked about becoming a West Country apple farmer. She's astounded that it's a dream he shared with Nick, too, but she's glad he did. And she's comforted that Nick thinks Vincent may have a future beyond the trial.

'I reached out to one of my father's old acquaintances in Bristol, who said there are several towns along the channel with free Negroes residing there, seemingly without trouble. I need to learn more about them, but once I have your approval of our approach,' he continues, head bent over the map, 'shall we away and see the bawd?'

'Approval of *our* approach?' Delphine fails to hide the surprise in her voice as she crouches beside him. 'I thought you would never ask.'

Chapter Nine

There is no study more entertaining or instructive than history.

—JOHN WILKES

Delphine
The following Monday, Delphine waits on the New Palace Yard for Nick in her best dress. Having agreed a rate of pay that Marion believes to be suitably extortionate, yet which Nick deems quite the bargain compared to more *qualified* assistants, she has been anxious to prove her worth to each of them. Delphine spent the weekend studying Nick's notes and snippets from recent parliamentary debates in newspapers. Reading, she has realised, is like a flower's first bloom: once budded it has the capacity to do so again – provided it has the right encouragement.

Among the crowds of sweating clerks in navy frock coats, almost buckling beneath the weight of their books, Delphine stands with her modest pile of papers, shifting nervously from foot to foot as the bell at St Margaret's announces eight o'clock, then eight fifteen, then eight thirty. The nine o'clock chimes are almost upon her when Nick finally appears, seemingly unaware he's nearly an hour late. He greets her heartily, and Delphine does the same. Maybe her first task as his assistant will be to ensure he arrives on time.

From the yard, they enter Westminster Hall. Late May sunlight floods through the huge, mediaeval windows on all sides, lighting up statues of important men in the great room's four corners. Her heels click on the stone floor, the coloured squares weaving together in a giant lattice.

The wealth in these walls is awe-inspiring, as is the rarity of a presence like hers inside them.

As they walk into a long corridor, she scans all the plinths and tables for memorable objects and notes which archway leads where — in case she gets lost or needs to find her way out alone. From the outside, Westminster appeared fortress-like, its spires and towers dominating the skyline for miles, but now she's inside the palace, it could only be described as a maze.

'Thankfully, both Houses are in recess today, so it's far quieter for conducting a tour,' Nick says. 'It's easy for conversations to be lost among the commotion. This morning, only clerks, a few ministers, and junior MPs like myself are in the building. You can tell who's who by the number of grey hairs...' He coughs. 'You were meant to say, *but Nick, you don't have any grey hairs. There's barely a wrinkle on you.*'

Delphine hadn't registered the joke. She laughs obligingly, still attempting to comprehend the layout of the place. 'Are you not too young to be an MP?'

'Well,' he says, smiling in appreciation, 'of the 550 or so members of the Commons, there are only a dozen under twenty-five, like myself. Fewer than one hundred under thirty.'

She nods, looking closer at the men passing them down the corridor. Grey hair and wrinkles indeed — they must be ministers. It strikes her then how little notice anyone is taking of her. When Nick suggested they base themselves in Parliament, she'd expected to make it but three steps inside the building before someone turfed her out, seizing back this opportunity as swiftly as it was granted. But these men are all engaged in discussions or else enveloped by their thoughts. Even the serving staff and porters are too busy to mind her. The knot of tension between her shoulders loosens slightly. She is often made to feel like the ceiling of a room — an attention-drawing feature or a blank space. She's content to be the latter today.

Nick shows her the offices leading to the court of the King's Bench, which is currently in session. The thick door is shut, intimidating and uninviting as the shields and swords carved upon it. She is almost glad they cannot go inside – they'll need to craft stronger armour of their own before Vincent's fate is decided here in a few months' time. Nick rattles on cheerfully as he often does, regardless of whether anyone is listening. 'These days, the Commons are far less elitist. In my father's heyday, he was one of the only professionals here.' He tugs proudly at his lapels. 'Whereas Saville, Bunbury, Glynn and I... We're a new class of party-less independents and radicals, pushing for reform.' He says all this as though Delphine has any idea who these men are; upon catching the excitable sparkle in his eye, she gathers they must be his fellow optimists.

'Of course,' he continues, 'it's not perfect quite yet. An independent's election campaign must be financed, of course. And votes must be bought with half-guineas and drinks tokens.'

'Must?' Delphine echoes, baffled at how normal it seems to bribe men for their votes – half a guinea would be three months' wages to Hetty the cook.

'Well, you can't expect a city doctor or country lawyer to win on policy alone, can you? Whigs and Tories have deep pockets, and independent candidates have to pay the cost of election somehow. Inevitably, that means trading the occasional principal to secure one's seat.'

Seeing the dismay in her eyes, Nick laughs tightly. 'I'm fortunate to stay out of all that. My father did good work for his constituents, and I like to think I do too, which is why they re-elected me.'

They veer right into a ruby-carpeted vestibule, and Nick says, 'Before I forget...' then halts so abruptly that Delphine loses her count of the corridors and almost bumps into him. Oblivious, Nick points a finger skyward before resting it on his chin. 'We must retrieve a copy of Glynn's latest speech from the Commons library. He said something about reforming the justice system I'd like to reference in Vincent's trial.' The floor squeaks as he turns on his heels and walks back in the direction they came. 'This way then.'

Seemingly infinite passages later, they stop, and Nick leads her into a library. There appears to be no other soul around them, and

Delphine relaxes further in the silence, releases her stomach little by little, and allows her spine to curve. She counts thirty-six bookcases crowded with thick-spined tomes as Nick drags a rolling ladder from the far end of the room to the bookcase behind Delphine. Like the shelves, the ladder almost reaches the ceiling, and its wheels slide easily over the floorboards. Nick places a foot on the ladder and looks over his shoulder as though he's about to say something when the clop of low-heeled shoes enters from another room.

Delphine's back straightens an inch with each step.

'Ah, young Mister Lyons,' the stranger says, thumping Nick on the back, then fails to stifle a cough. 'Just the man I wanted. The very man indeed!' He clears his throat, the sound like a nickering horse.

He seems not to have noticed Delphine, which gives her a chance to get a proper look at him. His nose is perfectly triangular in profile, and he has cunning, arched eyebrows. His face is cleanly shaven as a young man's, but his gaunt cheeks and tired eyes place him in middle age.

'A pleasure to see you, Sir William,' Nick nods respectfully. 'May I introduce you to my new assistant, Miss St Joseph. Miss St Joseph, Sir William Meredith, 3rd Baronet, former Lord of the Admiralty, now Member of Parliament for Liverpool.'

Nick flicks his head towards Sir William, suggesting she should come closer. People rarely utter her last name; in fact, it is rare for slaves to have last names at all. Vincent was given his at his christening, and Delphine's mother claimed St Joseph – the patron saint of the dying – for their family during one of the Catholic periods on the plantation. In a bloody and violent world, her mother had hoped it might bring solace to her sickest patients.

'It's an honour, sir.' She curtseys, dropping her gaze. Delphine doesn't need to have visited Liverpool to know the fate of the Blacks who live there.

'Erm...' the baronet stumbles. 'Erm, well.' His sunken eyes seem to be swimming with all the impossibilities before him. He chokes down his shock, then succumbs to a coughing fit so violent that Nick enquires if he needs assistance. The baronet bats Nick's words away, and Delphine glimpses wet crimson flecks on his palm. She looks away again, fearing that even the strongest poppy water tonic wouldn't help his ailment. Once recovered, he pulls out a handkerchief, straightening as he wipes his hand and says sternly, 'A word, Mister Lyons.'

Delphine swallows.

A baronet, a navy man, an MP and a knight — his authority is immense.

If he bids Nick dismiss her, he will likely have to comply.

Yet her new employer looks unconcerned. He promises to return shortly before striding with the baronet out the door.

To distract herself, Delphine sets about searching for the speech Nick wanted. An easy enough task — or it would be, had Nick told her which section she might find it in. There are thousands of books in this first room alone.

But she doesn't waste a moment. All the dull sage books along the first wall appear to be various volumes of 'State Acts and Measures', which cannot be the right place to find a speech challenging the state's current ways of operating. 'Buildings and Land Registry' follow 'Acts and Measures', then 'Councils and Committees'. With so many books on such riveting topics, it's no wonder the place is deserted.

Oh, how she wishes she were not alone in this moment. Why are there no librarians or ink-fingered researchers to point her in the right direction? Birds sing outside the stained-glass window — a mockingly upbeat tune to accompany her chore.

Then, a reckless thought stirs. An impulse so childish she almost immediately dismisses it. But when Nick returns she may already be out of a job, so why not have a few seconds of fun?

With a quick check outside the room and in the next one, Delphine giddily crosses back to the ladder. Taking a deep inhale, she grips the smooth edges, raises her left foot onto the second rung, pushes back with her right and *glides*. Glides around the room in this most serious of places, in this place that she may never see again. She bites her lip as the wheels bump over the wooden floorboards, then exhales as she comes to a stop, letting out her glee.

Her eyes crinkle as she smiles. She needed this.

A few seconds later, Delphine gives herself a reaffirming nod and heads to the next room. Perhaps she can find the speech among the bound handwritten copies in the 'Debates' section.

No such luck. Nor in the next.

Time stretches, and Nick is yet to return.

Entering the adjoining room, she spies a single desk piled high with unbound parchment in a cupboard-sized nook beneath a small window. Something tells her this is where she'll find her prize. Glynn's speech had better be worth it. Falling upon the papers with quick hands, she catches herself just in time to put every other document carefully back in its rightful place; there's no telling whose work she's disturbing.

With the state of her reading skills and the low lighting, it takes much concentration for Delphine to decipher the words. Usually, upon realising a document is not the one she's looking for, she replaces it. But some are fascinating enough to draw her in.

She squints to read the record of a speech made by Robert Nugent: *'Had the House of Lords not callously rejected the amendment to our poor laws, perhaps the quantity of executions at Tyburn would not so vastly outnumber those of every other European capital...'*

Another, which appears to be about the imprisoning of the radical MP John Wilkes, says: *'I think the Administration acted wrong in ignoring the voters' choice to re-elect Wilkes...'* The scribe's hand then becomes almost illegible, bunched together like it's been scrawled in a rush. *'... and while I do not wish, in these trying times at least, to purge off all Tory blood without cause, how can the Members of the majority of this House undermine our democracy and ban his return to office?'*

She leafs through a dozen more speeches before another catches her attention, this one with no title or name associated with it. *'Should the under-secretary truly wish to avoid an outcome of war in our Falklands negotiations with Spain, may this minister humbly suggest he cease investing in ships and arms for the time being?'*

Surely not? Delphine thinks, blinking the dancing words back into focus. Surely, no British government official would seek to *profit* from war? Intrigued and disgusted, she puts back the anonymous speech. She rises from her stool, stretches and reorientates herself; she feels hot, and the cotton of her dress is clinging to her body. How long has she been in this small, sweaty space?

She reaches for the pole to open the window, hooks it on the latch and pulls. A gust of air whooshes in, forcing the window to slam against the wall and, to Delphine's dismay, sending the pages scattering everywhere.

Excellent. This really is a first day to remember.

Crouching down to scoop up the pages, she begins sorting the papers into piles of matching handwriting. With absolutely no hope of putting them back in the right order, this is the best she can do to remedy the situation before Nick returns. What could have captured his attention for so long?

Each time her hand touches the floor she grimaces at the thickening layer of dirt in the whorls of her fingertips. Reluctant to wipe the grime on her dress, she glances around to check she's still alone. Then she sighs and frustratedly rubs her hand on the nearest wall panel.

The panel answers with a *click*.

The wooden panel she's just sullied has moved before her eyes and now juts out from the wall.

Delphine gasps. Has she just broken the wainscoting in the Houses of Parliament? What sort of punishment would await her for this? Her stomach drops. How could she hope to explain this away? She scrambles to her feet and frantically tries to push the wood back in place, but it only juts out further. She tries again, blood pressure rising, but it won't stay shut. Gripping with all her might, she attempts to jiggle it back, but all that does is send a smattering of dirt down from inside, over her hands and out onto some of the parchment. She pushes again and there's a low creak of a hinge and Delphine realises this is not a broken panel.

It's a door.

'Oh,' she says aloud, breathing heavily. 'Oh.'

In a six-hundred-year-old building, there are bound to be secrets. If she had a candle, she'd stick her head inside the hole in the wall and see what lies behind it, but she'd rather not risk looking like a chimney sweep. With a reluctant shrug, Delphine reasons that if force is what dislodged the door, it's a delicate touch that may close it.

No sooner has the panel clicked tight once more, and has Delphine set about gathering the final pieces of paper, than she hears the thudding of footsteps once more.

'What are you doing in here?' a man's voice says, his words knife-sharp.

In a panic, she wipes her hands on her petticoat and drags a sleeve across her forehead to dry the sweat. She drops her gaze and begins, 'I am the Member for Kettering's new assistant, tasked by him to retrieve a copy of a speech.' She makes sure to over-enunciate every syllable of every word. 'Unfortunately, a gust of wind sent the papers flying, so I've made a bit of a mess.' She picks up a random sheet with a tight smile and makes a show of tutting at her clumsiness, but the man is already closing the gap between them.

He snatches the paper from her, tilting his head to make out the text. 'Glynn, eh? Fancy yourself a troublemaker, do you?'

She could have laughed or cursed, but instead she keeps her mouth squeezed shut. Of course the parchment she arbitrarily selected is the one she'd been looking for this past hour.

The red-coated beefeater grabs her arm and grunts, 'We'll see what the Member for Kettering has to say about all this. You know what the punishment is for trespassing here. I know your type.'

'I assure you, sir—'

Before she can continue he's dragging her through the library, the document crumpled in his free hand. She can only hope Nick is close by — she's almost certain trespassing is one of the 220 crimes punishable by death.

Her legs tremble as he pulls her along the corridor and up a flight of stairs. Without knocking, he flings open a door and pushes Delphine into an office. She bangs her hip on the side of a desk and cups a hand over the pain.

'This one says she works for you,' the beefeater snipes, holding out Glynn's speech to Nick.

'Good god, man!' Nick says, slapping his book shut. He strides over to the guard, whose ears are flushing pink. 'What do you think you're doing? Throwing my assistant about like a rag.'

'Uh...' The man wavers, then stiffens.

Delphine doesn't fight the smirk that rises on her cheeks.

'Do not touch her again, or I'll have you out of here before you can say prosecution.'

'If I may say, sir—'

'You may not, sir,' Nick spits, seizing the speech and all but pushing the man out of the room.

'If I may,' he pleads.

'You may not.' Nick stamps his foot. 'Good day, warden.' He slams the door.

In the ensuing quiet, Delphine listens to the beefeater's footsteps retreating uncertainly down the stairwell. First comes relief, then a rising tide of anger. So much for this morning's invisibility.

Nick said he'd return to fetch her from the library, but evidently, he forgot. His thoughtlessness infuriates her, but what good would that do to rebuke him? Her position relies on his goodwill, and on his almost unique ability to see that she can be more than society claims she can be. This opportunity is not just for Vincent and his cause — it's for her. Before Nick offered it to her, the odds of Delphine being here, in Parliament, were beyond one in a lifetime.

And today is only her first day.

Delphine grits her teeth as Nick places a sorry hand on her shoulder.

'One day, Delphine, this will all change. They won't treat you like this. I promise.'

It may one day, but it won't be in her lifetime. Yet what can she say to those pitying eyes? How can she describe the revulsion curdling in her stomach at his satisfaction from having saved her?

With a mournful smile, Delphine pushes down the embarrassment, the fury, and the shame and says, 'I know.'

Because she does know. Today, Delphine chooses silence, as many have to when they are the first. In bearing that burden, Delphine determines a different future: one where things are better, one where she is not an unusual presence but belongs. Delphine can be that silent first, because she has hope there will never be a last.

Chapter Ten

To be DISPOSED OF,

A HANDSOME BLACK BOY, about thirteen years of age, very well qualified for making a household servant, serving table well and of a fine constitution, inured to the climate, and has had the smallpox. Any person inclining to purchase him may call at Mister William Reid's, ironmonger, opposite the door to the city guard.
—EDINBURGH ADVERTISER

Vincent

When Grey comes for Vincent, he commands him off the ship but doesn't tell him where he is being moved. The captain tosses him a rag to wipe his face with, instructs him onto an ill-maintained carriage, and climbs in beside him. Then they set off, winding through busy streets just before sunset. The reek of the vessel still clings to Vincent like wood smoke. And as the rickety wheels bump over the cobblestones of Westminster Bridge, dirt falls from his body, coating the seat like ash.

It's the first time Vincent remembers crossing the river.

Soon after, they reach their destination: the immense King's Bench prison. Its grey outer walls are built high and sturdy, topped with spikes resembling the sharp tip of a crown. Yet at such a forbidding sight, Vincent feels only peace.

He'd spent so many moments on board the *Ann and Mary* in stomach-churning dread. Every time the ship rocked, he'd feared they were setting sail. But here he is on solid ground, and the prospect of taking up residence within solid walls with solid rules could not be more appealing.

A prison guard invites him to step off the carriage; as he does so, he isn't grabbed or chained. The guard — a weighty fellow almost as wide as he is short — seems as confident as Vincent is that he won't run. But there's still an abruptness in the man's tone, reminding him that while he's not under arrest, he is undoubtedly a prisoner. Captain Grey tentatively wishes Vincent well for the trial, before shaking hands with the prison guard and taking his leave.

As the carriage trundles back in the river's direction, the guard introduces himself as the prison tapster, sticks out a meaty hand for Vincent to shake, then snatches it back when Vincent reaches for it, chortling.

'Name's Livey,' he says. Turning from the portcullis, Livey leads them through a narrow watch tower onto what Vincent assumes is the central square, but it's nothing like he imagined. Inside the fortress is a smart red brick building. A few women beat rugs on balconies from the four stories overlooking the courtyard, and pipe smoke curls into the night from glowing fire-lit cells.

A whistling man fills a bucket at the furthest of the yard's three water pumps, and from this distance, he seems neither weak nor starving. Neither do the half dozen children who pass them, squealing and chasing each other near the cell block entrance, their gawping at Vincent shortened by the fun of their game.

On the way to Vincent's cell, Livey points out the chandler's shop, a coffee house and two tap rooms, while explaining a few prison rules. Vincent struggles to hear them over the chorus of dogs yipping and barking inside several of the cells and the discordant scales of a men's choir.

'This is the one,' Livey says, stopping outside the last door on the second floor. He unclips a key ring from his belt and says, 'It's the billiards for you, mate,' as he struggles to locate Vincent's cell key among a hundred others.

'Sorry?' Vincent says.

'We're at capacity this month. At short notice, it's the best I can do. Hope you don't mind. Ah!' He finds the key at last. It clinks as it turns in the lock, then he ushers Vincent in.

A billiard's table sits at the centre of the otherwise scant room, with a barely-scuffed green playing field and shining legs so recently varnished the reek of camphor makes Vincent's eyes water.

Livey slaps him on the back, and Vincent's relieved his wounds have healed. The guard says, 'If you want ink and paper to write your mate back, that'll cost extra.'

'My mate?' Vincent asks, taking in his new surroundings. Unlike the courtyard facing cells, there's no balcony and no fire. Maybe those things cost more, too. The barred window and stone floor give the room a cellar-like chill.

'Aye. He's left you a letter by your bedroll.' Livey jangles the keys towards a thin, bare mattress in the far-left corner. Upon it, Vincent spots an envelope held in place beneath a couple of candle stubs – tallow, not wax, he assumes. The room is otherwise empty, bar the two billiard cues which rest against the opposite wall.

'Now,' Livey says, his chipper tone replaced by something low and serious. 'The Chief Justice has ordered that you'll have no liberties, so you can't leave the prison walls. But you can use the facilities from tomorrow, including the taproom.' He reclips the keys to his belt. 'Some of the lads may want to come in here and play billiards with you. Or,' he says, pity lacing his voice as he looks Vincent up and down before turning to leave, 'they may not.'

Vincent flinches as the guard slams his cell door shut, stealing most of the light.

Livey's wispy black hair and pockmarked forehead reappear between the grates at the top of the door. 'Keep your head down, Freedom Fighter,' he says, cheerfulness returned. Then his eyes bob in and out of view like he's failing to balance on his tiptoes. 'I reckon you'll be all right.'

When Vincent doesn't reply, Livey knocks his farewell on the wood and jingles down the hall.

Still standing by the door, Vincent crumples forward in relief. His shoulders hunch inward, and he cradles his stomach as he finally feels the worms of fear cease feeding on him. The touch of his own hands lets him know that this is real, that he's truly here. There's no way this prison can set off across the Atlantic at a moment's notice.

In this place, he hopes to God that Lord Harvey can't get to him. But his young nephew can.

When he feels strong enough to move, Vincent crosses the stone floor to retrieve the envelope from the bedroll, then returns to the door to read the letter in the light.

25th June 1 7 7 0

Dear Vincent,

If you are reading this, it means you have safely arrived at the prison.

My apologies for the lack of forewarning, but once I had secured your room, I could not risk my uncle discovering where you were being transported and ordering Captain Grey to set sail. I do hope the wardens are amiable. I have spoken to one — a Mister Livey, I believe — who informed me that if your room is not to your liking, the furniture and other comforts can be changed.

He was quick to provide a catalogue of sorts and insisted that I remember such adjustments would come at an additional cost. At a rate bordering on extortionate, I tell you.

As I am assuring you, I assured him that coin is of no concern thanks to the generous fund bestowed by your godparents. He seemed delighted by that prospect — as I have since learned, the King's Bench prison where you find yourself is predominantly for holding debtors. However, I have yet to discern how a man is meant to emerge from the trenches of debt while paying for room, board, roaming, and whatever else. Is it true that men bring their families to reside in their cells to avoid two sets of housing costs?

Pray remember the poor debtors, indeed!

Mark me, droning on about coin like a miser. I propose you obey the lord and, as Ecclesiastes so boldly says: eat, drink, and be merry, Vincent.

I will write again soon and endeavour to visit even sooner. Please ensure Mister Livey sends any bills to me.

Your faithful servant,
Nicholas Lyons

Hunched over the billiard's table the next morning, Vincent hovers his newly acquired quill over a blank piece of parchment, unsure how to begin his reply. Last night, he composed a dozen responses in his mind, but now they are as lost to him as yesterday's dream, his head as empty as his rumbling stomach.

Unsure how far his godparents' coin would go, he chose writing utensils over a sizzling hot breakfast.

He re-dips the quill, still considering his words. Once they're dried in ink, there's no way they can be taken back — unless he asks Mister Livey for another expensive sheet of parchment.

Supposing it's best to keep it light, he writes:

27th June 1 7 7 0

Dear Nick,
Pray sit if you are not doing so — I fear your heart may give out when you learn how much the ink, paper and postage cost.

Extortion indeed, my friend, extortion indeed.

Though Captain Grey had become amiable by my departure, I find myself in better spirits than I have done these last few months. Those spirits are, of course, as indebted to you as I am.

As my debts mount, I look forward to your visit when you can spare the time to attend me. If there is anything I can do from within these walls to help you to help me, I'll give all I can.

Your faithful servant,
Vincent

8th July 1 7 7 0

Dear Vincent,
It was good to see you last week. I'll repeat now — for the final time — there is no debt between us, my friend. Your support and guidance over the years — and occasional saving of my life (remember that incident with the red-headed woman on my 23rd birthday?) is more than enough.

Speaking of women, your Delphine is far more valuable than I initially gave her credit for. I do not mean this to sound invalidating (my mother's mind worked twice as quickly as my father's), but for one, uneducated and untried in the pool of the law... Well...

Today, she successfully secured the advice of one Mister Granville Sharp, whose name and reputation for service to Negroes in Britain, I'm sure, has not escaped your attention. Delphine passed on his regrets that he cannot be hands-on during your trial. Other cases need his support, ones where the Black may not have such well-taught friends(!)

I am sure I had not seen such a grin on a person as when she relayed that end of his message. But in lieu of his time, he has supplied us with a list of books and treatises to purchase, which Delphine is collecting from Hatchards tomorrow — along with an invitation to join the monthly abolitionist meeting hosted there. He is also keen to introduce me to a new correspondent on the other side of the Atlantic. A man founding a school for Negroes, if you can believe it. Let's hope these tides of progress reach our shores.

I hope to share more of our strategy in these coming letters.

I see from your bill you have only had three tankards in the taproom, Vincent, and I find this greatly disappointing. As my tutor at Oxford once said to me: do better.

Your faithful servant,
Nick

10th July 1 7 7 0

Dear Nick,

Or should I say Delphine? I'm not sure which of you composed your most recent letter. Please, for all our sakes, do not say all of these things to her out loud for she'll get a frightfully big head. And certainly do not tell her I said this. As the bard said: Hell hath no fury like a Delphine scorned.

That said, I'm glad Delphine is benefitting from your company.

I am pleased to report the furniture you requested for my cell has arrived. With so many hours for contemplation during the day, acquiring a desk to write at has brought me greater peace than I could have ever expected.

The long nights are still difficult. However, I have joined the men's choir to pass the time. Remarkably, I seem to have found friendship among the baritones, and as a result, the billiards table in my cell is at last being put to good use.

You'll be glad to hear that I have since visited the tap room with them — thank you for the suggestion. I do not, however, intend to get drunk enough that I feel the urge to piss off the side of a staircase without checking to see who may be passing below. I maintain that while I did save you from that red-headed woman's wrath, her anger was not misplaced.

I deeply wish that we may drink together again, my friend. I have missed your companionship. Thank you for all you are doing.

I look forward to your next letter.

Your faithful servant,
Vincent

2nd August 1 7 7 0

Dear Vincent,
I apologise for the delay in you receiving this letter.

Every time I sat down to write this correspondence, my mind became overwhelmed with other thoughts — how I may help you in the trial, how to balance that with my constituents' needs during the parliamentary recess, among other everyday mundanities. Do you ever find that despite having so much to do, you end up doing nothing at all? I'm afraid to say that has been my week.

Rest assured I do have good news. And, I have cleared away all thoughts temporarily to focus on writing this letter.

I wish to tell you of our latest stroke of luck. The Justices have been decided for your case. Supporting the Chief Justice will be Willes and Aston — an increasingly inseparable pair. They ruled in support of dismissing charges against Wilkes earlier this year, and tend to be rather brusque in pushing for reform. Then there's Justice de Grey, who I'm still forming an opinion of. Most importantly, the case will be heard by Lord Chief Justice Mansfield.

Mansfield is famed for his neutrality towards political concerns, but I've heard that he may now have a personal reason to sympathise with your cause. He's adopted his niece. A mulatto girl from the West Indies. We cannot say if this will sway him entirely, but one may hope.

Your faithful servant,
Nick

2nd August 1 7 7 0

Dear Vincent,
Apologies for penning two messages in one day. Perhaps I shall send this one tomorrow.

Earlier, I pulled out one of Locke's works to build rebuttals to some of the arguments my uncle's counsel will make and came across an interestingly contradictory statement. Locke, as you may know, does condone the enslavement of others — abhorrent as that may be — but he also writes:

'Every man has a property in his own person. This, nobody has a right to but himself.'

How a man may hold such opposing truths in his mind and wholeheartedly believe both is incomprehensible to me. Hypocritical philosophers aside, I thought I would make the most of this letter and inform you of our plans for your trial.

It will draw on four key themes: character, Christianity, commerce and contract.

As regards the third point, we have things well in hand. I've engaged an economist to calculate the benefits of your transportation versus your contribution to British society as a boxer. Then, he will multiply these figures by an estimate of the total number of Blacks in Britain, so we may have a more tangible view of the positive impact your people make here, even as freemen.

As for Christianity, there is much to be said about slavery in the Bible, both in favour and against it. Mister Sharp has referred me to his acquaintance, the Reverend Doctor Rutherford, for guidance in this area.

As for your character, Delphine is assisting your godparents in constructing their endorsement of your most amiable, gentlemanly qualities. Are there any others you believe would give testimony?

And finally: contract. While I believe all of London is aware your boxing career was in pursuit of your freedom, we need to be able to prove it. When you asked my advice on the terms all those years ago, I did the best I could without seeing it. Do you remember the specific wording?

That may be the best we can do in lieu of the physical product.

Your friend,
Nick

6th August 1 7 7 0

Dear Nick,
Thank you for both letters and for arranging Delphine's visit. It was a much-needed diversion from the solace. I have drawn up a list of those who may be

willing to speak against my master as follows (and have provided their addresses to Delphine):

    Lord Bernard Rennington
    Sir Morris Taylor
    Reverend Clarence Wallace
    Lady Clarice Winnington
    Baron Bruce Mayweather
    Colonel Bert Robinson

I have wracked my memories to try and remember the exact wording, but I'm afraid I cannot remember. The terms are burned into my mind: Win your weight in coin, and you will be free. After locking it in one of the cabinets in his study, he never mentioned the terms again. However, the next day, he did find a boxing instructor. I'm unsure if this information will aid you, but it is all I know.

I can't believe we're a little over a month from the trial. Although the days are darkening since the solstice, I do not seem to be getting any more sleep.

    Your friend,
    Vincent

11th August 1770

Dear Vincent,

Thank you for the list of names. We have reached out to each of them, and while some have agreed to contribute to your ongoing legal costs, none will speak for you. Your godparents will likely suffice, but I cannot help feeling disappointed by their lack of courage. You could probably be an African King, and they'd still value my uncle's homely power over that of yours.

We will have to make do without the contract. I petitioned for it to be seized by the authorities, but alas, I have been turned down. Professedly, there are insufficient legal grounds to raid St James's Square. If I had Delphine's rebellious spirit, I'd march over there and procure it myself, but I fear my uncle will destroy the document if he learns we are trying to steal it back. Supposing he hasn't done so already.

These obstacles aside, I am in good spirits, and you should be too. The newspapers appear to be mainly on our side — even the local newspapers as far as Ipswich are gearing up to publish daily bulletins on the trial, despite the efforts of those who wish to silence stories such as yours: those parliamentarians who call themselves the King's Friends, and the shareholders of EIC and ACM, to name a few.

If you were not before, I would say you are indeed becoming a celebrity, Vincent.

And so, like overprepared soldiers, Delphine and I are ready to march into your upcoming battle.

I will see you soon.

Nick

Delphine

It's been almost four months since Vincent was dragged from the Exoticies, and tomorrow, his trial will begin at last.

As Delphine lies awake in her bed at the bawdy house, an uncomfortable feeling bubbles in her stomach. A voice in her head nags that if Vincent is afraid tonight, no one is with him to soothe his worries. In these months of preparations, she has seen her brother less than a handful of times. She has no idea if her visits have succeeded in cheering him up or in making him believe that they can win this.

But she believes they can. She will be there for Vincent tomorrow, and the next day, and the next day.

As she tosses and turns in her bed, she considers all the reasons why.

Even before Vincent joined her family, to her, love was a silent thing: three words rarely spoken but fiercely felt. In her mother's pots of red bean stew started at sunrise and eaten well after sunset. In four pairs of floured hands shaping Friday night saltfish and johnnycakes. In long blinks and staggered breaths and burdens carried but never spoken about. Then Vincent joined their family, and Delphine came to know his silent love, too: in the giving of wooden birds, in little rebellions and best-laid plans.

And later, she shared a new kind of love with Pearl; secret, and cut short before she could speak of it out loud.

First because Pearl would not listen, and then because she was sent to an early, violent end. But even after Pearl's cruel death – the circumstances of which Delphine could not bear to voice, even now – Delphine has continued to love her quietly. She suspects a part of her always will.

There are many times in Delphine's life that she has felt alone. But never with her family. Never with Vincent. Because Vincent is her home. And home is a precious, quiet thing, which she will protect at all costs. As the lamplight fades, Delphine smiles in the darkness. For once, she is not so scared of what is to come. She has put her trust in Nick – just as she trusted that things would get easier after a terrible first day in Westminster, and they did. The papers and the public are on their side. Their arguments are well-prepared. They'll go into tomorrow with open eyes and hopeful hearts.

Chapter Eleven

Tomorrow morning, the Court of King's Bench will meet in the first course of the judgment of the Negro Boxer, Vincent Mourière, against the Hon. Lord Harvey Esq. The cause of the trial is to know how far a Black servant is the Property of the Purchaser by the Laws of England, because the Black refused to go back to the West Indies at his Master's command.

Known for his fighting prowess, the Freedom Fighter is now engaged in a Legal Battle of Blows. It may surprise readers that Mourière has instructed the counsel of one Nicholas Lyons, MP for Kettering and recently disinherited nephew of the Hon. lord aforesaid.

This paper has heard that the presiding Chief Justice, Lord Mansfield, has sought to resolve these matters outside of the courtroom and prevent a formal judgment and the far-reaching implications it may present. But both Mourière and Lord Harvey are relentless in their desire to knock out their opponent in court.

—GENERAL EVENING POST

Vincent
Vincent slides the newspaper across the table. Is this all the public thinks of his case? That the first day of his trial is no more important than a boxing match?

They await their summons to the King's Bench in a small back room. Along with the sparkling mirrors and usual array of portraits (once you've seen one battle-ready white man on a horse, you've seen them all), a gilded oval table dominates the space, surrounded by carved, cushioned chairs. After months away from such grandeur, Vincent takes a seat and relishes the smoothness of the leather upholstery. It's almost comfortable enough to make him forget that many of the chair's previous occupants may have also felt this way on the morning of their trials, only to be returned to iron and stone by nightfall.

Nick stands, hands clasped over the back of his chair, the cuffs of his black robe rolled up to his elbows. He's practising voices to use when addressing the Chief Justice.

'My lord,' he says, through his nose. 'Chief Justice.' His voice filled with gravel.

'Your lordship.' Now, every syllable is perfectly crisp and elongated. Sitting beside Nick, Delphine quickly nods, wordless confirmation that he's found the right one. How well they seem to work together. Nick clears his throat, turns his attention to Vincent, tilts his head, then leans over to pluck a stray hair from Vincent's shoulder.

Gone are his topaz livery coats and bright yellow bottoms. Today, his clothes are demure: a smart copper jacket and simple black breeches that sit flush with the stockings below his knee. Like Nick, he also wears a newly purchased wig in the rolled lamb's wool style of the moment. All this must have cost Nick a fair portion of the retainer from his godparents, but Nick assured him it was worth it.

First impressions mean everything.

Vincent appreciates the generosity of all involved, especially because his wig is black. White would have made a spectacle of him; black is respectable *and* different.

If he does earn his freedom, Vincent makes a mental note to wear this ensemble when he begins courting a potential wife.

The clock at the back of the room ticks on, approaching a quarter to ten.

'A final reminder,' Nick says, thumbing through a stack of papers without seeming to read any of them, 'it is best if you are silent today, Vincent.'

How could I forget? thinks Vincent. He is not to say more than a sentence on the first day of his own trial. Though he's uncertain he would be able to speak anyway. The knot in his throat is the size of a walnut.

'The opening arguments will do all the talking for you,' continues Nick. 'Instead, you must focus on remaining composed. But...'

Nick pauses his rifling to glance up at Vincent's facial expression. 'But don't look too stern, or you'll come across as a brute. Try holding the edges of your mouth into the beginning of a smile...' Dogearing the page he was on, he uses his index fingers to stretch his lips into a tight curve. Vincent copies, or thinks he does.

Nick drags his mouth into a frown. 'But don't appear too content either, or they will think you aren't taking your situation seriously.'

Vincent attempts to follow Nick's direction, the corners of his mouth settling into place.

'*Hmm.*' Nick crosses his arms and pensively taps a finger to his nose.

Vincent wonders what he is doing wrong. They practised this at great length during Nick's visits to the prison. He *knows* how to measure his tone, knows when his face is at risk of giving away his inner thoughts. After years of working in service, he is as skilled at appearing passive as any working man. But today, the art of indifference will be more crucial than ever to master.

It's hard to remember the shape of his days prior to his arrest, how different the world had seemed. When he last set foot on the grass, the trees had just released their spring blossom. Soon they'll be covered in the burning shades of autumn, his favourite season.

Depending on the trial's outcome, he might not be here to watch the leaves fall.

A knock at the door.

'The first call is for me,' Nick says, scooping up his papers and law books. He says in a reassuring tone, which Vincent suspects is for both their benefit, 'Chin up, my friend. All will be well.'

So long as I don't move my face and hands or speak.

Nick adjusts his robe with one hand, and Delphine gets up to open the door for him – but not before she hastily reorders his papers with a pointed look. Vincent spies the word OPENING on the page she places at the top. Nick disappears towards the courtroom, the door closing with a soft thud.

An encouraging start.

Vincent reminds himself that this experience is new to all of them. Nick became an MP soon after being called to the bar. It's not that he doubts his friend's passion or knowledge of the law, but Vincent can't let go of the creeping thought that his godparents' money could have paid for someone with more experience.

But then he'd not have this wig or the jacket. Then Delphine would still be working at the bawdy house. Then he wouldn't be going into the King's Bench today with someone he trusts.

How ungrateful he can be.

The clock chimes a quarter to the hour. A battle erupts in Vincent's stomach, clashing swords and swooping arrows. He hunches forward in his seat to contain them.

'I can't do this, Delphine,' he mutters into his sleeve as he presses his head to the cool wood of the table.

Delphine's skirt rustles as she moves beside him, her hand landing softly between his shoulder blades. When her voice comes, he welcomes its calmness. 'Of course you can, brother. No one on this Earth would do it better than you.'

He's not sure he believes it.

Though he is trying, Vincent does not feel brave. He can't even sit up straight for fear that he's about to fail every single person who has put their faith in him. On his way into Westminster this morning, he saw at least a hundred Negroes among the crowds cheering for him.

What if he lets them all down? What if he makes everything worse?

His next thought comes out unbidden. 'What if they're right and I'm not meant to be free?'

Delphine squeezes his shoulder. 'Vincent, I adore you, and I understand your fear, but I'm afraid if you say that again I may have to slap you.'

Vincent laughs into the wood, making a hollow sound. At twenty-six, he's had plenty of practice dealing with his worries alone, but he supposes he can let Delphine help him shoo the feelings away for once.

'There's no need to be ashamed of your anxieties.' Delphine's voice is kind and sure. 'Remember, we know something those men out there do not.' She crouches beside him and traces her thumb over his hand. 'You have always been capable of more than they gave you credit for. At twelve, you convinced Lord Harvey you should learn to read. At thirteen, you bested *four* Frenchmen who snuck onto the plantation with bayonets. You helped Pearl and I plan our escape. You worked your way from messenger, to clerk, to butler, to boxer, and you were good at it. So good, you earned enough to be freed.' She slides a hand beneath Vincent's chin to raise it. The faith he sees in her eyes threatens to bring tears to his own. His sister swallows. 'Today, there will be no fists, but you are strong enough without them. You *are* meant to be free.' She cups his cheek in her palm. 'You *deserve* to be free.'

The knot in his throat loosens. He's unsure if her determined gaze or her gentle words helped most, but for once, he is relieved not to be carrying this burden alone. He's glad he's told her how he feels.

There were also *five* Frenchmen, not four.

'You are the best of men, Vincent Mourière.' She nudges him lightly, noticing the return of his smile. 'And they'll be damned if they don't see it.'

Delphine

There's standing room only in the highest court of the land.

Five minutes until the trial's due to commence, spectators are still cramming themselves into the upper and lower galleries, overspilling onto the staircases and in the aisles.

Delphine would have had to stand with them if Nick hadn't reserved her a seat — the last spot on the front right pew. She draws in her stomach to squeeze past the robed men who are already seated on her row, rising onto the balls of her feet and apologising profusely.

With no official role in the trial, she half expects one of them to summon a court usher to remove her. But they let her pass — albeit with huffs of displeasure and without budging to make her passage easier.

Peering back over the flock of spectators' wigs, she's cheered to see a few of Nick's acquaintances from the Bill of Rights society present — some of whom have contributed to Vincent's fees at the King's Bench. A loaf of bread could be bought for sixpence in Southwark, but step inside the debtor's prison and suddenly it's three shillings. They've needed every farthing they can get.

Behind them are Vincent's benefactors: his godfather, the short, softly spoken Sir Wishaw, is wearing a drab olive-green ensemble, which Delphine suspects he has chosen to allow him to fade into the background. Beside him is Vincent's godmother, Eliza MacLeod, whose lace-trimmed finery overshadows her unremarkable features. They each give Delphine a shaky wave.

Delphine returns the gesture, then looks away. She is not in the mindset to placate their nerves when she is so preoccupied with her own.

There are many darker faces here today, too, and that brings Delphine comfort. With so few of them in this land, it is easy to feel alone.

Wedged into her space against the raised press docket, she leans over the railing to tap Nick on the shoulder. He's drumming the fingers of his left hand on the wooden desk while his right fiddles with a short length of twine. In their preparations, they'd soon concluded his mind works better when his body is in motion.

He twists around to face her.

'How are you feeling?' she asks, if only for confirmation he's as nervous as she is.

'Good, good,' Nick says, words rushing out in a flurry. 'Very well indeed.'

Just as nervous, then.

The pressure almost seems to be bulging out of his eyeballs.

But she has no more time to reassure him: Lord Harvey's counsel has just walked into the courtroom.

Chapter Twelve

> Liberty is the right of doing whatever the laws permit.
> —BARON DE MONTESQUIEU

Nick once described John Dunning as a skunk of a man.

Then, he had to explain what a skunk is to Delphine. 'It's not on account of his smell,' he'd said, 'but his attitude.'

Resourceful, yes; proud, certainly. But it's his tendency to spray odorous opinions about the inns of court that renders the comparison.

What she does know: less than a year ago, Dunning defended a Negro in a similar trial, arguing that his client could not be sold on English shores. This further proves Delphine's suspicion that for many influential men, allyship rests where profit lies.

Like a hare anticipating a fox, Delphine searches the hall for Lord Harvey, but first, she spies Vincent being led into the courtroom. Her chest tightens as he sits on the long, empty defendant's bench below the dais. The spectators quieten briefly – out of respect or disdain, Delphine can't be sure. His eyes are trained on the herringbone floorboards. As much as she wishes he'd look to her for support, she's sure her face would betray her own fear.

The clock chimes ten o'clock, and a clerk announces from the higher dais: 'All rise for the entrance of William Murray, 1st Earl of Mansfield, Lord Chief Justice for England and Wales.'

When Mansfield enters from behind the curtain, Delphine is surprised by how kind a face he has for someone with so much power. His wiry crescent spectacles are wide enough to reach the cusp of his eyebrows, which are faded, presumably from years scrunched over documents by candlelight. His full-bottomed wig sways like a poodle's tail as he strides across the courtroom, the ends wafting as he sits at his solitary bench.

The Chief Justice settles, as does the chattering courtroom. Delphine's heart pounds as all assembled await his lordship's opening remarks.

'The case of Mourière vs Harvey has been brought here today from the lower courts. Are both the complainant and the accused present?'

Vincent rises from the bench, and Lord Harvey does the same from his place beside the witness stand.

Delphine examines her former master. In image, he looks every part the composed lord, but Delphine knows the rage that lingers just beneath his surface. The sight of him stirs that same fury inside her. He stands upright but not defensively, in a newly made pale green coat embroidered with gold thread. His hands are crossed thoughtfully in front of him; not a strand of his wig is out of place; his solemn cheeks are smooth from a fresh shave.

Delphine tears her eyes away.

This is the face that would send Vincent to a slow and dehumanising death.

It twists her stomach.

The Chief Justice turns to Lord Harvey. 'I would urge the lord once again,' he says, in a way that sounds more like a demand than a suggestion, 'this matter can be resolved quickly, should he release the complainant from his ownership.'

The Justice pauses for a moment, and Delphine holds her breath. But Lord Harvey is as immovable today as he was the three times he'd declined the judge's suggestion in the lead-up to the trial. He stays stubbornly silent, mouth pressed in a hard line.

'So be it,' the Justice says, leaning back in his chair with a disappointed sigh. 'Well, if the parties will have judgment, they must both be prepared to bear the consequences. *Fiat justitia, ruat coelum.*' He turns his head next to the bench of newspapermen. 'And these are all the members of the press present?'

The wigless men cast their hands up.

The Chief Justice arches his threadbare brows. 'Then keep your scribbling quiet. Should the court be distracted by your incessant rustling, scratching, *oohing* and *aahing*, you will be removed. I trust I am understood.'

With the newspapermen chastened, his lordship calls the court into session, and invites Dunning to give his opening remarks.

'Thank you, your lordship.' The skunk rises, lifting and smoothing the tail of his jacket ahead of addressing the court. 'The question brought before the court today is a simple one: can a slave legally refuse the will of his master? The defendant, the Negro boxer Mister Mourière, has been in the possession of my client, Lord Harvey, for sixteen years. In that time, Mourière has been educated, provided for, and given access to opportunities far beyond those granted to the majority of Englishmen. Yet, on the sixth of May this year, he ran from his master's service. And when his master exerted his right to transfer his ownership to another — Mourière refused like a petulant child. But this counsel knows he is worse than that.' Dunning continues, voice fatherly and sharp. 'He is an animal. When faced with a choice, he will choose destruction over diplomacy every time. And that is not his fault: much like any beast, Negroes must have their tempers controlled through hard work, discipline and control. But my client, Lord Harvey, has taken on a heavier burden than most in this wild thing.

'By law, Mourière is my client's property. This counsel will argue that it is not only Lord Harvey's right by law to move such property wherever he sees fit, but that this is also his right — nay, his *duty* — given by God. Indeed, it is the honourable Lord Harvey's Christian *obligation* to complete his great task to mould Mourière into a moral being acceptable to God.'

Heat rises beneath Delphine's stays, and with it, that anger Dunning describes. She knows she is not *wild*, but how does anyone react when backed into a corner?

The Chief Justice is satisfied however, and invites Nick to say his piece.

Nick thanks Lord Mansfield and angles his head towards his speech for a few seconds. His shoulders slowly rise and fall, then, leaving the speech behind, he steps in front of the desk and starts pacing.

Delphine prepares to recite the young lawyer's speech in her head along with him.

'The picture the prosecution has painted of the defendant is a lie. Vincent Mourière is a Christian who espouses all the values we strive for as Englishmen. He is brave of heart, strong of mind and even stronger in body. He is a champion of those who need him, providing charity and goodwill to those he meets. He served most honourably in Lord Harvey's possession, and most importantly, Vincent Mourière serves God. And no place in the Bible allows for the enslavement of any Christian, not when in this world there are so many villains we could easily procure instead.'

Delphine frowns: that last part was off-script. Enslavement shouldn't be inflicted upon anyone, villain or otherwise. But Nick is gaining momentum now, gesticulating freely towards the mahogany beams that hold up the brilliant white ceiling.

'Vincent Mourière was denied his freedom when, by law, it should have been his nine years ago when first he set foot on British soil. The precedent I describe was declared by Chief Justice Holt, some forty years past. The arguments made here, my lord, are nothing new. They are repetitions of cases long established in the courts of England: Yorke vs Talbot; the Cartwright case of fifteen...' Nick freezes, face blank.

Has he forgotten? Nick always struggles with the dates. But this is not a theatre performance where the actor can improvise the next line – he must get it right. Usually the world is more tolerant of mistakes made by men like Nick – people would trust him after a dozen errors, while losing faith in Delphine after the first one. But in this courtroom, with his lack of experience, his credibility is like fresh-blown glass: fragile and easily shattered.

Nick's voice drops to a mutter. 'Of fifteen...'

Dunning curls a finger to his lips to cover his grin.

This might not be a theatre – but Delphine can still act as a prompt. As inconspicuously as she can manage, she coughs.

Immediately, he glances in her direction and she mouths the answer. 'Of 1569!' Nick blinks his thanks, then raises a hand in apology to the court. 'And John Lilburne in 1649; and so on and so on. The defendant seeks that this matter of law be put to rest once and for all – no more uncertainty. No more Christians sold on a whim or for want of profit. This is the argument of the defence.'

Murmurs of agreement echo through the gallery, but Vincent shifts in his chair, yet to look up from the floor.

'Thank you, counsellors, for your opening statements; they have been noted.' The Chief Justice makes a final stroke on his page and dips his quill again. 'Regarding this case and others like it, I would rather all masters think themselves enslaved, and all slaves think they are free – so that both may behave better.'

Laughter swells from the floor; a few newspapermen smirk, jotting down the Chief Justice's quip. Delphine doesn't snigger along with them.

'Counsel Dunning,' the Chief Justice booms, the authority in his voice silencing the crowd. 'Please present your case to the court.'

Dunning stands once more, adjusting a silver button on his waistcoat. As he turns to address the court, Delphine continues to glare at the small silver circle, the sale of which would likely feed a family for a month.

'The defence speaks of the Bible. Many here today are as familiar with our sacred text as we are with the backs of our hands. And the Bible, much like the law of this land, has been interpreted over centuries as a veritable source of truth for morality and justice. Slavery is as old as the Bible and accepted by it. It has been an essential component in the cultures of the Romans, the Egyptians and many great empires, including ours. But in our case, slavery is not only a *necessity* that drives our empire's greatness but also the will of God.'

Dunning extends a hand to the crowd, inviting them to buy into his performance. When he's confident he has their attention, he continues. 'After the Great Flood, Noah had three sons. Sem, Japhet and Ham. And it is through these brothers we learn not only why we have three races of men – the European, the Asian and the Black – but also why the Black must serve.'

Delphine braces herself for the familiar story.

'Ham was a bad son.' He chuckles, leaning casually with one hand on his table. 'That was an understatement. Ham was an *intolerable* son. He dishonoured his parents, so our Lord condemned Ham to be a servant of servants for all time. It is the burden of Japhet, the burden of Englishmen, to hold the sons of Ham accountable and obedient to the Lord's will – for He makes no mistakes.'

Applause erupts from a pew near the back of the hall, and Delphine shrinks, reminding herself that if their roles reversed, the men who are clapping and cheering would feel as she does now. Small. Disobedient. Vermin.

Her brother has spent years trying to avoid becoming a target, but from the way his lip trembles now, she can see Dunning's arrow has found his heart.

'Therefore, your lordship, before this trial proceeds further, I will ask all present to hold the story of Ham in their minds.' Dunning throws a dismissive hand towards Vincent, then Nick. 'Do not be misled by Mourière's dapper exterior or the arguments his counsel will make, lest we invoke the wrath of the Lord. In this demand for his freedom, Mourière demands we disobey God.'

'Your lordship,' Nick snaps, rising from his seat, 'is this not a court of law?'

His words are met with jeers from that adversarial back pew, prompting the clerks to shout for *order! Order or removal!*

'In a Christian nation such as ours,' the Chief Justice responds once the crowd quiets, 'each of us indeed has a duty to serve God. But as the defence counsel so keenly protests, this court's concern is to uphold *earthly* law. Which, despite an emphatic, acrobatic display of emotion on both sides, neither counsel is yet to achieve.'

The Chief Justice gives Nick the floor. The complainant's nephew powers over to the eastern arched window at the front of the hall. He gestures to the bookcases beneath it, lined with centuries of leather-bound decisions. 'It was 1596 when this court declared the air in England too pure to be inhaled by slaves. I pray, your lordship, that the wind does not blow worse since?' He takes an extravagant sniff to illustrate that the question is rhetorical. 'Unless there has been a change in the air, the moment a slave sets foot on English ground, he is free. Indeed, this ruling has been upheld and documented by these courts time and time again.' He runs his hand along the books. 'So, why are we *still* discussing it?'

Because there's money to be made, Delphine thinks.

Nick runs a hand through his hair. He seems to have recovered from his earlier nerves. 'Because Lord Harvey is a man of means. Not a man of God. He seeks to further his own interests – not God's or this court's.' He raises his voice to meet the jeers of the spectators. 'To keep one man in chains to satisfy the greed of another binds us all in hypocrisy. And, since the counsel for the prosecution is set on referring to the Bible, there is no passage clearer than this: *there is no Jew nor Greek, no slave nor free, no male nor female. We are all one in Christ.* That is God's will. Not only is slavery illegal on these shores, but it is also unchristian. It is immoral, and this man,' Nick taps the hollow wood of the dock, 'must be free. If Lord Harvey wishes to use his services, he should pay for them.'

For the first time since arriving in court, Vincent looks up at Mister Lyons, eyes shimmering with pride. Nick is performing, but his words make her feel seen, too – until Dunning's thick laughter quashes that rare sentiment.

'So, are we purporting now that a man may not preserve his interests?' Mock puzzlement flashes on the opposing counsel's face, and he brings a hand to his chest. 'That we should return to primitive society, where shares are given equally regardless of each man's contribution and heritage?' Casting a flippant hand in Vincent's direction, he continues, 'If the defence and this Negro's logic follows, we gentlemen should also pay our wives for performing their domestic duties. And believe me, your lordship, that would bankrupt many a man.'

A man guffaws in the gallery above, the sound swiftly followed by an *oomph* as the woman next to him, presumably his wife, elbows him in the ribs. Delphine glances at Mrs MacLeod in time to catch the approving smile on her lips.

'No.' Dunning scoffs. 'That would never be a question because *most* wives know their place.'

The woman in the gallery stiffens in her seat, clearly embarrassed.

What it is to be a woman in this country, Delphine thinks. But at least the white lady's displeasure was noticed. There's a uniqueness to her burden of being a woman and being Black. Double the disadvantage. Less than half a voice. Sometimes the men of this world make it difficult for her to remember all she has achieved despite them.

'It is the accused that is unchristian,' Dunning concludes with a pompous twirl of the wrist. 'He does not know our Lord.'

'He *does* know our Lord,' Nick counters, swiping a piece of parchment from his table and placing it in front of Lord Mansfield. The Chief Justice eyes it keenly, then passes it down to the other judges as Nick continues. 'This certificate proves that a year after arriving in England, Vincent Mourière was baptised a Christian on the fourteenth of August 1762.'

The Chief Justice *hmpfs* his acknowledgement. 'I presume there are witnesses who can attest to the authenticity of this document?'

'Yes, your lordship.' Nick smiles and summons Vincent's godparents to the stand. Mrs MacLeod blushes red as she bows her head to the court. Sir Wishaw digs both hands in his pocket and gives a bashful nod to the assembly.

The reasoning behind Vincent's baptism has long perplexed Delphine. Like pond water, it seems clear on the surface: Lord Harvey wanted an upstanding household, and publicly boasting a christened slave was one way to command the admiration of his peers. But the deeper you wade, the muddier the reasoning. If status is what he desired, why only baptise Vincent and not her?

Delphine supposes that if she wasn't worth the expense of tutoring, she wasn't worth the cost of a christening. Or perhaps it simply didn't occur to Lord Harvey to baptise a slave girl.

'Thank you for your introductions,' Nick says to his witnesses, drawing Delphine back to herself. 'Now, to the matter at hand. Has Mister Mourière, in your trusted opinions, ever done anything that you would regard to be in breach of the Christian faith or acted in a way that you would consider to be against God?'

'To my knowledge?' Mrs MacLeod tugs on her lace collar again until Wishaw interjects.

'I believe he is as good a man as any.'

'I agree,' Mrs MacLeod says. 'He has always behaved as a Christian should.'

They are telling the truth. Lord Harvey's pride must have stopped him from telling them what Vincent did. However, Delphine is sure that laying a single punch on a man like him should not be counted as a sin. Nick shakes Sir Wishaw's hand before they both return to their seats.

Nick returns to Vincent's side. 'There you have it, your lordship,' he says, opening his arms to the Chief Justice. 'A Christian and I think we can all agree faith unites us in ways our races may not. And if there is anything the Bible does not tolerate, it is the enslavement of Christians.'

When the Chief Justice dismisses the court at the end of the first day, Nick bounds around the back room as if Vincent's case has already been won.

In fact, Lord Mansfield called for an adjournment.

He and the other justices need to consider the legality of enslaving Christians and whether or not that legality changes based on the colour of one's skin — which means if they decide Vincent should be freed, the ruling will expand to apply, in theory, to all Black Christians in Britain. Delphine can envision the vicars now rushing to hide their holy water.

Nick believes that is the only conclusion the justices can reach. Vincent seemed optimistic, too. But while their faith heartens Delphine, ultimately they are not the ones who will decide Vincent's fate.

And now that Vincent has been sent back to the prison, her feelings on the matter are more confused. The arguments presented by Nick and Dunning echo loudly in her ears; every reaction from the justices, newspapermen and spectators looms large in her mind's eye. So before exiting Westminster Hall that evening, it's to clear her head that she returns to the courtroom alone.

The King's Bench is now deserted, save for the portraits of former justices that line the back wall. Clad in black robes with miniver fur collars, these men are the select few who built the country's entire legal system; the men who, according to Nick, *established the oldest democracy in the world*. She approaches each painting, searching each severe, pale face for guidance, clarity, or hope. *Would you have freed Vincent?* she wonders. *Would you have?*

She closes her eyes, stretches her neck to one side, then the other, and rolls her shoulders. Her back aches from carrying months of stress.

Then the door opens, and the ensuing sound pierces her with a spike of panic. She tenses as a man about Nick's height stands beside her. She doesn't need to look to know who it is; she knows his scent: honey and almond. The sweetness does little to mask his poison.

'Queer that you should stay behind to admire *this* portrait,' Lord Harvey says almost cordially. He and his pug-headed cane come one, two, three taps closer.

Delphine keeps quiet, staring straight ahead. She can't bring herself to face him.

He steps in front of the final portrait on Delphine's right and smiles fondly at it. She follows his gaze – barring a few additional crow's feet, the subject looks almost identical to the painting of Pearl's great- great-grandfather on the mantel in the lord's office. One of the founders of the East India Company, Lord Reginald Harvey I was a merchant turned justice turned lord. It was the current Lord Harvey IV who expanded the family's interests into the West Indies.

'My nephew has made quite the impression on the court,' he sneers. 'I don't think I've ever felt such utter disappointment in him.'

He's trying to provoke a reaction, Delphine tells herself. *Keep quiet.*

Harvey's eyes burrow into her like mites beneath her skin. She's desperate to gouge them out. He continues, unbothered. 'You may dress like us. Sit like us. Speak like us. I believe there is a saying about that – something about putting rouge on a pig. But mark me, girl, we will never be the same. There is always a master, always a slave. Freedom will not help Vincent. You may have proved too ungodly to restrain, but without me, you are nothing. And so is he.'

Delphine looks bleary-eyed at the vaulted ceiling. Counts each arch, each angel and gargoyle carved into stone, until she hears the portrait-perfect lord smirk and his cane *tap, tap, tap, tap* away.

Chapter Thirteen

The West-India merchants have, we hear, obtained a dubious promise from the Hon. Lord Harvey that the commodity of slavery will not change, regardless of the outcome of his legal cause. In the dockyards, rumours are circling that if the laws of England do not align with colony laws concerning property in slaves, no man of common sense will, in the future, lay out his money in so precarious a commodity. At least not without having moved abroad. The consequences will be the inevitable ruin of the British West Indies and Britain herself. For the sake of our nation, let us pray the Chief Justice sees sense.
—GENERAL EVENING POST

There have been four adjournments in six weeks. Each has persisted longer than the last. With so much ground to cover, the justices are digging up ancient statutes or considering the proposal of new laws to Parliament to keep up with Dunning and Nick's arguments. Over the last few hearings, they've examined religion, morality and the intelligence of the Negro.

October's chill hangs low in the courtroom, and both lawyers' tempers are shortening with the days. Were the court not so packed with spectators, Delphine might shiver after each frosty exchange.

'We are not solely discussing Vincent Mourière.' Dunning throws his hands up, robe flying behind him. 'This ruling bears far more consequence now. Counsel Lyons has ensured that much.'

Nick scoffs. 'Have you not read your client's grandstanding in the *Evening Post?*'

Dunning dips his head reverently at the Chief Justice before shooting Nick a withering look and continuing his tirade. If Delphine couldn't see the bags under his eyes, she might swear he enjoys it. The bags under Vincent's eyes are worse, and though it's hard for her to accept, their light is beginning to dim.

He's been at the centre of this debate all these weeks but has never been involved. It's hard enough for her to remain silent. What a toll it must take on his mind.

Dunning points to another historic ruling. 'In the Penny trial of 1677, ten slaves escaped and were returned to their master. When the matter was brought before the court, it ruled the slaves were considered the same status as chattel property or villeins – and as such, Blacks should always be returned to their owner. A chair does not decide in which room it is placed.'

'And a mere twenty years later,' Nick strikes back, 'Chief Justice Holt ruled the converse. For villeinage has long been extinct in this country, and therefore unenforceable in practice. I suppose Counsel Dunning would also imprison a man for playing football? Or eating a dinner of more than two courses? Agile as you may be, sir, you cannot twist the law to fit your view of the world. Like a villain of progress, you ask us to linger in the past when this court has the opportunity to set the course of the future.'

Dunning laughs, unphased. 'A naive dream. The *young* counsel here fails to recognise the economic foundations of our great Empire. Recent estimates say there are currently fourteen to fifteen thousand Negroes in London. The cost to set them all free would exceed £800,000. In London alone! If this precedent is set, then our fellow Englishmen will be financially castrated.'

Naturally contemplative and quiet, the Chief Justice raises a hand and says, 'Of course, one must deeply consider the disagreeable effects of such costs in one's decision making.'

Delphine grips the bench with irate fingers. Here, they are discussing paying *masters* for the inconvenience of losing their slaves. *Fifty pounds a head.* It's not the number that enrages her, so much as the lack of consideration for compensating slaves.

For while their masters may lose their chattel and future profits, it is the Negroes who have lost their lives.

But as she and Vincent have known all along, this trial is not really about them or Vincent's freedom. It is about white men's right to property.

The skunk scurries over to the press bench. 'Who would squeeze all the sugar from the cane once all the slaves are freed? Your sugar may be expensive now…' He pauses to let his noxious argument permeate the air and settle over the newspapermen. 'But imagine if you *paid* for it.'

'True liberty protects the labourer as well as his lord!' Nick shouts, but Dunning is on a roll now. He has most of the court on his side.

'How many good English minds are furthering our country's ambition in the colonies? How many of them will we lose forever, should this ruling promise to confiscate their property if they return home? Must we condemn them to exile?' Dunning places a hand tenderly over his heart, as if England is beating within it. 'It does not matter if a slave is in Kingston or Virginia or the far reaches of Russia—'

'Yet it *does* matter,' Nick interrupts, crossing his arms over his chest. 'To even consider applying the legislation of such places in an English court would be *reductio ad absurdum*, impossible. We must focus here on *English* justice. Let the Virginians and the Jamaicans keep their laws, as we may make and keep our own.'

'A slave is a slave is a slave!' Dunning snorts. 'A bulldog may not become a beagle by simply crossing country lines. It is not so much a geographical matter as biological and economic. And I am afeared to say, with this inexperienced counsellor's thinking, he would see this great Empire face financial ruin.'

Burbles of discontent ripple through the courtroom.

'The empire would face ruin?' Nick counters. 'Or the complainant's purse strings?' He strides to meet Dunning, but the Chief Justice interjects, his tone sharp.

'I too should be glad to be informed if this suit will be carried on at the expense of the West India merchants, or only at that of Lord Harvey?'

Dunning flushes. 'My client's, of course.'

'Oh?' Mansfield says, clapping his hands together in faux surprise. 'According to the complainant's recent press activities, it seems otherwise.' He raises a sceptical eyebrow towards the press docket, deep lines wrinkling unevenly on his forehead.

Delphine chances a glance at Lord Harvey, but his cheeks are as cool as alabaster.

The newspapermen emit a few awkward coughs, and their scribbling intensifies.

The Chief Justice sighs and shakes his head, then lowers his tone once more. 'If the merchants think the question at hand is of great economic consequence to commerce, they had better think of an application to those legislative powers down the hall.'

'Of course, my lord,' Dunning mutters as he scuttles back towards his counsellor's table and casts a disgruntled eye at Lord Harvey. Clearly, the lord's recent trumpeting to the *Evening Post* had been against his advice. 'Lord Harvey and the West India Merchants will make sure to carry their point at the next session of Parliament in December.'

Mansfield flicks his gavel towards Nick, who ceases fiddling with the length of twine in his hand, ready to continue.

'Thank you, my lord. As we were saying, the Empire's glory is enough to withstand the freeing of slaves in this country. And as Mister Dunning at last concedes, here we are not discussing colonial jurisprudence.' He tugs down on his lapels with renewed confidence. 'The crux of the matter is that in 1770, no man in England may be a slave. And that includes Mister Mourière.'

Delphine spies the corner of Vincent's lips tug into a tight smile, his hands clasping nervously together as he straightens in his seat.

'This case is farcical.' Nick throws his arms wide, voice unwavering as it booms across the courtroom. 'Lord Harvey promised Vincent Mourière his freedom. And Mister Mourière himself will attest to this.'

Whispers sweep through the hall once more.

Vincent

This is it. This is what Vincent has been waiting for since iron chains grasped his wrists over four months ago. Nick has done a good job presenting their side of the argument, thus far.

Vincent's primary goal is to not ruin everything.

All he needs to do is speak – he's been doing it for almost twenty-six years, it shouldn't be so hard.

But has his mouth ever been *this* dry?

He rubs his clammy hands down the length of his breeches. Will the sweat be misconstrued as duplicity?

Every breath Vincent takes on court days is vigilant; he's all too aware of what he represents. When he was in the ring, his rising status was a promise that inspired those around him. But in this court room, that promise has turned into something sinister.

Vincent blinks and finds himself in the witness stand.

'Please tell the court, Mister Mourière, of how Lord Harvey promised your freedom.'

Nick is holding out a hand, inviting every spectator to stare at him. But Vincent is still thinking about how he can summon Nick's confidence, and how he can look back at anyone when focusing on the ceiling or the floor is much more comfortable.

Nick clears his throat and tries again.

'Mister Mourière, please recount the truth of the agreement between yourself and Lord Harvey.'

With a single nod, Vincent mimics the same throat clearing and takes a breath.

'1766 and '67 were difficult years for the Harvey household. After Lord Harvey's daughter's accident, the family entertained less at 20 St James's Square. Lord Harvey's investments went neglected and his wife, Lady Katherine, moved in with her mother in Sussex. It would affect any man, to undergo such changes. And the lord sought to combat his melancholy.'

'How did Lord Harvey do that?' asks Nick.

Vincent shifts his gaze from Nick to his master for the first time today. His stare is met by a black and fiery scowl, its heat so intense Vincent feels it beneath his collar.

Tensing his jaw, Vincent pulls his eyes away. There is every reason for him to hate the man.

Yet, he can't help but feel a pang of sorrow.

He still remembers how proud he felt when, back in St Lucia, Lord Harvey elevated him from messenger to clerk. How insistent the lord had been for Vincent to accompany him back to England – how exceptional he'd made Vincent feel. Having spent so long seeking his master's approval, his obedience so engrained, speaking these words still feels like a betrayal.

But then Vincent recalls the other days. The beatings, the demands that could never be satisfied, and the broken promise that brought him to this witness stand. Lord Harvey may have owned him, but his loyalty was never deserved.

'I cannot say how he spent the period between June and August of '67 – when I was sent to attend to you and your estate, Mister Lyons. But the other months, he'd spent drinking, mostly,' he says to Nick. 'By the time I returned to St James's in September, we were receiving shipments of brandy and canary fortnightly. One barrel each time, sometimes two. The casks were empty by the time the next shipment would arrive. I know this because I carried the barrels in and out of the house. When the lord tired of drinking alone, he would attend his Private Members Club, Socrat's, where he would play dice or cards.'

A sense of calm settles over Vincent, now, his voice no longer shaking, and he even looks out into the crowd. If Dunning's to be believed, there could be as many as fifteen thousand faces like his in the city, and at least a dozen are smiling here today, invested in this cause. He cannot speak for their past experiences, but perhaps he can improve their futures.

'One such melancholy night, I accompanied the lord to Socrat's. Before leaving home, he had already consumed half a case of wine. My duty was to obey him and ensure his safety throughout our excursion.'

'How did you attend the club?'

'Gerard Forthright, who was then Lord Harvey's coachman, drove us there. I went to rouse him, but found he had not yet retired to bed. He had also been drinking his supply of ale. I wondered if he'd be well enough to man the coach, but he assured me he was, so we set off. The journey to Socrat's was only half a mile, but as usual, I hung to the back rails of the carriage for the duration, lest any villains attempt to take advantage of Lord Harvey. One cannot be too careful in London at night.'

Several spectators mutter their agreement.

'The lord bade me accompany him into the club, while Forthright minded the carriage at the adjoining stable yard. But uncommonly, after a point, Forthright too was invited in to partake in a game of cards, after which he joined us at Lord Harvey's table. That was when I saw Forthright steal the coin purse upon Lord Harvey's person and as was my duty, I proceeded to challenge the man — albeit discreetly. Lord Harvey would have disliked it if I caused a scene.'

He moves to cup his hands behind his head to support his thoughts better but remembers that this might make him appear too relaxed, perhaps uncaring, and crosses them in his lap instead.

'After I challenged Forthright, he did not deny his theft but offered me half of the loot in return for my silence. When I denied him, he took great offence and pushed me by the shoulder into the wall.'

Delphine sends Vincent an encouraging smile, which he catches like a rope thrown between them, the cords thickly braided, steady, and strong. *Kontiné lèspiwasyon*, she mouths. *Keep breathing.*

He speaks louder.

'To protect my master's honour, I pushed the coachman back, and a fight ensued. A crowd gathered, and I eventually claimed victory before returning the coin purse to my master. He was elated. He clapped me on the back and said we should return home immediately to discuss my reward, which he expressly said would be my freedom. Lord Harvey dismissed Forthright from his employment there and then, and after a footman from Socrat's had driven us back to 20 St James's Square, the deal was struck. One hundred and sixty pounds was the price I'd need to pay: one hundred and twenty for my release, and forty to ensure a decent start to my future. My boxing career started shortly after that.'

'Preposterous lies!' Lord Harvey snarls, and Vincent flinches in his seat. He could not help it. The response was so sudden, so involuntary, that the rest of the court could not have failed to notice it.

As the clerk reminds Lord Harvey to *respect this court's proprieties*, Nick gestures towards the press dock – in a manner that says, *This is what Vincent had to live with* – and cedes the floor for cross examination. To Vincent, he mouths, *Well done*.

They've built the wall of his testimony – now Vincent only needs to defend it from being knocked down. He steadies his breath to steel himself against Dunning – and his nerves.

Dunning rises, tucking his hands into his robe's pockets with an exaggerated shrug. 'You mentioned, Mister Mourière, that your master had been drinking on the night of your so-called agreement,' he says casually. 'Is that why you set the stage for this pack of lies that evening? Were you hoping that when Lord Harvey woke up the following day with a sore head and didn't *remember* making you any such offer, he would simply take your word for it?'

Vincent grips his hands tighter in his lap 'My testimony is no lie.'

'I beg to differ,' Dunning says coldly. 'Tell me, was Lord Harvey in the habit of freeing his slaves on a whim?'

'No sir,' Vincent says. 'To my knowledge, I was the only one.'

'How convenient,' says Dunning. 'That Lord Harvey should make such a fantastical exception for you, Mister Mourière. And one that was most out of character for him.' He turns to the assembly. 'That wine must have put him in a very generous mood, indeed!'

The laughter of a hundred white men echoes in Vincent' ears. Nick had prepared him for many eventualities, but they could not have practised for this. Vincent bites his lip to stay the tremor, the dull pain confirming that this is a waking nightmare.

'And this *crowd* of witnesses, you speak of. Can any of them attest to the veracity of your story, Mister Mourière?'

'I did not know the names of the gentlemen who gathered to watch the altercation between myself and Mister Forthright,' Vincent says, struggling to remain composed.

Dunning's green eyes remain glued to Vincent's as he addresses Nick. 'If I understand correctly, Counsel Lyons, you are asking the court to free this man – who we must remember is a slave – on his conjecture alone. Have you no testimony at all?'

'Your client can attest to it, Counsel Dunning,' Nick retorts, 'lest he risk perjuring himself. The coachman would have done too, were he not still a rogue, on the run from the law.'

'Would he now?' Dunning puffs out his chest. 'I am sorry to disappoint the defence counsel, but my next witness will now prove to the court that the coachman is running neither from the law, nor from the truth.'

Nick seems puzzled; in the pews, Delphine pales. Is this another surprise?

Dunning's grin widens, and his devious eyes flash as he says: 'Mister Forthright, kindly take to the stand.'

As the former coachman approaches the dock, Vincent notices his neat, cream-silver uniform. *Why is he wearing that?* Vincent tries to meet Forthright's eye, but the coachman averts his gaze.

Vincent's heart sinks as the realisation comes no one is going to believe his testimony by the end of the day.

He can almost see himself from outside his body, on a West Indies-bound ship, all chance of freedom sailing away. After Forthright has confirmed his name, Dunning leans with one elbow on the press dock.

'Can you confirm for the court what you were doing on the night of twenty-first September 1767, before Mister Mourière summoned you to transport your master to Socrat's?'

'I can,' Forthright says. 'Hetty, the cook, had brought me up a glass of warm milk. I'm partial to one before I go to bed. She lets the milk and oats for porridge sit overnight so they're full and thick. But that's by the by. I was having a glass of milk.'

Is he nervous? He's not jittering or fidgeting. It's hard to tell. What Vincent is sure of: Forthright is already lying.

'What time was this?'

'Not long before midnight.'

'And after you'd taken Lord Harvey to Socrat's, what happened?'

'Unexpectedly, I was invited in by a kindly gent. I forget his name. I'd been warming my hands by the fire out back — it was February and bone cold. There wasn't any snow but still, it was freezing. This gent took a leak by the fireside and ended up pissing on my shoe. He invited me in as an apology, I guess. I don't claim to know the minds of noblemen.'

With a flourishing hand, Counsel Dunning bids the coachman move on with the story.

'Er, so. I lost a hand and excused myself from the table. I had less to lose than the regular players, you understand. That's when I saw Mourière swipe Lord Harvey's coin purse. The master used to hang it on the back of his breeches you see — a great big lump under his frock coat. The boxer was a deft fellow, and easily nabbed it away.'

Or you did. The muscles tighten in Vincent's jaw, but he manages to keep his face neutral.

'And what did you do next?'

'I confronted the man, of course.' Forthright flings his arms out, apparently roused by the memory. 'The master's always been good to me. I didn't want to lose my position. If you don't mind me saying, and I'm a bit afeared to say it actually...'

'Do say it,' Dunning urges.

'I always thought the master was a bit too trusting of Mourière. Let him read all them books and saunter round the house and city like a freedman almost. It was unsettling. You know Hetty told me she reckoned he helped the other slave girl escape. Now, that don't strike me as someone loyal to his master, especially to one so giving. Vincent always came across as a bit of a beau-nasty. And you know Blacks, they don't abide by the same moral code as me and you.'

'Mister Forthright,' the Chief Justice admonishes, brows furrowing over the top of his spectacles. 'If I require your *opinion*, I will ask for it. Conjecture is not wanted or valued here, so I request you keep to the facts and the facts alone.'

'Sorry m'lord.' Gerard bows his head. 'I was just saying—'

'And now you are not,' he says firmly. 'Counsel Dunning, continue.'

Vincent's eyes grow owlish. Is Chief Justice Mansfield on his side?

Dunning gives a slight bow. Vincent catches the lawyer wordlessly mouthing something as he spins from the Chief Justice and then presses on. 'After you confronted Mourière, what happened?'

'He did not take kindly to it. Got a wicked air about him, grabbed me by the scuff of my neckerchief and near about flung me against the wall. When the master saw it, Mourière was given a beating and I was praised for my bravery.'

'So you were not dismissed from your post as Mister Mourière claimed?'

'Never.' Forthright sounds outraged at the suggestion, but his eyes are on his silver cufflinks, which look brand new to Vincent's eye.

Lies. Lies. Lies. Left with two choices – look away or scream – Vincent gazes up at the King's Bench rafters, focusing on the light flowing through the honeycomb-shaped window. *Do not be the person they believe you to be*, he tells himself. It all feels. It feels...

Wrong. Heavy. Too much. Shame swipes at his chest, a tiger clawing its already weakened prey.

'And can anyone else attest to this?'

'They can. Those men there.' Forthright points to the back-left corner of the court.

Though he doesn't want to, Vincent turns to look.

He recognises some of the faces from Socrat's that day. Things are going from bad to worse.

Over the next five hours, twelve witnesses are called to the dock.

Each one of them swears an oath to tell the truth. In the next breath, each of them breaks it.

On and on, the lies pour like sweet, poisoned wine from their mouths. Vincent feels like he might drown by the thirteenth witness, but Lord Mansfield bats a hand to send the man away. For even he has heard enough.

'The Crown requires no more testimony on this particular event, *thankfully*.'

From the dais, he gestures down to Nick with his quill. 'I trust you have the contract Mister Mourière acknowledged in his testimony.'

'No,' Nick says, head bowed. 'I do not.'

'Well, then I believe there is no more to discuss. I will be prepared to give my ruling when we next meet.'

With his eyes closed, Vincent tilts his head to the ceiling once more. So, it will come to nothing after all.

All he has achieved.

After a lifetime of hardship, all he has worked for has come undone in one day and thirteen lies. There is no word for this kind of heartbreak. No word could even come close.

'Chief Justice, if I may...' Nick rushes to approach the bench, his face as desperate as Vincent feels. 'May I offer a closing word?'

Lord Mansfield re-dips his quill in acquiescence.

Nick turns to address the court. 'The Blacks have been intrinsic to our success as an empire. I think, Dunning, even you will grant me that?' Dunning lifts his hands in response with a gentle, appeasing smile. Like he knows what Nick is about to say will not matter.

Like he's already won.

'Yes,' Nick says, frantically digging in his pocket for his piece of twine, which now looks as frayed as his nerves. He wraps and unwraps it around his fingers. 'Counsel Dunning argued that our Empire was built on the backs of slaves, to further the greatness of our King and country. Therefore, shouldn't we consider this another way?'

The court room seems to tilt their heads collectively.

'Surely, if we can acknowledge the strength of the Negro, their unrelenting wilfulness to work, their humility, then we must also be able to acknowledge what they may contribute to our society if they were freed. The Black, raised to match us, could be key to securing our nation's future as well as its present.'

Dunning leans back against his desk and turns over a piece of parchment without looking at Nick. 'Please, Counsel Lyons, we have spent an entire morning discussing the commercial impacts of emancipation. It is not a valuable use of the court's time. We have since spent this afternoon establishing that a Black cannot tell the truth.'

'According to your bribed witnesses!'

'Counsel Lyons!' Lord Mansfield scolds. 'Should you wish to make such outrageous claims, you had better have proof.'

Nick's eyes grow wide.

Vincent draws his jacket closer about him, gritting his teeth. Other than pushing his master, one of Vincent's biggest regrets is that he never stole the contract from Lord Harvey's belongings, or asked for a copy himself. If he had, then perhaps Nick wouldn't have been pushed to such distressed statements.

Dunning, unphased by Nick's outburst, continues. 'My lord, if the Blacks were freed our future would inevitably go to Hell.'

'Dunning,' the Chief Justice roars, jowls shaking. 'Have I allowed children into my court room? This is the King's Bench.' He slams his hand on his desk. 'It is an *honour* to present testimony here. Both of you will cease this callowness and act with the grace and decorum I expect. I do not care how late into the trial it is, I will have you both removed.'

'Apologies, my lord,' Dunning says, then smirks at Vincent in that skunkish way of his. 'I merely meant to remind the court of what we've established today: that the Black on trial here is a liar. And a violent one at that. We would be wise to recognise that we could not keep our Empire great, or ensure our nation's continued rule, if all the Blacks were freed.'

Nausea swirls in Vincent's throat like smoke.

'There is no way you can know this,' Nick says, but no one seems to pay him any attention.

'We have come this far with the Blacks beneath us. To allow them to rise will be ruinous for all.'

There's not a whisper, not a breath in the court room. All the newspapermen's scribbles have ceased; no one is shifting in their seats. Everyone's eyes are fixed on Dunning.

Everyone but Vincent and Delphine, who are looking straight at each other. There's a defiance in her eyes that he doesn't have the strength to match.

She mouths from behind Nick's bench, *'Même bête, même lam.'*

But Vincent cannot bring himself to mouth back his half of the promise.

'If we release this man...' Dunning moves towards Vincent and throws a pointed finger within touching distance of him. 'If we set the precedent that Blacks should be free, their violence will only grow. There are fifteen thousand now, but in ten years, twenty, there will be so many of them that even an army will struggle to stop them. That is what is at stake here. This case is not about me or you or even about Vincent Mourière. No. This trial is about what we wish our nation to be. It is about our future. It is about protecting what it means to be English – about protecting our heart.'

A burst of applause erupts from the gallery. A lady sighs, moved by Dunning's sentiment, and a gentleman cries *Hear, hear!* With a satisfied sneer, Dunning turns to Nick. 'Oh, apologies Counsel Lyons, weren't you about to say something?'

Chapter Fourteen

> In truth, laws are always useful to those with possessions and harmful to those who have nothing; from which it follows that the social state is advantageous to men only when all possess something and none has too much.
> —JEAN-JACQUES ROUSSEAU

Delphine

It's turning six o'clock when Delphine leaves the King's Bench. After today's disastrous turn, Nick had all but flung every book out of his office. She sensed Nick needed space, and Delphine certainly needed air, so now is heading out to the courtyard. Long clouds streak evenly over the marmalade sky, coating Westminster in a coral hue. As she walks down the steps to the pavestones, a domed, two-horse carriage clops into her path. On its door is a crest bearing a knight's helmet amid a lush green forest. The Mansfield coat of arms.

As if cued, the Chief Justice steps out of the courthouse. Gone are his poodle wig and billowing robe, though he still wears the same crescent glasses. He nods courteously to her as his coachman jumps down onto the street — a sore reminder of today's first horrible witness. But unlike Forthright, Mansfield's coachman is not so slick: while opening the carriage door, he misjudges a step and his eyes bulge as he hurtles face-first towards the pavement. With impressive dexterity, the Chief Justice catches him, and it's in the heartbeat or two it takes for the man to regain his composure that Delphine comes up with a plan.

'My lord?' Delphine calls. She tries to imitate the assertiveness Marion adopts when speaking to men of the law — the justices and constables she needs to keep sweet, to keep the doors of the Exoticies open.

The Chief Justice's foot hovers above the step to his carriage. It has been a long day.

An exhausting trial, and with Monday's judgment looming, she understands he is likely in no mood to entertain the ramblings of a woman who does not know her station.

But she has to try.

And since the Chief Justice does look back at her and smile – a weary but patient smile – Delphine takes this as her permission to proceed.

'A word, sir?' She inclines her head.

'All that has to be said on this trial will be recorded in the proper place, at the proper time,' he says, not unkindly.

'And if what Lord Harvey is doing is *im*proper? If Mister Forthright and all those others lied… Should one wait for justice then?'

Mansfield huffs.

'Can you prove that?'

'I—'

'Young lady,' he says, rubbing his eyes beneath his spectacles, 'the courts of this land are not as they once were. The only thing worth more than testimony is evidence. If you have some, it should be presented in the right way.'

'But my lord, it is the court that prevents us from seizing the evidence we need. The contract, if it still exists, is in Lord Harvey's possession. How can that be right?'

'My position is not to question or reinvent the law but to interpret it fairly within its sacrosanct confines. You heard me criticise Mister Forthright and both counsellors today for presenting me with unfounded opinions. You heard my comment that Lord Harvey should not have taken matters into his own hands and spoken to the press.' His lips tighten as he turns away from her once again and steps up into his carriage.

Delphine thinks of the books she's been studying over the course of the trial. How motivated she'd been to develop her skills, to distil the inked pages into her thoughts and beliefs. Before this man rides away, she needs to put into practice what she's learned. 'But is it not your responsibility to not only preserve the law, but also to set the Empire's standards for values and morality?'

Mansfield's eyes flicker with interest from his seat, which is gilded with roses and lilies. 'Only God can do such things.'

'But where God does not intervene, surely that falls to you. To your conscience, to your heart.'

'Be careful, child. That is mere breaths from blasphemy.'

Delphine raises a hand to her lips. It crosses her mind that despite his unthreatening demeanour, Lord Mansfield could have her arrested, even end her life if he wished. The King's Bench has allowed Catholics to be burned at the stake for saying less.

Mansfield's face softens.

'Dear girl, do not look for humanity where there is none. Regardless of what you and I believe, you need evidence. If you can present me with some, I shall consider it.'

'And if there's none?'

'Then my decision must be based on the facts I have been given.' Mansfield raps his knuckles on the hollow carriage roof. 'Good evening.'

She flinches as the coachman cracks his whip, and the horses fling themselves into action. She is unsure what to make of the conversation she's just had. She no longer feels Vincent is in as dire a situation, but he certainly is not safe either.

It all rests on one thing.

'Evidence,' she says to Nick when he eventually joins her at the roadside. 'We need evidence.'

'Twenty years ago a court would never have asked for evidence,' Nick laments. 'Testimony was what mattered above all else. I swear more rulings have been judged on evidence in the last two years than in the preceding two centuries.'

'That is good for us, is it not? If it can outweigh all the damage done today.'

'It would, if we had any,' he concedes. 'But we have presented all we can. Without the contract, I'm afraid we're doomed.'

But maybe they don't have to be. The contract might still exist.

They just need to find it.

'If Lord Harvey still has it, and we managed to secure it,' Delphine says carefully, 'would it matter *how* we'd done it?'

Nick is silent momentarily as if searching the sunset for an answer. 'There are no rules regarding how a defence counsel procures evidence.' Recognition dawns on him, then another look that reminds Delphine of the face he made when she suggested rescuing Vincent from the ship: disappointment. 'You can't seriously mean to break in?'

He's right: the idea is reckless and likely futile. But somewhere in 20 St James's Square, there might just be a piece of parchment that can free her brother.

'What choice do we have?' Delphine counters. Plenty and none.

Nick reluctantly nods, confirming that the ends would justify the means.

'If it's there, we must find it. No matter what,' Delphine says.

He hesitates. Is this a boundary he is willing to cross? Delphine prays it is, and that Nick can muster the courage to help Vincent one last time.

'How can you be certain no-one is home?' Delphine asks as she silently eases open the door to the servants' quarters.

'Undoubtedly, my uncle will be at Socrat's, partaking in his usual ritual of Sunday night revelry. Filling himself with canary wine and pheasant until the early hours of the morning. He never did need much sleep.'

Delphine remembers.

Once inside, they creep through the Harveys's kitchen. The curtains are still open, bathing the room in silver moonlight. On the largest table, dough for tomorrow's bread — Hetty's handiwork, no doubt — is rising beneath a cloth in a ceramic bowl. As they pass it, Delphine breathes in the scent of the yeast, along with traces of the evening's leftover stew. Once, this was a comforting smell, but now it sits uneasily in her lungs, and transports her back to the last time she was in this room.

It was the night before Ranelagh. She and Vincent were stuffing dried meat and fruit into Delphine's bag: supplies for her escape with Pearl.

It had taken Vincent several days to accept their plan to elope.

He'd spent a fortnight failing to convince them to stay, but Delphine had known he would support her in the end.

When they were younger, her mother told them stories of the Agojie, the legendary women warriors from her grandfather's birthland of Dahomey; stories of female husbands and male wives, of many different types of marriage. Her mother's tales taught her that Black hearts are capable of anything: like finding love where white men forbid it, and fighting for it against all odds.

And as Pearl's wedding drew closer, their time was running out: there was no better time to flee.

It had to be Ranelagh.

If Lord Harvey looked harder, he might have realised the mounting evidence of betrayal in his household — the thick air of anticipation due not to impending nuptials but to a union of another sort.

Delphine, Pearl and Vincent all knew that Vincent shouldn't help them. Knew what Pearl's father would do to him if he found out. But he did it anyway — selling some of Pearl's jewellery to purchase their stagecoach tickets, and handing over his outgrown breeches and shirts for them to wear as disguises. And even though Delphine had no choice but to escape alone when the critical moment arrived, Vincent's little rebellions changed her future. She could never thank him enough for them.

So, breaking into Lord Harvey's office is the least she can do in return.

It's almost pitch black when they enter the study. The house seesaws between eerie silence and a strange chorus of groans from the settling floorboards. Each creak freezes Delphine in place until she's satisfied that the only sounds remaining belong to Nick, or to the rapid thrumming of her pulse. After stumbling around the office to find and light a candle, she sets another aflame and passes it to Nick, whose face emerges golden in its soft glow.

'Which cabinet?' she asks. There are at least four in the room. 'The ebony one with some metal adornments. I think that's what Vincent said.'

They all look ebony in the dark but it doesn't take Delphine long to find the one he means. The one closest to Lord Harvey's desk, with gold handles and bronze ornamentation: near the bottom of the left door, a Roman centurion brandishing a sword; on the upper side of the right, an angel weeping heavenly tears. Delphine has seen this cabinet before, of course, but she never noticed such details when she lived here. During her little time in the master's study, her eyes were mostly fixed on the ground.

Nick stands beside her, and neither moves to open the doors for a while. Delphine suspects he is equally as afraid as she is of what they might find – and what they might not.

Tensing with her eyes squeezed shut, she flicks the latch. Nick comes closer, she opens one eye, and they both lift their candles to examine what is inside.

'I had no idea we still had one of these in the family,' Nick gasps.

'One what?'

'It's a curiosity cabinet,' he answers, matter-of-factly. *Of course Nick knows there's a name for it.* 'They were prevalent a while back, I'm sure. Lots of the nobility had them for storing oddities they had collected. Some even held human remains, I'm told, but I'm glad that's not what we see here.' They examine a colossal snail shell, an azure-blue egg, and a beaten shekere with half its cowrie shells missing. 'They'd wheel these out at parties and dinners, tell stories about their collections and how they procured them. They were used for gaining status – which is undoubtedly why my uncle still has one.'

'So that's what Vincent's contract was? A curiosity?'

'Apparently so. But I can't see it in here.'

Delphine clenches her jaw, hoping he can't see her shoulders sagging. 'Can I take a look?'

He moves aside, and she peers closer inside the cabinet. Every part of her knows that by now, the contract is probably a small pile of ash in Lord Harvey's hearth; every part of her is clinging to the hope that it isn't.

Beside the musical instrument, there's a figurine of a toga-clad woman, no larger than Delphine's palm; a ruby and bronze perfume bottle; and the skull of a small bird with a very long beak.

Beneath that, a drawer.

Inside is a gold ring attached to a scarlet ribbon. Without thinking, she pulls on it to discover what it's connected to.

A mechanism begins whirring, emitting a buzz so low she feels the hum from her fingertips to her collarbone. It knocks the statuette over and the perfume with it – what spills out before Delphine rights the bottle is not the toxic sweetness of Lord Harvey's, but something saltier, more floral, the smell she chooses to conjure when she thinks of St Lucia, of home.

The house seems to stir from below.

'What did you do?' Nick whispers as the base of the cabinet sinks towards the floor, revealing a previously hidden shelf.

'The only thing I could.'

Delphine lowers her candle – surely this will be where Lord Harvey has hidden the contract. But when she sees what is on the shelf, her excitement drains away. Instead, her body reels backwards. She tries in vain to blink away the memories. Scenes she never witnessed first-hand, but has spent years trying to banish from her imagination. *A newlywed man and girl, carriage-bound for Cornwall. A detached wheel rolling into a muddy ditch.*

The highwaymen circling, threatening, daggers drawn. The body of a dead baron and a bloody string of pearls.

'My God.'

Startled by the strength of Delphine's reaction, Nick drops his candle to the floor. 'What is it?'

Quick as a fuse, Delphine stomps out the flame. This room is half-filled with silks and oil paintings. It will easily go up in smoke if they aren't more careful. She rubs her throat and chest to regain her composure, and dares to look back at the shelf.

'It's Pearl's necklace. The one they found after she was killed.'

'Christ.' Nick swallows and grips a hand to his throat. 'How morbid.'

The house moans in agreement, the outer windows wheezing at a sudden gust of wind that sends a distant door clicking shut. They freeze again, limbs tight, waiting for the silence to return. A creak, a tap, then nothing.

'What else is there?' he asks, releasing his held breath.

Beside the necklace, they find an ornate box stuffed with papers and miscellaneous trinkets. One is the deed to 20 St James's Square. The next is a letter from Lady Katherine. And beneath that, the most surprising object yet: a wooden bird that's missing a wing.

Vincent's.

Delphine remembers this bird. Vincent's mother, Abigail, gave it to him mere days before she went missing. It was one of the few belongings he kept from their shared home and the first thing he packed when he learned that Lord Harvey had selected him for transportation to England. Delphine runs a fingernail over each groove in the wood. It feels much smaller than when she'd last gripped it, clutching it to her chest for days as they sailed away from everything she'd ever known.

She's not seen the bird since they first arrived here. And she doesn't remember the right wing being missing then. Why would Lord Harvey take this from him?

She will have to puzzle that out later.

Before Nick can question her, she pockets the bird, and, after a moment's hesitation, the necklace. One precious item for Vincent, another for herself.

It can't fill the absence of their loved ones, but at least now they'll have something physical to ground their losses.

She riffles through one, two, three more documents until at last, she finds an item that makes her heart stop.

Two items, in fact.

It can't be. She blinks in disbelief, drawing the candle so close she risks setting fire to it. Here, in Delphine's hands, is the impossible document they came here to find. The contract.

And beneath it, the tally of Vincent's boxing winnings.

Was it arrogance that stopped Lord Harvey from destroying these? The smug surety that the authorities would not come looking for them?

Right now, Delphine does not care. Resting the candle on the cabinet's middle shelf, she angles the paper carefully above the flame. 'Listen to this,' Delphine whispers to Nick. 'On the occasion Mister Vincent Mourière earns a total sum of his weight — estimated at one hundred and sixty pounds on the twenty-first September 1767 — I, Lord Reginald Harvey IV, do promise to grant the named Negro his freedom.'

'Yes!' Nick shouts, then he shushes himself. 'Yes. Sorry — I very much wanted this to go our way.'

'Me too,' Delphine agrees, giddy excitement in her veins. 'And look at this.' She swaps the pages so the earnings sheet is on top. Score tallies are lined up in rows of ten; corresponding dates in a column down the side. Scanning it, she shakes her head — mathematics is not her strong point, but the numbers aren't adding up. 'This can't be right.'

'What is it?' Nick says, squinting at the paper. 'I can't see from here.'

'How many tallies do you count?'

She hands him the list. He mutters the numbers as he counts. 'The fiend,' Nick spits. 'He's been underreporting the odds for months.'

'We can prove it too,' Delphine says. She explains she still has the betting slip from Vincent's final match tucked away in her box of keepsakes. It didn't feel right giving it to Vincent after everything that happened. Still, her face pinches with fury. The cruelty of it. The ease with which Lord Harvey denied Vincent his freedom despite having kept track of every last ha'penny; the length to which he's tried to keep him in chains. One day, she will strangle him with them.

'Incredible,' Nick sighs. But unlike Delphine, he's smiling.

Because this is all they need to secure Vincent's release.

Dunning may have argued his way out of ending slavery for good, but at least now they can give someone the life they deserve —the person Delphine loves most in the world.

She's about to fold the documents and slide them into her pocket when another door slams shut. This time, the noise is coming from nearer to the study. And it's followed by the staggering *tap, tap, tap* of Lord Harvey's cane.

'God's bones.' She's never heard Nick curse other than in this room. Lord Harvey truly brings out the worst in people. 'Get down, behind the desk,' he commands. 'I'll go and distract him.'

But Delphine's feet remain treacherously frozen to the floor. She cringes at each nearing step and feels like her knees might snap beneath her – the anger that had burned within her a few moments ago is now turned to ice.

Lord Harvey would never let her get away with this. Nick he might forgive, but for Delphine it'll be the noose if they're caught. He'll burn the contract, and the tallies, and Vincent will still end up on a plantation. It will all be for nothing. The papers tremble in her hands.

As if Nick has just realised the same thing, he snaps, 'Give them to me!'

'I can't.' They're too important. Even now, she's not sure she can trust him.

'You can,' Nick pleas. 'I'll deliver them to Mansfield tomorrow. All you have to do is wait for me to persuade him into the lower drawing room, then get yourself to safety. You cannot be caught.'

The footsteps draw closer, closer, closer still.

'You have my word,' he whispers, desperately throwing out his hand to her. 'I can use his signature on my letter of disinheritance to prove the integrity. You go home and fetch the betting slip. It's our best chance.'

Delphine looks at his outstretched palm and swallows. If she lets him have these documents now, she is handing him her brother's fate.

Terror doesn't begin to cover it. 'Delphine!' Nick begs.

It's not their best chance. It's their only chance. Delphine hands them over.

'Thank you.' Nick grips the papers to his chest, his released breath the sound of shuddering leaves, then tucks them into his jacket pocket. 'Wait until you hear us descend the lower stairs. You remember the way out?'

She nods at him before rushing to crouch behind the desk. Peering above it, she watches Nick wipe his brow then his hands on his breeches. Then he turns the door handle and leaves the room, taking with him the key to Vincent's manacles.

On her knees, Delphine listens. Nick's footsteps are hasty and heavy. She hears him flee down the corridor, and Lord Harvey's drunken, slurred speech brings him to a halt. 'What do you think you're doing here?'

Nick's reply comes loud and bright. 'Uncle, I'm here to make amends. I looked for you in your study but found it empty. Ah! I see your wine glass is empty. Let's away to the parlour — I'll rouse the housekeeper to build a fire. There's much we need to discuss.'

Chapter Fifteen

> Each player must accept the cards life deals. But once the cards are in hand, he alone must decide how to play them in order to win the game.
>
> —M. DE VOLTAIRE

Delphine's fear is a suit of armour. She sheds it plate by plate as she distances herself from St James's Square.

After Nick had led Lord Harvey away, she'd struggled for several pulse-pounding minutes with the ribbon mechanism before successfully closing the secret compartment of the curiosity cabinet. Only when she was satisfied that all the lord's treasures appeared just as she had found them, did she slip out into the night.

Though the bird and the necklace are burning a hole in her pocket, the weight of Vincent's trial is beginning to lift; at last, Delphine thinks he might win.

And that kind of news cannot wait until morning.

As she approaches the prison, she spies the spiked facade piercing the darkness. The portcullis is raised, set to bite.

Opening the door to the poky, candlelit galley, Delphine is greeted by the weighty tapster. Livey is sitting alone at a game of cards. He looks up at her from between hunched shoulders, head almost invisible beneath a whirl of smoke from his pipe, and says, 'Evening, love. You here to see Mister Mourière again?'

'Yes, sir,' she coughs, squinting at him. 'I have joyous news for him.'

'We don't have much of that around here. I'll escort you.'

He gathers his playing cards, shuffles them into a neat pile and places them back down in their pewter tin on the table. 'It was a losing game.'

'Most of them are.'

'Ain't that the truth.' He shrugs. 'Patience is the right name for sure.' Despite the brisk eventide, some of the ground floor cells have their doors open wide, illuminating tables where a dozen and a half prisoners are engaged in what seems to be a game night. Passing them on the way into the main block, Delphine glimpses their enjoyment playing Trictrac and Mississippi. While they swig from glinting tankards, belches and deep-bellied laughter tangle in the night air.

As they move around the prison, Livey continues to blow puffs of smoke out of his mouth and nose like a dragon. 'Your fella seems to be getting a lot of visitors lately,' he remarks casually. 'Most do during their trial.'

Delphine wonders who he could mean. She's about to ask when a dog yowls, bursting out of a nearby cell. Delphine springs out of the path of a huge grey mop, water flying from its mane as it hurtles past. Momentarily it's followed by a soaking wet man, who chases the hound barefoot, wearing only a nightcap and a flapping, fur-covered banyan.

'Bath night again, eh, James?' Livey shouts after him.

The man flings a rude gesture over his shoulder before disappearing around the corner.

Delphine stifles a laugh. It's fortunate that the Chief Justice allowed Vincent to remain on the wealthier side of the prison, and not in the squalor of a cell in Newgate or in that fetid box aboard the *Ann and Mary*. Livey clears his throat as they stop at Vincent's door, and Delphine reaches for her coin purse. If she's learned anything from her visits here, it is that everything has a cost.

She pulls out a shilling (her entire earnings for this week, minus Marion's cut) and, with gracious resignation, pushes it into his hand. Twisting the key in the lock, he gives a final nod and says, 'Vincent can escort you back down. Don't stay too long, or you'll have to pay for the night.'

Delphine raises her hand to knock, but Vincent's already opening the door before her knuckles reach the wood – he must have overheard them in the corridor. He looks surprised to see her, but his confused frown quickly becomes a welcoming smile. 'There's a face I'm glad to see,' he says, wrapping her in his arms. 'What cheer, sister?'

Squeezing him tight, Delphine realises he's much thinner than he once was. Still strong, but the muscles that once rose and fell like hills on his arms have eroded. His eyes, brown as earth, are still sunken from that tough day in court.

'Did you come all this way alone?' he says, reassuming the role of big brother. She imagines most incarcerated people would be impatient to discover what their visitor had brought for them – gifts, home comforts, word from friends. But Vincent is one of those rare personalities who will never ask anything of you except your safety.

'I needed to speak with you before tomorrow,' she says. 'We found the contract.'

The fatigue in Vincent's eyes falls away. 'You mean that?'

'Yes!' She scoops up his hands in hers and tells him all about the documents. She was right to trust Nick – he's not let them down so far, and Vincent deserves to share that hope. 'Nick will present them to Lord Mansfield tomorrow. You're going to win, Vincent. You're going to win.'

'Thank you, Delphine. I—'

A thunderous noise erupts outside the prison. They exchange a look, and Delphine knows that for just a small instant, he too is back at Ranelagh.

Fireworks.

On a darker day, she might have tensed up at the sound, deemed it a bad omen. A sign that their well-laid plans are about to go awry. But after the day's earlier battles, the win claimed at 20 St James's Square, she decides to see it as a new start.

They move to the window. It's weeks before bonfire night, but the celebrations seem to start earlier every year. A gunpowder phoenix screeches through the sky, its tail soaring gold, followed by exploding white stars and crackling red fountains – casting the black city below in a devilish light.

They marvel at the display, and Delphine etches this moment into her memory: the good news she's delivered, replacing the hurt from Ranelagh and the girl who broke her heart there.

When the colours fade to grey streaks in the darkened sky, leaving the air tinged with sulphur, Vincent pulls himself away from the window and walks over to his desk. It's littered with scrunched parchment, writing equipment and a half-melted candle, dripping wax onto the woodwork. Vincent pushes a finger into the puddle to remove it before it dries.

'I am so grateful to you and Nick,' he says, rolling the soft wax between his fingertips. 'There's something I wanted to tell you before tomorrow. Before...' His voice trails off as he sets the tiny ball onto one of the pieces of paper.

'Go on,' Delphine says, wondering where this is going. She senses he needs space, so she leans against the cell wall instead of going to him, shivering as her back touches the stone.

'I have never been good with words.' He shakes his head and laughs, a gesture laced with dark mirth. 'But you've helped me realise something these past few months. About myself. When we were children, I never really told you how I was feeling, did I?'

There was never the chance. When Vincent's mother left the plantation, Lord Harvey and the overseers gave him no time to mourn Abigail's loss. For months after moving into her parents' cabin, Vincent was stolid. No matter how many johnnycakes her mother fried, or how often her father tried to coax him into one of their games. It was like La Soufrière's molten core brewed inside him, and if he let out even a flicker of emotion, he'd erupt.

'But I want you to know that I *do* feel,' he says. 'Everything. I always have. It just always seemed wrong, or ungrateful, of me to voice it. Because we were the lucky ones: we never worked the fields, we got to go to England. To say we wanted more than that...' His voice wavers, his hand clenching into a fist on the desk. 'My mama told me never to show them my weaknesses. Your parents did, too. Because no matter what, you've got to keep fighting and moving, pushing everything down and carrying on. So I did. We both do.'

It's as though Vincent is putting her most private thoughts into words. Countless times, she has needed to block out or ignore the pain until it becomes something manageable. But unlike Vincent, Delphine has always had someone to share that burden with afterwards: Pearl, Charity, and him.

Delphine wants to reach out to him, but instead, she feels for the bird in her pocket and grips the wood with her fingers. Vincent shuffles his feet as if trying to rebalance himself before continuing. 'I thought that if I were as strong and brave as everyone said I was, then there would be no room for anything else within me. But I don't want to spend the rest of my life like that. I don't want to *start* my life like that. I just want to be... Me, I suppose. And I can't do that unless I've told you everything I know, everything *you* deserved to know years ago.' He clears his throat. 'So I've written a letter for you. I don't want to leave anything unsaid. I was expecting to give you it tomorrow but...' He trails off, expression torn.

Knowing the courage it took Vincent to say all that, Delphine feels a tender ache in her chest. She is so proud of who her brother is becoming, that he is finding the strength to express his vulnerabilities.

Though she wishes to hear more in this moment, she suspects right now he feels exposed – and he's putting his trust in her not to push him too far. She says lightly, 'Do you want to read it to me now?'

'I did. I do, but saying all this out loud...' He strains a smile. 'It's like there's this vice that's trying to strangle every word as it comes out. Um...' He straightens and grabs a piece of paper from his desk.

'Oi!' Livey's bark rips through the air between them. From outside the door he grumbles, 'I did say you'll have to pay if you decide to spend the night.'

Delphine swallows. Her time is running out – that shilling was all she had – and she still needs to give Vincent the bird. 'We found some other things in Lord Harvey's office, with the documents. Pearl's necklace, and this.'

'Pearl's—' Vincent blinks in surprise, but his mouth closes as Delphine reveals his mother's gift. The letter falls from his fingers to the floor as he takes the bird from Delphine and turns it over in his hands. Though he's looking down at it, he doesn't seem to be seeing the carved creature.

'So that's why,' is all he whispers.

'Vincent?' His eyes are glassy, far away. Clearly, he hadn't known Lord Harvey still had the bird. Instantly she regrets burdening him with this knowledge before the trial was over. It was too much. Obviously it *is* too much. A thoughtless mistake. At last, she puts a hand on his shoulder. 'Vincent?'

'I mean it,' Livey growls, turning from innkeeper to prison warden in a breath. 'Don't make me come in there!'

Vincent is still absorbed in his thoughts. He says nothing, as though he's not heard her or the guard. But Livey won't let her stay a minute longer – she has to go. 'I'm sorry,' she says softly, 'I shouldn't have given you it.'

With Vincent's body stiff as it is, she won't move to hug him goodbye. Instead, she crouches to pick up the letter before she leaves.

'Don't,' Vincent says, abruptly. His shoulders slump as he tightens his grip on the bird. 'Don't take it yet. There's more I need to write.'

Chapter Sixteen

AN OPINION ON THE NEGRO CASE
Printed anonymously at the submitter's request

How disgraceful of those who profess Christianity, and whose pride it is to be called civilised, to carry on trafficking in the human species; to make slaves of those whom Heaven created of the same flesh and blood, and who are equally with us the sons of God. This trade, I am sure, is repugnant to all the laws of Nature and Humanity, and I abhor any man who claims divine authority permits it. What power can make laws to punish those Blacks who refuse to obey their masters? Who are all too often treated worse than hounds? Surely Heaven will not look upon them as culpable in using all means to regain their liberty... I hope that the opinion of the Chief Justice today will be such, as will best agree with the good of mankind.

—LONDON GAZETTE

The morning sun brings Vincent's day of judgment. Today's session is due to commence at a quarter past ten, fifteen minutes later than previous court days, but by half past nine, the King's Bench is already filled to bursting with chattering spectators. Today, the front rows, usually populated by robed white men, represent a broader cross-section of society: the conflicted, the curious and the concerned. None more so than Delphine, who is haphazardly perched on the end of the third row as, for the first time since the trial began, Nick hasn't succeeded in reserving her a seat. She'd be more comfortable if the rather large Black man beside her would cease invading her space with his wide-spread legs.

Her unease grows with every guffaw of laughter, every click of a heel on the courtroom floor, every whiff of sweet perfume or musky cologne. There is no sign yet of Nick, nor of Lord Harvey. Delphine fiddles with the fabric of her emerald skirt — she tucked the betting slip among Nick's hearing notes in his office this morning, but now she wishes she'd kept it safe in her pocket. She's tempted to rush to the back room to find him herself when, at last, Mister Lyons appears, his eyes decorated with dark, sleepless circles that match his robe.

She's never seen him this way, pale as if drained of all his passions, his walk stooped like his books are much heavier than they were yesterday. And there, barely a heartbeat behind him, is Lord Harvey. Smug as ever, in a newly powdered wig and vibrant red coat, with bright eyes that belong to someone half his age.

Lumps like caterpillars squirm in the back of Delphine's throat. At this moment, Lord Harvey reminds her of a sasabonsam, a violent creature with pink skin and iron teeth that renews its strength by feeding on its victims. Those monsters only dwell in stories, but her former master must be something close — the self-satisfied wretch.

Oh God. If Nick has been with Lord Harvey all night, did the lord see through his ruse? Perhaps he discovered Nick's theft and forced him to give back the documents. And if the evidence is not presented today, there's almost nothing to compel the Chief Justice to grant Vincent's release. Mansfield helped build the Empire's economy. He would not threaten its strength because of one Black man.

How foolish she'd been to hope.

Nick doesn't make eye contact with her as he sits. He's betrayed them, then. And Vincent's fate is sealed. What had Lord Harvey offered that was worth more than her brother's life? The caterpillars transform into butterflies, flapping in her throat to get out.

A bang of the gavel silences the hum of the courtroom, and Vincent is led in. He's unchained still, his features relaxed. The shock she gave him yesterday when she handed him the bird seems to have dissipated. There's no urgency to his movements – the trial will begin, the Chief Justice will say his piece, and he will be freed: that is what they'd said last night. How Delphine wishes to just grab him and run.

Panic flashes on her brother's face when he notices she's not in her usual seat. He scans the crowd, his brightness returning only when he spots her. Delphine forces her lips to curve up into a smile. For a moment, she swears that he sees the lie behind it. But Vincent smiles back, unaware.

The second hit of the gavel punctuates the entrance of the Chief Justice.

In he walks, solemn as stone.

There's a long silence after he sits down, as if he's still pondering what is to come.

'The ruling of Harvey vs Mourière will be made today. Unless – for the last time I ask you, Lord Harvey – you wish to save the time of the court, defer the ruling, and release the Negro?'

'I do not, my Lord Justice,' Lord Harvey says, with all the sincerity of a snake.

The Chief Justice nods. 'So be it. Counsel Dunning, please make your closing arguments.'

Dunning stands in his finery and brushes an imaginary speck of dust from his robe. 'Thank you, my Lord Justice,' he says with a bow, then raises his hands to the rafters like he's about to summon a miracle. 'This country, the one I am proud to call my home, stands on the clifftop of uncertainty. We stand now at a point in history which will either establish our Empire as the greatest to have ever existed, or throw it to annals of mediocrity.' Next, he rehashes his well-worn arguments for the umpteenth time: *Negroes are violent and untrustworthy; it'd be an economic disaster to free them; God commands white people to enslave Black people.*

Delphine's eyes glaze over until he closes with a plea, facing the Chief Justice with his hands clasped. 'Do not rule against the honourable Lord Harvey. Do not rule against all we have built.'

Silence follows. No applause or cheering like he'd garnered in earlier weeks, but silence — a wall of it — thick with anticipation of the Chief Justice's ruling. Dunning straightens his robe and sits at his bench, a rosy flush creeping up his neck.

Good. Let him be embarrassed.

The Chief Justice says nothing, just motions for Nick to begin.

Nick pulls himself to his feet and wipes a bead of sweat from his brow, face still pale. Has he come down with a case of influenza overnight? Or something worse — something more treacherous?

'The questions arising from this case do not merely concern the poor, unfortunate soul who finds himself the subject of it,' he begins, wearily, twine dangling limply from his hand. 'The right claimed by Lord Harvey to detain Mister Mourière is based on the condition of slavery. The condition Vincent was born into in St Lucia. But the unfortunate circumstances of Vincent's birth should not supersede the protections afforded him by the country where he now resides. We previously established a precedent that no man may be a slave on English shores. If that right is recognised by the court today, then along with it, we banish an evil that has been imported into this country. To think, a mere thirty years after the Portuguese and Spaniards commenced the trading of human chattel, Spain's own Emperor Charles V intervened to stop its horrid chain of progress and ordered all slaves on the American Isles to be freed. And yet, one hundred and eighty years later, that unwelcome spectre still haunts this land.

'I implore the court to recognise the most fundamental rule of our Lord: to treat your neighbour as you wish to be treated. Who here would condemn his neighbour to a life of servitude, where he may meet hardships unnumbered and grief untold? Nobody. For we are civilised, tolerable, human — and English. Vincent Mourière took in his first lung of free English air almost a decade ago. Do not let his last one belong to another. The English may not have instigated slavery, but today we can become the first to end it.'

He did not mention the contract or Lord Harvey lowering the odds of Vincent's boxing matches. Has he forgotten to add those salient points to his speech? Or has he left them out on purpose?

The Chief Justice peers at Nick over his spectacles. 'Are you quite finished, Counsel Lyons?' His tone is soft but stern, like a grandfather who has witnessed a child steal a treat from a confectioner's bowl.

No, Delphine wills him to say.

'Yes, your lordship,' he says. Delphine curses under her breath.

'In that case, the court is now ready to make its ruling.'

At this, Delphine looks to Vincent, who seems to be staring above the crowd into nothingness.

She wonders what he would have said, if he was allowed to make a closing statement of his own. Perhaps he will tell her after the ruling – or perhaps, if the verdict is in Lord Harvey's favour, she will never have the chance to ask him.

'A little over six months ago,' Lord Mansfield continues, 'Vincent Mourière was forcibly removed from 35 Carnaby Street and chained aboard Lord Reginald Harvey's ship, the *Ann and Mary*. From there, he was set to be transported back to the West Indian island whence he had originated. It has been the argument of Lord Harvey and his counsel that he has the right to assert where and how Mister Mourière's days are spent, as from birth, it has always been. This power of dominion, exerted by a master over his slave, is so extraordinary that it could only be permitted if such a right were recognised by the law of the country where it is used: England.'

He pauses, now addressing the black-coated West India merchants who are standing angrily in one corner of the courtroom – the individuals have varied over the course of the trial, but they're easily identifiable by the way they raise their noses as a Negro passes them, how they rub imaginary stains from their jackets. 'I am aware of the economic consequences that pertain to this ruling, but this court is beholden to the law of this land, not to the masters and plantation owners who dwell in it. Nor is it beholden to the slaves—' he looks directly at Vincent, here, '—no matter how educated and well-presented they may be.'

'This case has been complicated, not least due to improper displays of emotion on the part of both the defence and the prosecution. In addition, the testimonies of certain parties have been proven to be calculated falsehoods.' The Chief Justice looks sternly at Vincent again; Vincent's brow creases for a moment. Is he thinking what Delphine's thinking – that she was wrong to get his hopes up?

'It is, therefore, on the presentation of that evidence and the arguments exhibited in this court these last months that I now give the following rulings...'

Delphine leans forward on the bench. Silently praying one last time for Mansfield to make the right decision.

'Though the tradition of slavery has been upheld in England for centuries, tradition is not the same as law. What's more, this court finds the state of slavery to be so outdated, so odious that nothing can be suffered to support it. Therefore, whatever inconveniences may follow from this decision, the court agrees to uphold the 1596 ruling that a slave shall be free as he sets foot on English ground, that the transportation and selling of slaves is not legal on these shores. Therefore, the Black must be discharged.'

Stunned silence lingers in the courtroom as the spectators take in the monumental impact of the words that have just been spoken.

Delphine's heart soars, lifting her to her feet. The eyes drawn to her are unimportant. They do not matter. Neither does it matter whether or not Nick delivered the contract, the score tallies or the betting slip to the court. All that matters is this: every Negro in England is now free.

She claps once, twice, three times before the cheering starts, before the man beside her rises to join in. Then the brown-skinned woman next to him, the olive-toned man next to her, and on and on – wave after wave of unrestrained jubilation.

Some dance on the benches, some weep into their kerchiefs. Delphine makes eye contact with a white gentleman she's encountered at the Exoticies. Since becoming the housekeeper, she's more familiar with his face than other parts. However, his blushing recognition still adds to her joy before they both return to their celebrations.

Within this sea of triumph are the indignant shouts of the red-faced sugar merchants and chattel traders. But their words cannot hurt Vincent now: they are hurling abuse from the wrong side of history.

The Chief Justice must have banged his gavel at some point because the ushers begin to beckon for quiet. It's at least a minute before the court settles down, and even then, there's not quite silence.

Vincent remains seated, luminous, with a cheek-aching smile.

He has changed the world.

Evidently realising this happy hum is as quiet as the assembly will get, the Chief Justice projects out to the courtroom. 'Then there is the matter of the contract. I had been willing to overlook Mister Mourière's testimony that such a document existed until this morning, when I found it directly before me. The signatures thereon are undeniably and verifiably those of Lord Harvey and Mourière.' A grateful shiver passes through Delphine – like she's stepped into a fire-warmed room after being caught in the rain. From the way the colour has returned to Nick's cheeks, she can tell he's relieved too. Perhaps Mansfield hadn't outright agreed to take the evidence into consideration when Nick presented it.

'Vile snake!' Lord Harvey spits, twisting his head towards Nick. 'Insolent thief!'

His nephew ignores him. As does Mansfield.

'And on the matter of the contract,' Lord Mansfield continues, holding the document aloft for the court to see, 'this document clearly states that Lord Harvey was to pay the sum of one hundred and sixty pounds to Mister Mourière upon his earning that amount through boxing matches. Mister Mourière has not only earned but exceeded this sum, despite Lord Harvey's best efforts to conceal that fact—' Here he holds up the score tally and betting slip, '—by various fraudulent and deceitful means. This court upholds that contract, and orders that Lord Harvey settle his debt to the defendant, which now stands at two hundred pounds.'

'Ludicrous!' Lord Harvey shouts, face turning the same shade of vermillion as his jacket.

'An outrage!' cries another white man. But the outrage is drowned out once more by the thunder of applause.

As Mansfield rises from his bench with a weary grimace, Delphine reasons that this decision was not easy for him. The retaliation he'll face from the gentry will be significant. But at this moment, those ramifications feel all too distant from her to dwell upon.

Next, the other Justices stand to vacate the court, and hosts of Black and brown spectators bow to them from their pews. Delphine joins in, for once lowering her head out of choice – these men have earned her respect.

She badly wants to leap the barriers and embrace Vincent, but it's already too late – he is gleefully allowing the ushers to guide him towards the clerks' exit. She watches him take his first steps as a freedman.

A free man.

The light from the honeycomb window glints in his eyes, and he clutches his heart, tipping his head to Delphine before ducking out of the courtroom.

Lifting a hand to her cheek, Delphine finds it wet with warm, happy tears.

Then she startles – somehow, Nick has clambered over the barrier and is by her side, grinning.

'We did it,' he says.

She returns his smile. 'We did.'

Looking at Nick in this moment, she is drawn back once again to that day at the docks. When he asked for her trust, and she gave it. Those first attempts at friendship felt so unnatural then.

Delphine may not be able to hug one brother right now, but she can embrace a friend.

Before she can extend her arm towards him, Nick is tugged away by his robe. He stumbles backwards into the crowd and Delphine comes face to face with another man – a man who is now one slave down and two hundred pounds poorer.

If Vincent was shining with joy, Lord Harvey is all shadow. The absence of emotion in his voice frightens her far more than his rage ever did.

'A reckoning is coming, girl,' he says. 'And you will be the first to feel it.'

Chapter Seventeen

My freedom is a privilege which nothing else can equal.
—VENTURE SMITH
1729-1805, enslaved 1735-1765

Vincent
Free.

Vincent is free.

It's as if an orb of light has bloomed inside him, beaming through his body, tingling down his arms and cheeks, spilling out in golden steps as he is led from the courtroom. It is eleven o'clock on the twenty-second of October, 1770. The start of the rest of his life.

'Free,' he whispers, savouring the word on his tongue.

It is a breeze through a wheat field.

Cool water gliding over skin.

It is heaven.

Walking along the corridor, he mentally rehearses his thanks to Nick, his compatriots, and his godparents.

Before Mansfield gave his ruling, he'd been riling himself up to ask if he could speak to the court. To tell his story – in the way he wanted to, at last – before he learned his fate. But something stopped him. It wasn't fear or doubt but acceptance. A calm sense that no matter what he said, it would not change the trial's outcome. That he would survive, no matter what came next.

Perhaps one day, he will voice those words. But first, he needs to find his sister.

Make plans for their adventures to come in Somerset.

Buy all the lemon bonbons they can eat.

And give her the letter waiting on his desk at the prison.

So she can learn exactly who visited him in his cell the other day, and also what he's learned from that bird.

He wonders what she will do with that information.

But such conundrums can wait. For the first time in Vincent's life, he does not look down as he walks. That effortless confidence he's seen in so many men and women of paler complexion is his now. Finally, he's been granted the sense of autonomy he's been reaching for since birth.

His mother was right, after all, when she told him he wouldn't always be a slave.

He slips a hand into his pocket to touch the little wooden bird. The court usher is guiding him towards the small back room where he, Nick and Delphine have all but taken up residence these last months. But when they arrive there, the usher walks on.

'Where are we going?' he asks, every syllable said with a smile.

'The Lord Chief Justice requests an audience with you.'

Requests. Not demands. Not orders. With every heartbeat, he finds something new to celebrate.

The usher raps on the arched door to Mansfield's chambers with his ringed fingers. 'Good show, Mister Mourière,' he says softly to Vincent, then a clerk opens the door and bids Vincent to come inside.

Entering the room, Vincent looks down at the white wainscoting – Lord Harvey had the same style on the lower drawing room walls at 20 St James's Square. Perhaps one day he'll own a home with something similar – if only to delight in tearing off each panel with a crowbar.

Lord Mansfield is sitting in front of the fireplace at the far end of the room in one of two forest-green jacquard velvet armchairs. He still wears his robe but has removed his wig and spectacles. They perch neatly on the small Pembroke table beside him.

'Sit with me if you will, Mister Mourière.' He gestures to the unoccupied chair.

To suppress a grin, Vincent purses his lips together. How long will this elation last, he wonders?

The lord gives a little nod as Vincent sits down, then narrows his eyes slightly and takes a deep breath.

Evidently he is considering what he will say next carefully.

In the beat of silence, Vincent's left leg begins to shake up and down in his seat. He's restless for his new life to begin.

'Now,' the Chief Justice says, picking up his spectacles to clean them on his robe. 'Mister Mourière. May I call you Vincent?' He glances up briefly to seek Vincent's agreement before continuing. 'This divide we men have made between ourselves. Black and white. Master and slave. I have come to learn recently that it is entirely of our divination.' Vincent waits for the lord to continue. If the rumour about his mulatto niece is true, perhaps that's what gave him this newfound perspective.

But to assume anything about the man would be a mistake – Vincent senses there's more complexity to Mansfield than that.

'It is significant, this ruling,' the Justice says. 'Not only for slaves in England, but throughout the world. For England has long been a tastemaker of *what is done*, and now that we have definitively declared domestic slavery to be wrong... Well, one can imagine what might come next.'

His glasses cleaned, he tilts his head to examine his handiwork and, seemingly satisfied, places them back on his face. He blinks and makes a little *ah* noise, like he is only just seeing Vincent for the first time.

'When you have ruled on as many cases as I have, Vincent, when you have had a career as long and if I may say – not so humbly – as great as my own, you come to learn a few things about human nature.' He briefly approaches the fire, warming his hands before returning them to his lap. 'And so, to my point. There will be many who are upset by what has happened here today. You would do well to remain inconspicuous until the newspapers and nobility have something else to gossip about.'

Fame, or rather infamy, is not what Vincent seeks. It is fickle and fleeting, another kind of chain. He'd not sought it while boxing. Nor does he want that attention now. Vincent is content with his mark upon the world, to let the rest of his story belong to him alone.

'A wise suggestion, my lord.'

The Chief Justice smiles warmly. 'Once they have moved on, I have no say over what you do with your time, but I would implore you to use the freedom you have been given. That is not to say you cannot have a small life, if peace and quiet are your greatest wishes. But grasp this ruling and do something with it.'

He rises, joints creaking as he accompanies Vincent to the door.

'I cannot promise you an easy life, Vincent.' Lord Mansfield turns the handle, and rests a familial hand on Vincent's shoulder before using it to urge him over the threshold. 'But the one you have now is your own.'

When the Chief Justice has pressed the door shut, Vincent lingers in the corridor to lean against the wall, thinking of the future and of Somerset.

So this money he has earned will be put to good use. For him. His future children. For now, *at last*, Vincent permits himself to imagine them.

A cottage. An orchard. To reap what he sows, create and cultivate new life.

On exiting the courthouse, Vincent lifts his face to the sun, basking in its warmth.

Delphine and Nick are in the middle of the yard, conversing with who he assumes to be a newspaperman. He attempts to hurry towards them, but on his first step forward, he is swarmed by well-wishers.

'Congratulations!' one Black man cheers.

'Freedom Fighter!' another calls out.

'The best of men,' says another, seizing Vincent's hand. 'The very best.' Unsure what to say, Vincent allows his hand to be shaken. Again and again and again. He stammers words of thanks. Even kisses a baby's head when the child is thrust in his face.

A white man nudges his way to the front of the crowd, takes off his tricorne and holds it to his heart. 'You must come to my tavern to celebrate, sir! It's The Dolphin on Red Lion Street.' The man grins with crooked teeth.

'Of course,' Vincent agrees. He feels tears spring in his eyes, unsure if it's from gratification or from the man's rancid breath. In a dozen steps forward, he's invited to twice as many parties and dinners. The crowd doesn't look like it's thinning out, and as wonderful as it is to be inundated with pleasantries, he would very much like to go and hug his sister.

Craning his neck to see over his new friends' heads, he gives her and Nick a little wave.

They wave back. His sister mouths for him to enjoy this moment before throwing a triumphant punch in the air.

The jubilation continues. Vincent is heaped with praise and congratulated for being exactly what this country needs. Most of their faces are Black or brown, but paler ones are growing in number among them. He reaches out to shake one of their hands — but soon regrets it. The white man's grip is too firm. Just overexcited, Vincent thinks. There is a lot to be excited about.

Another white man appears, this one wearing a grey highwayman mask. Vincent is on edge now: the man's forehead and eyes are covered, exposing a crooked nose, and his broad shoulders are arched with menace. The masked man takes a step towards him, followed by two more. He stops a foot too close for polite conversation, and Vincent retreats to diffuse the tension but finds himself backed up against another masked individual.

'What cheer, sirs?' His voice wavers as he lifts a hand half in greeting, half in self-defence.

A dark cloud descends over the sky; goose pimples prickle on Vincent's skin.

'What cheer indeed,' the first man croaks, scowling at Vincent with his beady black eyes. The man behind grabs at Vincent's coat, pulls it off him. As Vincent staggers forward to get away, his little wooden bird flies from his pocket, past the first man's boots, before clattering on the cobblestones. Vincent's chin hits the ground a moment after, sending his skull rattling.

'What are you doing?' someone in the crowd shouts.

'Stop!'

'Help!'

The kick comes anyway. Then another thud. A scream. Next come the pain and four more men.

Strange purple and red lights sparkle in Vincent's vision. He blinks and Westminster falls away.

He's in the countryside, collecting the last apples of autumn.

Gone are the city crowds, the endless warren of tightly packed buildings and the sludge-sullied pavements. Instead, the undulating hills are singing in all their sun-dripped glory.

This is life, Vincent thinks. *This. Is. Everything.*

Hillsend Farm is not the biggest in the county. Not by any stretch. But it is home – a home he has built with his own two hands, and it means so much. Every day, when he first wakes up, he can scarcely believe he was able to achieve his dream. But even after reimbursing Nick and splitting the remainder of his boxing winnings with Delphine, there was enough to begin a comfortable life outside London.

As well as the apples, they make a living harvesting a small plot of wheat, raising chickens and milking Mary, the goat – so named by Vincent's youngest child when she bore two kids last summer despite there being no billies on the farm. When Nella brought their third and final child into the world, Vincent was glad it was a daughter. Abigail, they christened her, after his mother.

Abigail has a keenness for livery. Small for her nine years, barely a head above her father's waist, and so softly spoken that sometimes Vincent swears only the animals can hear her. But his daughter possesses that brilliant mix of softness and intuition, and can tell if an animal is sick before they've shown a single symptom. Where the hens would flee from Vincent or his sons, Arthur and Henry, they flock to her.

And she's wild herself, too. Her curly hair is braided in the morning; by evening, it's matted with hay or mud. And the cycle starts again.

What a life.

Vincent flinches, feeling something crack. 'Abbie,' Henry calls from beneath the tallest apple tree. 'Abbie, climb up.'

And she does.

Much like her auntie Delphine climbed when she was a child.

Abigail reaches the highest branch and claims her prize: the last rosy apple. It's easy to be brave when you're sure that if you fall, your brothers will catch you. If there is one thing Vincent wanted to teach his children, it was that.

He stands up straighter. Now he thinks about it, his back and his knees are beginning to ache. His eyesight is bleary, too — when he blinks, the hills on the horizon are hazy. They used to stand vivid in their beauty. Perhaps it is time to go in for dinner.

'Abbie!' Nella calls from the farmhouse. 'Arthur, Henry, Vincent — this rabbit will go cold.'

Nella will be upset if they're late. Abbie climbs down and wraps her fingers around his, tiny calluses on her hands. Together with the boys, they amble towards home, smoke curling from the chimney on the thatched roof.

The aroma of the kitchen already fills Vincent's nostrils: carrots and onions braised for hours, rich and gamey rabbit. Nella has prepared his favourite.

What a woman she is. After three children and fifteen years of marriage, there is nothing they cannot discuss. They choose not to talk much about the first twenty-six years of his life, though. Born free on English soil, she can't begin to imagine what that was like for him, and he doesn't like to nowadays, either. It has been far more pleasant to create new memories of their own.

He can still see her the day they first met in Frome market. Tumbles of auburn hair, light brown skin, and a smile that could bring any man to his knees.

One knee, in Vincent's case.

What a life, Vincent thinks, though he's certain he's getting a headache.

The farmhouse door is within reach. He pushes it open, the faded blue paint catching the light of the evening sun.

Nella turns to greet him, and Vincent's life is spun from gold.

The beating doesn't hurt anymore. Now that he thinks about it, nothing does. He senses the blows, but instead of pain, white and hot, there's a warmth now. It feels sunny, like Hillsend's shears of wheat.

Vincent turns his head, sees Delphine through the legs of the masked men surrounding him. There are a dozen of them now. Vincent wonders why she is screaming, why Nick is pulling her away.

He never gave her his letter. Maybe that's why she's upset. Emotions have been running high today. He'll give it to her later. But first, he has to get up. Why won't anyone help him up?

Tears and rain feather his face, and Vincent blinks, the dull ache of realisation settling over him.

Is this truly my end?

Death is not the peace he was expecting.

I can't breathe, he wants to shout, but chokes on liquid iron as he opens his mouth.

He blinks again.

I will get up, he insists – part command, part desperate bargain.

Not yet.

I have so much more to give.

Vincent blinks one last time, hope fading.

And there is Abigail, leading him into the light.

Part Two
Deeds, not Words

Chapter Eighteen

AN UPDATE ON THE NEGRO CASE
Printed on behalf of Nicholas Lyons, MP for Kettering
Tomorrow evening, on the fifth of November, a vigil is being held in memoriam of the late Vincent Mourière after his passing on the steps of the King's Bench two weeks past. Those wishing to attend should make their way to Carnaby Street, Soho, for five o'clock in the evening.
—ENGLISH CHRONICLE

The body is a miraculous thing. Delphine has always admired how much one can withstand. From the first time she studied her mother administering tinctures and tying bandages to the limbs of other slaves, she has thought it incredible. So much pain. So much brutality. Yet, despite all this, despite the loudest of protestations, it keeps breathing.

Until of course, it can't.

For the last two weeks, Delphine has willed herself to stop breathing. Taken one last breath and held it and held it and held it until she feels her head dizzying, her throat tightening, her heart aching and then... disappointment. Emptiness returns to her with that next unwanted breath. On the outside, she appears calm. Her shoulders are straight against the back of the chair. She has got out of bed and dressed every day – though she rarely changes her clothes. Beneath her headwrap, dust gathers between the braids of her unwashed hair. While in company, she tries to prevent her eyes from welling up.

On the outside, Delphine appears to be coping. On the inside, everything is on fire.

Vincent's story has not left the newspapers since he died. There's little focus on the ruling, the monumental victory his trial secured for every Negro in England. They only want to talk about the protests that came after. Despite his murder occurring in broad daylight, few have come forward as witnesses.

No one has been arrested for his killing.

Since Pearl's killers were never brought to justice either, Delphine holds out little hope of a conviction.

Vincent's attackers stole everything from him — even the jacket from his back. And there was no trace of the letter he'd written for her at the prison. She'll never know what he wanted to say.

When Delphine remembers her brother's last moments, she sees his eyes — the utter fear and lack of understanding — and wonders at what point he stopped being human to his murderers. Perhaps he'd never been human to them at all.

The ruling has changed nothing.

Since then, Nick has granted her a leave of absence. With the trial over, he's recommended her for a teaching position in Philadelphia, where one of his abolitionist acquaintances has founded a new school for Negroes. But since mentioning it, he's been so preoccupied — planning the petition and tonight's vigil, attending abolitionist meetings at Hatchards, working on a reformation charter over glasses of port with the Bill of Rights Society. They've barely had a chance to discuss what it would be like for Delphine in America. Not that it's troubled her. She can't imagine a meaningful future in any place without Vincent.

Instead, she has kept herself busy with chores around the bawdy house. Her only official role here since working for Nick has been brewing remedies for the women's ailments. Over the summer, the tiny rooftop garden she keeps outside her attic room grew in abundance. And since word spread that Vincent was captured at the Exoticies, the Temple has risen to new levels of infamy, and the beds have scarcely been empty. For Delphine, that has meant grinding up more sunny calendula flowers to soothe chafed thighs, gathering more bright cornflower petals to fight cramps and infections, and brewing more chamomile tea for a well-earned sleep.

Marion's been giving Delphine space, content with her increasing surplus of coin. And the other women are too engaged with culls to pay her much attention.

But Delphine is used to her labour being unseen, and has learned to measure her worth only by her usefulness. So, she starches the bed linen, darns the clothing and does anything she can to keep going. Anything that means she doesn't have to sit, dwell, or reckon with the darkness that's been festering in her since the funeral. She barely remembers that awful day.

'Delphine,' Nick says now, reaching out to her across the dining room table. 'Did you hear me?'

It wasn't until he squeezed her arm that she realised he was speaking; she replies with a small shake of the head.

'Six thousand,' he says, gesturing to the piles of paper surrounding her pot of undrunk tea. 'Six thousand and forty-nine signatures. In two weeks!' He sighs when she doesn't respond. 'I'll present the petition to the Speaker of the House ahead of tonight's vigil.'

Lord Harvey and the West India merchants will likely try to overrule Mansfield's decision, using their presence and influence inside the Commons and Lords. The petition is Nick's attempt to discredit any such attacks by capturing the public sentiment. He hopes it will incite parliament to take things further in the right direction – to abolish the practice of slavery across the entirety of the British Empire.

This evening's vigil will allow Vincent's supporters to come together. Both to commemorate his life and to show his killers that despite what they did to him, his people will not be silenced.

Delphine looks down at Nick's hand, still gently resting on hers, and notices the black ink staining his skin like a bruise. Many of the petition's signatories could not write their names, so he did it for them.

If this had happened to anyone but her brother, she might have been moved by London's collective horror. She might have been impressed by how much interest there's been in obtaining true justice. She certainly would have contributed to the fund for Vincent's upkeep in prison or his funeral. She might have joined the first protests, small and spontaneous in Mile End, Stepney and other pockets of Black London. But loss is selfish and all-consuming. So, she didn't. There's little consolation in knowing how others will remember him.

Delphine and Nick are still sitting quietly at the table when Charity — one of the three girls Marion has granted the night off — flies into the dining room. She has swapped her signature fuchsia gown for sombre, Prussian blue. 'Come, Delphine,' she says. 'Marion and the others are almost ready. I've laid out clothes for you in your chamber. But first, you will *need* to bathe.'

Charity scrapes Delphine's chair out from beneath the table. Delphine says nothing as Charity manoeuvres her by the shoulders out of the kitchen, towards the stairs.

'This is the change we've been waiting for,' Nick calls after them as Delphine puts a hand on the banister. 'Six thousand voices are too many to go unheard. *For a nation to become truly great, one must stand with people, not above them.*'

Delphine doesn't look back at him as she mutters. 'Montesquieu isn't the answer to all the world's problems, Nick.' However, the words of one other philosopher come to mind: *man is born free, and everywhere he is in chains.*

If Delphine is to march with hundreds of people later, she must practice speaking with one. So, when Charity strongly suggested washing Delphine's hair a few minutes ago, she conceded on the condition they attempt regular conversation. Seemingly relieved at her acquiescence, Charity had accepted these terms all too eagerly.

'As the only girl in this house who gets paid, D, let me tell you how queer it is that you spend most of your wages on soap,' Charity says. With Delphine's head resting on the back of the pewter washbowl, her friend uses a thick wooden comb to separate her curls into six equal sections. 'If it were my money,' she continues, lathering a lemon-scented ball in her hands, 'I'd get a new broach every season.'

Delphine pops one eye open and attempts a sardonic tone. 'You think I'm paid enough to buy a broach every season?'

Charity smirks. 'I find it hard to believe Marion allows you to keep any of that salary!'

As Charity works through each strand of her hair, the comb gets caught on a particularly stubborn knot. She tugs and tugs until Delphine winces at the fire of it, attempts to block the comb's path with her fingers.

'Eh!' Charity scolds, batting Delphine's knuckles with the comb's wooden teeth. 'Don't be so tender headed.'

Delphine hisses an apology as the comb breaks through the knot, and they fall back into easy small talk. They chat about how unforgivably rude one of the girls is for always taking Charity's rouge. How long they each think the new door bully will last (Delphine thinks two more weeks; Charity, two more days). Hair unmatted, Charity massages Delphine's scalp with a softness that reminds her of her mother, and her shoulders relax with the reassurance that she has not forgotten the basics of human dialogue. She almost wishes she could remain in this moment forever: firmly cared for and unencumbered.

But then Charity shifts in the chair behind her, and a hesitation creeps into her voice. 'Have you thought any more about Nick's idea – about teaching in America? I think you'd do such a lot of good there. Vincent would have been so proud.'

Delphine tenses at the mention of her brother's name. She sits up, and a streak of lukewarm water snakes down her neck. 'He would have been worried about it, too,' she says. 'You don't know what it's like to cross the ocean on a ship.' Charity has never left London – she has no idea how volatile sailors get when the water runs low between ports when no one can clean themselves or quench their thirst as the sun bears down on the cloudless Atlantic. Though the conditions of carriage would be different this time, she's not sure she could do it again. Beyond the journey, it would mean leaving everyone Delphine cares about far behind for a land that treats Negroes far worse. She's just helped abolish slavery on English shores; how could she risk being captured elsewhere?

Charity wrings out the excess water from Delphine's hair and pats it dry with a towel. 'Promise you'll keep thinking about it?' she presses as she helps Delphine up. 'Because if...'

'If?' Delphine says, reaching for her hair pomatum.

'I was just fancying that if it were *me*... But that's stupid.' Charity scoffs at herself, and with a pang of guilt, Delphine understands what Charity is not saying. She would be seizing the opportunity with both hands if it were her. But with no education and somewhat of a reputation, Charity would likely never receive such an offer. Despite the mountain Delphine has already climbed, it's her responsibility to keep paving the way for others — even if it's not the path she wishes to take.

Contrite, Charity massages the oil into Delphine's curls then parts her hair into two sections. They each quickly twist Delphine's curls into a braided crown and once her hair is secure beneath a head wrap, she assures Charity she'll continue to think about it.

'Good.' Charity fetches the shoes she'd selected to match Delphine's charcoal dress. Sliding out of the grimy ensemble she's been wearing all week, Delphine supposes that since her hair is clean, she may as well use a bit of the water to wipe her face and underarms. Then she plucks a few leaves from the lavender plant on the windowsill — which, like most of the summer bloomers, desperately needs pruning — then crushes and rubs the silvery strands on her neck and wrists.

Charity returns with black leather boots hung over one arm, and is ushering Delphine into her skirt when a bang erupts outside the window. 'I guess it is after sunset,' Charity says. 'Oh, Lord! *Sunset!* We've got to get back downstairs, or we'll be late.' She scrambles to lace up Delphine's back, then pushes her — ready or not — out of the attic room with the shoes still over her arm.

'About time,' Marion says, pouncing as Charity passes Delphine over like a rag doll at the bottom of the stairs. 'Let's get this over with.'

'Excellent, you're here,' Nick says from behind the bawd. 'I need to get going now, I'm afraid, or there'll be no chance of me reaching Westminster before my appointment with the speaker.' He readjusts the reams of parchment in his arms. 'My footman has just been in to inform me that my driver is waiting on Golden Square. The carriage can't get any closer — the streets are overflowing.'

'There are that many people?' Delphine asks, but as they pass the receiving room, she can believe it. The Exoticies is full to bursting point. At a glance, she spots the other two girls Marion has excused from work tonight, the farmer Delphine purchases her seeds from at Carnaby Market, some of the neighbouring tavern's regulars, and even a few culls. Some of Nick's wealthier friends linger awkwardly near the door.

This is more support than she'd ever thought possible. It seems injustice can sink its teeth into the bones of those it affects, moving them from discomfort, to pain, to action.

'And there will be even more now,' Nick says, as another firework crackles in the distance. 'Do you remember the route?' he asks Delphine. 'It's only those roads you've been granted permission to march down.' Delphine nods. She has been useless while the others have planned the vigil, but leading the march is the least she could do.

Before Nick slips between guests to the door, he meets each of their gazes in turn. 'It goes without saying, but I will say it anyway for my peace of mind. I have taken a tremendous risk by so publicly organising this vigil, on today of all days.'

'*Remember, remember,*' Charity chants softly. Delphine has heard the fireworks on this day every year and seen the bonfires where they burn effigies of the Guy, but she's never spent much time considering the meaning behind it. Now, the rest of the sinister rhyme plays out in her head.

'Because of the gunpowder plot?' she asks.

'Yes,' Nick says, lowering his voice. 'Because on this day, we remember the consequences of treason. One group of conspirators decided they were above the law, so we're annually reminded that persecution is no excuse for recklessness.'

'Even when the law don't help nothing but itself,' Marion mutters.

Charity nudges the bawd to quieten her.

'*Even so*,' Nick says, bristling slightly at Marion's blunt truth-telling, 'I chose today because there is no more powerful reminder than bonfire night that Parliament's mandate to legislate comes from the people. They elect us – and so we must listen and represent their views. With the turmoil this country has seen of late, it took me a great deal of effort to obtain approval for all this. I had to seek special permission from the Prime Minister for the march to end outside Westminster, and I imagine he and His Majesty will be more on edge after learning how many are in attendance.'

'So what should we do?' Charity says, hands cradling her elbows.

She's never been one for trouble.

'Keep order. Follow the law. Today is a chance to foster unity beneath the banner of equality and Vincent's cause.'

The supporters gathered nearby have ceased their conversations to hear Nick's warning; always happy to speak in front of an audience, he projects his voice further, and a hush falls over the room.

'Remember, remember, my friends,' he calls out, 'there are forces that would relish disbanding you, and they will do anything they can to overturn Mansfield's ruling. Do not give them cause or aid. For the sake of your safety and your future freedom, you must follow Miss Delphine St Joseph's every direction meticulously during tonight's vigil.'

Nerves flutter in Delphine's stomach. Nick is looking at her in a way that suggests he trusts her directions will be wise. But she can hardly manage her day, let alone those of three hundred men. She fears he sees something in her that she lacks.

But there's no time to correct him. Nick bids them all luck as he leaves the bawdy house, disappearing down Carnaby Street into a quickly descending fog. The crowds outside seem to be getting louder, and the fireworks louder with them. Delphine checks the clock on Marion's mantel: in half an hour, the march will commence.

Chapter Nineteen

To the wicked, everything serves as pretext.
—M. DE VOLTAIRE

The next half hour passed in a blur. Delphine spent it greeting protesters outside the bawdy house, shaking their hands and then folding candles into them like weapons. Nick must have bought four hundred boxes of matches and at least thirty firestrikers because the misty streets were lit with an army of tiny flames when the clock chimed five o'clock. They'd expected a few hundred people to come, but there must be at least two thousand. Delphine steadies herself at the front and tucks a spare matchbox into her pocket.

Marion is beside her, but Charity isn't.

The bawd whispers that Nick's warning compelled her friend to stay behind. 'Don't be too hard on the girl. It's her way.'

Delphine agrees, crestfallen.

But despite the disappointment, she must march.

They take the first step. Then another. Then another. The crowd follows their lead, one foot after the other, one row, then the next. Until every torn, tattered or tailored shoe along every winding street for half a mile is in step.

As she walks, Delphine feels the sadness that has been holding her still for the last fortnight begin to flow outward: through her fingertips, through the candle, and up with the smoke into the night. She pulls her shawl tightly around her shoulders with her free hand. November's chill has set in, and despite all the bodies around her, she still feels its sting.

'How are you doing?' she asks the bawd. 'Cold,' Marion grumbles. 'Likewise,' Delphine says. 'But it's worth it. Because this is *for Vincent.*' Marion lifts her candle closer to Delphine's face and peers at her. Then she takes her arm. 'For Vincent,' they echo in unison.

It does not go unheard.

The words spread from their lips to those at the very back of the crowd. Hearing his name uttered so many times, like an incantation, forces Delphine to acknowledge that her brother is much more than a man now.

He is a symbol.

And they are quietly marching towards another.

Halfway through the forty-minute journey to Westminster, she notices more tiny flames flickering inside some of the houses they pass. Men and women stand with their arms wrapped around each other, nodding their heads from behind the safety of windowpanes. They are with her, too, in their way.

The crowd swells as they reach New Palace Yard. No other people are in sight. Delphine grabs an empty, discarded crate from one of the trader's stalls. They'll need it later. Reflections from their candles bounce off the scaffolding surrounding the House of Lords, making its towers seem taller and more menacing in the darkness. Delphine takes comfort knowing that Nick is within, presenting his petition to the Speaker of the House.

When the abbey bells announce six o'clock, he will join them. Some of the signatories will tell their stories, relating to all of Westminster what Vincent's success meant to them. Delphine sensed an expectation from the others that she should speak too, but the words in her heart are not meant for crowds – she'll save them for her brother's graveside.

Somewhere in the crowd, people begin to sing. A sombre tune carried from plantation to plantation, across islands and oceans. Delphine sets down her crate and closes her eyes, humming along to the melody, and though she hasn't heard the song in years the lyrics easily resurface:

> *Massa buy me, he won't killa me,*
> *O'*
> *Massa buy me, he won't killa me,*
> *O'*
> *Massa buy me, he won't killa me,*
> *O'*
> *'For he kill me he whip me regular*

The bells chime after the third repetition, and there is no sign of Nick. There could be any number of reasons why he's been delayed, but tendrils of unease creep into Delphine's voice. She tries to shake them off by singing louder. The low notes of the second verse reverberate deep in her chest.

> *'For I live with a bad man,*
> *Oh la lie!*
> *'For I live with a bad man,*
> *Obudda bo*
> *'For I live with a bad man,*
> *Oh la lie!*
> *But the bad man gon' reap what he deserve*

The singing halts when a man emerges from a balcony window above them, dressed in red balloon breeches trimmed with gold. The crowd cheers, and Delphine steps onto the wooden box and raises her hand to call for silence. The hush falls quickly; her nerves do not. The man looks so tiny from where she stands, dwarfed beneath the twisting pillars of the medieval building.

So much for Nick's idea that governments are not above the people, she thinks.

Marion nudges her. 'What do you think he'll say?'

'I'm not sure,' Delphine whispers.

'Where's Nick?' she mutters through her teeth.

'I don't know.' But Delphine is sure Nick will be here any moment.

The man on the balcony clears his throat, and his nasal voice rings across the square.

'Our Sovereign Lord the King charges and commands all assembled here to immediately disperse...'

Anger slithers down Delphine's spine – the Riot Act. The man is reading them the Riot Act. It's been impossible to avoid the tumults that swept through the city these last few years, but this is no riot. Delphine can still hear the shouts of 'bread or blood' from the rioting women in 1766, when the army could barely control the uprisings after the price of wheat rose so high that only the rich could afford bread.

Or two years ago, when fifteen thousand angry white men mobbed the streets after Wilkes, the anti-monarchist MP was first imprisoned. After the first night of shooting, even Marion was forced to close the Temple doors.

And it's not like during the silk weavers' bloody revolt over wages and conditions in Spitalfields. Delphine still passes by many streets with boarded-up windows because of it.

No blood has been shed here. Yet Parliament is demanding they leave.

Is it possible all the people gathered here are in the wrong? What does that man see from his Westminster balcony that she does not?

'... peacefully depart to your homes or your lawful businesses, upon the pains contained within the Act and...'

The vigil's attendees are getting restless now. The lights on the walls dart about as some people shake their candles like fists; shouts of *We not doing nothing, leave us be*, and *For Vincent*, fly up into the air.

'... at the will of his Majesty, King George III, for preventing tumults and riotous assemblies.'

The cries grow louder, and the bodies push closer into one mass of shock and outrage. Delphine's pulse quickens – she wants justice, too, but not like this.

If this becomes a riot, there is no way Parliament will hear these people's stories, no way for Vincent to rest in peace. Nick told her to control the crowd, but how can she? She is just one person. There is no reason for them to listen to her.

'You have one hour to depart. God save the King.' No one repeats his words.

No one moves.

The man turns and slams the balcony door behind him. The thud is lost among the rising commotion.

'Should we go?' Marion says to Delphine.

Should we? Delphine wonders as the shouts grow louder, as she turns to Marion and sees fear flickering in her eyes. This is how it starts, she thinks as the air thickens with uncertainty. This is how a protest becomes a riot. We agree to follow their rules and then they change them. Force the discontented masses to choose between compliance or violence, leaving no options in between. 'We've done nothing wrong.' But Nick did tell them to obey commands. And this is definitely one of them.

'We did something wrong as soon as we were cut from our mothers' wombs,' Marion hisses. Delphine has never seen the bawd so vexed, and a fire is building in her, too. It's been there all along, deep in the pit of her stomach, just as Vincent described it on the eve of his death. She has gone to great lengths to put that fire out daily. To suppress the flames of her anger with pursed lips, tensed shoulders and a held tongue. It has left her exhausted – the slave's burden.

But no more.

Tonight, she will not be silenced.

'I'm not leaving,' Delphine says, loud enough for those around her to hear. She steps back onto the crate and lifts her candle to the sky.

'Delphine!' Marion snaps, tugging at her skirts. 'Remember what Lyons said.'

She hasn't forgotten, but Nick isn't here. She can guess why he hasn't joined them – it is safer within Parliament's walls – and she's not going to wait for him any longer.

The crowd is quiet again, all eyes on Delphine. Then, row by row, they raise their candles in solidarity, flames shimmering in the night. She has their attention — but what to do with it?

There must be a way to heed Nick's warning without abandoning their cause. She couldn't save Vincent's life; at the very least, she needs to save his memory. And that's what all these people came here to do.

Her heart won't calm, but her thoughts are racing towards an idea. A beautiful, horrific idea.

'We will not riot tonight,' she calls out. 'The men in this building have decided who we are, but we shall prove them wrong.' Her voice is strong and carries across the yard. 'You do not have to remain here, but if you choose to stay I am asking for your help. Help me show these men what it was like for our parents, our grandparents, and all those who came before them. We will... lie down.'

'What?' Marion points indignantly to the delicate lace trim on her dress, as the rest of the crowd mumbles their confusion.

The bawd has never told Delphine of her journey from Jamaica to Britain. She doesn't know if Marion has ever experienced the tight packing method — where slaves are forced to lie, squashed side by side, for dangerous lengths of time in the belly of a ship. Having been born in St Lucia, Delphine hasn't. But she has seen the chain-linked lines of broken men as they were forced off the vessels. She has dabbed water onto their cracked lips and has cleaned the layers of shit and puss from their untreated wounds.

This is what they are protesting. This is why her brother died. 'Can you do this?' Delphine asks Marion after explaining her idea.

The bawd pales, then nods her sombre agreement.

'Then let's spread the word. Make sure everyone knows they can leave if they have to.'

Delphine goes left, and Marion goes right.

All around the square, people lay down their bodies, as close as possible to one another. Delphine feels the crook in the bawd's elbow, the calf of the man on her other side, and the scent of his sweat.

Delphine takes each of their hands and closes her eyes as she trembles at the thought of living this. The strength it would take to survive it, what would be left of her on the other side.

When that man reappears on the balcony, guarded by his velvet pomp and privilege, he will see this:

Thousands of people lying head to toe, legs overlapping, heart next to crying, beating heart.

They are not faceless drawings in a book. They are not cargo to be claimed on insurance.

They are as they have always been: real, breathing beings with lives, struggles and stories.

She hopes that when the man comes back he sees that this is not a riot.

This is humanity. Resilience. Desperation.

As the last few protestors join them on the ground, there's not a whisper among the crowd. Only the far-off boom of fireworks: each thunder and peal an echo of the explosion that never happened but will never be forgot. Because once, it might have destroyed this very building, disrupting the very heart of the empire.

Too soon, the fireworks are drowned out by marching feet and clopping hooves. She looks up to see the Horse Guard blocking the road on the north side of the square, the ranks of soldiers amassing on the east. Hundreds of black boots and silver bayonets glinting in the candlelight.

When the hour is up, they give no final warning. Gunpowder and lead explode overhead. A cacophony of screams rises, and her control over the crowd is gone.

When you don't know whose blood just spattered your hands and face, instinct takes over.

Delphine runs, desperate to make it out of New Palace Yard.

Marion is already out of sight, as are the other girls and all the faces she recognised earlier.

How quickly peace can turn to violence.

She fights through the crowd, ducking and dodging the soldiers' bullets and swords. With no weapons, the protestors are throwing their candles, pocket contents, and rocks from the ground to defend themselves.

'We're not doing anything, we're not doing anything, we're not doing anything!' a woman begs, one arm over her face, desperately trying to drag a companion from a soldier's grip with the other.

Delphine runs, skin flushed and slick with sweat. She breathes hard, but there's too little air to fuel her flight in the crush.

Trying to block out the sounds of knuckles cracking against skulls, she scrambles over falling bodies. She cringes every time she hears the roar of a gun.

'Move! Get the hell out of here!' a redcoat yells, the noise burning like magma in her ears. His bayonet is on its side, and he slams the butt into her spine, then the back of her head. Delphine stumbles dizzily out of his eyeline before he can change his mind and pull the trigger.

The man beside her is injured. She reaches out to him, but the crowd surges, pushing her forward. It swallows him up like he's being pulled under a wave.

She keeps pushing, keeps being pushed, until at last she breaks from the crowd, and finds herself sprinting across Westminster Bridge.

Though her lungs are on fire and the wind shoots icy daggers at her cheeks, she does not stop. If she does, she is dead. She slows only once she reaches the south side of the bridge, gripping the stone barrier to try and steady the swirling mess of her thoughts. Blood is trickling from the back of her head; she feels faint. As she looks back at parliament, all she can make out against the night sky is its silhouette – spikes, spires, and smoke.

What Delphine wishes to see instead: Westminster in flames.

It almost happened over a hundred and fifty years ago on this very day.

Remember, remember.

Across the city, church bells toll. Seven deep chimes for seven o'clock.

They didn't even give us an hour.

A scream builds in her lungs, but she holds it. For too long Delphine has kept her head down in the face of injustice. She has tried, oh, how she has tried to reconcile her impulses to rebel with the reality of her status, to accept that she has no power. But she cannot any longer. She will not.

And why should she?

All they asked for was to be heard.

But instead of listening, the government Nick asked her to trust opened fire. Shooting to kill in the name of the King.

She knows now it does not matter which rules she follows. The noose drops all the same.

Because her very skin is a rebellion; her breaths evidence of resistance; her thoughts a living reminder of ancestral hope.

The protesters' crying hasn't stopped.

More of them are fleeing over the bridge, pursued by soldiers on horseback. She doesn't need to see their faces, hear their voices, or know their fear. She was born knowing the scent of it: sulphur and ammonia, sweat and iron. She will take that fear and craft it into a weapon.

They will be here soon.

Delphine lets the scream out, primal and vicious and wild. With one last look at Westminster, before she runs again, Delphine makes herself a promise: this Empire will fall.

Chapter Twenty

> There is no greater tyranny than that which is perpetrated under the shield of the law and in the name of justice.
> —BARON DE MONTESQUIEU

Delphine wakes with the dawn. The unlocked boatman's hut she sheltered in overnight kept out the worst of the cold, but she was thankful she still had her shawl and could wrap herself in its woolly warmth. The scattered dreams she'd snatched looked the same as her waking thoughts. All are of justice. Yesterday, she'd been weighed down by grief and expectation. Today, it's only her mud-caked skirts that hold her back.

Fear carried her the two miles from Westminster to London Bridge. She hadn't intended to sleep there, only to avoid any lingering soldiers on her way back to the bawdy house. But as the cold and the delirium from her head wound set in, her priorities changed from returning home to finding shelter.

Her damp clothes begin to dry on her journey to the Temple of Exoticies, the numbness within her replaced by a flurry of unanswered questions. She needs to know if Marion and the others made it back safely.

London's bare streets are beautiful as the early sun creeps along the rooftops. Chamber pots have yet to be emptied, and the rain has washed much of yesterday's filth away. Despite last night's chaos, the city around her seems at peace.

For the forty-minute walk across London, a new rhyme of her invention plays in Delphine's mind.

Remember, remember the fifth of November;
the gunpowder treason and plot.
I know of no reason why
the gunpowder treason
should ever have been stopped.

It leads her to question: how far would *she* go to change things?

Maybe Delphine should seek a fresh start in Philadelphia. Her attempts to change things on this side of the Atlantic have been thwarted repeatedly. Perhaps she is trying to change the wrong thing, focusing on the law and the system, not the people living within it. Maybe it is too late for her to improve her lot in life, but she can equip the next generation for a better one. Yet the thought of leaving her friends – the closest people she has now to a family – ushers a weariness into her bones. As she continues down the row of Palladian-columned shop fronts along Piccadilly, the weariness spreads, the wound on the back of her head throbbing with each step.

She must look unkempt and even more out of place in the prestigious St James's parish than usual. She puts a hand to her hair to check for fresh blood and winces. The wound is dry, but she does not feel well at all. A passing washerwoman clutches her laundry basket tighter to her hip and crosses the street, giving her a wide berth.

Through bleary eyes, Delphine recognises the trio of bookshops up ahead. She frequented them all during Vincent's trial, but there's only one she feels safe enough to go into and rest. As her vision swims and her breath shallows, Delphine pushes Hatchards's jet-black door open. The bell tinkles, and the tinny sound echoes for far longer than it should. Delphine sways as a middle-aged bookseller emerges at the top of the staircase, holding a scalpel and leather book spine as if he'd been operating on it. He jogs down to greet her. Delphine replies by swooning into his arms.

With an astonished grunt, they both collapse to the floor. His binding and scalpel fly across the room, as does Delphine's shawl.

After a stunned moment, the bookseller says, 'Can't say I've been greeted like that before.' He blinks down at her, motionless in his aproned lap. 'Do you need a chair, Miss... St Joseph, isn't it? A doctor? A biscuit?'

'Just a second,' Delphine says, shuffling from his lap to the floor, which to her surprise and gratitude is spotless. She rests her cheek on the hardwood and doesn't say anything until the trio of gentlemen before her merge back into one. 'I'm sorry, sir,' she says, considering his suggestions. 'A chair, please.'

Without another word, the man stands, scouts around for his items, then disappears back up the steps to his workshop. Meanwhile, she pulls herself into a sitting position and leans gingerly against a row of clothbound myths and legends. She almost wishes she had fallen unconscious to save her from this embarrassment.

When the bookseller returns, he has a cushioned stool in one hand and a plate of biscuits in the other. 'I hope these might make up for the lack of a physician,' he says, helping her up before passing her the golden tower of shortbread.

She bites into one of the buttery biscuits, and it crumbles between her teeth. 'Thank you.'

'I'll be honest, Miss St Joseph, I was not expecting my first customer of the day to have partaken in last night's antics. I presume that is why you are... unwell?' He picks up her blood-stained shawl from the floor between finger and thumb, and passes it back to her. 'It's the talk of the town, you know.'

'What are they saying?' she says, the wooziness returning now in the pit of her stomach. She'd forgotten how fast word spreads along the Thames.

'That it was a riot like any other. Though not many make it to the steps of Parliament.' He tilts his head, a double chin forming as he tucks it close to his neck. 'So, well done you.'

Delphine smiles in recognition of his support. But beneath it, her anger still simmers. Nothing had gone to plan yesterday, certainly nothing to be congratulated for. She'd not heeded Nick's warning, and now, things will inevitably get worse. She sighs and is rubbing at her temples when the shop bell rings again, this time short and crisp. A pale woman in a paisley dress strolls in with an eager-faced young boy. 'Mister Walvin?' the woman calls out.

'I'm afraid I'm needed over there,' the bookseller says. 'Unless... was there a book you wanted for Mister Lyons? Or a recommendation for yourself, perhaps?'

Not yet ready to stand and face the outside world again, Delphine chooses a distraction. 'Maybe something about teaching?'

'Ha! Alas, teaching is something you do, not something you read about.' Mister Walvin's gaze darts between the new customers and Delphine, and he bids the former wait a moment longer, which makes Delphine smile but elicits an audible huff from the boy. Offering Delphine his arm, the bookseller helps her to her feet and leads her carefully towards the back of the store. 'I fancied myself a teacher once,' he says. 'History, if you can believe it.'

'What stopped you?' she asks.

The boy moans, 'What's taking so long?' and his mother hastily shushes him.

'An avid lack of patience for children,' he says wryly, stopping in front of a case with dozens of crimson spines. 'But the minds of the future should be moulded by the past, don't you think? Maybe then they'll be less inclined to repeat our mistakes.' His voice drops low as he mutters, 'I wonder what the 1770—79 edition will say about last night.'

Before Delphine can ask him anything more, he excuses himself to serve the mother and child. 'Feel free to hide here for as long you need.'

Alone at the back of the shop, Delphine lingers on the bookseller's words as she scans the red-bound books before her. They are somewhat intimidating to her eye, all entitled 'State Histories' and at least a palm's width in thickness. Each volume holds a decade's history in a series that stretches back two hundred years. The man is right, of course — people *should* learn about the past to inform their future. Should she teach, then?

Just as Nick told her, she is a quick study. And since she began working with him, she has learned how men perceive the world. She can recite Montesquieu and Locke's views on liberty, and quote Kant and Rousseau's thoughts on justice; she sees their influence when she examines old trials, reads laws, and looks for precedents. With every underlined paragraph and dog-eared page, her mind has slowly been reshaping itself. Making sense of the differences between her world and the words on the page.

She understands why Nick loves to read. There's solace in finding parts of yourself in the words of another. It provides comfort for some and courage for others. For Delphine, it has uncovered a new truth.

Ideals are words without action. Laws alone don't guarantee change. Vincent's trial and last night showed her that.

Philosophy and politics cannot keep her safe, nor can they do the same for others. Her stomach twists at the memory of Nick *helping* Vincent find the least risky way to sit in court. It will never be enough to teach children how to avoid hatred, to watch for signs of rage and to elude violence.

She will not teach children in Philadelphia how to be good slaves. She'd never been a good one herself.

There's a seed of an idea she's searching for, one planted around a hundred and fifty years ago. Delphine starts with 1620—29, learns of the Archbishop of Canterbury's acquittal after killing a keeper with a crossbow, of the Lord Chancellor being impeached for taking bribes, of a tribe of Algonquian Indians destroying an English settlement after the English burned down their own. Another war with Spain. But no gunpowder plot.

Back another decade, she opens the volume for 1610—19 and learns of women burned and hanged for witchcraft, of trading posts set up on the West Coast of Africa, but no gunpowder plot.

In 1600—1609, Delphine turns through the heavy pages until she reaches November 1605. And there is the seed: so tiny, so muddied by darkness that the chance of it growing successfully is too small to imagine. It has been inside her for a while, fed by every impulse that has driven her to rebel.

Little rebellions can only go so far. It is not enough to keep snatching at false victories in this unfair, losing game. She's done fighting against guns with her wits alone. She's done waiting for Nick or another well-meaning white man to save her.

It is a ridiculous thought. An impossible one born of disappointment, desperation and disillusionment. To *think* of treason is enough to be punished for it. To be tortured, hanged, drawn and quartered or, for a woman, to be burned at the stake.

But she keeps reading. Turning the pages of 'State Histories', Delphine reads about Guy Fawkes and Robert Catesby, their plot and its downfall. Their plan was seemingly futile, but came so close to success. Formed over a year by a dozen or so men, all of whom had been subjected to varying degrees of injustice by the state. Apparently, they dug a tunnel from a rented house to an underground chamber beneath the House of Lords, where they stored thirty-six barrels of gunpowder. No evidence of the tunnel was ever found.

Having walked Westminster's halls for months now, she would not be surprised to find that other tunnels and secret entry points exist there. That loose wall panel she found in the Commons Library, for example. What would the Catholics have used that for if they knew about it? And could it be used for a second attempt, now?

What am I doing? She shivers, imaginary flames licking at her skin. But still, the thoughts do not stop. A born planner, Delphine allows herself to think of the how and when.

The House is out of session until mid-December. To act now, to set fire to an empty building, would change nothing. They would simply rebuild it and move on. No lessons learned; no new laws passed – just more of the same injustice. To start again, like the conspirators of the past, she would need all the Empire's influential figures to be gathered there. Could she erase them in a single moment, as swift as blotting out a sentence on paper?

Fawkes chose the State Opening. And that is only five weeks away. The King and nobility will all be there, along with the highest-ranked members of the Church, Parliament and the Judiciary, ambassadors and diplomats and members of the trading companies.

A chance to establish *tabula rasa* while staining herself with blood.

It is as abhorrent as it is darkly thrilling. Only a thought, but a thought that's fast transforming in her mind, into something stomach-twistingly unconscionable.

Unsettling. Unforgivable. Unrelenting.

Her heart knows the why, the vagaries of how. But most of all, there are the what-ifs:

What if there is another, peaceful way to change the system? Or what if she carried out the plot and somehow succeeded — would she be able to live with herself? Or what if she failed, and things got worse than ever?

But what if she does nothing?

Slavery may be illegal on English shores, but a hundred thousand souls are still traded by the British each year. That's almost a million between today and her thirtieth year. A million lives. And what if things get *worse*? What if the trade companies grow greedier? What if the violence against Black people in England intensifies, and more are killed? What if, what if, what if?

From reading about the Catholic plot, she already sees the similarities between their causes — their lack of representation, voice, and freedom. It has been a hundred and forty years since that failed plot, and still, a Catholic man — a white man — may not hold land or vote. Even now, priests are captured and imprisoned. What hope is there for Delphine, then? For Black men and women and countless others?

Though Fawkes and Catesby were trying to change the country, not bring down a whole empire, their plan still involved great risk. It cost them their lives. But it *almost* worked.

Catesby, the plot's originator, said this: *Let us give an attempt, and where it faileth, pass no further.*

But what if she *can* pass further? What if she can learn from their mistakes? She might allow this dark spark of an idea to burn a little while longer. She needn't tell anyone about it; should her conscience overwhelm her, she can simply snuff it out. A snuffed spark can do no harm.

So, what if?

Taking risks gave Delphine her freedom. It has enabled her to achieve the impossible before.

What if she could fix this broken system by taking her biggest risk yet?

What if, armed with an impossible idea from the past, Delphine can fix everything?

Chapter Twenty-One

The passion of fear, like pride and envy, hath slain its thousands

—PRINCE HALL

c. 1735-1807, enslaved c. 1746-1770

'Did you get hit over the head with a bayonet?' Marion screeches, almost spilling her tea across the kitchen table. She flings her hands up. 'You know what they'd do to you, to us?'

Marion's reaction doesn't surprise her. Three days ago, if someone had asked Delphine to join a conspiracy to bring down an empire, she'd have thought they'd been hit with a bayonet too.

And since it would not help her case to remind Marion that she *had* been hit over the head, she decides to keep that fact to herself.

Working at the countertop at the other end of the room, Delphine chooses her next words carefully. She's far enough from Marion that her scolding drink wouldn't reach her if the bawd threw it, but the ceramic cup might.

These last few days, Delphine has thought long and hard. While tending to Marion's and the girls' injuries – which, thankfully, were as mild and easy to treat as her own – she memorised every page on the gunpowder plot in her newly acquired copy of 'State Histories'. She has looked at every alternative path too, of course: she could lead protests, which will be ignored or answered with bullets; campaign for reforms, which will only paper over cracks or do nothing and let her anger rot her away from the inside. Two innocent protesters were killed by soldiers on Monday night, both of whom were Black: a forty-two-year-old carpenter named William Frett and a twenty-four-year-old seamstress named Maud Donovan. Delphine did not meet either of them, but every time their names return to haunt her, *she* returns to her final option: she could try and end the British Empire. But she cannot do it alone.

The tides of the Empire are changing. There is the crisis in the Falklands. The increasingly frequent clashes between the English forces and settlers in America. Vincent's ruling. After his release from prison in January, Nick's fellow radical MP, John Wilkes, published a damning criticism of the King's underhanded influence on government, simultaneously condemning Parliament's nepotism and self-serving agenda. A year ago, the newspapers were banned from publishing parliamentary debates, but the press has fought for transparency, and the public has echoed its demands. Now, they publish stories of corruption, stagnated reform and controversy almost every day.

The desire is there.

The British Empire at its tipping point. All she needs to do is push.

And for that, Delphine needs gunpowder. She needs Marion's smugglers, for someone to tell her if this is even possible before she takes it any further. Marion's the only person she knows with the connections to make it happen. She's the only person she trusts enough to give voice to her plot.

'You know what I've learned these last six months?' Delphine says. She stops grinding the white willow bark in the mortar in front of her – its powder, when soaked, will make a poultice to lessen the inflammation around Marion's blood bruise. She'd been pushed into an empty trader's stall in the commotion, the skin over her rib cage caught on a wooden post.

'Every time a tragedy occurs, they create a new law, or some man publishes a pamphlet condemning tyrannical governments.' Delphine laughs to herself. 'Six months ago, I'd never even heard the word tyrannical. Yet aren't we the ones who've experienced tyranny the most?'

'Everyone's got troubles.' Marion tuts and bats Delphine's words away. 'And yet, you nuh see the white women ruffling dem skirt. Or white men sharpening fi dem swords.'

'But they have,' Delphine says. On Wednesday, she returned to Hatchards and, aided by Mister Walvin's recommendations, learned about Britain's rich history of political and civil unrest.

How had she never known before yesterday that an English King had lost his head?

'The people have gone to war with the King twice in the last century!' Delphine says. 'They thought the crown had too much power, so they gave it to the government. But what's changed? There's still no power for the majority who cannot read. No vote for those without land to their name or members between their legs. No time for us to think, because we are too busy working harder and harder to counter each increase in the price of bread. If you'd just let me speak to the smugglers, see if it's possible, then—'

'Ain't no one else who need hear that speech, Delphine. You nuh need no smuggling gang to tell you rebellions nuh work.'

'Because we settle!' Delphine says, voice rising. 'Because we're afraid to see what happens when we take the next step.' She turns away and throws a stick of cinnamon into the mortar with the willow bark, grinding it in time with her teeth.

'And so we should be!' Marion fumes. 'Because we aren't the ones with the ships and the armies and the weapons. Stop running your mouth before the wrong person overhear it.'

Marion is right. She might as well suggest that an ant try to topple an elephant. But there's a difference between knowledge and acceptance. Delphine should drop the subject now to save herself from facing more of Marion's ire, but she doesn't think she can. Not yet. Delphine's lip trembles; she tucks a needle between her teeth to stop it.

With the mortar in one hand, damp linen and a clean wooden spoon in the other, Delphine crosses the chipped stone floor to Marion, who gracefully turns and lifts one leg to straddle the wooden bench. The bawd rolls up the bodice section of her dress with a painful hiss.

Setting the items on the table, Delphine removes the needle from her mouth and pins the cotton bodice – in the colours and style of fine China porcelain – out of the way. 'Better or worse than yesterday?'

'Near enough the same,' Marion admits.

Delphine squints to examine the bruise, three fingers wide but starting to heal. On the right side, the curved end of an old lash scar almost touches its deep violet edge. Delphine slathers some of the grainy mixture in her mortar onto Marion's skin. The bawd winces, either from the cold or the pressure, she's not sure. Brows knitted together, she says, 'I never did tell you how I got taken to Jamaica.'

'You didn't,' Delphine says, unsure if this is a story she ever wanted to hear.

'It were my father who sold me to the slavers. I won't waste a breath telling you what him like; him nuh waste a breath on me to say goodbye. I was ten. Then a man pale as teeth push a gun into my father's hand and clap me in iron.'

Delphine tries to stay focused on her work, not to conjure the image. 'Dem herd us onboard. After the ship set sail, I start listening to the other women, who were talking quiet about taking over the ship, turning back toward land.' She cradles her cup of tea so firmly her knuckles start to whiten. 'That first night, my teeth had never rung so much from cold... This were before I come to England, of course.' Marion smiles, but Delphine can't find it within herself to return it – she can already tell this story will not end happily.

'When the men started taking us to their sleeping quarters, dem had to loosen wi chains. It were a few days later that one of the women – tall as a tree with arms strong as roots – grab a sailor from behind and use the chain to strangle him. Then, when he was dead, she tore the key from his belt and got us free. The other women used anything they could to take out the sailors.' Marion stands a little straighter, her voice hardening. 'I'm not ashamed to say I didn't. I hid. The women nay win. The one who started it – the one who'd stood tall like a tree – she didn't float like one. Half the others were taken below with the men. The rest of us were separated and kept on deck in chains.'

Delphine's breath catches. Although the memory is not her own, somehow, she can see every bit of it. She lays down her pestle and rests her hand over the bawd's. 'I'm so sorry, Marion.'

Marion flips her hand over, locking her fingers with Delphine's over blue cornflower and creamy chamomile petals, left over from another remedy. 'What surprised me most when I got to Jamaica was how many tales told the same: women unchained on deck, then fighting back. You'd think the crews woulda learned.' She squeezes Delphine's hand, then breaks away. 'A woman is never a threat fi dem, just another piece of cargo, like barrels of wine or crates of spices.' Marion laughs, a sad, small sound. 'But dem tales all end the same, too — women back in chain or at the bottom of the sea. I didn't know much then, but I've always known this: you don't survive going against the people with guns. And that is what you're asking me to do.'

Delphine doesn't know what to say. Tears warm her eyes as she holds her breath, thinking over all she knows of Marion's life on the plantation and what came after — how she wooed a slaver into wedlock, convinced him to go to England, and opened a brothel so that she could build a business and a life. Marion still has so much to lose. Delphine understands why she is saying no.

'I know your heart, Delphine,' Marion says. 'I know there's no evil in that chest of yours, but believe me, the world is full of it. What goes bad in a morning, gon' stay bad in the evening. You be sure no change gon' come in the afternoon.'

'But aren't you tired of being the one who pays the most and gets the least?'

'I'm tired,' Marion says, an edge creeping into her voice, 'of being charged more because some girl don't know her place.'

But Delphine does know her place. She just wants a better one. And she thinks Marion does, too. 'But what if they don't find out?'

she says. 'You're right. Change doesn't happen overnight, but it does happen. You've seen it. You've lived it. What if it brings us closer to equal footing? They're not going to stop killing and chaining us – isn't it time we made them? If one man can rule an Empire, why can't one woman bring it down?'

'And you think you that woman? Ha! All you'll bring is trouble!' She grabs the pestle and thrusts it into Delphine's chest. 'Stick with what you're good at, Delphine: fixing for no babies and giving the girls soft dreams.'

Delphine stiffens. Today, she won't make herself smaller. 'No.' The air around them tenses.

'*No?*'

'I can't keep brewing potions and patching up wounds. I need to know if I can do more.'

'*More?*' Marion snarls. 'You tell me you need *more?* When I give you a roof over your head? After you aks me to save your brother? You dare say no to me when it's *my* business getting trampled by Runners and *my* girls put outta work at your fool's protest.' Marion kisses her teeth. 'You have me act like we back in a damned hell hole of a ship. Cause all that trouble, then disappear, don't even let us know you're alive. And now you come moaning about the price of bread when you don't even buy the flour.' The bawd slams her cup on the table, all sympathy vanished.

'Marion...'

'Ah-ah!' Marion spits, her chest heaving. 'You say no? You say *you're* done? But still you want my help. Asking me to risk *my* life, my girls' lives, because you nuh care about yours! Fine, Delphine. I'll sort the meeting. You want dem smugglers to tell you there's no good to be got from this plan? Fine. But no more.' She picks up a cornflower petal, crushing it between her fingers. 'Don't think you can stir up a hurricane and expect me not to lock my door. So how much do you want this? It worth your family? Your job? This roof? Because that's my price. You wan' me do this. I want you gone.'

Delphine looks down at the table. When Nick offered her the chance to go to Philadelphia, it was the thought of losing her family and her friends that first held her back. If she does this, she'll lose them anyway. But if she doesn't... Delphine meant what she said: no herbal remedy can fix this feeling inside her.

Four years ago, before Marion took Delphine in, Delphine had shared an alleyway behind a baker's yard with a scrappy stray dog. Every day, the mutt would take a beating from the baker to steal his burned scraps from the gutters. After a few days, she figured out why the dog kept returning. It is better to be beaten, knowing you'll eat afterwards than to avoid a thrashing and risk starvation. It troubled her to dwell on how the dog had learned that.

One dreary day, the skies were half dark with rain clouds and smoke. Delphine heard a whelp and a thud in the unlit alley as the baker pushed the matted dog a little too far. The man tripped, falling to his knees on the cobbles, and the dog pounced. He tore, snarled, and snapped at the man, turning his floury overalls from white to red. Delphine rushed to the baker's aid, but the dog had gone for his neck — short of ripping off her stays and tying them around the gushing wound, all Delphine could do was run into the yard and find his wife.

He died before they'd made it back.

It was inevitable. After one push too many, a dog will always bite back.

And like that dog, Delphine has been pushed too hard, too many times. What she wants now is to see those bakers bleed.

Delphine meets the bawd's gaze. 'Set up the meeting.'

Chapter Twenty-Two

> RUN OFF from his Master's Service in Newcastle, a NEGRO MAN, about six feet high, speaks broken English and is about twenty-seven years of age. Had on a lilac coat with matching breeches and waistcoat. Whoever shall secure him may have half a guinea reward. He went by the name of Castillia, but it is now believed he styles himself Jack Steel.
>
> —NEWCASTLE CHRONICLE

Delphine has crossed most of London to find the smugglers' hideout. The streets are packed and it's taken almost an hour and a half on foot.

When she approaches the Thames and sees the low sails of Dutch fishing boats dotting the skyline, she knows she's close. A few steps later comes the smell. Squid and saltwater. Salmon and sweat.

Did the entrance have to be so close to Billingsgate?

Delphine weaves between women with hefty behinds and gin-flushed cheeks. One wide-set fishwife lurches by with a corset so tight her breasts look firm and round as marbles. She uses one hand to steady a trout-laden basket on her head; the other she uses to take a long swig from a glass bottle. She doesn't stop walking to chug.

Delphine glances over to the clock face, hanging like a shop sign off the steeple of St Magnus' church. A little before one o'clock. Elsewhere, she might judge someone so inebriated at this time, but if she spent every day hauling around fish carcasses, she'd want to take away the edge, too. She could use a drink now, having moved her few belongings to an inn near Holborn this morning.

Marion didn't immediately throw her out of the Exoticies after their conversation, but she didn't want to see Delphine's face either. So Delphine spent most of these last two days reading 'State Histories' in her room. Every time she heard a ripple of laughter from downstairs, or one of the women asked her for a home-brewed herbal remedy, her resolve wavered. She questioned if leaving them all behind was the right thing to do. But then she remembered Vincent or thought about the future, and the balance shifted again.

That didn't make saying goodbye to Charity any easier. If her friend had any desire to tell Delphine *I told you so* since the vigil, she's done a remarkable job of keeping quiet. And therein lies the problem. Charity may avoid trouble, but she rarely avoids the truth. Without her guidance, Delphine feels like she's looking for flaws in her reasoning through a muslin-coated mirror.

After she told Charity her new address, Charity had simply kissed her on the cheek and walked away.

But Delphine hardly felt the sting of her friend's apparent indifference: she has been abandoned in far more painful ways before.

'Fresh eels!' a young boy calls from one of the stalls. 'Yer Gal'll squeal fo' a bit o'eel!'

The boy's next cry is so rude that even Delphine blushes. That's Billingsgate. Even a girl who's lived in a brothel can be surprised here. The rush of servants, dockworkers and shrimp girls pulls her towards the centre of the market, but Delphine continues forward, remaining focused on the task at hand. Marion's parting words were strict instructions on how to find the gang's den. Instead of turning left into the thick of the crowds, she carries on down Thames Street, until she sees the unmissable outline of the Tower of London emerging from behind the sails. A thrill of terror seizes her. If she fails, like Marion assures her she will, that'll be where Delphine meets her end. The type of torture that's inflicted behind the Tower's walls is far worse than anything Lord Harvey could dream up.

After passing a slim man in a long, brown coat selling whining puppies from a pig pen, she turns right into an abandoned alley. Sparkling fish scales and bones litter the flagstones here, and the buzz of the market is drowned out by the murmuring flies. Delphine lingers on the corner, scanning the street until she's satisfied she's not been followed. Then, as if granting her wish for anonymity, the sun tucks itself behind a cloud, cloaking her and the rest of the alleyway in a chilly darkness. Delphine draws in her shawl and shivers. It's bound to be even colder underground.

The door to the smugglers' den is here. She finds it in the middle of the alley's left-hand wall, boarded with an expansive timber plank. It looks entirely unremarkable to the average passer-by. Although Delphine has only the faintest notion of what awaits her behind this door, the sight of it sets her heart pounding. She looks down at her damask emerald skirts – if Vincent's godparents knew where she was about to take their gift, what would they say? She lifts the hem and raises one of her winter boots beneath to slide the plank loose with her foot. As it falls to the ground, relief floods her veins. At least Marion's instructions have come good so far.

The door is coated in dust and grime, which dislodges when she wipes it with her boot. She grimaces, trying not to think of the mystery materials that make up the muck. Tilting her foot to the left, she feels the latch, long and thin like a pencil. With a firm kick, she slides it out, and the door opens – revealing the murky stairwell that leads to the tunnels.

She'd had the foresight to bring a candle, matches and a striker with her, and as she treads down into the shadows, the small light flickers wildly. The wind catches it in so many directions the flame looks as lost as Delphine feels.

After descending what must have been a hundred steps, she looks over her shoulder, thighs already burning at the thought of reascending them. This can't be the only way in, she reasons – she can't imagine the smugglers lugging gallons of rum down into this sewer-like hole. She's hopeful she'll be allowed to leave another way — if she is allowed to leave at all.

At the bottom of the stairs she reaches another door, its bolts blackened with rust. Delphine drags it open, and the hinges screech against their metal, the heavy wood spreading recently settled dirt across the floor. Delphine steps over the threshold, and the warm light of a sconce dwarfs her flickering candle in what appears to be a short, narrow tunnel.

Empty, save the motionless guard at the end.

There's a thick red curtain to his right, and he leans against the brickwork with one hand deep in his pocket. His other hand rests on the side of a revolver hanging from his belt.

Pulse rising, she steps closer. Is this truly what she wants to do?

The guard throws her a glance without shifting his position. He's already assessed that she's not a threat.

'State your business,' the guard says. His accent is strange — the words come out almost like a song, one that should be sung on the edge of a clifftop in the open sea air. He's not from London, Wales, or any far place in the North — maybe one of the farming towns to the Southwest?

'I've an invitation,' Delphine says in a voice much deeper and more confident than her own.

'*Mmhm*,' says the guard, his tone inscrutable. "And it over.' His jawline is so precise she swears it could cut paper.

Delphine takes a controlled breath in and reaches into her pocket, very, very slowly — an instinct that comes from generations of Negroes moving too quickly around white men and their guns — to reveal the letter Marion wrote for her.

The guard takes the crumpled paper from her — which bears a short, scrawled note of introduction and a few small drawings Delphine could not decipher — and glances at it. 'Who ye here to see?'

'The boss,' Delphine says. Marion hadn't said anything about *who* she should ask for.

'Marching straight to the top now, are ye?'

She didn't mean to come across as arrogant. Or does he suspect she's here to cause trouble? The words sound benign, but Delphine's too on edge to ascertain whether the man is irritated or amused. And if she were to go missing down here, Marion's sending no one to look for her.

After an agonising moment, the man harrumphs and says simply: 'Follow me.' He lets go of the revolver and pulls back the curtain.

Delphine audibly gasps, witnessing the marvel that lies behind it. It looks like an ancient Roman bathhouse. A vast, vaulted chamber, every inch lit up by billowing metal torches lining the mosaic-tiled walls. Immediately, her eyes are drawn to the gleaming bronze statue at the centre: a nude woman reclining on a rock. Transfixed by its intricacy, Delphine takes a few steps towards it. Twisted tendrils of seaweed drape over the woman's bare breasts, and she holds a sharp trident encrusted with finely cut seashells.

'That's Suerva, our patron of sorts,' the guard says. Without further explanation, he yanks her by the arm past the statue. They walk between two of the four deep baths in each corner of the room, piled high with crates, barrels, and large square objects wrapped in parchment – stolen mirrors, or perhaps works of art? Delphine has many questions: how did they find this place, with its chipped Roman columns and semi-crumbling archways? Where did the statue come from, and how did they get it here? Surely not down those steps?

This is a far cry from the dank, dark hovel she'd imagined finding in a smugglers' den.

Delphine counts five doors leading off from this chamber. The guard leads her to the second one and knocks four times. The first two knocks are rapid, the next two slow. He presses his ear to the wood and waits for what Delphine assumes is permission to enter.

The door opens, and a lean, dark-skinned man appears behind it. He is around fifty years of age, his fox-like features suspiciously searching Delphine's. He folds his arms and stands back, wordlessly allowing Delphine and the guard to come in.

This room is just as well-lit as the previous, but decorated with a hodgepodge of shabby and extravagant furnishings: a suit of armour standing to attention, guarded by four knee-high clay urns: from a distance, Delphine can't make out the detailing, only that whatever scenes they depict are painted in black. An oval cherrywood table with mismatched chairs is in the middle of the room. Stacks of books are strewn on the floor, and the air carries a faint scent of brandy.

The person Delphine assumes to be the boss is sitting on the other side of the table, with his back turned to them. He is seated in front of a woven tapestry: a scene of two claret-clad white women embroidering cushions beneath an oak tree. He's hunched over, busily working on something that sounds like a wood carving. His knees are spread wide on either side of the box's edges, and he's dressed in unmarked cream breeches and a silk, cyan jacket. He looks much smaller than the other two men, but the superior quality of his apparel sets him apart. Delphine's breath waves like a gull bobbing on the sea's surface. She's starting to feel out of her depth, and could easily be dragged under.

'A visitor for you, *boss*,' says the guard, setting Marion's note down before him.

So, Delphine was right. The foxlike man also turns his head to the fellow in cream breeches and waits.

'Marion sent me,' Delphine says quickly. Her eyes scan the room for an escape route, but there's no window, no other door.

The boss lays down his whittling knife and a small brown object that Delphine can't make out. 'I'd begun to wonder if you'd ever find your way here.'

Delphine startles. The voice doesn't sound like a man's but more like a woman's. Husky and rich and rounded by wealth. It's eerily comparable to a voice that has haunted Delphine's dreams for years, and the sound of it inflames an old scar over her heart.

The boss wipes curled wood shavings from their breeches, then stands up and turns.

First, Delphine notices the loose corset over the top of her stays. Then, an impossible face.

Grey eyes framed by golden, shoulder-length hair. Delphine gasps. Blinks.

Blinks again. The face doesn't change.

'Pearl?'

Chapter Twenty-Three

> The necessity of pursuing true happiness is the foundation of all liberty. Happiness, in its full extent, is the utmost pleasure we are capable of.
>
> —JOHN LOCKE

'Pearl?' Delphine says again. She shakes her head, half expecting this ghostly apparition to fade and the smuggler's true face to return.

This cannot be Pearl.

Pearl's body lies in an unmarked grave, God knows where. Buried beneath flowers on a quiet roadside, or deep in a tangled forest, or held down by rocks at the bottom of a river.

She's spent four years mourning the loss. Spent four years trying to repair the scars left by grief. No. This is surely some trick of the light? Or perhaps the thin air down here has turned Delphine mad. It is the only truth she can bear. How else could she explain this?

The ghost takes a step forward and then another. Its feet land solidly on the tiles.

The air grows thinner, and Delphine cannot breathe. She suddenly wishes she was somewhere, anywhere, else. What is happening? Her mind spins. What is happening? *How* is this happening?

The ghost skirts the table, lifts a hand and reaches for Delphine's face. It's warm and soft. Alive.

It's everything she remembers.

It's everything she used to want.

The ghost says, 'Hello, Delphine,' and flings her back into her memories.

Into the night when everything changed between them.

Ranelagh Pleasure Gardens, London
4th June 1766

Delphine waits for Pearl at the entrance to the maze. It is not where they had planned to meet — beside the spouting fountain in the maze's southern corner — but Pearl is late. Two compositions late. Delphine's eyes had taken several minutes to adjust to the darkness. The rest of Ranelagh Pleasure Gardens is lit up to the heavens to celebrate the King's birthday, but Delphine cares little about that. She just hopes Pearl isn't lost among the hedgerows.

As Mozart's third piece comes to a triumphant marshal end, Pearl appears, as if cued by the audience's applause: a blonde vision in a caramel-coloured gown, she closes the distance between them with all the grace of a young woman who'd rather be in breeches.

Delphine loves that walk of hers.

'It's like we're in a play,' Delphine muses. 'The heroines reunited before their getaway.'

But as Pearl stops beside her, she doesn't return Delphine's smile.

Instead, she gazes skyward and rubs her arm up and down.

Pearl Harvey is always cold. Delphine takes a step closer, reaching for her hand to warm it up. Even in the dark, it's plain that she's trembling. Six or seven hours, and they'll be at a tavern in Marlow, and she can trace circles over those goose pimples in front of a fire.

But for now, it's not the end of the world — there's a shawl and a spare jacket in their getaway bag.

Delphine bends down to retrieve them and asks, 'Are you well?'

Pearl's eyes turn to glass, and at last, she mumbles, 'I don't think I can do this.'

Delphine tries to hand over the shawl, but Pearl bats it away. The glass has seemingly frozen over, replaced with icy certainty.

'What do you mean?' she asks gently, trying to hide the lump in her throat.

'I can't.' Pearl turns from her and breaks into a run, vanishing into the shadows of the maze.

'Wait. Pearl, please.' Without thinking, without the bag, Delphine rushes after her.

The further they run from the illuminations, the harder it is to see. Delphine hurtles into something warm — she hopes it's Pearl, but before her eyes adjust, the sounds and smells tell her it's a drunken couple in the throes of passion. She mutters an apology as she darts past, feeling her way along the maze's leafy walls.

In the distance, she can still hear the din of the orchestra. Closer, though, is the rush of water. After one more turn, she spies Pearl's outline, seated on the stone bench surrounding the fountain, face buried in her hands.

'What happened?' Delphine says when she catches up to her. 'Talk to me.'

If Pearl's been stung by another barbed remark from one of the girls she came here with, Delphine could handle it. But, if it's not...

'What is there to talk about?' Pearl snaps her head up. 'This was never going to work. What made us think we'd be able to do this?'

Delphine sits beside Pearl, fighting to regain her breath and her composure. 'Of course we can. It was your idea. Remember that article you read me about those Poplar women, Mary East and her wife? We can do it too.'

'But they were caught!' Pearl cries, throwing her hands skyward and leaning back on the stone. 'They were all caught! It may take three days or thirty years, but it will happen in the end. I don't want to live that way. I don't want to spend every moment of my life worried about when we'll be separated.'

That is how we live now, Delphine thinks. But she doesn't say that. Instead, she tries to soothe Pearl.

'We only hear about the women they caught. For every story like that, there'll be hundreds we don't know. We can be two of them.'

Believing every word she has just said, Delphine inches her fingers along the grainy bench towards Pearl's, but she turns away.

To Pearl's back, she says softly, 'If you're worried Marlow's too close, we'll go further. We could go to Manchester. Dammit, Pearl, I'd go to Iceland if we have to, China, the moon — whatever it takes for this to work. Is it the breeches?' Delphine is flailing now, summoning the last of her resolve. 'Or cutting your hair?'

One of them must play the husband for this new life to work. It seemed natural it would be Pearl. She always preferred menswear, and she'd even said breeches unbound her from the feeling she was failing as a girl.

But if that's what's stopping her, Delphine will perform that role in a heartbeat. She only wants Pearl. 'I can do it. If you take off the breeches, I'll wear them.'

'It isn't enough.'

Pearl's reply is a whisper, though it knocks Delphine back like a gust of wind.

Because what Delphine hears is: *I am not enough.*

Delphine's future unstitches within her: one with messages drawn on frosted cottage windows, of armchairs and fireplaces and holding wrinkled hands, of greying hair and fat tabby cats, a home where their decisions were made as equals.

But if Pearl doesn't want that life, doesn't want *her*, then what power does Delphine have to change her mind?

She has nothing to offer except all of her heart.

'So,' Delphine sniffs and wipes a tear away with her sleeve. 'What now?'

After a long moment, Pearl says, 'Can we go back to how we were?'

'And do what?' Delphine unravels. 'I watch you get married to that rake baron? I lie awake in the next room while you make love to him? While you grow older and have children with a man, we both know you'll never love.'

Pearl grips her own throat with anxious fingers. 'But at least we'd still be together,' she chokes out. 'We'd be safe.'

'No. *You* would be.' Delphine stands up. 'Even if I'm given as a wedding gift to your husband, there's no promise he'll keep me.'

It is Pearl's turn now to step forward and reach out for support. Delphine takes it and clutches Pearl's hand to her breastbone as if stemming the blood from a wound.

Pearl says, 'I won't let him get rid of you.'

Get rid of you. Like claw-marked furniture or last season's ostrich-feather hat.

'You'd not be able to stop him.'

'We'll find a way, I promise.'

'I thought we already did. *This* is that promise.' She kisses Pearl's fingertips, and they taste of honey and roasted chestnuts. 'This is the moment we choose the direction of the rest of our lives. It's *our* choice, Pearl.' She grips her hand and squeezes. 'So come with me.' *Choose me.*

'I *can't.*' Pearl sobs. 'We won't make it on our own. It'll be too hard. We're not ready.'

'For what?' Delphine says, letting Pearl's hand fall. 'We'll get by without feathered beds and silver trays.'

'You benefit from them too. We share the same bed!' That is not what Delphine means, and Pearl knows it.

If she is stumbling into this unknown future, let there be no denying the truth of their past. 'I am a slave!' she yells, her voice finally cracking. 'I thought you understood what that means. My life has been controlled, Pearl. I lost my family. I was sent across an ocean. And it was all because your father wanted to present me as a gift to you.'

Saying this fact out loud, Delphine realises she has never allowed herself to dwell on it before. The realisation halts her tears in place. 'There's no safety for me after you're married. It doesn't matter how luxurious the chain is – it binds me as any other would. This is it for me, Pearl. For us.'

Pearl says nothing.

Delphine straightens and blinks away that white-fenced cottage again. 'I thought you would be the great love of my life. I knew it would be difficult when you asked me to run away with you. I knew that life would grant us no easy path, but I was going to take it,' her voice strains, 'because you said we could be together, and I was naïve enough to believe it.'

'We can be together,' Pearl pleads, but Delphine shakes her head. 'Please, we can, Delphine. Just... please don't go.' Pearl gushes more empty promises, but Delphine cannot listen. She turns and runs away.

It takes every ounce of her will not to glance back. But this is her choice.

Her very first one after claiming her freedom.

Disoriented and alone, it had taken Delphine over an hour to escape that maze, but she did not hear Pearl's footsteps behind her. The longer the silence pursued her, the more certain she'd been that she'd done the right thing. But her confidence had wavered when she discovered the getaway bag was no longer at the maze entrance.

Then came the fireworks, the crowds and the King.

Penniless and free was better than cushioned and caged, but Delphine's cheeks grew sallower by the day. A month later, Lady Pearl Harvey became Baroness Chalmers. In a ceremony with all the pomp and circumstance a Mayfair marriage deserves, Pearl promised to have and to hold her baron, for richer and richer still, until that fateful carriage ride to Cornwall when death did them part.

Attacked by highwaymen, her body was unrecovered.

Delphine's heart had broken again when she learned of Pearl's demise. It turns out that was a lie, too.

Somewhere near Billingsgate Market, London
11th November 1770

'How is this possible?' is all Delphine can think to say. Pearl's hand remains on her cheek, but Delphine's face hardens. It's been too long since Pearl's touch could make her melt. 'How is this possible?'

'You know each other?' the Black smuggler says with an American drawl. His eyes flick between the two of them.

Pearl nods. 'She used to be...' Delphine knows the words she is looking for, but Pearl can't seem to make them come out. 'She worked for my father.'

'You mean...' The white smuggler's brow furrows. '*This* is the slave?' The American flinches at the word, as does Pearl.

Letting go, Pearl avoids Delphine's gaze and says nothing. Still unable to face the truth.

A stone settles in Delphine's stomach, the weight making her want to keel over.

'What's she doing here then?' the American asks.

It's now that Delphine notices the white man's hand has returned to the hilt of his revolver. He shifts his weight forward, and three fingers tap the steel. Did the men think she'd come here for revenge? Did Pearl?

'That remains to be seen,' Pearl says. Curiosity tints her voice. She circles Delphine as if trying to take the measure of her and says, 'But I am most keen to find out.'

As her former master's daughter observes her, Delphine watches her, too. Pearl's hair is still wavy, but the crop is new; her face, once doughy, has leaned out to reveal a sloping jaw and a defined chin. It is the same person, but entirely different. Freed from the constraints of corset strings and petticoats, this Pearl appeared only in rare moments as they relaxed on her four-poster bed in breeches Delphine had sewn secretly. To see her like this, living contentedly in a world of men, makes her wonder if she wasn't ready then. Or was it that Pearl simply didn't want her?

Whatever the answer, Delphine is irked to find that it still hurts.

And what does Pearl see in her, she wonders? A filthy emerald dress, someone pretending to be someone more than herself. It only took one word for the guard to reduce her, an instant to deconstruct her disguise. Though Delphine once gave Pearl her heart willingly – as a friend and then a lover – she will always be the woman Pearl and her family used to own. It lingers over them, a noxious cloud, poisoning everything.

'You're a smuggler now?' Delphine says, breaking from that painful thought.

'Among other things,' Pearl chuckles, 'though I prefer the term "Robin Hood". You've met two of our merry men – Jules—' the American nods at Delphine, '— and his husband, Colin.'

The white man grunts, then bares his teeth in a handsomely crooked smile.

'But...' As surprised as Delphine is to hear that these two men are a *couple*, she has more pressing questions. 'How did you end up here?' she insists, still struggling to comprehend it.

A dark look passes over Pearl's face before she cracks a smile. It looks forced. 'All in good time.'

Delphine gapes at Pearl. How long will it take her to explain all this? When Delphine finally told Nick what happened at Ranelagh, she had given him the bare bones of the truth – it had taken days for him to wrap his head around it. Time they don't have now.

Then again, how can Delphine begin to explain why she's here? Ask *Pearl* for help, of all people?

Before she entered this den, she knew it would be difficult to convince a group of strangers to join her plot. Delphine's still not certain she can bring *herself* to take part in it. But for Pearl, so much more is at stake. It won't just be a building, powerful men, gunpowder and a fire.

It will mean killing her father.

'This way, then.' Pearl gestures to the tapestry hanging on the wall behind her.

Delphine is hardly surprised when Pearl peels the hanging back, revealing yet another door with a ring knocker at its heart. How many more secrets will she encounter today?

Colin makes to follow them, but Pearl stops him. 'I've not seen this woman in four years. Privacy would be appreciated.'

Colin snorts and lets out an animalistic jeer.

Jules shoots him a warning glare, but Pearl is unruffled. Without turning back, she says dryly, 'Not that kind of privacy, Colin.'

Delphine swallows and looks down at the floor. Do these men know what she and Pearl once were to each other?

'Don't pay any attention to him.' Pearl is evidently amused until she catches Delphine's torn expression, whereupon she turns serious. 'You have nothing to fear here. I promise.'

Delphine's heard that one before.

She shrugs, then follows Pearl deeper into the ancient tunnels.

Chapter Twenty-Four

> Rules for happiness: something to do, someone to love, something to hope for.
> —IMMANUEL KANT

If Delphine imagined that Pearl had faked her death and joined a gang of smugglers, this bedroom is precisely how Delphine would have pictured it.

The room is no larger than one of the baths Delphine had passed on entering the den, but Pearl has evidently furnished it as best she can on a bootlegger's budget. Beneath the low coffered ceiling is a small cot with four wooden posts clumsily hammered into each corner. A dozen rags dyed in various shades of red are sewn into a draping canopy over the top and sides as if Pearl is trying to recreate the harrateen over her childhood bed. Six or seven lifeless pillows are stacked on each other – Pearl's always had the odd habit of sleeping nearly upright – along with a pile of blankets.

Beside the bed is an Ottoman rug and wooden-box-turned-night-table with a gold oil lamp surrounded by half-burned candles. The light reveals undoubtedly stolen art dotted between various-sized crates. They're mostly still lifes of everyday objects, but there's also a hand-drawn map of St. Lucia. This piques Delphine's curiosity, and she walks towards it. Pearl and Lady Katherine never set foot on the island.

'We've got hundreds of maps and architecture diagrams,' Pearl says, joining her in front of it. 'I decided to keep this one to myself.'

'The island is smaller than I remember,' Delphine says.

'It's smaller than most in the British West Indies.'

'*French*,' Delphine corrects. The Seven Years' War primarily unscathed the island, but Delphine still vividly recollects those few nights of cannon fire. When it became apparent that Britain would sign the island back to France, Lord Harvey sold the plantation. He departed for England soon after that, with Delphine and Vincent in tow.

'French,' Pearl concedes. 'Please, sit.' She drags a crate over for Delphine and perches on the edge of her bed.

Delphine does as she's told and tries to breathe through the nervous energy in her veins. *It's really Pearl.* 'You've been here the whole time?' Delphine asks, wanting clarity before they discuss why she is here too.

'Mostly,' Pearl says, her voice settling into its familiar husky tone. 'After the carriage was ambushed, I managed to get away. Colin saw the whole sordid ordeal and had been waiting for leftover loot. He supposed if I could handle myself against highwaymen, I could handle myself here. It took the others longer before they thought the same thing.' She chuckles lightly to herself. 'I was the last one to agree Colin was right. But I couldn't bear to go home again, after all that had happened, with you, and then the wedding. Being married once was hard enough, but the thought of my family forcing me to marry again...' She swallows as if in pain, and shakes her head. 'And what was it you used to say? *What's for you, won't pass you by.* Well, it took on a new meaning in those woods.'

Pearl recalls the story nonchalantly, as though it happened to someone else. There's no sadness in her voice for the fate of her husband, no hint of remembered fear. But what is still unclear to Delphine is how she went from an outsider to the boss of this smuggling gang in a few short years.

'I'm just glad you survived,' Delphine says, meaning it. 'And now you lead this group?'

'I beg your pardon?'

From the perplexed look on Pearl's face, Delphine immediately wonders if she misremembered her conversation with the guard. 'Colin said...'

'Colin?' Pearl scoffs. 'Colin's an ass.'

'But he gave you Marion's note?'

'Our messages are coded,' Pearl says, unfolding Marion's note from her back pocket and angling it towards Delphine. 'See here at the top right? These are Persian numbers; each client has a unique one, so we know who the message is from. Usually, there would be other symbols to represent location markers or the required goods. In this case, there's the double-headed arrow – here – used to request a meeting. But Marion has written text too, which is unusual. Colin couldn't decipher it, so he gave it to me because I was the only literate one there: *by introduction, I present Miss Delphine.*'

'It's all very... sophisticated.' Delphine says.

Pearl shrugs. 'It's a business like any other. We just operate in a less *conventional* manner than most. But enough about that.' She tucks the note beneath a candle on her bedside table, then says, matter-of-factly, 'Let's talk about you. You've been working at a bawdy house in Soho. And more recently for my cousin.'

Delphine blinks. 'How did you—'

'Vincent.' Pearl's lip quirks. 'He told me. I'm so sorry for your loss, Delphine.'

'*Vincent?*' Delphine's voice cracks. Her brother knew Pearl was alive and didn't tell her. Pearl knew *she* was only a few miles away, and didn't seek her out. She feels the betrayal, like two knives cutting her on both sides.

'I'd been following his trial since the beginning,' says Pearl. 'I was negotiating a deal in a tavern off Trinity Lane. A paper boy was reading the day's news, and the client bid us listen until we heard the results of some rowing race up north.' She shuffles backwards to make herself comfortable against the pillows. 'At first, I paid little attention, but at the third repetition of the name *Harvey* and *his Negro*, I realised they must be talking about Vincent and my father.' Pearl shudders. 'There's a word I've not used in a while. Anyhow,' she uses one hand to wave away the distracting thoughts, 'it wasn't too difficult to discover where Vincent was being held after that. It didn't seem the trial was going too well, and I couldn't bring myself to do nothing. So I took the risk and reached out, told him the truth of my situation, and offered him the chance to disappear with me and the gang. He said no, of course – he was too worried about the repercussions for Nick. And for you.'

It's too much to take in. The secrecy of Pearl's story, the tragic consequences. The lamp flickers, highlighting the side of Pearl's face, and Delphine considers her as if through a stranger's eyes. There's a new scar at her temple, and a maturity in her eyes that's unfamiliar to Delphine.

'I can imagine what you're feeling...' Pearl says, drawing a sideways, sympathetic smile. 'But we're an underground group. So, after he declined, I swore him to secrecy. He insisted he couldn't keep this from you forever. I agreed he could tell you if he wished, but only *after* the trial – when there wasn't such a pressing situation for you both to worry about.'

Delphine recalls her last visit to the prison.

That letter Vincent had written, about *everything you deserved to know years ago.*

The tapster's strange comment. *Your fella seems to be getting a lot of visitors lately.*

'You could have come to me,' Delphine says, failing to mask the hurt. 'If you knew where I was.'

Did Pearl not *want* to see her again? If seeing Colin and Jules' life together did not inspire Pearl to make contact, does that mean she never regretted her decision to abandon Delphine?

Before Pearl responds, she picks at a stray thread on her pillow, avoiding Delphine's gaze. Then she says quietly: 'I didn't think you'd want me to.'

So, the shadow of their parting looms over her, too.

Of course Delphine would have wanted her to. There has not been a single day where Pearl hasn't crossed her mind. Though their separation was necessary, she still wished it were not.

'But Vincent didn't explain to me *why* you're still here. After we…' Pearl seems to fumble for the right words, '…said goodbye. I thought you intended to leave London.'

She had. But when the King closed the waterways, Delphine missed their scheduled stagecoach to Berkshire. Trapped in London, she'd tried to find employment, but discovered that even if you have a decade's experience in domestic work, very few places will hire without a reference. It felt too early, too risky to find Vincent and ask for help. So, she was stuck, starving, penniless and alone. Then she met Marion.

Delphine traces a hand over her neck. 'I tried. Things didn't go to plan.'

Pearl opens her mouth, then presses her lips shut. How easily they've returned to their pattern of leaving things unsaid. For the longest time, they look anywhere in the room but at each other.

Eventually, Pearl says, 'Why are you here, Delphine?'

Delphine recounts everything that has happened in the last year, filling in the gaps left by Vincent. Pearl already knew all about the boxing match, about Vincent's arrest and his murder. Apparently, she was at the vigil, too, but there's no way for Delphine to tell if that's true.

As Delphine talks, Pearl listens intently. Occasionally, she asks a question, brows furrowed in focus. A couple of times, Pearl wells up, and Delphine asks if she's well, almost reaching out to hold her hand, either through lingering fondness or old habits. Pearl nods and tells her that as hard as it is for her to hear the story, Delphine needn't worry about her state of being.

Another surprise. Another difference in this new Pearl.

When she's finished, an exhausting hour has passed. Drained and unsettled, Delphine breathes out and then voices her plan. It comes out a little easier this time, but every word is still as heavy as lead.

'It has to stop, Pearl. I need gunpowder. I need your help.'

Instead of looking shocked or horrified, Pearl makes a little *hmm* noise and curls a slender finger beneath her chin. It makes Delphine wonder what she may have seen in these last years to harden her so.

'But Nick's petition?' Pearl says carefully like her thoughts are still forming. 'Vincent's ruling?'

'Will do nothing.' Delphine gets up and paces the room. She has barely had time to think of Nick. Every time she does, she remembers his absence at the vigil. The memory leaves a sour taste in her mouth. Nor has he even sent a letter to check on her health.

'You can still push for change, surely?' Pearl says. 'The public and the papers are on your side. I've been following everything. You should put pressure on Parliament while you can.'

'Parliament doesn't open for five weeks yet,' Delphine says, 'and Britain's memory of bloodshed is short when the blood is foreign. The papers and the public will have moved on to the next sob story by then.'

'I understand, Delphine; honestly, I do, but there must be another way. What you're saying is impossible.'

'Unthinkable, maybe, but it's not impossible.'

Pearl huffs. 'You can't just get rid of the government.'

'I don't want to get rid of *the* government. I want to get rid of *this* government and the Crown and the institutions that support them.'

'But how will things change? How do you even know things would be better?'

Delphine can clearly see almost every part of her plan, but this aspect is hazy. A future without the Empire seems unimaginable. Its existence is so ingrained into their lives that it's almost impossible to think they could continue without it. There are so many parts at play and unseen obstacles that there's no way of telling with certainty what will happen next.

In her mind, she sees three paths.

The first: whichever high-ranking members of the Army and Navy weren't caught in the explosion swiftly take over the country and enforce some new militaristic emergency government. At the same time, the seats and noble houses are quickly refilled. Nothing changes; her plan fails.

The second: violence and anarchy descend over the country until another nation, most likely France, decides to conquer Britain for its own empire. Her plan still fails.

Or third – the one that she hopes will happen: after the nation recovers from the shock and ensuing unrest, it will face the prospect of collapse or transformation. Britain's people could come together to form something new. Something untested, something better. Where liberty is built into the foundations, instead of a precariously attached afterthought.

She says all of this to Pearl, then finishes with, 'I don't know which would come to pass, but I have to believe there's a future better than this. There are men at the bawdy house I can leverage information from, maybe Nick too.' Delphine could have the best plan in the world, and there'd still be little she could do in the aftermath without the help of someone in power.

That someone is never going to be her.

Seemingly unable to sit any longer, Pearl strides across the room to join Delphine. 'You'd need to do more than blow up a building to get the result you want. The outcry would be huge.'

'That's what I'd be counting on. If we could stoke up the people's unrest before the explosion, it could be enough to push the new government in the right direction – and stop the blame from landing with any one group or community.' People from all walks of life are already angry with the government. As Marion said, Negroes are not the only ones with struggles. But all this thinking is useless unless the smugglers can help her. Planning and good intentions can only get her so far.

'Jules has contacts,' Pearl muses. 'He's originally from Georgia and since arriving in London, he's tried his hand at almost every job. From cooper to beekeeper to rat catcher. If we were to do this, his advice could be a start.'

'Wait.' Delphine stops, unsure if she heard Pearl's last sentence correctly. 'Did you say: *if* we were to do this? You're not saying no?'

'What I am saying is...' Pearl runs a hand through her cropped hair. 'There have been many times when I made the wrong choice by you. When I've regretted saying no.'

So, she *does* have regrets. Infuriatingly, this still matters to Delphine. She makes a concerted effort to keep her face neutral and not give away how much.

'I am not saying we will help,' Pearl continues. 'I am not even saying I'm sure I *want* to...'

'But?' says Delphine, amazed by the turns this conversation is taking.

'But... I think we *could* do it. I'm hearing you out because I know you, but the others don't. Their trust won't come so easily. And we're a collective. We decide on jobs in groups. You'd need a unanimous vote for something as risky as this.'

That's a sobering prospect. Every person they tell puts them more at risk. Catesby and Fawkes had a dozen conspirators, all trusted and well-known to each of them. These strangers, a gang of criminals no less, are not the most natural allies. But they are necessary ones. Delphine has no war experience or military contacts to work with like the original conspirators did.

'Unanimous?' she asks. 'How many of you are there?'

Pearl glances up to the ceiling as if counting. 'Twenty or so. But we're rarely here at the same time. And I don't mean you'd need the whole gang's vote, just the people who would be involved. I reckon you'd need four people, including myself. The others wouldn't have to know.'

Four. A much lower number than twenty, but that doesn't ease the tension in Delphine's jaw.

'Don't worry,' Pearl says, 'it's our prerogative to keep secrets. We've smuggled worse things than gunpowder to places more difficult than Westminster.'

'Sounds ominous.' Delphine's nerves settle enough for her to ask, 'Who are the other three?'

'First, Colin. He was a miner for a time, then a powder shifter who did the occasional job for the gang before joining. If you need a gunpowder expert, there's none better. But bear in mind he is exceedingly short tempered.'

Which makes Delphine question why he's on the door armed with a gun.

'Where Colin goes, Jules does too,' Pearl continues, 'but he's a man of his own merits. He has friends in every borough. He could drum up the loudest and unhappiest workers he knows.'

'He could convince them to protest?' Delphine asks. In addition to the attack on Parliament, protest will be vital to her plan. To divert and divide attention away from the conspirators while giving others space to voice their discontent. There's always a small group or two outside of Westminster on any given day. They can safely start to increase the pressure, working different angles to remain inconspicuous, and maybe encourage others to come out of the woodwork.

Pearl flashes a wry grin. 'Persuasion's more my forte. I can be very charming, my dear.'

Delphine swallows. 'So, you'd work together – his contacts, your... charm.'

'Precisely,' Pearl says, her grin turning wicked.

Delphine has to avert her gaze. When did Pearl become so at ease in her skin? 'And the last person?'

'Bela. She's a few years our senior. Deft and quick and fiercely serious. She'll be the one who needs the most convincing.'

'And what would she do?'

'Whatever's needed. She was born into this life – her mother travelled from Persia while pregnant and settled with a highwayman in Glasgow. By the time she came here at just sixteen, she had all the skills a criminal could need. She was the one who invented our secret code. These days, though, she mostly acts as tubsman.' Before Delphine can ask, Pearl elaborates, 'She drives the cart to shift larger cargo and moves smaller loot by sewing it into her skirts. It's imperative she's on board because she, Colin and Jules are close – they work on almost every job together. I can't see either of them agreeing without her support.'

'And you trust them?' Delphine says, shifting from foot to foot.

Without a hint of doubt, Pearl says, 'They're better than family. But... family bonds take time to forge, and that's something you don't have. I understand why you need to target everyone in a single attack. That makes sense. I also know that the State Opening is the only time of year you can do that. But Delphine, since we're talking about family, I must ask: what of my cousin?'

Delphine has already considered this, of course. She's certain Nick would never get on board with her plot – how they see the world is too different. However, she'll try to keep Nick safe. No matter how vile the system is, not every politician and church minister at the State Opening deserves such a terrible end. Lord Mansfield, for one, John Glynn and Sir Bunbury, and a few other radicals, reformers and reverends who preach equality over economic advancement.

Deciding who lives and dies is a delicate and unfair line. Delphine doesn't have the right. But when universal rules are applied without exception, exceptional men are murdered. Men like Vincent. And if she doesn't try to preserve life where she can, how could this new world be any better than their present one? And she's confident that with *just* the right amount of slippery elm and blackberry leaf, she can bring on the kind of stomach upset that ensures one man doesn't stray too far from his chamber pot that day.

'I have a plan involving a herbally-induced malady to keep Nick and a few others safe,' she says. 'But I'll need help with the distribution. Many of them dine together at the Beef Steak Club at Appleby's, and drink at the London Tavern when they're in town – maybe that's where your Bela would come in. Or maybe Jules knows a server there who could tell us more about the regulars.' But Pearl's question about Nick also raises another. 'What about your father?'

'As far as I'm concerned, we're just hastening his descent to Hell.'

There's bile in Pearl's words, but the hatred doesn't quite match the look in her eyes.

'You're sure?' Delphine presses.

But Pearl has turned away from her. 'I buried that part of my life a long time ago, and all ties to Lord Reginald Harvey IV along with it,' Pearl says. The words come out confident, but she is fidgeting with her collar. Pearl was never one to say what she needed, and Delphine knows her well enough to recognise the tells of doubt.

It's enough to make her question everything.

If Delphine can convince the smugglers to help, she *may* have just found the perfect group to aid her plan. But when Pearl decides on a path, she will only rush down it unblinkered until reality gets in the way. Maybe trusting Pearl will once again be her downfall.

Turning the door handle, Pearl laughs. 'So, you're plotting the deadliest event in recent history, and it might just be my path to redemption. What could possibly go wrong?'

Chapter Twenty-Five

> It is dangerous to be right in matters on which the established authorities are wrong.
> —M. DE VOLTAIRE

'Absolutely not,' Colin says, slamming his hand down on the table.

The following day, Delphine is back at the smugglers' den. The room where she was first introduced to Pearl's new life of crime is apparently where the smugglers conduct their planning meetings. Sitting across from Delphine at the table are Pearl, Colin, Jules, and the final conspirator Pearl has called upon: Bela. A tawny-skinned woman with sleek dark hair that shimmers like the Thames at midnight. She's lean, with long fingers that Delphine imagines can nimbly pluck a man's coin purse or slide off a lady's diamond ring. Her deep russet dress gives her a noble bearing that matches her regally bored expression.

Barely a breath ago, Delphine explained what she intends to do.

Colin's reaction came before she'd spoken the *why* or the *how*.

Pearl holds up a hand to calm Colin. 'Hear her out, that's all I'm asking.'

'No, Pearl,' Bela says. 'Your old flame turns up out of the blue, demands we blow up the fucking houses of parliament, the King and his countrymen. I will not listen. She's a lunatic.'

Delphine swallows down embarrassment like a lump of coal. Not only because of the insult, not even because her life's most precious secret — the love she once held for Pearl — has just been so crudely exposed. But because Bela's blunt, Scottish twang is one she's heard before.

'It's you,' she says to the woman she met in Marion's darkened cellar, on the night of Vincent's boxing match. The woman Delphine had assumed to be a harlot.

'Aye, it's me,' Bela tuts, unimpressed. 'Marion must be on her way tae Bedlam too if she's sent ye 'ere.'

Even without Pearl's warning about Bela's skepticism, Delphine would have expected this reaction. It would be more disturbing if anyone immediately said yes.

'My thinking is clear,' Delphine says.

The smugglers glare wordlessly at her.

Pearl leans forward and lays her hands squarely on the table. 'Delphine and I discussed her proposal in great detail yesterday,' she says. She speaks slowly but with authority and natural charisma – evidently, she wasn't lying about her newfound persuasive charms. 'I examined her aims and motivations. And I had to admit that for the kind of progress that she wants – that *I* want, that everyone around this table wants – for our country...' Pearl pauses, catching each of her comrades' eyes in turn. 'Such radical change could not be achieved any other way. Not within our lifetimes.'

'Even if that is true,' Jules says in a measured tone, 'revolutions ain't our lot.'

'Jules is right,' Bela snaps, shooting daggers at Pearl. 'We dinnae need this sort o' heat.'

'The risks would be great,' Pearl agrees. 'But Delphine is careful. I trust her.'

'Trust won't cut it,' Colin scolds. Bela and Jules murmur in agreement. 'And neither do any high-minded ideas of heroics. What's really in it for us?'

Delphine is ready for this question. 'Picture this, Colin: our plot has succeeded. The Empire's fallen, and with it, its selling power. The entire system's fallen into chaos. No trade companies are left to dominate the ports. The market will be free, and who'll be ready to swoop in? You.

Imagine how many deals would be yours for the taking. How much coin you'd make.'

Now she's got their attention. Even Bela looks vaguely interested. Colin's eyes flicker with excitement as the grand scope of the opportunity unfolds in his mind. Then his expression softens as his gaze meets Jules's.

'It's tempting,' Pearl says, cracking a smile. She nudges Jules. 'Imagine how it'd feel to be able to trade on the surface. To feel coins in your pocket *and* sunshine on your face.'

Jules steeples his fingers together. He seems to be considering his next words carefully. 'I see the potential for reward. And you weren't wrong when you said that none of us got love for politicians. It ain't nothing to me if Westminster burns. But as Colin says, trust don't cut it.' He fixes Delphine with his cunning gaze. 'I wager you don't know the first thing about breaking into a building. Even with our help, how could you possibly hope to pull this off?'

Delphine's heartbeat stutters, like she's falling in a dream. *I don't know*, whispers a voice in her head. That question is what she's been asking herself all week. But she can't let it show – not when six suspicious eyes are boring into her. 'I can get into Westminster.'

'She's been working for my cousin,' Pearl says, unphased by the others' reactions. 'Remember the MP?'

Delphine watches them nod and doesn't elaborate: she reasons that now would not be the wisest moment to mention her unconfirmed employment status.

'And he'll let her in?' Bela says. The woman is meticulous – can she smell Delphine's self-doubt?

Pearl rolls her eyes. 'We get in there all the time, Bela.'

'Tisnae a matter of what *we* can do,' Bela retorts. 'It's nae about getting the powder in. In the end, she's the one that needs to be able to light it. It sure as hell ain't aff to be any o'us.'

'What do you need?' Delphine asks before the conversation can veer further off course. 'What must I show you to prove I can do it?'

'I doubt you can.'

Irritation cuts through Delphine's nerves. The woman is meticulous *and* rude. 'Try me.'

'A plan, fae one.'

'Well, that's easy,' Delphine says, not quite meaning it. Nothing about this is going to be easy. 'Pearl said you keep maps. Do you have one of Parliament?'

Colin disappears next door to the central bathing chamber and returns moments later with a piece of charcoal and a scroll, which he unrolls on the table. It's a floor plan of Westminster.

Delphine had expected an outline or an off-cut from one of Rocque's maps. This is much more extensive and detailed, but it's outdated. Since then, a new building facing St Margaret Street has been erected, and new gardens are laid around the back. She takes the charcoal and adjusts the map accordingly.

'You ken your way around, then,' Bela says. 'So what?'

'So,' Delphine presses on, 'I also know that Parliament is built on tradition. Unless a plague breaks out in the next month, the State Opening will follow its exact schedule every year.'

'How does it work?' Pearl asks.

'Like this.' She drops her voice a little lower and tries to recall Nick's words from memory. 'First, the politicians arrive along with the nobility and the clergy, between ten thirty and eleven o'clock. Usually, the MPs gather in the Commons and the rest in the House of Lords. But this year, the Lords' roof is undergoing renovations and is covered in scaffolding so that most people will be gathered in Westminster Hall. The King arrives at eleven fifteen and is led in through the Sovereign's Entrance to the Robing Room.'

'And?' Colin says.

'And, once he's seated on his throne at eleven thirty, the hall will be packed like a Church on Christmas Day. Black Sword, or Black Rod, or whatever their name is, leads the MPs to the main hall to listen to the speech, and no one can slip in or out of the room until the ceremony is over. Nick says the King's speech runs longer than a vicar's sermon. Plenty of time for someone to get in and out before the explosion.'

'Fae *you* to get in and out, you mean.' Bela raises an eyebrow.

'Indeed,' Delphine agrees. 'Even if anyone did manage to get out of the main hall, I know these rooms well enough to find a way out without being detected. I was there almost every day during Vincent's trial.'

She pauses after saying her brother's name. Now is not the time for Delphine to crumble. Such moments of darkness are reserved for her sleepless nights when the world has quietened, but her mind cannot.

Not now.

'All we need to do,' she says, rallying herself, 'is place enough gunpowder in enough places to ensure that the main hall's roof comes down. Then…'

'Then… boom?' Colin mimics an explosion with his hands.

'Then, boom,' Delphine repeats, the sound hollow on her tongue. As if a single word can encompass the devastation it would bring. But it's the only way. 'This has been done before, or almost has. It can be done again. Pearl says you've smuggled worse than gunpowder into harder places than Parliament.'

Colin proudly crosses his arms over his chest. 'She's right about that.'

Delphine resists the urge to ask what *worse* could mean to this gang. 'Then you have the expertise I need,' she says, looking around the room at all of them. 'I'll set the explosion if you show me how. It's my plan – I will take on that risk. What I need from you is to get the gunpowder in place, and to help with the protests.'

Colin leans over the table, takes the pencil and marks an *x* on several of the walls around Westminster Palace. He tilts his head from one side to the other as if considering something. 'We've used these—'

'Colin, haud yer weesht,' Bela chides.

'What? We have!' he says, pressing a mucky finger on the library where Delphine searched for Glynn's speech. Where she found the mysterious broken wall panel.

So that's how they get in, Delphine realises. 'I've seen the secret door in the library,' she says. 'That's a smuggling route? And there are more?'

Bela says nothing, so Colin concedes. 'You're half right. We use some of 'em for shifting cargo, but most are sealed off. Leftover from when it were a royal residence.'

'Escape routes, then.' Delphine shakes her head, wishing she'd put two and two together. Fawkes and Catesby and their gang dug no tunnels. They must have used the passages that were already there. Catesby was from a family of rebels, a line that stretched back centuries. Delphine read that the Catesbys were known for hiding priests in their manor, but according to 'State Histories', no one knows where. Maybe his home had such passages, too. Maybe he knew where to look.

Staring down at the floorplan, Delphine notes the locations of other secret passageways. There's one near the undercroft and cellars, one in the Speaker's Chambers, and one in St Stephen's Chapel. Colin explains they are all interlinked in an underground network, leading to a hidden exit far out of view from passers-by. 'And we could store powder between the walls? No one else knows about them?'

Jules purses his lips and then gives a silent nod.

'No one who might rumble ye, at least,' Colin says as Jules circles the table to stand beside him.

Jules seems to swallow before he says in a lowered voice, 'This might be our big break.'

Colin's eyes widen and brighten with something like hope. 'Aye?'

'Aye,' Jules says, resting his hand over Colin's. 'It *could* work.'

Delphine feels a wave of relief, but it's short-lived. She had no idea if her plot was feasible until Jules just confirmed it. And that fact alone is a glaring reminder of how far out of her depth she is, how mad she would be to attempt this. This gang breaks the law for a living – they don't care about the morality or immorality of the plan, only that they don't get caught. Hearing them talk about destroying a building and the people inside it so easily, it chills her. But not enough for her to back down. Not yet.

Bela is still not convinced. 'If Colin and Jules say it's possible, I believe them. But I'm agreeing to nothing until we have proof of your capabilities. Prove to us that you're as free to roam Westminster as you say you are. If you can show us you can be in the right place at the right time, then maybe we'll do it. Does that sound fair, O mighty Pearl?'

Pearl raises her eyebrows and shoots a small smile at Delphine. 'That sounds entirely fair to me, Bela.'

'Good,' Bela says, then rounds on Delphine once more. 'Bring us something you can only find in Westminster in two days.'

'Two days?' Sweat prickles on Delphine's forehead. This is moving quicker than she imagined.

Bela leans back in her chair, arms folded. 'You said the State Opening is in four weeks?'

'How long will it take to get that much powder, Col?' Pearl asks.

'Two? Maybe three weeks?' says Colin, thinking out loud. 'And just under one to move it all into place. That leaves just a few days' leeway.'

'Two days.' Bela thrusts two fingers in Delphine's face. 'And if you manage that—'

'*Then* we'll vote,' Jules says.

'Then we'll vote,' Colin agrees.

Bela huffs and Pearl winks as if it say, *well done*.

There's no hesitation before Delphine smiles back. 'I'll do it.'

Chapter Twenty-Six

There are men who appear outwardly to love liberty for all, but who are inwardly its sworn enemies.
—TOUSSAINT L'OUVERTURE

Delphine's not sure she can do it.

But at noon the next day, as she stands unannounced outside Nick's apartment building, a welcome surprise distracts her from the task ahead. It is not the sour-faced landlady who greets her at the door, but Hetty.

'...And when both housekeepers quit, the old bear didn't bother replacing 'em!' They are halfway up the stairs to Nick's apartment before the cook draws breath. '*Hetty can do it*, is what he said! Three jobs. Same pay.'

'And so you came to work for Mister Lyons instead?'

'Too right! Twenty years of service gone in a blink. I've still got to be the housekeeper *and* cook, but it's much easier managing an apartment. And anything's better than working for that miserable cunt.'

Delphine can't disagree. She laughs out loud, but Hetty seems to detect the nerves in her voice. 'Mister Lyons will be thrilled to see you. Neither of us ain't barely slept since the vigil. He's been pacing about and scribbling all night. I told him you'd be fine, because Lord knows you've been through worse.' She gives Delphine a knowing look. 'And here you are! Barely a scratch on you. Our unbreakable Delphine.'

Delphine's not sure about *unbreakable*. She's felt more broken since Vincent's death than ever before.

Hetty lets them into Nick's apartment, which has markedly improved since Delphine's last visit. Even the cornices on the hallway ceiling are spotless – from experience, Delphine knows how difficult these are to clean and how much spiders enjoy curling up in their crevices.

'Thank the Heavens!' Nick cries from his drawbrary, as he hears them approaching.

When Hetty and Delphine reach the door, he skids barefoot across the room. Despite the hour, he's in silk pyjamas and a matching Japanese-style banyan. Dark bags cradle his eyes.

'Are you well?' he says. 'I've been consumed with anxiety.'

This isn't what she expected. She'd expected to be scolded for her actions or to be caught in the current of one of Nick's meandering academic spiels. But instead, he's been worried. Not enough to stop his colleagues from sending an army after her, or to check on her in person. But admittedly, he says he had written to her yesterday to enquire after her – a whole week after the vigil had passed.

Delphine says, 'I'm glad you're safe too.'

He leads her to the lion-clawed sopha beneath the bay window. Their path to it is clear – Hetty must have convinced him to tidy away the maps from the floor. They sit down and Hetty re-enters, setting a tray of tea and a confectionary box on the table between them. Without taking his eyes away from Delphine, he says to Hetty, 'I think whisky would be more appropriate, don't you, Hetty?'

Hetty nods, blinking just a little too often, as if it will shut her annoyance away. She's always been good at hiding her displeasure – at least in front of the master. Now, there'll be two sets of washing up instead of one, not to mention the waste of good tea, which the cook never drinks.

'Things escalated so quickly at the vigil,' Nick says. 'I had no time to respond. Those devilish King's Friends decided to call in the troops before you'd set foot in Old Palace Yard.'

'They told you this?' Delphine says. It's what she suspected deep down, but she'd hoped she'd been wrong. It would have been impossible to amass that many soldiers so quickly. Whitehall's Horse Guard she could understand, but the foot soldiers who came from the west? Even if the regiment was on high alert before the vigil started, there's no way they could have covered that distance before the shooting began.

Nick nods darkly. 'If I'd known they'd always planned to read Riot Act, I would have warned you.'

'It wasn't your fault,' Delphine replies, almost meaning it. Nick trusted in the system, and she trusted in him. Now, she knows better. 'The game was rigged from the start.'

'And we were their pawns.' Nick puts his head in his hands.

Perhaps they were.

But even a pawn can take the King.

Hetty arrives with the whisky, then curtsies and leaves them. Delphine gingerly takes a sip – it's a far cry from the throat-catching spirit she's tried at the Exoticies. Smokey on the tongue, it still burns as it glides down her throat, but the sensation warms her blood. She takes another sip to bolster her.

'They're a bunch of charlatans, too fond of Old Corruption,' Nick continues. 'This country still has very far to go, Delphine.'

A promising start.

'What's done is done,' is all Delphine can say, but now she's in Nick's drawbrary hearing his version of events, a foolish hope grows in her. Maybe Nick would be sympathetic to her plan – but it's too soon to say anything. There's still a whole conversation to unfold. 'Let's look to the future.'

He shakes his head. 'I'm more concerned about the present. The papers have been filled with disturbing discourse on the protests, and I saw the most uncomfortable advertisement yesterday. I've circled the relevant pieces. Here.' He leans over to the tea table and passes her the first newspaper in the pile.

TO BE SOLD
*A BLACK GIRL, the property of J.B., eleven years
of age, who is extremely handy, works at
her needle tolerably and speaks English*

> *perfectly well; is of an excellent temper and willing disposition. Enquire at the Angel Inn, behind St Clements Church on the Strand.*
>
> — PUBLIC ADVERTISER

Delphine rests her hand on the vile advertisement. Her sadness almost pulses out onto the page.

The *Advertiser* reported on every day of Vincent's trial. They knew about the ruling the moment it happened. It has been barely three weeks since Vincent's passing, and the papers have already forgotten and moved on. If a London paper can be so brazen, what are the chances they've started advertising again in Bristol? Or Liverpool? Or Glasgow?

Nick swoops in, ready to assuage her melancholy. 'I've written a strongly worded letter to the editor, threatening legal action if they print such things again.'

Then he gives her the next paper.

TO THE PRINTER OF THE LONDON GAZETTE

A conversation between an American, a Scotsman and an Englishman

American: In light of recent events, I am of the opinion we should do more to help England's freed slaves. What a terrible plight they suffer!

Scotsman: What plight? It is the poor who suffer the most. Wretches who dig coal in dark underground caverns! Children forced up chimneys! The Negro may be the freest among us. It is the rest of us in chains.

Englishman: It cannot be so! We are the wealthiest nation in the world.

American: England is rich, indeed. For while you boast of freeing your slaves, you continue selling slaves to us by the boatload. England is a nation of hypocrites.

Scotsman:	And yet, so is America. For if it displeases you to buy slaves from England, why continue purchasing them?
American:	You are right! Let's say the three of us were to start a revolution. America would cease to buy England's slaves.
Scotsman:	Scotland would empower the poor. But what would the English do?
Englishman:	Can you not guess? We'd make a law, change nothing, and then claim ignorance of the consequences.

Delphine puts aside the newspaper and glances at Nick, who is eyeing her intensely.

'Do you think it's true?' he asks.

'What's true?'

'That the law is inconsequential. That Parliament does nothing but oppress and enslave.'

How can Delphine even begin to answer that question? She must be careful not to arouse Nick's suspicions, but she is curious to know his position.

'What do *you* think?'

'I think it's more complex than that,' he says. 'Men, dominant as they are, always find reason to complain when others instruct them what to do. They claim infringement of liberty when anything else would mean chaos.'

'I thought you were in favour of liberty?' she says — *Beef and Liberty* is the motto of that Beef Steak Club he's so fond of dining at.

'I'm in favour of liberty through moderate government. Not unlimited freedoms. As Montesquieu said...' Nick sits up as if he's about to launch into another quotation, but Delphine interrupts.

'That's not what Montesquieu said.'

Nick's mouth snaps shut. 'Pardon?'

'He said that even in moderate government, there can only be liberty if there's no abuse of power. After Vincent's vigil, do you believe there's no abuse of power among your fellow Members? When they invoked violence at a peaceful protest on behalf of the King?'

Easy now, she tells herself — she needs to stay on Nick's good side.

'Well, Montesquieu is all theory, of course. In practice, humans are not perfect. Politicians included. Nor was it every member,' he says. 'Only some.'

'And this?' She passes the *Gazette* back to him. Next to the satirical conversation, he's circled another piece. **AN UPDATE ON THE NEGRO RIOTS.** It says 4,000 people attended the protest. Nine hundred and fifty soldiers broke it up. Eleven new names have been added to the death toll, and hundreds injured. 'Surely, it's not the theory that matters here, Nick. It's real life. And real death.'

Delphine considers the final words of the Englishman. Then, the scale of the members' response to the vigil. If there were such a revolution, England would certainly not do *nothing*.

He sighs. 'It *was* a catastrophic turn of events. If only you'd left after the proclamation...'

'You believe we were wrong to stay?' she says. The whisky has loosened her tongue, making it harder to temper her tone. 'You think they deserved to die?'

'I believe that staying was breaking the law.' He takes a deep breath and pours another dram. 'Yes, it was a foul trick to read the Riot Act. But you should have followed the rules. Disobeying did nothing for your cause. You didn't see what it looked like from up there. Whether or not the decision was predetermined, it was a fright to see all those threatening faces.'

There, Delphine was, believing that it was *their* cause, not hers. It's easy to read between the lines of what he's saying. He says threatening faces, but what he means is Black. Before the Riot Act was read, they were singing. They were protesting peacefully, and even Nick perceived it as a threat.

He *still* perceives them as a threat.

'Change can only happen from the top.' Nick finishes his drink. 'Damn the *Gazette*'s satirist, it has to be through legislation.'

Delphine has made up her mind. Under no circumstances can she tell him about the plot. Well-meaning as he is, Nick doesn't see the real problem – that this kind of change can never happen from within. If he doesn't see it by now, perhaps he never will.

'I agree,' Delphine lies, even though he wasn't asking her opinion. This is the way it's to be. She's got two days to return to the smugglers with the loot, or the whole plan is off. Guilt swirls in her veins, though – she didn't want to deceive him. She recognises that they both want change. In the conversation between the American, the Scot, and the Englishman, she hoped he had seen how the rest of the world perceives England and understood that they must do more than simply change a law. But if Nick still believes in serving the current government, she'll use that to her advantage.

Delphine takes another sip of whisky to still her nerves. 'I'd like—'

'Anything,' Nick says. 'Anything to move on from this debate.'

'I'd like to come back. As your assistant.'

Nick pours a third dram in as many minutes. 'What?'

'You said I was a great help during the trial, and I can continue to be. Change doesn't need to start at the top – it needs to start with work like ours.'

She'd never considered herself a sales clerk, but she has convinced herself.

'But what about Philadelphia?' Nick says. 'I am quite sure my friend Mister Benezet at the Free Negro School will write back to me soon, and they'll be thrilled to have you. Wouldn't you find teaching more diverting?'

'I...' Although the duplicity of it turns Delphine's stomach, she doesn't want to appear ungrateful. 'I am giving serious thought to the idea of teaching and am very appreciative of your recommendation. But if I did go to America, it wouldn't be until the spring term. I need to do something of value in the meantime. I wouldn't ask for much in the way of pay. Please, Nick.'

'I understand.' Nick deflates. 'It's not a question of money. I could scrape together the funds for a modest salary. But Delphine, I don't know if it's possible right now. When I mentioned that I was concerned about the present, I'm afraid there's another reason.'

Delphine's lips press into a grimace, her heart shrinking. What bad news is set to come next? 'Tell me.' She tries her utmost to keep her voice neutral.

'It seems the staging of the riot was only the beginning.' He rubs the back of his neck. 'When I went to hand in the petition, I learned that a motion has been filed for debate after the State Opening. They're planning to overturn Mansfield's ruling.'

Delphine has to clasp her hands in her lap to stop them from shaking. They've both feared this since the Chief Justice told Dunning that the West India merchants could apply to Parliament to object to the economic consequences of his ruling. But somehow, together with the news that the papers are already advertising *servants* again, it strikes Delphine as a terrible shock.

Vincent is gone and buried after being murdered in the street. Somehow, she has to live the rest of her life without him. Every time she tries to rest, she sees those last moments as the light faded from his eyes. When her brother finally lost hope.

It has been three weeks since then.

And the only reason Delphine has carried on since was because it had meant something. Vincent was an unwilling martyr, but if they overturn Mansfield's ruling, then what is he? Another Negro who died because a white man didn't like what he had to say. There are already too many of them to name.

If almost a thousand troops could be assembled in an hour, how long would it take the King's Friends to convince other MPs to vote in their favour? How easily could they wipe out Vincent's legacy?

Suddenly, Delphine's plot is no longer about justice. It's a last resort. But she cannot tell Nick. And she *must* get her job back.

'Lord Harvey sits in the Upper House,' she says. 'How can he introduce a bill in the Commons?'

'The Trading Companies' interests extend to most places. I don't know the numbers, but at least half the Foreign Affairs office has investments in the Trade. I'm rallying anyone I can to stop it from happening, writing letters and proposing alliances outside of my usual circle. But I'm a second-term MP of little significance.' He leans back on the sopha, his voice wavering. 'I don't know what else I can do.'

Fight it, Delphine wants to scream. *Fight them.* 'Bring me back, Nick. They don't even see me when I'm in Westminster. Let me find the ammunition for your alliances. I can help.'

Nick scoffs. 'If they didn't see you before, I'm sure they'll see you now.'

'Then let them see we are moving forward instead of clinging to the past. You are not an inconsequential MP – you already helped to change the law when you argued for Mansfield's ruling. Let me show them that I am no slave. Let them know I won't ever be.'

When Nick looks at her, she sees the conflict in him. Nick wants to make the world better, but he also wants to be Prime Minister one day. He cannot do that without friends in high places. Writing letters is one thing; resisting is another.

He grasps at his nape again, then swallows as if he's about to be sick.

Draining the rest of his drink, he says, 'Tomorrow then?'

'Tomorrow,' Delphine agrees, finally allowing herself to breathe. 'You're a good man, Nick Lyons.' *As good as he is willing to be.*

He raises his empty glass in a sardonic toast, then opens the confectionary box on the tea table. Inside are fragrant, yellow, sugar-dusted sweets. Lemon bonbons.

At the sight, a strange blend of feelings overcomes her – guilt and grief and sadness, but something else too. It's a sense of anticipation, of becoming. Delphine was never caught for those first little rebellions when she stole these sweets from Lady Harvey. Perhaps their appearance now is a sign this is meant to be.

'They were Vincent's favourite.'

'The man had excellent taste,' Nick says, relaxing just a little. As if hearing Vincent's name has just confirmed for him that hiring Delphine back was the right thing to do. He picks up a bonbon. 'To Vincent.'

One step closer to enacting her plot, Delphine knows how far she still has to go. If Nick's right that everyone in Westminster will be watching, it'll be even harder to complete Bela's task. There are still protests to organise. There's agonising over who to save and how to save them. There's getting the powder into Parliament, keeping it hidden and dry – a fatal mistake in Fawkes's plot.

There's doing all that and still doing everything possible to ensure a fairer future. But Delphine is ready to try.

She takes a bonbon. *'For* Vincent.'

Chapter Twenty-Seven

> Every person has a right to risk their own life for the preservation of it.
> —JEAN-JACQUES ROUSSEAU

Outside Parliament, the cries of dissent carry on the wind.

When Delphine first sought Nick out in May, only the occasional protest took place in the Palace Yards. Today, there are three groups, and Delphine's had nothing to do with it. Over by Bridge Street are the abolitionists and the coalheavers objecting to being paid in ale and coal over coin. By the stairs leading down to the river are the notorious silk weavers. Last year, they set fire to their looms due to despicable work conditions, earning them a reputation as the most riotous professionals on the Thames.

Between the abolitionists' and coalheavers' chants, they shout, *Choose people! Not profits!* and the more rhythmic, *Pay us now our daily bread, or we'll make all your silks unthread!*

Delphine distances herself from all the protesters and waits for Nick close to Westminster Hall's entrance. Although their cries strengthen her resolve, she must work harder than ever to remain inconspicuous. What she intends to do today may help all of them achieve their goals. If that means Delphine needs to bite her tongue for the next few weeks, then so be it.

She has come prepared, having clipped her most over-sized pocket into her petticoat this morning. It's almost as deep as a luggage trunk, perfect for smuggling whatever contraband Bela requires and proving her worth to the gang.

But even if she fails, there is already loot inside. Before leaving the Exoticies, she'd slipped the precious necklace she'd stolen from St James's Square into the bottom of the pocket. It feels wrong to hold onto it, knowing Pearl is alive. She will return it to Pearl later, along with whatever she manages to steal today.

The workers on the chapel roof cover their ears as the bells ring out for eight o'clock. Delphine turns back to the yard, and on the seventh chime, she spies Nick striding towards her – the most on time he's ever been. As he passes the weavers, he wrinkles his nose and draws his simple black jacket closer about his person, as if trying to protect himself from their scorn. When he reaches her, he casts a backwards glance, shakes his head and says, 'You know the Riot Act was created because of those silk weavers? Layabouts and scoundrels, the lot of them.'

How quick he is to dismiss causes that aren't his own, she thinks. She already knew Nick had many sides to him: the rude student, the worried friend, the passionate lawyer. He didn't seem to mind the weavers' handiwork yesterday when *he* was laying about in his pyjamas. But looking at him now, she feels this is the first time she is genuinely meeting *Nicholas Lyons, MP for Kettering*.

She keeps that thought to herself, and bids him good morning. 'Are you ready to face the wolves?' he says.

'Of course,' she responds quickly and firmly. Then, for the first time since Vincent's trial, she and Nick venture inside Westminster.

Delphine curses under her breath as they walk into the main hall. The Houses have been in recess for months, and she'd thought most of London's elites would be out of the city until December. Often, Lord Harvey would move to one of his many country homes for the entire autumn season. But unfortunately, today, the place is bustling with people. What she'd hoped, perhaps naively, was that she'd find something small and valuable in one of these first chambers to steal. She could pocket it, feign sickness, and be back in the smugglers' den by lunchtime. But how will she steal anything here, when there are eyes everywhere?

It strikes her that until now, she hasn't adequately considered just how many people work in Parliament. People who aren't involved in making laws or responsible for upholding a barbarous system; people who are just getting by and doing their job. The cooks and the cleaners and the clerks. How many of them will be in attendance at the State Opening? How many innocent lives would her plot snuff out? Guilt has taken up permanent residence in the pit of her stomach, but here, in these halls, it has forced its way into her heart.

How easy it's been for her to detach humanity from these humans. She supposes she learned from the best.

Does that make her no less despicable than the powers she's fighting against? That thought will certainly keep her up at night.

'Before we set to work,' Nick says, 'I want to show you St Stephen's Chapel.' They have stopped outside the chapel's great interior door, cut in the shape of a shield. Every inch of the oak and the surrounding stone frame has been carefully crafted with flowers, sceptres and scrolls. Delphine has walked past this door at least three dozen times – it's not too far from the Commons library – but there'd been no reason for her to go in before. She'd always been curious about it since the chapel is the meeting place of the House of Commons, but she'd been afraid to go alone to most places in the building.

It was worth the wait. Nick pushes open the door to reveal a room with beautifully panelled, dark wood walls with gold-topped columns, which rise from the polished floor to support the spectators' gallery. Delphine gazes up at the enormous 100-candle chandelier that hangs in the middle of the high ceiling, between the Speaker's Chair and a table covered with an emerald cloth, upon which two golden, ornamental forks sit. Unlike the teeming hall and chambers outside, the chapel is deserted.

If there's something to steal in this building, she's likely to find it here.

'It's a remarkable place,' Delphine says. She eyes the forks on the House table – they appear to be fixed in place. Are they distinctive enough to impress the smugglers? Could she find a way to prise them free if only Nick weren't looking right over her shoulder?

'Yes, and it is good to see it quiet like this.' Nick comes to meet her at the House table and rests his arms on the cloth. 'It reminds me it's not the room that has power, but the choices we make in it.' He smiles contentedly at Delphine, and she smiles back. If only he weren't so blind, he'd be an excellent ally.

'The mace is also remarkable.'

'Mace?' Delphine asks. Unable to resist, she leans on the table and strokes the soft velvet, her fingers inching closer to the forks. The cloth's gold tassels flutter against her skirt. She can't see a mace anywhere in the room. 'Is it a weapon?'

'Technically, yes,' Nick chortles. 'But also no. It's ceremonial, of course. It signifies the monarch's authority over parliament and His Majesty's confidence in us legislating on his behalf. When the Commons is in session, it is laid upon these forks, here, as a symbol of our loyalty to the Crown.'

'And where is the mace kept?' she asks, her question flecked with excitement.

Such a crucial ceremonial object would fit Bela's brief perfectly: *something you can only find in Westminster.*

Nick seems pleased by her interest. 'It's upstairs, in the Speaker's residence. Would you like to see it?'

Delphine feels her mouth twitch in disappointment, and hopes he didn't notice. She'd hoped it would be somewhere in this abandoned chapel – robbing a private residence would be far more difficult. 'Will the Speaker not mind?'

'No. The residence is purely ceremonial, too. No Speaker has ever lived in the building. And thank goodness for that – can you imagine how miserable it would be to live right above where you work? Lord Grantley lives in Soho, not far from where you used to... oh.' The tops of his ears flush pink. Presumably because, on mentioning the Temple of Exoticies — where Delphine used to live *and* work — he has realised he's just insulted her once again.

She sighs and says nothing of it. 'I would love to see it.'

Nick's entire face turns peony as they leave the chapel. They pass through four more doors, each leading them in a different direction. Westminster truly is a maze. The final corridor opens into a grand lobby decorated with matching thick, scarlet curtains and carpets. In the corner, beside the staircase, stands a red-coated guard, whose face shifts from vacant to disapproving as Nick leads Delphine right past him. Nick doesn't seem to notice as they mount the steps. He never does.

Faced with another oak door, Nick opens it and gestures that Delphine go in first — which doesn't usually happen when they're working.

'You're not coming?' Delphine asks. She'd expected Nick to chew her ear off about the mace's history and not leave her alone.

'It's a pretty thing, I grant, but I've seen it a thousand times. I would like to pick up a far more interesting scroll from the library before we commence our work for the day. Would you mind going alone then meeting me at the office?'

Not at all, Delphine thinks, though it brings to mind the ordeal of her first day in Westminster, how different a person she is now. 'See you there,' is what she says. 'I won't be long.'

Mercifully, the Speaker's House seems as deserted as the chapel. She finds nothing in the first room besides two large sophas, so she heads straight through an open door into a smaller chamber decorated with woven red flooring and paisley wallpaper.

Another chandelier hangs at the centre of this room, and on entering, Delphine first sees a large mahogany table with gold claw feet. It's topped with an oil lamp, half a dozen letter openers, and other stationery. The walls are lined with bookshelves and various open cabinets filled with ceramics and other knickknacks. She steps further inside the room. There's another open door to the left, and to the right... She sees her prize.

The ceremonial mace. It's exquisite.

The finest craftsmanship she's ever seen.

The mace is fashioned from pure gold. The four national emblems circle a crucifix at the top. Its handle is carved with raised roses and thistles, bound by spiralling ribbons.

But at the sight of it, her heart sinks.

Not because it's locked away or bolted down. It's unprotected and attached to its cabinet only with a removable metal grip.

But because it's at least five feet in length. Delphine is barely four inches taller than the thing.

Even with her enormously deep pocket, there is no way she can get this out of the building unseen.

She throws her palms against the wall on either side of the cabinet and leans her forehead against the top of the cool, unstealable mace, thinking for a few moments with her eyes shut.

Nothing else in these rooms could only be found at parliament. She could take a parliamentary seal, but you could find one of those in any politician's home. It's not unique, valuable or impressive.

A long sigh slips between her lips. She will have to go back for the forks. She turns to leave the room, heels hushing against the carpet.

But then she hears voices downstairs.

'Saw her go up there,' comes the first gruff remark.

'And he ain't with her?' says another.

Delphine's muscles tense, the hairs on her arms raised. She doubts those men have good intentions. Recalling Colin's map, she's sure this room has an escape panel. But where? She dashes back over to the bookcases, twisting every porcelain bust and pulling out every discoloured book she can find. The passages were always behind the bookcase in the novels Pearl read to her. But not here.

There's a sniff and the sound of belts jingling, of hesitant footsteps coming up the stairs. Feeling along the oak walls, she searches for the same loose panel she encountered in the Commons library and swipes a letter opener from a nearby desk, just in case.

'I ain't losing my job for this,' grunts a third voice – Delphine recognises this as the warden who stopped her on her first day in Westminster.

'They'll bleeding promote us.'

Ducking beneath the desk, she presses against the wall. And there, thank the Heavens, is a hairline crack in the panel. She pushes down hard on it, and in half a second, the wainscoting clicks open. The footsteps are coming closer and closer; her pulse is thudding in her throat. Bunching her skirts and crouching, she lifts one foot over the skirting board, hesitantly feeling for firm ground behind it. She almost sighs aloud in relief when her heel hits the floor, and she manoeuvres herself inside.

'In here,' the first voice says, just as Delphine clicks the panel shut, a primal dread creeping in as she envelops herself in darkness. 'I swear I saw her go in.'

'Well, where is she then?' says number two.

Delphine hears the men lumber into the room. She sits back on her heels and waits, trying not to think about the dust, filth and spiders that share her hiding place.

Number one's voice drops to a whisper, so low Delphine can't make it out.

'What?' says number two.

'I says you probably scared her away with your yapping!' barks number one.

'How'd you even know it was her?' says the third, this voice even closer.

Delphine uses her skirt to muffle her breaths, holding it between her teeth to stop them chattering.

'How many Caribees do *you* see knocking about?'

'Well, there ain't no one here.'

There's a sound like a head being scratched. Then, a sigh. 'Goddammit,' says the first voice. 'I could've used that extra coin.'

'What coin?' the second says.

'For protecting propriety and property or the like.'

'So no one even sent you after her?' says the third, irritated.

'Cretin,' huffs the second voice. 'Dragging us away from our posts...'

Delphine's jaw unclenches, just a little, as the footsteps recede. Not willing to risk being caught, Delphine stands up behind the panel. There's enough room for her to keep her skirt bunched in one hand, and she feels her way along the cold wall with the other. Now that she's here, she is struggling to picture Colin's map clearly, and she wants to know where this passageway leads.

She considers removing her shoes to stay as silent as possible, but decides she couldn't handle it. There are small, hard pellets on the floor, and she can hear the distant scuttling of paws. So she turns right, and sets off toward St Stephen's Chapel. Her eyes are beginning to adjust to the darkness, and soon enough, there is an opening in the wall, where the passage forks down a narrow spiral staircase. Feeling each step carefully with her feet, she slowly descends.

After the stairs, the passage continues to wind this way and that. Before long she is lost, and with a prickle of fear, Delphine wonders if she will ever find her way out. She reminds herself that all these passageways lead to the same exit, trying to stay calm. After what feels like forever, she sees two narrow streams of light in the wall up ahead: a metal grate. Peering through the hole, Delphine realises she's exactly where she hoped to be: back in St Stephen's Chapel. Turning her ear to the grate next, she listens for voices and footsteps, but there's nothing. It requires barely any force to open the grate and climb through. Blinking in the light, she shivers as she looks down at herself. While most of her dress and arms are clean, dirt coats her hips and the places where her shoulder brushed the walls. She will have to make her escape quickly if she is to avoid attracting the wrong attention.

Even if the guards have given up looking for her, Nick might be searching too by now.

She scrapes the underside of her heels with the grate before fixing it on the wall to prevent treading unknown muck through the chamber and leaving a trail that points back to the tunnels. Colin said most people don't know of their existence, and she'd rather keep it that way.

Then, adjusting her shawl to hide the worst of the dirt on her clothes, she rushes to the House table, where the ceremonial forks remain untouched. With a glance around the chamber to ensure the guards haven't somehow followed her, she clutches the letter opener, ready to levy the forks from the table.

Their edges are decorated with the same stems of rose and thistle as the mace, but they are each only the length of her hand.

Valuable, unique.

Pocket-ready and perfect.

The next consideration, then, is whether to take one or both. One is all she needs, but would it be more suspicious if half the pair is missing? Or is it more likely to raise the alarm if both have been misplaced? She decides both lost seems more reasonable. Maybe someone took them away for polishing, and they disappeared on their return.

Unlikely, but not impossible. Delphine's favourite odds.

And if she has any chance of carrying out her plans – of making this country a safer place for herself and thousands like her, of preventing more deaths like Vincent's and her fellow protesters – this is it.

It's now or never.

With a sickening feeling – of excitement, fear, triumph and regret – she pockets the forks.

Chapter Twenty-Eight

To be sold by auction at George Dunbar's office. Thursday next at one o'clock. A Black BOY about 14 years old, and a large Mountain Tiger CAT.
—LIVERPOOL GENERAL ADVERTISER

Three smugglers are staring at Delphine. Colin, Bela and Pearl were all in the den when she returned, while Jules is out on a job. Delphine holds up the stolen forks with both hands, and they glint under the candlelight. Delphine sets them down with a half-smile and slides them across the table towards Bela.

'Well?' Delphine says.

Bela waves a hand dismissively. 'And these are?'

'These two forks support the most important object in the British Empire.'

Bela snorts. 'They hold up the King's cock?'

Delphine lifts her chin and gives them the same explanation she'd heard from Nick. Pearl gives a low whistle of appreciation, and despite herself, Delphine has to bite her cheek to stop her mouth from breaking into a smirk.

Colin and Bela, however, seem unmoved. Bela narrows her eyes. 'What? Were you expecting a round of applause?'

The question momentarily unsteadies Delphine. She wasn't expecting them to clap, but she'd at least thought they would all look impressed. That seems ridiculous now, though. While she feels like she's pulled off a considerable feat, this is only a typical day's work to them.

'I'm *expecting* that vote you promised,' Delphine says, attempting to match Bela's tone.

Bela and Colin say nothing.

'No need,' Pearl interjects. She's wearing a pale blue shirt, unbuttoned to the breastbone, with an unfastened waistcoat and breeches. 'We voted before Jules went out this morning and agreed that if you completed the task successfully, we'd join you. Colin here's been your biggest advocate.'

'I love any excuse for an explosion,' says Colin, 'but this one will be especially worthwhile.'

'I'll work with her for Colin and Jules' sake,' mutters Bela, 'but that don't mean I have to like her.' She lets out an unimpressed *hmpf*. 'I've got other jobs on today. Let me know when you need me.' Then, without meeting Delphine's eye, she stomps out of the room, her shoes squelching over the damp flagstones.

Delphine watches her go and sighs. This is not the best start to a working relationship with a treasonous co-conspirator. But before she has time to dwell on it, Colin unrolls the map of Westminster Palace on the table.

Pearl places their newly acquired forks on top as paperweights at each side and says, 'What next?'

With a deep breath, Delphine leans forward and examines the map. 'Next, we decide where to hide the gunpowder. As I said, the State Opening will occur in the Main Hall.' She taps it on the diagram. 'In the Catholic conspiracy, they stored all the powder in the cellars beneath the hall, which they accessed via a building next door.'

Delphine was reading 'State Histories' again last night. She's memorised its pages so well that its censorious descriptions of Fawkes and Catesby's tactics could almost be a guide... Almost. After all, the fault in Fawkes and Catesby's plot was not just in their planning but also in the people they trusted.

It was their fellow conspirator, Francis Tresham, who betrayed them. Not because he'd abandoned the cause but because he couldn't abandon his family. Tresham sent an anonymous letter warning his brother-in-law to avoid Westminster on the day of the State Opening. That letter eventually ended up in the hands of the King.

But other than Pearl, no one who knows about Delphine's plot has links to anyone attending. So, although Delphine is paying close attention to Pearl's movements, she is more concerned about getting the execution right.

'However,' she continues, 'we won't be able to put our powder in the same place. The yeoman wardens sweep the cellars every year on the day of the Opening.'

'So your plan is?' Pearl urges.

Delphine smiles. 'See these two towers at the far side of the hall? The one next to the King's Bench, and the other leading outside to St Stephen's Court?'

Pearl and Colin nod.

She'd paced between those towers more times than she could count during Vincent's trial. The one day when she'd needed to be alone, she'd practically ripped the door from its hinges to get inside. When she did, there was only dust and darkness.

'These towers are completely disused. If we place a few of the barrels there, it guarantees the roof's collapse.'

She blinks away the image of the crowd looking up when the first barrel explodes. The closer they get, the more vivid the picture.

'The rest of the powder we'll need to space around the tunnels near the hall. There's one that's ideally located, running from the Speaker's House to the chapel.'

'Keen eyes you've got,' says Colin. 'That's one of the tunnels we use.'

'How many of us will need to help smuggle the powder in?' Delphine asks. As resourceful as she's sure Colin is, it's unlikely he can move it all alone.

'Me and Jules. Maybe Bela, but she usually watches for trouble at the cart. Maybe Pearl if she fancies getting her hands dirty. James is a strong lad if we need him, then there's Marcus, Xia and Joe. I could rope in a couple of others, too.'

Delphine glances at Pearl. That's twice as many as she mentioned before. Twice the risk. 'Can you do it with three?'

'*Yes,*' Colin says, adjusting his collar. 'But it'll take that much longer to move.'

'But you can do it?'

Reluctantly, Colin concedes and rubs a hand comically over his kidneys. 'Let's just hope my back doesn't blow out before we place the fiftieth barrel.'

'That many?' she asks. Fawkes only had thirty-six.

'Fifty,' he says firmly. 'You can take my word for it. If it has not been made abundantly clear, dove: gunpowder is my speciality.' He twirls his two index fingers before shooting them towards Pearl.

Pearl sighs. 'I told you that Col was a miner. Well, the story goes that one day, his tasks grew too mundane for him, and he determined to see how big a hole he could create with an entire cart of powder. Now, he takes credit for creating a little gap in the land known as Treyarnon Bay.'

Colin makes the exploding noise again. 'Truer words ain't never been said. Don't worry. I did it at night, and no one else was about. We ain't all as murderous as you.' He winks.

Delphine has no idea how to respond, but she doesn't wink back.

'Not that that's a bad thing, mind,' he says. 'Someone's gotta take a stand against the villains. If I'd hurt someone, do you think any of them mine owners woulda gave a fuck? Those puff guts cared about nothing other than their wallets. That's when I decided explosives were the right profession for me. Spent the next few years working at the gunpowder mill in Faversham before I came here, and the lads there still owe me a few favours. So, what I'm trying to say is, don't you worry about us getting what we need. All *we* need from *you*, our revolutionary turtle dove, is to practise laying the fuse.'

Delphine tilts her head. 'That takes practice?'

'If you want to live, I'd recommend it. If you light it so it burns down real slow, you'll be able to get out before it hits the barrels. Then...' He raises his eyebrows and waits for Delphine to say it.

'Boom?'

'*Boom.* We'll need to make sure the fuse is the right length. We don't know how much fuse you'll need until we agree on where you want to light it. So you'll need to practise laying it in the House. It might take a few goes unless you want to risk this being a suicide job.'

She definitely does not.

'So, what's the fuse made of?' Delphine says.

Casually, Colin draws a handful of gunpowder from his breech pocket.

Delphine wonders why he isn't worried about going up in flames himself.

He spits in the powder, then holds it out as if inviting Delphine and Pearl to do the same. They cast a glance at each other before Colin laughs to himself. 'I jest, I jest.'

Next, he pulls a hip flask out of his jacket and pours a clear liquid that makes Delphine's nose wrinkle as it hits the spit and gunpowder mix. He leaves the room for a moment, spit-slurry-mix in hand, before returning with a miniature barrel under his arm and two lengths of thread over his shoulder.

Delphine sits, fascinated, as he scrapes the mixture into the barrel and mixes it with more powder and water. Then, he dips a long strand of white cotton inside until every thread is coated in deep black slime.

'Slurry,' he says, pointing to the mixture. 'Dip in the cotton, light it, and it'll burn nice and slow – if it's the right thickness, that is.' He is about to lay the thread on the table when Pearl gives an affronted cough. He huffs in concession, then balances it over the back of a chair and takes the other length of cotton from his shoulder.

'Here's one I made earlier,' he chortles, laying the stiffened fuse on the ground before flipping open his pocket watch and passing it to Delphine. 'You watch the ticking hand and tell me how long this beauty takes to burn.' He steps away and crouches over the thread. 'I reckon fifty seconds.'

'Why not use the other one?' Delphine asks.

'It's best to wait 'til it's dry. You're wanting a sausage, not a snake.' Delphine blinks twice, thinking she'd misheard.

Colin doesn't say anything but flicks his eyes to the watch again before striking a match and lowering the flame to the thread.

It sizzles like sausages in a pan.

Delphine can't help but laugh. She watches the cotton burn down, white, orange, and black, while keeping one eye on the pocket watch. When it fizzles out, Colin says, 'How long were it?'

'Forty-seven seconds.'

Colin scrunches his brow. 'I'll make it a trifle thicker next time.'

Delphine purses her lips, impressed. She didn't think he meant *exactly* fifty.

'Then this one.' Colin grabs the other wet fuse for good measure. He lights it, and it hisses snake-like as it burns — twice as fast as the other. 'See?'

She does.

'I'll make your slurry,' Colin bows, 'then I'm away to supper.'

'Thanks, Col,' Pearl says.

'Thank you,' agrees Delphine.

Once he's finished making it and slipped out of the room, the air shifts, warming with the realisation she and Pearl are now alone.

If Pearl's uncomfortable, she doesn't say so. Her shoulders relax, and she shakes off her waistcoat before looping it over a chair. 'It's my only one,' she says, drawing her hands to her waist. 'I'd rather not dirty it.'

Delphine winces as she says this, shutting away thoughts of how carefully she'd had to scrub out any traces of their lovemaking at Lord Harvey's house — grass stains on Pearl's skirt, dirt in her hair. Pearl had teased her for her obsessive cleanliness, despite knowing that wasn't the real reason Delphine had to clean up after them both. However, the idea of Pearl having just one of anything is new. So is her taking such care not to damage her things in the first place.

The pearl necklace suddenly feels heavy in Delphine's pocket. There will be no better moment than now to confess. She squares her jaw and says, a little too quickly, 'There's something else I stole.'

'Oh?' Pearl cocks a puckish eyebrow, her intrigue piqued.

'Not from Westminster,' Delphine says, then takes a deep breath. 'From Lord Harvey. During the trial. I don't know why I took it, but it's yours. Here.' The string of pearls clicks as she hastily gathers it in one hand and holds it out to her.

Pearl's face freezes. Then flashes with something Delphine can't quite decipher — grief, longing, or shame.

'He found it?' she says in a small voice.

'He did.'

'I can't take it back,' says Pearl after a few seconds of strained silence. 'I'm grateful you brought it here, but that life is not mine anymore. It never should have been.'

This catches Delphine off guard. Her hand still hovers in the air between them, weighed down by the gleaming, pale stones. Pearl loved this necklace. For the years they lived together, it was as much a part of her identity as her name. Delphine knew, of course, that it was paid for with the pain of her people, but she didn't think that had ever occurred to Pearl. Did it occur to her now?

'You should sell it,' Pearl continues, a forced levity in her voice. 'Or keep it. Toss it in the Thames, for all I care. Whatever you wish.'

Still confused, Delphine tucks the necklace back into her pocket. She has no idea what she wishes to do with it now. Delphine doesn't want any gift from Pearl, and certainly not one born of guilt — but she can't open that Pandora's box now. She must try to put the pearls, and all they signify, out of her mind.

'Your skirt,' Pearl says abruptly.

'My skirt?'

'You need a new lining,' Pearl says, gathering up the rest of Colin's mess. 'If you're going to try out different fuse lengths, you'll need a way to get the thread into Westminster safely. Pockets are easily searched, but skirt linings are not. It won't take long.' Pearl starts towards the tapestry that leads to her bedroom, the barrel of slurry tucked under her arm.

'And I'll need to...'

'Take it off, yes,' Pearl says without looking at her. Are those nerves Delphine hears in her voice? 'I've breeches you can borrow so you won't freeze in your chemise. If you prefer, we can prepare the test fuses first?'

Delphine follows Pearl into her bed chambers. 'Let's start with the fuses.'

'As you wish.'

Throughout an afternoon in the tunnels, Pearl and Delphine take turns dipping long, winding bits of thread into Colin's slurry mixture, laying them out on a mahogany wash stand to dry. Their chatter is easy and constant, about everything from the oddly perfect (and perfectly odd) match the comedic Colin and sensitive Jules make, to reminiscing about Hetty's macarons. Every mention of the past brings a tightness to Delphine's throat, but they are both careful not to touch on the sore topics. And with every shared memory, it gets easier.

Once half of the rack is covered, the windowless chamber stinks of sulphur. Delphine's head spins from the fumes, the candlelight blurring into the yellowed stone.

'You seem tired,' Pearl observes. She draws back the patchwork blankets on her bed. 'We've enough fuse for now. I can move on to the skirt if you'd like to rest a while?'

'Just a while,' Delphine says, closing her eyes. The pressure behind them is already beginning to subside. Exhausted, she relaxes her head into the pile of pillows.

Pearl clears her throat. 'Though I'm afraid I'll need those skirts.'

'*Mmhm*,' Delphine hums unhooking one layer, then another and the last beneath the covers. It's not that she's afraid of Pearl seeing her – though they're older now, they've seen each other's shape a hundred times before. Nor is Delphine ashamed of her body – not when it has endured and carried her through so much.

But there is discomfort between them, Delphine thinks, wiggling the skirts drowsily over her hips. A barrier that keeps Delphine at a safe distance, and the more complicated things left unsaid. It's easier to talk of baked goods than of unrequited heartbreak.

Delphine's head thrums lightly, and she kicks her skirts out from under the covers.

Pearl may have said something further, but Delphine is already falling asleep to the sound of her first snore.

Pearl isn't in her chamber when Delphine wakes up. The scent of the slurry mix has vanished, too, along with her headache. Delphine stretches her limbs out, then holds back a smile when she sits up, noticing the present Pearl has left on the end of the bed – a pair of neatly folded breeches.

Delphine shuffles into them, enjoying the comfortable fabric and the shape of her silhouette in the looking glass. Then, she follows the sound of laughter coming from behind the tapestry.

'The idiot thought he had us worried,' Pearl chuckles, 'but Bela strode over, flicked her pocket-knife to his throat and said if he told anyone he'd so much as met us before, she'd turn his Adam's apple into a third tallywag.'

'And you know she meant it!' Colin roars.

As Delphine pushes the tapestry aside and ducks beneath it, she sees Bela sitting on the table with one of Delphine's underskirts in her lap. Bela juts her chin at Delphine. 'Aye, I did. Because you dinnae threaten family.'

Warning received. Delphine pulls herself upright and wipes sleep from her eye. 'Good to know.'

'We were just talking about an ex-client,' Pearl chuckles. 'Care to examine our progress?' She scoops up one of the skirts and angles her head, inviting Delphine to come closer.

Still half-dazed from her nap, Delphine joins Pearl at her side and looks over the thin new layer of material snaking up the petticoat. Pearl beams, then curls and uncurls her hands like they're stiff. 'My sewing isn't usually this neat,' she says. Delphine spots the outline where the needle has pressed into her fingertip.

'It's not,' Jules agrees, cutting a final fingernail's length of thread from Delphine's petticoat and knotting the end.

'Time you left, I'd wager,' Bela says, sliding down from the table. 'It's late.'

'How late?' Delphine asks.

'Just gone eleven,' Colin says, glancing at his pocket watch.

Delphine winces, calculating whether there's enough time for her to get dressed, out of the den and back to the Mitre Inn before midnight. She'd rather not get locked out.

Bela scoffs. 'Don't say you're afraid of the dark!'

'I'm not!' Delphine objects. 'It's just late.'

'Have you forgotten your key to the Exoticies?' Pearl asks.

'No, I—'

'You should get a chain for it,' interrupts Colin, 'keep it round your neck.'

'I know, I mean, I did have one.'

'So, you lost the chain?' Jules asks.

'That's not like you,' says Pearl.

'It's not because I didn't,' Delphine says, slightly exasperated. She folds her arms over her chest and says, 'I'm not lodging at the bawdy house anymore.'

Pearl's brows knit together, a crease forming between them. 'Where are you staying?'

Bela shoots a look at Pearl, then a worse one at Delphine. 'Since when?'

'The Mitre in Holborn,' Delphine says, answering Pearl first. 'It closes at midnight.'

'Not the best place, not the worst,' Jules says, unconcerned.

'What else isn't she telling us?' Bela says.

'I'm right here,' Delphine snaps.

'So, what aren't you telling us? What happened with Marion?' Bela's voice drops, increasingly threatening.

Suddenly, Delphine is weary once more. She could devise an elaborate lie explaining why she's not staying with Marion, but it's pointless. Knowing Bela, she'll go back and check with Marion anyway. Bela already dislikes her, and Delphine doesn't want to give her another reason to. So, she chooses honesty. 'She didn't object to the plot but didn't want it happening under her roof. Marion values her business more than most other things. I don't hold it against her.'

Bela considers this momentarily, then says, 'She was probably wise to be rid of you. Living in an inn is better for you right now. It grants you anonymity.'

'Even so,' Pearl says, 'There's no point in risking a night on the streets. You might as well stay here. And if you like, you can come with us on the job tomorrow night, too.'

Delphine blinks, surprised. She knew they were scoping out Parliament over the next few days but didn't know it was happening so soon.

'You didn't think it was as simple as rolling barrels of gunpowder into Westminster the day before the State Opening, did you?' Bela says.

'Of course n—' Delphine says, but Bela's already gone.

Colin snickers. 'I know where there's half a bed for you tonight.'

'Ignore my husband,' says Jules.

'Yes, shove off, Colin,' Pearl says, shaking her head. 'Sorry, Delphine.' And it's as Pearl says that Delphine comes to a realisation.

The Pearl she knew had never touched a needle, or stitched a hem. The Pearl she knew never asked Delphine to take a break while she took over, and Delphine rested on the bed. The Pearl she knew had never apologised.

Not once.

Chapter Twenty-Nine

Sir George Saville, Member for the city of York, said in the House of Commons, 'This House, by meanness, wickedness or corruption, has betrayed its duty and its sense of moral pride.' In response, the King's Friends called for Sir Saville to be sent to the Tower, asserting the House had never been attacked with such impunity and boldness. However, several other members stood up to applaud him.
—IPSWICH JOURNAL

'Is it right at the Long Gallery or left?' Colin says, stabbing a palm-sized map against the arched tunnel wall.

It's just past midnight, and the gang are preparing to go to Parliament and scope out where to hide the barrels of gunpowder. They are gathered in the long, cavernous underground tunnel where the gang's horse-drawn cart is kept. It leads from the smugglers' den to Blackfriars Street, a twenty-minute ride from Westminster.

'How've you ended up there?' Jules says, moving closer to Colin and peering at the map. Beside them, one of the horses lets out an impatient huff.

Colin hastily reels off the rooms that are linked by the network of passages running from one end of Westminster to the other. 'Start at the Painted Chamber, then the Commons Library, down to the cellars, up to the Long Gallery, then the lobby and the chapel, then the lobby again before the big hall?'

'Long Gallery's the other side of the Painted Chamber, love. You don't need to go there at all,' Jules says quietly.

Colin cocks his head. 'So left at the Painted Chamber?'

'Right,' Jules says, stroking the small of his back.

'Right.' Colin laughs. 'Just had it upside down!' He flips the map over and stabs it four or five more times before turning to Delphine, who's sitting in the back of the canopied cart, watching their interaction with much amusement.

Their plan for tonight is simple: Colin and Jules will sneak into Westminster and check if the hiding places they've selected are viable. They've got into Parliament plenty of times before, but these centuries-old routes can become obstructed between one job and the next. The map helps them memorise the route so they can find their way around the labyrinth of dark passages by touch.

Delphine's role will be to man the getaway vehicle. She's dressed inconspicuously as a driver in a brown cloak, hat and breeches. Meanwhile, Bela will keep a lookout from the scaffolding on St Stephen's Chapel, and Pearl will distract any witnesses on the ground.

'Where's Pearl, Delphine?' Colin asks, but Pearl emerges from behind the wagon, where she'd been fastening her earrings. To maximise her distracting capabilities, she's swapped her long trousers for a pastel blue, wide-skirted dress with a neatly coiffed hairstyle and a dusting of rouge on her cheeks.

Earlier, Delphine had stiffened as Pearl stepped out from behind her tapestry in this ladylike disguise, and their conversation had come to an abrupt halt mid-flow. It was the first time since meeting her again that Pearl had looked like Lord Harvey's daughter. It was also the first time Delphine hadn't needed to dress her in such clothes.

'She's not my keeper,' says Pearl.

'You just follow her around like a pup of your own accord, then?' Colin winks.

Pearl only sighs and wiggles uncomfortably as she adjusts her corset. 'Wretched thing.'

'I don't think she's talking about the corset,' Delphine says.

'Oh!' Colin smacks his sides. 'Let's hope Miss Revolution can watch the cart as well as she jests!'

'We heading out?' Bela says, emerging abruptly from the shadows of the tunnel, dressed in a dark cloak and boots. She tickles one of the horses on the nose, then holds back a grin as she sees Pearl.

'Don't.' Pearl shoots a warning look over the horse's muzzle but there's a smile on her face.

'Sorry, m'lady,' Bela snorts. 'You've not worn that dress since Colin's *accident*.'

'It weren't an accident, it was the bloody ferret, and you know it,' Colin protests, jumping up on the front of the cart and grabbing the reins.

'What happened?' Delphine asks.

Sitting beside Colin, Jules casually says, 'A ferret-infested treasure chest is what.'

'The ferret took a liking to Col and refused to leave him alone.' Pearl laughs, the husky sound accompanied by a wicked grin. 'It would've been endearing had the creature not had such a tiny bladder.'

'My breeches stank of piss for days,' Colin laments. 'Worst job I've ever done, that. Now hurry up and get on.'

'It can't be the worst, though!' Bela says as she and Pearl vault over the back of the cart to sit opposite Delphine. 'I *wished* I'd been on that job instead of Xia.'

Delphine met their fellow smuggler, Xia, at breakfast this morning: a middle-aged Chinese woman with silver-streaked hair down to her waist. She was ladling porridge with one hand and snorting snuff with the other. She offered Delphine some of both. The more time Delphine spends with the gang, the less they resemble the band of pale, peg-legged pirates she'd imagined. Along with Bela, Pearl and Xia, she's seen five other women scuttling around the tunnels, and between them all, it seems there are faces from every corner of the British Empire and beyond.

But the more Delphine thinks about it, the more sense that makes. Career choices for women are hardly bounteous above ground. And since goods float into the Thames from everywhere – the Americas, Arab Peninsula, West and East Indies and the Orient – it's not uncommon for seasoned sailors to eventually make London their home. In the melting pot that is the London Docks, who could be better at negotiating contracts smuggling foreign goods than those who know the relevant cultures and languages?

'I'd say it was the *worst-best* job for you, Col,' Jules says now. 'Awful smell, but great loot. That's what we do, ain't it? Bad good things.'

Like smuggling things worse than gunpowder into Westminster, Delphine thinks. Colin starts the horses, and the cart trundles up the tunnel.

'What's your worst-best job, Pearl?' he asks.

Pearl loops a lock of golden hair around her finger. 'You know, I'd rather not say.'

'Oh, come on, it weren't even that bad!' Colin says. 'Jules over here has armed maroons, Bela's gone and freed priests, and you're embarrassed about a little election rigging.'

'What?' Delphine's mouth drops open as she turns her head towards Pearl. 'Surely this wasn't about Nick?' She raises her brows, awaiting confirmation, but it doesn't come. 'Does he know?'

Pearl shakes her head, focusing on the wooden wagon floor.

Colin guffaws, but Jules grips his arm and whispers something inaudible before pulling the string to the canopy cover shut. Bela leans back on the bench, her eyes closed – apparently resolving to ignore them all.

Pearl and Delphine sit in silence as the cart clops over stone. The finger-width gap between the canopy curtains flashes yellow, orange, then black as they ride, the tunnel seemingly endless beneath the city.

'What Colin just told you is powerful information,' Pearl says, finally looking at her. 'You can't tell Nick.'

Delphine's not sure if that's a command or a wish until Pearl continues. 'Please, don't tell him. I was only trying to help.'

'By rigging his election?' Delphine asks, her mind spinning. When Pearl said her special skill was persuasion, she hadn't imagined anything this duplicitous. The first time Nick showed her around Westminster, he'd told her how proud he was that he'd been re-elected in his own right. 'Why?'

'Because Parliament needs more good hearts,' Pearl says as the cart stops – they must have reached the mouth of the tunnel. 'And because my father wouldn't back him, which meant neither would his constituents. He wasn't going to win without me.'

'So how did you...?' Delphine keeps her voice level. Outside, a wooden gate creaks open, and the wagon bounces as someone jumps back on.

'I traded a few secrets to open the door to him,' Pearl says, quieter now that the cart is pulling out onto the street.

'You said you've been trying to be a better person.'

'And I have,' Pearl says. 'Look at all the good he's done.'

He *has* done a lot of good, Delphine thinks. He's the one who persuaded the Bill of Rights Society to start compiling a proposal for universal suffrage – rather than just funding John Wilkes' prison fees. He might never have agreed to fight Vincent's case in court if he hadn't met them or the abolitionist groups and reformers he votes with. And he's even been invited to interview for a seat on a Foreign Trade Committee the week after next – all because of his good work in Parliament.

Besides, if Pearl *hadn't* rigged the election, they might not be having this conversation at all. Nick might have never got Delphine into Parliament; the smugglers would never have agreed to help her.

'And anyhow,' says Pearl, 'are elections ever fair? You or I certainly wouldn't have been able to influence it any other way. Do you know, Delphine, now that I'm legally dead, I have more power to influence this country than I did when I was alive? I suppose I couldn't resist using that power at last.'

Delphine cracks a small smile. 'I can relate to that.'

'I just wanted to *do something*. There are so many things I didn't do in my old life. Not just because I couldn't, but because I was frightened too – of society's expectations, or my father's...' She trails off, as one example rings clear in both their minds. 'Now, I have the power to help good people make real changes. *We* can make real changes.'

'I just think...' But Delphine's thoughts are too many, too conflicting. Pearl is talking about the kind of Old Corruption Nick hates – underhanded deals and tactics that undermine democracy, and which he wants to root out. But isn't what Delphine is planning even worse? Some things are easier to justify than others. She is in no position to judge.

'We're here,' Colin says, and the cart stops again. He peeks between the curtains at them. 'We good?'

Bela opens one eye and settles it questioningly on Delphine. 'We're good,' Delphine says, sounding as uncertain as she feels.

The plan is going smoothly... for the most part.

They are parked on Abingdon Street, which offers a clear view of the scaffolding on the chapel. Delphine is in the driver's seat, posing with her chin tucked into her cloak, hat over her face, like a driver dozing on his break.

But it would be easier to feign sleep if she weren't so cold her nail beds have turned purple. And if she couldn't hear Pearl's teeth chattering in her skull.

'They couldn't have held the State Opening in July?' Pearl whispers, shifting behind Delphine so the wagon jostles slightly. 'Why choose one of the coldest months of the year?'

'To make the most of their summer homes, I expect,' Delphine quips. 'Shh.'

'How long has it been? Twenty minutes, thirty?'

'Or thereabouts. Shh!'

'Scoping's the worst part of any job,' Pearl huffs a clouded breath, which lands pleasantly on Delphine's cold neck.

'Is this why they don't take you very often?' Delphine whispers, and it comes out harsher than she means it to. Her patience is short tonight, especially with Pearl dressed as she is. It reminds Delphine too much of the past.

'I have other talents! I...' Pearl falls silent as three rapid flashes of light shine out from the scaffolding. 'Shit, that's Bela's signal.' Pearl hoists herself from the back of the wagon to join Delphine in the driver's seat before tentatively stepping down to the pavement. 'You know what to do for plan B?'

'Yes,' Delphine replies, though she'd hoped it wouldn't come to that.

'Good. Stick to it,' Pearl says over her shoulder before dashing towards Westminster Palace.

Plan B means Bela's spotted a night warden too close to Jules and Colin's exit, and Pearl is off to distract them by pretending to be a lost, slightly intoxicated lady needing assistance. If it works out, there'll be no need for plan C, plan D or any other eventualities they'd envisaged.

Bela says the worst thing you can be is unprepared.

After several minutes, Delphine sees Pearl reappear at the furthest reaches of her eyeline. Her arms are clasped around the warden's neck, and she's begging him in a high, girlish voice not to tell her mother of her indiscretions. He tries pushing her off, grunting an offer to find a comfortable sedan chair to deposit her on, but she starts to cry, rattling off a long, loud story about why he can't possibly leave her alone.

She's brought him down to sit on the paving stones with her just as a clatter rings out from the scaffolding.

Each of them stiffens.

There's no clattering in plan B. Another guard shouts in the distance.

Pearl has done well with the guard so far – for all the gang's joking, they wouldn't have brought her along if she wasn't suitable for the job. Delphine hopes the same can be said for her. Simply manning the cart is no longer an option. She runs through plan C – distracting the guards by spooking the horses – but it's no good because that only works if Colin or Jules have already returned. Delphine has no clue how to steer a cart. Plans D, E and F won't help if Bela's caught by another night warden – or if she's already in trouble.

Delphine curses under her breath. That leaves plan G.

Gunpowder.

She jumps up from the driver's seat and flicks the latch on the bench, before lifting the lid and revealing the equipment she needs to enact their last-ditch plan: a jewellery box filled with gunpowder. It's wedged beneath a sewing kit, knotted bandages, two half-full gin bottles and a handful of ammunition boxes. Freezing and on edge, Delphine takes a swig of gin. The bitterness sends an involuntary shiver down her limbs as she grabs the powder and digs about in the trunk to find a matchbox, fuse and striker.

Plan G was only to be executed if Jules and Colin hadn't returned *and* Pearl and Bela needed help. Delphine had not anticipated this happening, but experienced as the gang is, things can change quickly on a job like this. So, Delphine leaves the horse and cart. As she turns into an alley that leads past a timber workshop down to the wharf, the wind whips her cloak, and the icy night air mixes with the smell of recently cut wood. When she reaches the Thames side, she deposits the jewellery box into the nearest sailboat, which she finds bobbing in the water. Silently voicing an apology to its owner, she runs the fuse from beneath the box's gilded ceramic lid to the other end of the boat and onto the wharf. Then she rubs her hands together to get the blood flowing, before unspooling a third of the dock line so the boat unmoors and floats two feet away from the riverbank, but no further.

Once she lights the fuse, she'll only have ninety seconds to release as much of the dock line as possible, sending the boat far enough away that it doesn't set the whole timber wharf on fire. For a first attempt at lighting a fuse, this is going to be tricky.

She listens for the movement of night wardens and the smugglers' shouts, but she's too far away. Craning her head over the dock, she can just about make out the bank side of Westminster.

Hesitating before reaching into her pocket, Delphine grabs the matches and striker and takes a deep breath. The match hisses to life, and she lowers it until the fuse sizzles.

Ninety seconds. *Is this happening?*

She throws the fuse onto the boat. Sparks fly, only narrowly avoiding the jewellery box. Then, swallowing her nerves, she rapidly unspools another six or seven feet of rope from the metal bollard.

The moment the boat reaches a safe distance from the bank, she sprints back towards the wagon. A stream of justifications and excuses for what she's done floods her thoughts. She's read enough newspapers this year to be sure that dust explosions happen often. Small fires occur every day. No one is going to be harmed. Even so, she's never set a fuse before. She's never had to reckon with the consequences if this goes wrong. What if the fire spreads? And how can she carry out her plot if she can't handle the guilt of starting *this* fire?

Delphine makes it back to the horse and cart, just in time for the explosion. She feels it first, the quakes rippling from the river to the cobbles beneath her feet, then there's a boom so loud she covers her ears. The timber yard isn't in sight, but the explosion is. A burst of bright, burnt orange soars high into the night, then is consumed by ascending clouds of smoke and debris.

Pressing a palm to her heart, Delphine laughs a little, relieved at her success.

It's the distraction they needed. Mere minutes later, Jules and Colin return to the cart. After returning Delphine's stolen forks, they'd finished their task but got trapped by a guard at the exit from the passage in the chapel.

Pearl returns next, wide-eyed and paler than usual. The night warden left her for the explosion, she explains, and before Delphine can object, Pearl envelops her in her arms. Only when Pearl lets go does Delphine realise how much they're both shaking — and how good it feels to be held.

Finally, Bela jumps into the cart, and not a beat passes before Colin lifts the reins, and they pull away. Over the journey back to the den, Bela says she managed to get off the scaffolding but got stuck hiding behind a statue because she'd drawn two wardens' attention. One of them even began climbing the scaffolding to investigate before the explosion.

'Had a good night then?' Colin asks Delphine when the cart arrives back in the tunnels.

Good isn't how Delphine would describe it. It's been an overwhelming night. Though she's more confident now in the smugglers — their skills, their plans, and their backup plans — the sight of the explosion burns in her memory every time she shuts her eyes. The height of it. The roar. Even now, the sulfuric scent of it lingers on her cloak — all that power released from a single jewellery box of powder. It's a haunting new perspective on what's to come.

Chapter Thirty

> Equality, because without it there can be no liberty.
> —JEAN-JACQUES ROUSSEAU

It's all anyone can talk about at Westminster the next day. *It was an accident*, the traders gossip in the main hall.

Some fool left a candle burning after cutting timber all day, the palace cleaners agree.

The same thing happened at a bakery in Venice a few years ago, Delphine hears one minister reminding another. Remember how it put our sons off visiting the city on their Grand Tour?

A shame, gripe the day wardens outside the library. It would've made for an interesting shift.

Good thing no-one was hurt, Nick says as they part ways in the evening.

Not close enough to Westminster, the protesting silk weavers whisper as she passes them, on her way to fetch her belongings from the tavern.

The gang has agreed to let Delphine stay with them until the plot is carried out.

She's packing her emerald dress into her travel trunk when a knock thuds at the door.

It's probably the innkeeper about to angle for another shilling.

She'd paid a month in advance, but still, he had demanded an additional fee when she said she was leaving. The knock comes again.

'Delphine?' the voice says. 'Are you in there?' Charity?

'Finally, you're here,' her friend says when she opens the door, marching past Delphine in her fuchsia gown. 'I came last night, but you weren't in.' Charity takes a turn about the room, with its Tudor beams and unfurnished, once-white walls. She wrinkles her nose at the threadbare patchwork quilt before picking up one of the scratched brass candlesticks. 'This is nice, at least.' She grimaces, before replacing it on the end table and plopping herself on the bed. The mattress slumps. 'It's good to see you.'

'You too,' replies Delphine, but she's also taken aback.

Truthfully, Delphine never thought she'd see Charity again. She had surmised their friendship was one of proximity, not choice.

Since Delphine left the Exoticies, it's like she's been holding her breath. For all the bawdy house's problems, Marion did one thing right: she created a space where Delphine could remove the mask she presents to the outside world and settle in her skin. Seeing Charity now reminds her of that loss.

'Going somewhere?' Charity points to the open wardrobe and Delphine's half-packed trunk.

'I've found a new place to stay.'

'With them smugglers?'

Delphine gasps. What has Marion told her? She can't afford for word of her plot to travel any further than it absolutely needs to.

Charity lets a laugh fly as she sees the fearful look on Delphine's face. 'I overheard you arguing that day in the kitchen. Marion hasn't told the others.'

Delphine curses herself. She must be much more careful about who she talks to and where.

Charity shifts on the bed, folding her arms onto her lap. 'Why did you not tell me?' she says. 'We could've gone to Marion together. You know you get under her skin.'

'And you would've helped?' Delphine asks. She knows Charity too well to believe it. Delphine's instinct is usually to fight; Charity's is to flee.

'I... No. I suppose I wouldn't have.'

'And now?'

'And now,' Charity begins, 'I think...' She looks Delphine in the eye. 'You won't like what I've got to say, but I came to say it anyway. Vincent got them to change the law, and did it without violence. What you're doing is wrong.'

Delphine braces herself for an argument. 'But he—'

'What they did to him was terrible, D,' Charity says. 'The worst pain anyone can know. And I'm sorry it happened, and for what went on at the vigil. But that don't mean you're doing the right thing. I know you've had struggles with your mood, but you can't burn half the world and not get licked yourself.'

Delphine has not been struggling with her mood; the melancholy has come quite effortlessly. Though admittedly, panic is threatening to overwhelm her right now. 'Why'd you come here, Charity? To take me to Bow Street?'

'I wouldn't snitch, and you know it,' Charity says. Delphine desperately wants to believe her. Charity narrows her eyes and beats a fist over her heart. 'I just wanted to say my piece. I know you well enough to know I can't change your mind. I'd practised a million times before leaving the Temple and couldn't think of anything that'd work. But I wanted to come anyway, to make sure you're all right. To make sure you're keeping as safe as possible. Ain't that what you do for us?' She takes a breath before continuing. 'So, are you all right?'

'All right?' Delphine parrots, disarmed. It's been a long time since she's considered that question.

'Yes,' Charity says, creased lines appearing on her forehead. 'Delphine, you lost your brother, your home. You're plotting to get yourself killed. Of course, I am asking if you're all right.' She places her hand on Delphine's, and in that moment, when it's clear that her friend has not come here to hurt or betray her, Delphine feels exhausted. All she wants is to curl up in Charity's hand. She wants to say that sometimes she misses Vincent so much she can hardly breathe and that even though the smugglers are on her side, even though her plot might be on track, she still senses something is off, like when the air thickens before a storm.

She wants to tell her about Pearl, to share that part of herself with her friend and seek her advice about what she should do, but she doubts Charity could ever understand. So, no, nothing is wrong, but neither is anything right. Delphine decides: she doesn't feel right.

But because she cannot say any of that to Charity without admitting it to herself, all that Delphine responds with is, 'I'm getting by. How're you?'

'I'm...' Charity's jaw tenses, her mouth opening and shutting a few times before she speaks again. 'Someone needs you to bring down the flower.'

Delphine rubs her temples, then her cheeks. 'How?' Every time this happens, she feels sad for whichever poor girl is in trouble. But before she left the Temple, she made enough carrot seed tea to last a few months. She'd even used some of Vincent's money to buy more alum water, just in case. Mistakes rarely happen – Delphine knows her craft, and the women are careful. There's no place for babies at the Exoticies.

She almost asks who it's for, but it doesn't matter. She always starts with the safest option, prescribing something that wouldn't interact with any other health complaint. It complicates things because she can't be there to help administer the dose. There's no such thing as a perfect solution, but she'll do what she can. Whoever it is.

Cradling her arms over her chest, Delphine considers her options. Savin's the safest herb, but that's out of season. She avoids gin and metal and other more dangerous methods. Rue and calamint then: harsher than savin but as light on the body as it can be while still doing the job. 'I'll get it as soon as I can.'

At times like this, Delphine thinks of her mother. There were few pregnancies on the plantation, but given the choice between a birth aided by a white doctor or Delphine's mother, they'd choose her every time. She wonders if her mother would be proud or ashamed of how Delphine uses the knowledge she gave her.

'Thank you,' Charity says, tipping her head back, relieved. Then she stiffens a little. She's not done saying her piece. 'Your plot,' she starts again. 'You say you're doing it to free slaves, but what I want to know is... why wouldn't you do it for us?' Charity glances around the room, at Delphine's trunk, then back down at her hands. 'Why Vincent's cause, but not ours? You say they sell Negroes in newspapers, but Harris's list puts girls from Soho to St Pauls at risk every year. Why not us?'

Delphine's heart sinks. Charity is right. Harris's list is a public review of harlots, which shames and endangers every girl it features. Each year, women are attacked, arrested, and even killed after being exposed in its pages. Harloting might be the world's oldest profession, but it's still vilified. There are no laws to protect prostitutes; pimps don't need to pay them, and bawds keep them in dresses to keep them in debt. It's slavery of another kind and one the law won't even recognise.

And Delphine has failed to recognise this, too.

She's not sure she has an answer. This time, her rage turns inward. She's been blind, focused on freeing one set of people without considering who else is left in chains. What she's been doing is not good enough – asking Jules to encourage other communities to protest their discontent in the streets. It's not enough to blow up a building, to end the lives of so many in it. Not if it won't help free everyone else.

'I'm sorry,' Delphine says. Though sorry doesn't cut deep enough.

'Don't be sorry,' Charity says. 'Help me do something.'

'What did you have in mind?'

'I've got an idea,' Charity says, squeezing Delphine's hand. 'But for it to work, I need to learn to write. Here's what I want to do...'

As Charity tells Delphine of her rebellious plans, Delphine eyes the locked drawer beside her bed. Pearl's necklace has been coiled inside it, untouched, since Pearl gave it back to her. Selling it might not be such a bad idea, after all. And what's more, Delphine knows exactly where Charity should go first to put the proceeds to good use.

Chapter Thirty-One

At this moment, no honest man should remain silent or inactive. The time has come when the body of the English people must assert their strength, and not surrender their birthright to ministers, parliament, or kings.
—PUBLIC ADVERTISER

Over the next week and a half, London descends deeper into unrest. The protests are gaining momentum, so much so that Delphine considers that Jules can't be responsible for all of them. He and Pearl may have been spreading rumours around the dockyards and coaching inns to stir disruption, but having learned from her conversation with Charity, Delphine asked that they try and solve problems too. Listening to the workers' troubles and connecting them with other trades to see if anyone can help. So far, the brushmakers have helped the scriveners secure a pay increase of 2s a week. But the wins have been few and far between, so there are still men from almost every guild present at the protests. A united front of disgruntled labourers.

When Delphine arrives at Westminster in the mornings and when she leaves in the evenings, she can hardly move for the sheer number of angry people outside Parliament. She weaves around blacksmiths protesting ironwork decline, holds her breath as she passes the skinners calling for hygiene protections at work, and squeezes past coopers crying out for fairer pay because their wages have been lowered for the second time this year.

And these are just the regulars. Some days, Old Palace Yard also draws in more unlikely rebels: beggars, shoppers, and even the occasional band of white-gloved ladies.

Meanwhile, the papers are reporting frequent stories of matchstick girls smashing factory windows, of lascars defacing the white bricks of East India House, of a landlord chased out of his own home for overcharging Black tenants in Mile End.

One thing's certain in Delphine's mind: the people of London are unhappy with the status quo, and they want their voices heard.

Delphine has been busy, too. With what little spare time she's had between working for Nick and preparing for the attack on Parliament, she's been helping Charity to pull off her small revolution. Charity wants to publish her own Harris's list — only hers will review culls, not harlots.

Inspired by the smugglers' code that Bela developed, Delphine has helped Charity create her own system of hand-drawn symbols, so she can safely send messages to other brothels without fear of them being intercepted. It's a slow process, but it's working. Her friend and several other girls from the Temple are gradually compiling stories on the cruellest culls in the capital, including the notorious Mister Harris himself.

The sale of Pearl's necklace is helping too. The smugglers sold it for more than enough to enable the pamphlet's printing and distribution. Delphine is acting as scribe, and Mister Walvin, the bookseller at Hatchards, has agreed to help Charity secure a printer and sell a copy or two. Charity's cause is certainly on the path to achieving her aims: providing safe housing and care for workers who have experienced abuse.

Then, late into the night, Delphine meets with Jules and Pearl in the den to conspire over the future they hope to build. They talk of the law of inheritance being scrapped, of women inheriting seats and gaining the right to vote. Jules has been speaking with his contacts in the guilds, gathering information on as many MPs, noblemen and clergymen as possible ahead of the State Opening. Any man who is a proven ally to those less fortunate than himself — who has a track record of working towards a fairer, freer society — goes on Delphine's list of men to try and save from the explosion. Despite their best efforts, the list so far is woefully short.

Only when Delphine is alone, tossing and turning in her bed, does she allow her fear to catch up with her. For every success in her plan, for every second she isn't caught, she feels closer to the unspeakable possibility of failure. Her nightmares are haunted by Fawkes and Catesby, mutilated and screaming in the throes of torture. When she wakes, she still sees their faces in her mind's eye. She sees a burning building, a blackened crown, ruins and riots.

And all of it rests on today if Delphine can complete her next challenge.

It is two o'clock, and Delphine is sitting with Nick in his new office. Last week, Pearl traded a stolen painting with one of Westminster's wardens to move Nick to this room because situated on its south wall is the escape panel closest to the Thames-side secret exit. Nick does not like the room one bit: it's windowless, tiny, and a clear demotion compared to his old office near the King's Bench. He believes the relocation is because the Prime Minister dislikes him. As a result, he's been in a bad mood all day. Luckily, Nick will shortly be heading out for his Foreign Trade Committee interview. Which will grant Delphine both a reprieve from his grumbling and a perfect opportunity to tackle her next all-important task. She needs to check that the tunnel to the exit is still clear since Colin and Jules' stake out and measure the length she needs for the fuse. She is wearing the skirt that Pearl and Bela made for her, with thirty-six feet of fuse coiled safely inside.

'Ugh,' Nick scoffs, striking through the notes he's been working on all morning. He scrunches the parchment into a ball in his hand. 'I'd almost forgotten. That Lang boy will be at the committee today. He is the one they are comparing me to at the interview. A pimple-nosed child!' He almost spits the words. 'Not even twenty-one with a seat of his own and does nothing for it. You cannot be elected and handed everything in exchange for nothing!'

If Nick beats the pimple-nosed child onto this committee, he'll be able to influence colonial law, extending from the London docks to India, the Americas and the Falklands. That would be an undeniable victory for both his and Delphine's causes. But his last sentence gnaws away at Delphine's conscience — would he still want his seat on the committee if he knew what Pearl did? Would he still want to be in politics at all?

'It is utterly ridiculous,' Nick says, tossing the ball to the floor in time with the protestors' drumbeat. 'If the criteria for a committee role is only needless want, we may as well let every housewife and domestic in when they need a new broom.' He laughs now in that self-assured way men do when they believe they have made a most humorous and insightful joke.

Delphine bends to retrieve the parchment and hands it back to him, once again relieved to have kept her mouth shut. She wishes he would just leave for his meeting so she can get on with the job she's really here to do. Nick scrunches the notes into an even tighter ball, then rises. 'Of course, I don't mean you. Just...' He searches for the words, which he seems to think are hidden somewhere in the wrinkled parchment ball. 'For most women, their sphere is in the home, and... That joke works better in less fair company.' He fixes his gaze on the wall.

'Less fair, or fouler?' Delphine retorts. 'Isn't it time you were on your way?'

He discards the parchment on the desk and then pulls out a gold timepiece from his waistcoat. 'My word, yes!' He springs into action, smoothing back his hair. 'I'll be engaged for quite a while. If I've not returned by six, please retire for the evening. I'll see you tomorrow.'

That is almost four hours from now.

Surely, she can get the job done in that time? 'Best of luck. You'll do brilliantly,' she smiles.

Nick smiles, too, and then rushes away down the corridor.

The instant the door shuts, Delphine heaves her desk away from the wall of the small office, revealing the secret panel.

She tentatively pushes down on it and prays.

The door groans. Delphine does, too.

Then it clicks and juts out barely an inch from the wall.

Not wanting to waste a moment, she finds a candle nub, a matchbox and a striker.

With the door open, she can finally rid herself of her sulphur-lined skirt and test the length of the fuse.

She hoists her skirts to her waist and uses her teeth to rip open the hem of the bottom petticoat. The sensation of fabric tearing makes her skin crawl, but thankfully, the little patch they'd sewn on gives easily, revealing the end of the fuse.

She now has another burning decision. How does she hold the candle without setting the thread aflame? All it would take is an ember to waft down onto the thread, and her entire skirt, and likely the rest of her, would be up in smoke.

Delphine shudders and guesses the safest way is to prod the candle with something so it remains at arm's length ahead of her. If she keeps the skirt and cotton above her knees, there's very little chance of a spark. And it'll keep her dress clean so Nick isn't suspicious when he returns.

It is a crudely drawn plan, but it will have to do.

Grabbing a measuring rod from beneath the desk, she crouches down, takes one last look around the room and hopes it's not the last one she sees. Then, Delphine crawls into the blackness of the passage. She doesn't know why, but she holds her breath.

According to the map, she must walk left down the passageway a short distance before descending a staircase and taking two turns before she reaches the exit. With the ruler, she manages to keep the candle at a safe distance as she shuffles, one cautious knee then another. This tunnel is narrower than the last one she was in. She can't imagine a king crawling through a space like this. Though she supposes people may crawl through most things to save their lives. The further she goes, the more she attempts to focus on two things only: the light of the flame and the thread in her hand. To let her mind wander into the shadows, to think of what creatures may be creeping in the darkness, would send her running back out into Nick's office, plan be damned.

The floor gives way beneath her and, in fright, she almost drops the candle. Then, her foot lands a few inches below.

The stairs.

In the half light, she drops down onto her haunches and feels with her hand for the next step down. A splinter pierces her finger, and she winces, but the sound of the protestors yelling outside bolsters her.

She crawls down two steps before realising there's more space above her. With one hand still on her skirt, the other pressed to the wall, she rises, and treads cautiously.

At the bottom, it's another ten or so paces until she reaches the first corner, a few more steps until the next, and then, at last, the door. Or, not quite a door, for in the small ring of light thrown out by the candle, the secret exit appears to be disguised as a coal chute – small but large enough to crawl through.

Delphine pulls down the sizeable rusty handle with all her strength, opens it a crack, and then peeks outside.

The river is right there. Perfect for making her escape after lighting the fuse.

Delighted, she shuts the door again. Unsure how many feet she's travelled, she begins to unfurl the fuse as she backs towards the stairs. There's still plenty of thread as she places a foot on the first, but then she hears movement above her. Surely Nick can't be back so soon?

'You'll never believe this. A fight has broken out among the protestors, and they're not letting us cross the Yard! Here I was, thinking they were fighting the *government*, not each other. Really, I can't...' Nick's voice trails off. 'Delphine?'

Her heart stops. Her mind searches for a reasonable explanation, but there is none. She freezes until she hears again, 'Delphine, are you in *there?*'

The candle is gone. There is no need for her to move slowly. She wiggles her way up the steps and out of the darkness. She wishes it would consume her instead – anything other than explaining this to Nick.

Her voice shakes as she approaches the secret panel. 'I thought I heard a cat.'

'A cat, you say?' Nick's voice is louder now.

'Yes, a cat in the walls.' The lie forms on her tongue as she speaks it. 'I heard something yowling and scratching. You didn't realise there was a door behind the panel?'

She edges back out of the passageway.

'What have you done?' he says, looking at the splotches of brown and black all over her skirt, her stays, her skin. Maybe her plan for staying clean wasn't as considered as she thought.

'I couldn't let the poor thing starve in there.'

'Well, where is it?' Nick says, peering into the darkness.

'Where's what?' Delphine says. She uses her shawl to remove the cobwebs from around her wrists, hair, everywhere.

'The damned cat, Delphine. You look like a chimney sweep. They'll confuse you with the protestors.' He laughs. 'I suppose I'll have to find the thing myself.'

'No!' Delphine yelps. 'It must have been my imagination. It's far too dark to explore down there. Hardly fit for searching, don't you think?' She forces an uneasy laugh and points to her dress. Her heart pounds against her chest.

'You find a secret passage in my new office and expect me not to explore it? You've inhaled too many cobwebs.'

Panicked, she blocks his path. 'You can't go down there.'

'Why, what have you...' He pauses a moment and lifts her hand to his face. 'What's that smell?'

'Rat droppings.' Delphine grimaces.

'No, that's not it.' He looks at her again, stepping closer. 'What's this?' he says, squatting down and pulling on the cotton thread protruding from the hem of her dress. Thirty-six feet was too long, after all. She swallows.

'Oh, my hem is unravelling. Never mind, I'll mend it.'

'This smells like...' He searches his memories for the scent. '...like gunpowder, Delphine.'

His face hardens.

'Why is there gunpowder in your skirt?'

This is it. The moment she decides whether to confront Nick or ask him to join her. She hopes that deep down, he is on her side and he'll see what she sees. That he doesn't turn her in to be executed. After everything that has happened, maybe his heart is in the right place. Even after every joke and poorly spun word, despite it all. She wants to trust him.

So, with no chance of him believing her lies anymore, she tells him the truth. No more than she needs to – she tells him nothing of Pearl and the other smugglers' involvement – just how her idea grew, like many of his own, and how he'd caught her enacting her plan. He listens in gobsmacked silence, twisting the black cotton fuse between his fingertips, just as he had with his length of twine in the courtroom.

When she's finished Nick's expression morphs from gobsmacked to enraged. 'So your answer is to just blow it all up? Did you pause to think for even a second how I'd feel about this? It's not just you who feels excluded, Delphine. *I* don't fit in here, either.' His voice breaks at the top, words straining to get out. 'Every man who walks through these doors has a knighthood, a barony, a dukedom. And what am I? The commoner in the corner whose mother was a sibling to a lord. I have to fight for every single win in these walls. But I don't want to destroy them – I'm here, showing up, changing it from within.'

Delphine strides over to Nick, throwing her hands up to mirror his.

'But at least they'll tolerate you, won't they?' she hisses. 'We both know the real reason they let me in here. It's not because they think I'm your *parliamentary assistant*. They still think of me as your slave.'

The words shatter between them, but they don't assuage the fury in Nick's eyes.

'But you're here, aren't you?' he cries. 'I can protect you in these walls. I am protecting you.'

Protecting her? How can he protect her from a threat he still fails to see?

'We can make it better, without—' here he lowers his voice to an appalled whisper, '—committing a thousand murders.'

288

'We'd be stopping a million others!' she says, without breaking for thought. 'Look outside Nick. The nation is angry, begging for change.'

'And when you've done this, do you expect the whole country to thank you? Pat you on the back after you've demolished the institutions that keep us safe from invaders and tyrants? What is it you want? Your own seat of power?'

Delphine shakes her head.

'You'll burn for this,' he says. 'There's no doubt about it, and then everything will be a hundred times worse than before. These hopes you have, of freedom, of fairness, of creating a new nation. They'll be dashed before this building stops smouldering. Do you know what happened to the Catholics? One hundred years of persecution. *And they started with rights.* What do you think will happen to all those who look like you? To the people outside today? Is that what you want Vincent's legacy to be? And mine?'

Delphine slams her hand on the table. 'It's not about you, Nick. It's never been about you!'

He throws his books off the table and onto the floor. 'How is it not? Am I not one of the poor souls you intend to blow up?'

'Of course not!' she says. 'I had a plan! I—'

'So I'm different?' He is mocking her now. 'Forgive me, I didn't realise I'd employed St Peter as my assistant! What gives you the right?' His face curls into a sneer, horridly similar to the one his uncle wears. 'I have dedicated the last six months of my life to this. I have been your ally, held you up. And Vincent. And this – *this* – is the thanks I get?'

Delphine hardly cares who may overhear them now. She's ready to explode.

'I never asked you to save me! All I asked for was a job. To earn things on my own.'

Nick's reply is barely a whisper but loaded with venom. 'And even that was a lie. You used me and my office to commit murder. Treason! You've risked everything *I* have earned on my own, too.' He doesn't look at her as he's speaking, and Delphine grits her teeth, resisting the urge to reveal the truth of his election as he continues his tirade. 'How could you be so ungrateful,' he says, 'after all I have done for you?'

'That's just it,' Delphine hisses. 'It's always *our* ungratefulness. You know that's what your uncle said to Vincent the night all of this started? He called him ungrateful. All but ordained that Vincent was indebted to his *generous* master from here unto eternity. Is that what you want, Nick? A snivelling, grateful Black girl, humble at your feet?'

She puts a hand to her heart and balls it into a fist. 'Every time I hear another Negro has been murdered in broad daylight, I swear part of my soul dies with them. The death always hurts, but that's not what leaves the mark. That comes later. After the public cries for reform die down, the papers move on, and politicians backtrack on their promise that things will improve. Those freshly sewn seeds of hope in me die, withered and trampled again. They kill us and beat us, then give us just enough freedom to keep us in line. We're not allowed to resist. Not openly. Vincent taught me that.'

She pauses, offering Nick the opportunity to speak, but he says nothing. His face is red, and he's breathing hard. She's quiet for a moment, then heads to the door. 'Were you aware, Mister Lyons, that I don't know the real name of the island where I was born? They took that away too – gave it something they could control.'

Nick says nothing still; the look in his eyes is hollow and defeated. 'The way I see it,' she says, 'there are two options for you. You can find a way to join us. To get off your white breeched bottom and see the world the way it is, the way it *truly* is. Or you can tell the King. That'll most certainly get you the premiership and influence you desire.' Delphine trembles as she says it, for all her fears of being caught have now come much closer to the surface. They curl around her like phantom hands, twitching to drag her down. From here on out, there are only two paths for her, too: victory or ruin.

Chapter Thirty-Two

> All my misfortunes come from having thought too well of my fellows.
> —JEAN-JACQUES ROUSSEAU

Delphine's thoughts are bees, swarming. Attacking her as she storms away from Westminster, as rage radiates from her skin. How could she have let Nick in? What did she expect to come of her stupidity? Of course it was never going to work. Of course he will tell the King. In stinging Nick, all she has done is bring death upon herself.

When Delphine finally stops walking, she finds herself outside the crimson door to the bawdy house. Her feet have brought her to a former haven while she fights the war in her head. She can't go back to the smugglers yet. Not like this. What could she even say to them? She might be on the cusp of losing everything.

All because Nick returned early, and she left the panel open behind her.

All because she had told him her truth.

Even though Nick knows Delphine was staying at The Mitre, the last thing she wants is to bring the King's men to Marion's door if they don't find her there. She's about to turn away from the Exoticies when the door bully opens the door and – rather brusquely – ushers her inside.

As Delphine makes her way upstairs, past creaking bed frames and muffled moans, she allows herself a smile. When Charity came to see her at the inn, she'd failed to mention that the door bully had still not quit – making Delphine the winner of their wager.

'I thought I said don't come back here,' the bawd says the moment Delphine enters her chamber. It's grander than she remembers. The sun-faded coral wallpaper updated to a bright sunflower hue and the scuffed wooden wardrobe replaced with a gleaming new one. Then the bawd turns from the window, where she must have been watching Delphine from above, and shuffles towards her. She is clad in the gold dress she normally reserves for Sundays, or important culls.

Delphine clenches her jaw. She's in no mood for one of the bawd's lectures.

'What's the matter?' Marion says, lifting Delphine's chin with one finger. 'You look tired. Life not treating you well?' She lets her hand fall and shrugs. 'Can't say I'm surprised.'

'Nothing's the matter,' Delphine lies. 'I only wanted to check on the girls.' That, at least, is the truth. If Delphine's about to be executed, the very least she can do is ensure her potion helped the woman who needed it.

Marion clucks her tongue. 'I'm not such a monster, Delphine. They're fine enough without you.' And given the rest of the room's new furnishings, Delphine assumes that to be true.

Marion turns towards the two high-backed armchairs beneath the window, looks over her shoulder and says, 'Come. There's something we need to discuss.'

Delphine follows Marion and sits in the left chair – she knows the right is Marion's favourite.

'I found this in Charity's room,' the bawd says, picking up a thick pamphlet from the table. 'Do you know anything about it?'

'I—'

'I know she's been to you in Holborn. I know you helped with Lizzie.'

Lizzie. Delphine steadies her face so as not to give away her surprise. Lizzie is barely nineteen. This would have been her first. Or at least, her first since taking up at the Exoticies. 'Did the remedy take?'

'Like I said,' the bawd shrugs, 'they're fine enough without you.' Then, she pushes the pamphlet towards Delphine.

Unsatisfied with Marion's answer, Delphine bites down her questions for now and takes the pamphlet. It's thread-bound with a yellow cover and an illustration of a harlot winking behind a fan. The title, printed in block capitals, reads: **HARRIS'S LIST OF COVENT GARDEN LADIES.**

'We both know the girl can't read, so what's she doing with this?'

'I don't know,' Delphine says.

Marion's mouth draws tight. 'You're to come to me if she asks you for so much as a ribbon. We don't need more trouble under this roof. Understood?'

Trouble seems to be brewing everywhere – Delphine can't be held responsible for all of it – but she nods. She doesn't need another enemy today.

'Good,' Marion says, lifting herself from the chair. She almost stumbles, so Delphine jumps up to support her. Some days, Marion is the strongest woman alive; simply standing up can defeat her on others. It's the bargain that comes with age. Though Marion doesn't want to hear it, Delphine needs to tell her what happened with Nick. He knows that she moved out of the bawdy house into lodgings at the tavern, but if he tells the Crown and they can't find her there, this is where the soldiers will come next. Delphine opens her mouth to speak, but Marion raises her hand to cut her off.

'If you're not here for Charity, I don't want to know. You can have half an hour to see to Lizzie, then it's time for you to leave.'

Clearly her former boss is in no mood to chat. Delphine nods.

'Take care, girl,' Marion says, and stares at Delphine briefly before shaking her head. 'Don't forget, I tried to warn you.' Then she ambles from the room.

When Delphine arrives back at the den, she finds Colin polishing the handle of his pistol in the central chamber in front of the statue of

Suerva. 'What cheer, dove?' For some reason, it doesn't irritate Delphine when he calls her that. 'You figure out the panel and the fuse?' Delphine shrugs, but Colin takes this as a yes and says, 'Nice work. The rest of us can get on now. Tomorrow night, we'll get the first five barrels into the tunnel off that fella's office.'

She tenses. 'Maybe leave it for a few days.'

Colin cocks a brow. 'Why?'

The words snake out of her, another half-truth. 'It's damp down there. You said that if the barrel gets wet, it can't ignite. We should do the exit tunnel last.'

This way, if Nick gets someone to search the passage in the meantime, they'll find nothing.

Having left a muddy trail from the tunnel's far exit, Pearl arrives beside them, covered in muck. It seems she's overheard their conversation. 'You got in with no trouble, then?' Pearl asks Delphine, rubbing her hands down her slops, then looks at her palms and grimaces. She wipes her forehead with her elbow, replacing sweat with dirt.

A beat passes.

'Aye, she did,' says Colin, then he agrees with Delphine: 'Escape route last.'

'Perfect,' Pearl says. 'Come. We've lots to discuss.'

She leads them through the main chamber and the meeting room with the oval table. Delphine spies the floor plan of Parliament still sprawled out over it. New charcoal crosses and circles mark what Delphine assumes are the smuggling routes they intend to use next. Pearl clears her throat and draws back the tapestry to her room.

'Everything well?' she says.

Delphine hesitates. She will tell Pearl about Nick, but only once she knows what to do about it. She didn't tell Nick about the smugglers — as far as Nick's concerned, Pearl is still dead — so for now, at least, they're safe in the den. Maybe Delphine will speak to Nick again tomorrow and devise a solution. Then, she can present a Plan B to Pearl, not just a problem. Delphine knows Pearl's track record when facing unknown obstacles – if she tells her this now, she might panic. And she doesn't want that because things are improving between them. Delphine is finding herself *wanting* things to improve between them.

'Yes. I was just… Never mind. What did you want to talk about?' It's evident once she scans the room. On top of one of the crates, there's a wicker basket packed with so much white thread that the bundles look like freshly picked cotton. Her head dizzies from the stench of the slurry. 'You've made more fuses? The last one was long enough.'

'But was it exactly right? It takes twenty seconds to burn per foot. Too long and you risk someone coming across it, too short and… Well, I think the timber wharf demonstrated that.'

Delphine thinks about the distance between Nick's office and the secret door that leads to the Thames.

Thirty-six feet of fuse. Twelve whole minutes to get caught.

'I suppose six feet less couldn't hurt.'

'Good. I have one that measures exactly thirty.' Pearl picks up a rag to wipe the muck from one arm, then reaches out to Delphine, angling her head as if asking for permission to touch her. Despite the uncomfortable spark this ignites in her belly, Delphine nods.

Pearl wraps a hand around her waist, taking care not to get so close that she dirties her clothes. Delphine can't deny it feels good, to have some of their easy intimacy back. But she is determined not to think of just *how* good it once was.

'It's nice seeing you here,' Pearl says. 'I miss you when you're gone.'

More sparks fizz, warming Delphine from the inside. It's not often she is missed, but the thought of *Pearl* missing her? It's a fantasy she gave up on long ago. 'You do?'

'Yes, of course,' Pearl breathes and breaks away. She lifts a hand momentarily to Delphine's cheek, then quickly withdraws it and resumes cleaning herself with the rag. 'To think I'd almost forgotten this face.'

Delphine could never forget Pearl's – her cheek tingles where Pearl's fingers brushed it. For the first time since their reunion, dirty or not, Delphine wishes Pearl would touch her again. 'I missed you too.'

But as she says the words, the truth of them frightens her. She's had her guard up with Pearl, but it's been weakened after everything with Nick. If she lets these sparks catch, will she be burned again? Or might they light the way to something new between them? She *wants* to leave the past behind, but she also wants a new relationship with Pearl. A friendship, maybe. But possibly more. The idea makes her ache, like she's thumbing an old bruise.

Pearl wets her lips, glances down at Delphine's, and then meets her gaze. It's soft. It's familiar. It's Pearl. Delphine's breath thickens. Those lips. Those eyes. Those memories. Delphine leans closer, but then Pearl pulls back and sighs.

'Come on, then,' Pearl says. 'Help me with this thread.'

Delphine releases her breath — the moment is gone; the sparks stamped out. She follows Pearl to the basket and draws out a cotton bundle; Pearl takes the end before stepping backwards and unfurling it around the room.

'What were you doing before?' Delphine asks, hoping her tone sounds carefree. 'You look like a gravedigger.'

'You're not far off,' Pearl laughs. Then laughs harder upon seeing Delphine's concern. 'Sometimes we receive contraband in boxes of earth. No one wants to rummage through them at ports, so it's a good way to conceal it. If rather filthy at our end. These ones are headed up north.'

She lays the thread's end on the floor, moves to her bed, dips down, and pulls out a measuring rod before checking the length from one end to the other. About halfway across, she looks up. 'When will you next be in Parliament? I remember this concoction gives you a headache. You shouldn't carry it around with you all the time. Find somewhere dry to store it until the day.'

'I'll be back there soon,' Delphine says, then chides herself. *That* did not sound carefree.

Pearl makes a *hmm* noise and pauses a few feet away from Delphine. 'Now that I've mentioned it, why aren't you there today? What time is it?' She tilts her head. 'Not yet five? Won't my cousin be missing you?'

Her heart thuds. 'He has his interview today and is out all afternoon. He said I was free to go early.'

There's a pause before Pearl speaks again. 'Why don't you know when you'll next be at Westminster?'

Silence.

'Is everything well with the plan?' Pearl lays the thread on the ground.

Delphine tries to pick it up, but Pearl grabs her arm. 'Delphine. If we are to work as a team, we need to talk to one another.'

For the second time today, Delphine is backed into a corner. This is the moment they are both to be tested. How will Pearl handle the truth? How can Delphine admit to her mistake? She imagines them again as children: Pearl in her night shift, hair braided to her waist instead of cropped at the shoulders. Delphine's emerald dress replaced by the crisp white of her servant's uniform and cap.

Their first kiss. After Pearl's mother scolded her for eating *like a heifer* at breakfast, and instructed Hetty that she wasn't to be fed for the next two days. After Lord Harvey smacked Delphine for not curtseying low enough when she passed him in the corridor, cradling a bowl of near-boiling water under one arm, fresh linen piled beneath the other.

The daily household drum beat of chastisement and rejection drew their lips together at the end of Pearl's bed.

A love found in loneliness.

Delphine looks at the floor. She wants to tell Pearl the truth, to trust they will work through this together, but the truth and explanations often equate to violence or loss, and despite all the desire and all the will to change, Delphine's instinct for self-preservation wins. She cannot open her mouth.

'Delphine?' Pearl's grip on her arm tightens. 'Please answer me.'

Delphine winces from the pressure and forces the words out. 'I was going to find another way in.'

'What do you mean *another* way in?' Pearl drops her arm.

Honesty tumbles from her lips. 'Nick learned the truth. He isn't on board.'

Pearl's gaze darkens. 'What?'

Delphine's need to solve, to fix, to plan, sets in. She rushes towards the door. 'We'll find another way in. Don't worry, not yet.'

'No. There's definitely something to worry about. What did he say?'

Thinking back on it, Nick didn't say much, but she remembers *her* last words clearly. *There are two options. You can find a way to join us ... Or you can tell the King.*

Pearl doesn't wait for Delphine to respond. 'Why didn't you trust me with this?' She runs a hand beneath her curls and twists them into a knot above her head. 'That's it, isn't it?' She throws the rag to the floor. 'You don't trust me.'

'I do... I'm trying.' Delphine's voice trembles. It happened barely two hours ago, and she's barely recovered herself. She just needs time to think.

'But why? Why can't you?' Pearl shakes her head. 'Because of what happened at Ranelagh?'

Delphine folds her lips. She doesn't want to say yes but cannot say no. Pearl scoffs, anger flooding her voice. 'That was years ago! Trust me or don't trust me. You've put all our lives at risk by holding onto this. It was foolish. Selfish.'

That pushes Delphine over the edge. 'Selfish? *I'm* selfish?'

Pearl rolls her eyes and turns away from her. 'Oh, don't start.'

'Start what?' Delphine snaps. 'You brought it up! I would have told you. I was going to tell you. I just needed an hour or two to gather my thoughts.'

'Do you know what can happen in an hour or two?' Pearl shoots a dangerous look over her shoulder. 'Enough to get an entire gang killed. Enough to change everything.'

'You would know,' Delphine mutters.

Pearl hisses through her teeth, 'What's that supposed to mean?'

'Two hours,' Delphine says, finally giving voice to it. 'Two hours before we were meant to run away, you promised me it's what you wanted to do. And you've been doing the same here — all along, you've been saying we're a team, a family, you'd help, you've changed, that you've—'

'It's not the same!' Pearl flings her arms up and marches away from Delphine towards the tapestry. 'This is different, this is—'

'Is it? How?' Delphine says, following her. This is not how she's planned to have this conversation; it's not how she *wants* to, but now that they've started, she can't stop the hurt spilling out. 'How is this different to you running away at the first sign of trouble? Because a plan no longer seems easy.'

'Easy? Nothing about this is easy. I'd moved on with my life, I'd left everything behind — everything — but I'd started again. And then you come back.'

'You told Vincent he could tell me.'

'And would you have come if he'd said to?'

'It doesn't matter,' Delphine sighs, 'because I'm here now.'

'It matters *because* you are here. Because I never thought I'd have the chance to make things right, to tell you how sorry I was, how sorry I *am* for what happened. I wasn't ready then. I didn't know how to be the person you needed. I didn't know how to be the person I *wanted* to be. I am not the same person anymore, Delphine! I've been trying to show you.'

'Then who are you? A smuggler? A charmer? An election rigger? You've called yourself so many things these last weeks, apologised more than I have ever known you to, made your point about tying your own corset strings and wiping your own tears, but saying nothing real.'

'What do you want from me?' Pearl pleas, hands in the air.

'The truth!' Delphine yells. 'Who are you? The daughter of a lord? The widow of a baron? My mistress? My friend? The love of my life? What are you?'

'What I am is sorry!'

'For what, Pearl?' Delphine clutches the sides of her neck and scrunches her eyes tight. 'What is it that you are so sorry for, that you constructed a whole new life to get away from? What was so bad that it wasn't enough to leave with me, but to run off with a gang of smugglers?' She's heard it's supposed to feel lighter when you get things off your chest, but Delphine's words are rib-crushing, the weight of mountains.

'Me,' Pearl croaks. 'I needed to get away from *that* me. From the weak person who let everyone else make their decisions, who couldn't see beyond their cage. From the person who knew they could never be a wife but got too scared when you told me another option was possible.' Pearl's voice thickens. 'Who let you leave because if *wife* didn't fit, what if *husband* didn't feel right either? Then what would we have been?'

'Together,' Delphine says, a knot untying in her chest. 'We would have been free together. However we chose to live, whoever you decided you were. I never wanted anything else.' She's never wanted *anyone* else.

'I didn't know what that meant until I came here.' Pearl arches her head back, shoulders circling as if to steady herself. 'Until Colin and Jules, until Bela said we can be one way out there, but ourselves down here. I thought I knew what it was like for you because although I suffered so much less, we both were in a type of cage.' She chews the side of her cheek, looks up at the vaulted ceiling, then down at her unmade bed and the stone floor. 'I know it's not good enough, but it's the truth. It was easier to keep apologising, to show you I could draw my own bath or pin my own hair than to admit...' Pearl takes a deep breath. 'It was wrong, what we were. That even if you had wanted me, I kissed you first, and you couldn't have said no. There are no good masters, Delphine. I expected you to run with me, and I didn't even ask my father to free you first. You must have thought about that. Surely? I hadn't even considered it.'

Delphine had never asked. It was too big a request. Too great a risk. Still, every night they lay in Pearl's bed, Pearl's cold feet warming themselves between her legs, she thought about it. Every time a breeze whispered over her skin while sewing on the window seat, she thought about it. Every time, she brushed Pearl's hand while watching the acrobats in St James's Park. Every time Pearl rejected a suitor until her parents' patience ran out.

But Delphine never asked. 'He never would have said yes,' she says. 'But he would have asked why. He would have found out about us. He might have sent you to a madhouse.'

'But either way,' says Pearl, 'you would always have paid a higher price. It took four years for me to learn that others always do. So, I rigged an election to give Britain a radical MP. I use this voice, this body, to change what I can. But none of that changes the fact that I failed you.'

'You were a child,' Delphine says.

They both were. Unprotected and unvalued.

Pearl shakes her head. 'I was old enough to do better.' They stand in silence, taking in the weight of this truth.

Until they're interrupted by a thud from somewhere in the tunnels.

Pearl breathes out. 'That'll be Bela. We'll figure out what to do about Nick.'

The noise comes again. And again. A steady *thud, thud, thud.*

Delphine hears Colin yell from the meeting room. She and Pearl hastily follow him to the main bathing chamber.

'Oi!' Colin calls. 'The lads are back. Why isn't someone on the door?'

Thud, thud— Crack.

They move into the entrance chamber. And then the door shatters.

Chapter Thirty-Three

The only thing necessary for the triumph of evil is for good men to do nothing.

—ANON

The plank barring the door splinters in two, spitting wood across the room. The brass hinges break free from the frame and spew over the stones.

Delphine's first thought should be to flee, to find safety, but instead, she thinks of Nick.

Nick who reveres fairness above all else. Nick, who must always have a cause.

Nick, who has chosen to protect the Crown. He must have had someone follow her here.

Pearl was right. Delphine has put them all in danger.

The invaders pour in. She would have assumed they were soldiers, but they're not dressed in standard red uniforms. Instead, they wear frock coats, tricornes and hatred-filled glares etched into deep lines on their faces. There are seven of them. Each of them holds a sword, a bayonet or a pistol. Delphine has heard of secret battalions: king's men who move in the shadows, swiftly solving private matters and squashing potential public unrest. She'd thought they were a myth. Until now.

'Hands up!' one of them shouts, brandishing his pistol and driving them back into the main chamber. Several other smugglers are there, too, having heard the commotion. 'All those in this room are suspected of treason. You have two choices. Resist or submit. Die or face capture.

Make your decision now.' He beats his chest with his free hand. 'It makes no difference to me.'

The navy fabric under his fist draws Delphine to thoughts of the ocean's dark and threatening depth. She stares at him, this king's man, this upholder of the peace. She feels paralysed, overwhelmed and sucked under by a sinking feeling.

Colin presses forward and stops in front of the statue they call Suerva. 'It bloody well does make a difference, you King's cunt.'

He raises his pistol. Aims. The man follows suit.

Delphine's breath wedges tight in her throat, like a lead ball down the barrel of a gun.

Bang.

The intruder fires first.

It's not Delphine who is hit, but she recoils, can't stop the cry that escapes her.

For a moment, Colin seems unharmed, but as he turns away from the invaders, he clutches a hand to his chest. His flesh stains scarlet in an instant. He tries to say something but only hisses out air. His eyes grow wide, and he lifts his red hand to his mouth before he keels over, his beloved gun tumbling with him. Blood runs a ring around the base of the bronze statue.

'*Hmpf,*' the man says, kicking Colin from behind.

The Cornishman's nose hits the statue's plinth with a *smack*.

It's followed by silence.

There's no rasping, no groaning, and from where Delphine stands, she cannot make out if there is a rise and fall to his chest.

The air slows and thickens around Delphine. It's suddenly very cold. A wail breaks out somewhere behind her, and with it, a realisation spreads to the eyes of every smuggler in the room.

Colin warned Delphine this may be a suicide mission.

She'd prepared to sacrifice her own life but was not ready for this.

Colin is... The words begin to form in her mind. *Colin might be...* Thank God Jules is out with Bela, away from this mess.

'Who's next?' the man smirks. His eyes are black, small, and beady like a pig's. He steps over Colin's body like he's avoiding a puddle on the street. In a series of nods and finger movements, an unspoken decision passes between Pearl and the gang. They have a plan. Of course, they have a plan. The threat of capture didn't first emerge when Delphine entered their tunnels.

Because this gang is a family. And these invaders attacked one of their own.

A whirlwind of movement rips through the bathhouse. The smugglers scatter like spiders to the five routes leading off the central chamber. One invader pursues them in each direction. In the frenzy, Delphine has already lost sight of Pearl. She isn't sure which way to go. The first door leads to the tunnel where the horses are kept. But there's no guarantee the horses will still be there, and the tunnel is far too long to make a quick escape on foot. The second door leads to the meeting room and Pearl's room — where she would be trapped. The only other way out she knows is through the third door — which leads back to Billingsgate — and the intruders are blocking that exit.

Shots ring out. Screams follow.

Delphine can't tell whose.

'Delphine!' Pearl yells — she's still in this room, calling up from inside one of the enormous sunken baths.

Instinct takes over, and Delphine dashes towards the sound.

Down in the ancient bath, Pearl has knocked an intruder's sword from his hand and he's reaching for her throat. He's at least a foot taller than her, and his hand spans her neck.

As he squeezes, Delphine swears the grip catches her, too. 'Delphi—' Pearl's cry descends to a choke. She tries to pry off his hand but can't, so she pulls him with her headfirst onto the ground. Delphine jumps in after them, her ankle rolling in an unnatural direction as she lands. Heat shoots up her calf from the outside of her foot. She sets her jaw and forces the searing sensation down as though it were just another avoidable feeling.

The invader is on top of Pearl now, her body convulsing beneath him. Delphine's panic hardens into resolve. She will not lose Pearl again. Summoning all her strength, she barges into the man from behind. He flies forward off of Pearl, who chokes out a rasping breath. The invader rolls on his side, pushing up onto his haunches then onto his feet. The demonic look in his eyes as he faces her is one of complete hatred — a look that Delphine is wearing, too.

Let him come for her.

She will show him the depths of true rage.

When the man lunges at her, Delphine turns to the side and angles a foot in his path. She's ready to catch his head when he trips, to slam it into the ancient tiled floor. Once, twice, and she screams as his nose cracks on the third time. Pearl crawls along the floor, gasping, and throws her body over his to stop him from fighting back or getting up. The urge to carry on, to slam his head down over and over again, is magnetic. Delphine's blood is fire. Her hands are powerful.

She bashes his head once more, and he stops struggling, a pool of blood spreading beneath him.

He's unconscious.

She could take his life — it would be so easy — or she could run with Pearl's.

'We've got to get out of here,' Pearl says.

Delphine falters and goes to pick up his sword. 'Not without the plans.'

If they lose them now and let the men discover them, her plot will truly be over. She's not ready to give up. Not yet.

'Forget them,' Pearl demands as she climbs out of the bath.

Pearl reaches down and grips Delphine tightly as she hoists her up. Their eyes meet in an unspoken apology, which is broken by a heart-wrenching keen.

Jules.

They turn to see six smugglers standing around the statue of Suerva. They are frozen in place, stolen artwork dropped at their feet.

Five Delphine recognises, but only three she knows well. Colin, lying motionless on the floor; Bela, mouth agape, her chest heaving, her limbs trembling; and Jules, on his knees.

The wail that leaves Jules almost breaks her. The pain in those lungs stands every one of her hairs on end. It's all her fault. What has she done?

'Retreat!' Pearl yells, breaking Delphine's paralysis. 'Retreat!'

'Get him out of here,' Delphine hears Bela yell. Two smugglers drag Jules away from Colin, leaving the precious artwork on the bloody tiles. Bela runs forward, black hair streaming behind her like a Valkyrie, drawing a dagger from beneath her skirt as she goes straight for one of the intruders, whose swords are crossed with another smuggler, Xia. Bela jumps him from behind and snatches back his hair to pull her dagger along his throat. The blood comes out in a violent spurt all over Xia's dress.

'I've got to help the others,' Pearl says.

'No,' Delphine says. 'You've no weapon. You've got to get out.'

Reluctantly, Pearl nods. Before she turns and flees, she pulls Delphine into one last hug. Then she turns on her heels and runs through the fifth door – Delphine does not know where that leads. Meanwhile, Bela and Xia have also disappeared.

The plans are in Delphine's eyeline through the meeting room's open door, still lying on the table. She has a sword, and with Pearl out of the way, she has nothing left to lose. She can't undo the damage she's done, but she will hide the evidence against the survivors. Or die trying.

Two intruders and Colin lie dead or unconscious on the floor. Besides them, Delphine is now alone in the main chamber. Listening to the clash of metal and grunts in the other chambers, most of the remaining invaders seem to have assembled near the furnace, several chambers away.

But closer than that, there's a sudden bang – an explosion that seems to rattle the foundations of the tunnels. As Delphine skids across the tiles away from the noise, five smugglers, including Bela, dash into the main chamber via the fifth door, but only one intruder makes it out behind them before they slam the door shut, trapping the others inside.

Pearl and Jules are not among them. Delphine prays that means they've made it out safely.

A ruddy-complexioned woman with chestnut hair stabs the man with a ruby-hilted knife. It's only a matter of time until the others break out. But with three intruders dead, they now have the advantage in number.

Delphine runs into the meeting room, grabs the plans, stuffs them into her pocket, and runs back into the main chamber. If they can barricade the third door, they might be able to escape via another. But then she hears a cough near her feet. Colin shudders back to consciousness.

'Bela!' Delphine shouts, dropping her sword. 'Help me move him!' Bela breaks away from the door and runs to Delphine and the miner.

The other smugglers push harder to keep the invaders at bay. Delphine's thighs burn and her shoulders strain as they heave Colin up, writhing in pain and spluttering blood over the mosaic. With one arm holding Colin, Delphine scoops up his gun with the other.

'This way!' commands Bela, hoisting Colin towards the fifth door.

'Where does it lead?' Delphine asks.

'To the storehouse,' pants Bela. 'There's a grate in there that connects to Leaden Hall Street.'

They are just inside the door when the intruders burst into the main chamber.

'Christ,' Bela exclaims, echoing Delphine's thoughts. 'We won't make it.'

'We will. Keep going. The others will fight them off.' A part of Delphine knows this may not be true, but to survive, she has to believe it. She has already lived through so much; Delphine will not give up. Not on Colin and Bela, not on Pearl, not on Jules, not on the plans or herself. Together, they drag Colin back down the tunnel towards the grate where the other smugglers have escaped. Colin is drifting in and out of consciousness again, and even with two of them carrying him, he weighs them down like an anchor.

Bela points to the grate, and they are almost there when they hear footsteps closing in.

'Keep 'er alive,' one of them shouts. The man's words echo in the tunnel. 'He says to keep the darkest bitch alive.'

The Crown wants a ringleader. They want her.

The footsteps tread louder and closer, surfacing behind them in moments. Two intruders: the pig-eyed one, pointing a bayonet, and another wielding a bloody sword. With no other choice, Delphine and Bela drop Colin to the floor and drag him towards the grate.

Closer, closer, closer still.

'Stop her!' one of the men yells as they reach the exit.

Bela jumps down the hatch to heave Colin through. When Delphine peers inside, Pearl is there, waiting in the darkness.

Pearl reaches out a sweat-slicked hand. Delphine reaches for hers, too.

But she is pulled back by another.

Her head wrap was lost in the commotion, leaving her bun exposed. Her scalp burns as the intruder yanks on her hair. The other has her arm in his grip.

She screams.

She screams as they drag her back, and she kicks and thrashes against them.

She manages to kick the grate shut; Pearl's grey eyes and golden hair disappear into the darkness. At least they have escaped. At least Colin is alive. At least Pearl is safe.

Pig Eyes lifts his bayonet over his head and strikes her with the blunt end. Delphine flails to free herself, frantic, aimless and useless. Pig Eyes laughs and hits her again. Delphine's time has run out, and the world swallows her, dark and whole.

Chapter Thirty-Four

Weak minds exaggerate too much the wrong done to the Africans.
—BARON DE MONTESQUIEU

The prison smells like death and damp, and Delphine is in chains. There are no windows. She can see no other cells or prisoners. No way out except the way she was dragged in – through a black, metal door, which is now locked.

Her neck is fastened into a vice with spikes which burrow into her flesh every time she turns her face. The pain twists her stomach. Her chains are so short she cannot walk and so low down on the wall they force her to kneel. The damp-ridden stone miry on her skin.

There has been silence since they locked her in. Was it a few hours ago, or had it been a day? Longer?

All she knows is there has been no more violence. Nor food. Nor water.

What's left are her failures, taunting her in her mind, all pointed fingers and snarling faces. She'd curl up and hide from them if she could, but a drooping head is her only option. Bowed in deference to the Crown and to the inevitability of Empire, whose roots are too deep, too corrupted to change.

'Get up,' Pig Eyes grunts after heaving the cell door open. The iron screeches against the stone. 'Up,' he demands again.

'I can't,' she whispers as the numbness returns to her knees. The chains don't allow her to stand.

With a furious groan, he strides over and yanks Delphine up by her hair. The sudden movement forces the spikes to stab into her neck. She yelps.

'I can't! The chain!'

Pig Eyes stifles a laugh, and he mutters a forgetful *oh* before releasing her from the wall.

On her initial attempt to rise, Delphine collapses to the ground. She cannot feel the lower half of her body. It's been trapped beneath her since she arrived.

It happens a second time. A third. Pig Eyes only watches. His beady black dots wrinkle in amusement.

Yesterday, she may have had the will to spit at him. Today, she murmurs for help.

He all but drags her out of the cell. At first, her feet have forgotten their purpose. As they move down the corridor, they begin to work again and eventually, she walks weakly on her own.

The Tower of London is not how she pictured it.

She imagined endless narrow corridors. Oppressive darkness.

Screams from every cell.

Where they walk is as vast and empty as a warehouse, and light flows between the roof beams from angled windows high above. There are more iron doors, but no screams. Only the sounds of workers outside and below. The Tower is next to one of the busiest dockyards in the city.

How jarring to hear the world carry on outside as she walks towards her probable death.

'*Kontiné lèspiwasyon,*' She mutters. *Keep breathing.* For as long as she can.

'What did you say?' Pig Eyes scowls at her.

'I wasn't talking to you,' Delphine croaks, but immediately regrets talking back. Her voice is coarse like sandpaper, a thick fuzz over her tongue. She is parched with thirst.

Pig Eyes' blotchy face drains ivory. 'I'll kill you if you've given me any curse.'

She'd meant she was talking to herself. Why are white men obsessed with dark magic? Does he not think she'd have done more than curse him by now if she possessed supernatural powers?

His superstition cheers her a little, though.

'Colder all of a sudden, ain't it?' she smirks. Let him think she's a witch.

'Shut up,' he says, dragging her forward. He leads her down the stairs to another door, and there, they stop walking. The hubbub outside the building grows louder, but she still cannot see out of the window.

With another grunt, Pig Eyes struggles to remove a key chain from his belt. He flicks through the keys until he finds the one that bursts open the spiked collar around her neck.

She gasps in relief, and he leads her through the door.

Warmth hits her as she enters the room. There's a roaring fire at its hearth that warms every single stone. The window is covered by a cloth sack, casting the whole space in an umber light.

Pig Eyes pushes her towards a long wooden table with two leather binds at one end and rope at the other. A basin of water sits upon it. She wants to struggle against him, but she's too weak and too desperate to drink the contents of the bowl.

He forces her onto a chair in front of the bowl and makes a show of his sword's hilt as he clamps her feet into chains.

'Well, wash then,' Pig Eyes answers her unspoken question. 'He says he wants you clean.'

'Who?' she asks. Guy Fawkes was interrogated by the King himself. Tortured in the Tower for three months. The vice they've used on her already, but she read of manacles, thumb screws and the rack. She should have always seen the 'State Histories' for what they really are: not a guidebook but a warning.

How long before she succumbs to the pain? Or will she make it all the way to the stake?

'You'll see soon enough.' Pig Eyes leers at her from the door frame, then slams it shut behind him.

She throws her head into the water, taking in great gulps. It's hot and scalds her throat, but the pain doesn't matter. Even her stomach gurgles in thanks. Almost half the bowl is gone when her thirst is quenched.

A square cloth lies beneath the bowl, and Delphine submerges it in the water until it doubles in size before cleaning her face. She could almost cry as the dirt falls away. It's a difficult choice where to clean next. Her neck with its wounds from the vice, her bruised legs, her aching arms? In the end, she works from top to bottom, every smudge of dirt removed bringing her back to herself.

As she washes, it gives Delphine time to get used to her new surroundings. She wiggles her feet in the chains, but she's cuffed tight.

Other than the table, fire and window there's also a silver trolley on the other side of the room. Long metal objects hang from the walls, the type of items a blacksmith might work with. There are no positives to be gained dwelling on how her torturer may use them, so she quickly averts her gaze.

The door opens again, and Pig Eyes steps inside.

This time, he's joined by a man with a sea-beaten face and a grey beard. The man who kept Vincent imprisoned on his ship. Who lifted her onto the cart after she was torn from her family.

Captain Grey.

The warmth fades from her body.

After torture, she'd expected death. But transportation would be far worse. And that means…

Pig Eyes sneers at her. 'I told you, you'd not wait long.'

A shout builds inside her, but it dies in her throat upon hearing the *tap, tap, tap* of a familiar cane.

Lord Harvey taunts her as he enters. '*Remember, remember, the fifth of November; the gunpowder, treason and plot. I know of no reason why the gunpowder treason should ever be forgot.*'

Nick didn't tell the King. He told his uncle.

Did he think it would be better for her this way? Or simply not care that it'd be far worse?

With a vicious grin, Lord Harvey says, 'I'd never taken you for a revolutionary.'

She hisses, 'But I've always taken you for a murderer.'

His cane comes to a deadly stop.

'Is that so?' Lord Harvey says, folding his hands over the silver hilt. 'And how many died because of your actions at the riot? Ten? Twenty?'

Thirteen, Delphine thinks. Thirteen people whose names she will never forget. Splitting Vincent's small inheritance amongst their families was nowhere near enough.

'It was not a riot.'

'Yet they died anyway. I wonder how many of your sewer-rat friends were exterminated in the raid, too.'

Delphine flinches. Not knowing how many of the smugglers she sent to their deaths, not knowing how heavy her guilt weighs, is more than she can bear.

Edging closer, Harvey says, 'I must admit when I learned of your plans I was surprised – plotting to blow up Parliament! At first, I considered forcing you to confess before turning you over to the King. But then everyone would know I'd had two defective Negroes in my household. Our legacy wouldn't withstand the shame.'

Though Delphine knows better than to antagonise him, she has nothing left to lose. If she stays silent, panic will consume her. If she loses her voice now, it may be for the last time. 'So your ego is bigger than your civic duty?'

'Quiet,' Pig Eyes barks, punching her in the stomach. Delphine yelps, swallowing the blow.

'It's funny,' Harvey says, with no hint of humour in his cold, grey eyes. 'The difference I have surmised between Blacks and dogs, is that while both require taming, canines at least are loyal to their masters. Failing that, loyal to other dogs.'

The lord lunges, extending his hand like a pincer as he tries to grip her cheeks.

Instinctively, Delphine bites down.

'Arrgh!' he yells, ripping his hand away. 'Beast.'

No, not a beast, she thinks, *a monster. I am what you made me.*

'Tell me,' he says, recovering quickly. 'Do you know what a cabinet of curiosities is?'

She remembers the term. Nick told her it as they searched for Vincent's contract at 20 St James's Square. It feels like a lifetime ago.

'Of course you do,' he continues. 'You will recall that my nephew stole from my father's. His was an unordered and dull collection – the conch shells, marsupial taxidermy and whatever odd trinkets he could find on his drunken travels around the continent. A waste of an exhibition, I thought. Completely meaningless.'

'Like this story,' Delphine spits.

Pig Eyes raises his hand again but Delphine doesn't flinch, only lifts her chin to meet his gaze and whispers, '*Kontiné lèspiwasyon.*'

And he freezes.

Lord Harvey gives a mirthless laugh. 'Let us see for how long.'

Delphine's blood chills, too. Her mother's language was never meant for him.

'Hanley,' Lord Harvey says, 'fetch the pear.'

Pig Eyes, or Hanley as he seems to be named, rushes over to the trolley.

'I threw most of my father's belongings out after he died, but then I remembered this.'

He snaps his fingers, and Pig Eyes hands him a metal object shaped like a pear.

But Lord Harvey doesn't mean to feed her.

Holding the thing in front of her face, he twists it in all directions before tilting it so Delphine sees the metal dial at the top. He turns it once, twice, three times. The pear opens up, expanding like a flower. Delphine's fear grows with it.

'Grey,' Harvey commands, 'hold her still.'

She tries and fails to break free from her restraints and bites her lip to stop it from quivering. With dirt-crusted fingers, Captain Grey grips Delphine's head. It takes a few tries, but Pig Eyes manages to pry open her jaw, and Lord Harvey shoves the pear into Delphine's mouth.

No, no, no.

She tries to spit it out but it slides around, tasting of dust and iron.

'My father was a weak man. Collecting useless keepsakes while pissing away our wealth and influence. He despaired at how grotesque this pear was, so he stored it away with other items he deemed defects of humanity. It was he who was the defect — the reason I sought the St Lucia plantation, the reason I had to rebuild our name. Only there, I discovered more of humanity's defects.'

No, she tries to yell again, but all that comes out is an unintelligible mumble and saliva.

'Quiet!' he commands, fixing his hand over the dial. 'If you don't stay quiet, I'll have to open it.' He turns the dial just a little and the edges of her mouth stretch. *Oh, God.*

'Better.' He crosses his arms over his chest. 'Before you interrupted, we were discussing dogs and slaves.'

Lord Harvey turns to Captain Grey. 'In your opinion, Captain, which is the superior creature?'

Grey says nothing, still standing behind Delphine.

Lord Harvey frowns.

Hanley chips in, 'Dogs, my lord.'

Lord Harvey nods thoughtfully. 'Dogs indeed.' He runs a knuckle down Delphine's cheek and her stomach turns. 'Do you know how much it cost for the Black bawd to sell you?'

Black bawd? It takes a heartbeat for Delphine to understand Lord Harvey's meaning, then her mind erupts into a barrage of questions. Marion? How does he know Marion? Delphine cries out from the pain of her betrayal. She hadn't known it was possible for her heart to break again, into this many pieces.

The lord steps away from the table to get a better look at her reaction. He pouts and says with mock affection, 'I suppose I shouldn't be surprised. Your kind have been selling each other since time began.'

Delphine blamed Nick.

Wished curses and plagues upon him.

But Nick isn't the reason she is here. It's Marion.

The bawd had told her if things weren't going to plan, she would save her own neck. Delphine accepted that risk. Maybe Marion's suspicions were raised the last time Delphine visited the bawdy house. The *why* Delphine understands, but not the *how*.

'For weeks, she has been selling your secrets. During the trial I discovered she ran the establishment where Vincent was captured, and since then, she has been sending me updates on your whereabouts. That you'd fallen in with a crowd of smugglers and kept up the pretence of an assistant role with Nicholas. Idiot boy. Did he know what you were up to? Or was he too stupid to see what you'd been planning right under his nose? Watching his fortune run dry shall bring me great pleasure. And so will this.' As if already prepared for this next act of humiliation, Hanley holds up the parliamentary escape plans. He must have seized them from her pocket.

A cry escapes from Delphine, muffled by metal.

Snatching the plans, Lord Harvey throws the papers on the fire, and the moment they catch it feels as if he is searing her soul. As the flames turn the parchment from cream, to brown, to black, sobs overwhelm her. It is everything, and nothing. All she'd hoped for was burning away.

As the lord watches the fire, the captain bends down to her ear. 'Just stay quiet,' Grey whispers.

Just as he said when she was eleven, and being stolen away from her family.

When the plans have turned to ash, Lord Harvey bids Hanley bring over his carving set. With a satisfied huff, the beady-eyed man trundles to the trolley, returning with a box.

Lord Harvey takes it and presents the simple wooden container to Delphine as if he were a jeweller about to showcase his wares. 'Oh, this is better than informing the King. He would have simply had you burned.' He lays it down on the table and flicks open the latch to reveal a multitude of silver instruments. All polished to a shine against black velvet. 'That would have been too easy. And far less than you deserve.'

He takes his time to select an instrument before settling on a scalpel with roses carved on the handle.

She calls out, but the words cannot escape.

'Don't look so worried, Delphine, we'll start small. The best thing for you would be to cut out your tongue.' He taps the pear and grins as she writhes. Then whispers, 'But not yet. There are still many days until the State Opening. We won't have all the fun now.' He holds the blade beneath her eye, then her ear, cheek, and chin. As if selecting where to cut.

Delphine holds her body corpse-still. Waits.

And waits.

To her surprise, Lord Harvey steps away. 'There is one thing I have been waiting to try. You might remember my mentioning it before. An enthralling little punishment from Jamaica.'

He reaches into the box again and pulls out, of all things, a lime. Lord Harvey slices it in two on the table. 'You won't believe how much pain the juice can inflict when squeezed over fresh cuts.'

One last time, she struggles in her restraints, but she is too bruised, too debilitated to have any chance of escaping.

'How does it feel? To know that your life has been utterly inconsequential? That your aspirations will never be anything more than fantasy? There was no way you were ever going to win. To take on the Empire, it first needs to acknowledge you exist. You don't. You are dust. Beyond notice. Beyond care.'

Her mind is starting to shut down to protect her from the inevitable pain to come. She clenches her eyes shut and wills her consciousness to float away, to not be present for what comes next.

'But first, we have something even more special to give you. Hanley, bring the chamber pot.'

Grey whimpers but forms no words. He knows what this man is capable of.

Lord Harvey's voice descends to a low growl. 'It's time to give the beast her dose.'

Chapter Thirty-Five

> A slave named Derby catched eating canes. Had him well flogged and [lime] pickled, then made Hector shit in his mouth.
>
> —DIARY OF THOMAS THISTLEWOOD

The torture is an endless cycle. Time passes, though she doesn't know how many days. Only that they force her to drink, shove food down her throat and pour alcohol on her wounds to keep her alive.

With her power and dignity now stripped away, Delphine wishes they wouldn't.

Her whole life, she has escaped death, dodging its skeletal hand as it snatches away the people she loves.

There have been days when the pain has been so great, when her emotions were so strong they threatened to overwhelm her. Dark moments where she almost succumbed and invited her end in. But she has always been more robust than that. Until now.

She knew the risks of her plot.

She listened when Marion, Charity and Nick warned she would wind up being executed. She heard Colin when he said the explosion might destroy her. She would have been ready for it all, if it meant she had achieved something.

But all she has done is ruin the lives of those around her.

Vincent died for nothing. Nick and Pearl offered her their support and friendship, and she pushed them away. All because she was unable to move on. She let grief and anger harden her beyond recognition, withering her heart away to a blackened, broken stone.

So when the door creaks open today, Delphine is sure that she deserves death. Welcomes it. There is no reason left for her to live.

'Only me,' Captain Grey says as he re-enters her prison. She's gathered now that this is not the Tower of London — that she is not under arrest, but kidnapped — but there's still no escaping these walls. Delphine doesn't look at him, only stares blankly at the ceiling above. His pretence at benevolence sickens her.

'You going to eat this time? Or...' His voice trails off.

His footsteps cross the room towards the silver trolley. There's the clang of ceramic dropping on metal. The sour-meat smell of bone broth. As if she could swallow anything as she rots in a room spattered with her blood.

Grey sighs. 'Come on. Let's get you in the chair.' Delphine doesn't resist.

He puts one arm around her waist and another beneath her knees. Two places she has yet to be cut. Still, as he lifts her from the table to place her in the chair, the wounds on her arms press against his torso. She winces, exhaling a pained hiss.

To allow her to eat, he secures a strap around her shoulders instead of her wrists, with a padlock to which only her captors have the key. Even if she had the strength for an escape attempt, she would find herself trapped. The captain bends down and chains her feet.

'It'll be over soon,' he says.

Good, she thinks.

Grey retrieves a jug of water from the trolley, as well as the bowl of soup and a wooden spoon, and sets them in front of Delphine. 'Every drop.' he insists. 'I'm going for a leak. By the time I'm back you best have had both. Okay, Trouble?'

It's the first time he's called her that since she was kidnapped. It makes her despise him even more, but at least he is leaving her in peace. When Pig Eyes brings the food, he glares at her impatiently. He'll give her a few moments to feed herself before he pinches her nose and forces her to open her mouth so he can shove the soup in.

Delphine eyes the oily broth. On top of today's concoction, they've thrown bits of torn-up bread. The sight makes her gag.

After watching Delphine a few seconds longer, Grey turns from the table with a huff.

'Every drop,' he repeats with a peculiar emphasis, then makes his way to the door and scratches his back. A piece of paper floats out from beneath his jacket. He doesn't notice, nor does he turn to look at Delphine before leaving the room. She won't say a word about it – whatever it is, he'll find it when he's back.

Grey's footsteps recede, and her world returns to silence.

Warmth steams from the soup, but Delphine doesn't touch it. Her stomach grumbles, but she has no desire to eat. Her mouth is dry, but she doesn't drink.

Minutes pass.

She hears nothing.

Daylight fades from behind the sack-covered window – still, nothing.

Captain Grey has still not returned. Delphine's soup is cold.

Suspicion climbs up from her growling belly. With a slight shift in her shoulders, the strap loosens barely a finger's breadth. Her mind questions, but she does not allow it to hope. Raising a cautious hand, she lightly tugs at the leather. The strap falls slack at her side. Delphine collapses forward in her seat.

Can this be happening?

Are they playing a cruel trick?

Or has she gone mad from the torture?

The aching pain of her limbs tells her it's the first.

She flicks open the lock on the chains of one foot and then the other. Delphine braces herself, stands, and then spills her guts all over the floor, bile and fear leaving her. When she rises again her head spins, and her throat and tongue are coated in a bitter taste.

So she grabs the soup.

It's a struggle, but she gulps it down. Every drop reminds her that she is alive.

Kontiné lèspiwasyon. The promise she made to herself and assumed she'd break soon.

And then she remembers the paper the captain dropped on his way out — *every drop.*

Stumbling before she finds her feet, Delphine painfully inches across the room. She scoops up the paper from the stone. It's an envelope addressed to her — sealed shut. She recognises the handwriting instantly. It is slanted and round and full. Each letter is drawn with the care of a person who knows how rare a gift it is in this world to be able to write.

It's Vincent's. The letter he wrote for her, but could never give.

It looks like it's been opened and resealed at least once.

But how?

How?

It's a question she'll likely never know the answer to, but she hugs her brother's words to her chest anyway. Elation pulses through her. And with it, an utter absence of fear. She is about to hear from her brother again — a wonderful, impossible thing.

But she can't read it now. There's no knowing how long she has to escape. Pig Eyes or Lord Harvey could return at any moment, and she will not get this chance again.

Delphine pulls open the door, and the cuts on her arms tingle.

She forces herself down the corridor and the first flight of stairs. Then her dizziness returns and she stops, pressing her head into the rough bricks until she can move again.

Another flight of stairs.

Then another, revealing that this prison is in fact a warehouse. Crates, boxes, barrels and chests are piled high on the bottom floor. Moonlight seeps in through the enormous arched windows that look straight out onto the Thames docks. And stacked neatly on the floor by the door, she sees another surprise: a folded black jacket and a pair of shoes, waiting to help her cross the winter night to safety.

First, she pulls on the jacket, then each shoe, gritting her teeth through the sharp pain of her soles connecting with the leather. They're too big for her, clearly meant for a man. It takes her a few steps to find balance in them before she heaves open the double doors.

A gust of cold night air hits her face. Stars fill the sky above her. A sight she resigned herself to never seeing again.

The beauty of those silver dots brings her the greatest relief.

To think she had given up.

An unrestrainable smile fills her face when she spots the North Star. Then Delphine heads west. Back towards civilisation. Towards... where?

She cannot return to the bawdy house. She cannot return to the den. She has no idea where Pearl is.

There is nowhere else in the world for her to go. Her plan has been ruined, but if she tries hard enough, one friendship may yet be repaired.

She needs to go and see Nick.

Delphine leaves the warehouse as fast as her injured body can carry her. Her bones tremble with cold, and she turns down an alley, hoping it will lead her to the main road where she can find her bearings. Though her feet keep moving, the alley stretches in front of her and her vision blurs. She loses her balance and has to prop herself against the wall.

'Kontiné lèspiwasyon,' she whispers. She has to survive.

Find somewhere light and safe enough to read Vincent's letter.

It's impossible to tell how long she has been walking when she realises there's not a recognisable landmark in view.

No shadow from St Paul's.

No outline of the Parliament or the Tower, either.

As she continues, a few passers-by stare as she stumbles, but everyone leaves her alone. Even the pickpockets seem to sense she has nothing to rob. Delphine touches her face and peels off a fleck of dried blood that takes some downy hair with it. She could be the wealthiest woman in the world, but looking like this, no one she asks would aid her. Though Delphine is on the brink of hallucination, she's under no illusion: she must clean herself up before finding help.

It could be yards to Cold Bath Street, or it could be miles. Either way, she's certain she can't make it alone.

So she finds the nearest open barrel of water and breaks its frozen skin with her elbow. It sends shivers through her, but she scoops the water with both hands and drinks. She runs her fingers through her matted hair, which comes out in painful, uncombed clumps. Her hands almost turn to ice as she washes her face and the more exposed parts of her body until she no longer sees dark patches in her rippling reflection.

At last, she can think and plan.

The next step is to find a cab. To find a way to Nick's home.

The minutes stretch in front of her, and her knuckles are freezing. There aren't many sedan chairs or coaches that pass her, but the ones that do take one look at her, ragged, limping and wounded, and move on.

All except two men carrying an open-topped sedan with no curtain on the window. She's unsure if pity or the promise to pay double makes them say yes, but regardless of their reason, it is enough. They carry her to Cold Bath Street.

When she arrives on the cusp of unconsciousness, a startled Hetty answers the door. Bile-ish light spills from the hallway across the cobblestones. The front driver explains where they found Delphine, and Hetty covers her mouth with her hands before she rushes back into the house and remerges with a coin purse and another cloak.

Both drivers nod, satisfied, and support Delphine to the stairs. There, Hetty takes over, and Delphine winces as she leads her up each step, but she doesn't say that the housekeeper's fingers are pressing into her cuts. With a hand gripped around Delphine's waist, Hetty waves the drivers away, and when she looks back at Delphine, tears glaze her eyes. 'Poor girl,' she whines. 'Our little D.'

Delphine doesn't speak, only shivers.

They ascend the two flights of stairs, and Hetty yells for Nick in the hallway. He's already waiting by the front door, concern etched into his face. Nick takes her hand and guides her into his drawbrary, where one concerned face becomes two, and Delphine's world goes dark.

Part Three

Knowledge and Revolution

Chapter Thirty-Six

AN OPINION ON THE NEGRO CAUSE
TO THE PRINTER OF THE DERBY MERCURY
If it be true that last month the Negroes of the Virginia plantations have staged a revolt, and that the Abolitionists and Negroes of London are continually expressing their dissatisfaction for their situation both here and in the colonies, then, Mister Printer, should our Parliament not seek to address those dissatisfactions before tensions continue to escalate? I am, at present, against any emancipation of slaves. Still, I am of the opinion that Parliament should start preparing Negrokind for future freedoms, so at least they can make good use of it.
—A FRIEND TO THE ISLANDS

Delphine dreams of the ocean: of roiling storm clouds over black waters; of thick, salty air that crusts on her lips; of wooden ships crossing the Atlantic that splinter apart and are swallowed hungrily by waves.

Delphine dreams of fire: of smoke rising between trees; of emerald forests cloaked in fumes; of a blaze running down a mountain, engulfing an island in flames.

Delphine wakes to dull pain on a soft mattress, and stiff bones heated by a warm bedpan. She also wakes to whispers. She does not open her eyes.

'Nicholas, be quiet,' Pearl shushes, 'You'll wake her.' Pearl? Here with Nick? Maybe Delphine is still dreaming.

'We *should* wake her. It's been almost three days,' he says.

'Look at her. She needs the rest.'

Delphine could let them know she is awake, but once she opens her eyes, she'll have to resume her place in the world. She's not quite ready for that yet, because then she'll have to explain where she was and what Lord Harvey did to her. To not only relive it but then live through, and live after. Those horrors would be hard to reveal to anyone, especially Nick and Pearl.

'What do you think, then?' Pearl asks, still whispering. 'Could it have been the Crown?'

'No. It's all but impossible to escape the Tower. Her arrest would have been printed in the news. I've been following the papers daily.'

'Then who could it have been?'

'Well, if you could *remember* what the raiders looked like or what they were wearing...'

'We've been through this,' Pearl hisses. 'I was more concerned with getting away from them than noting their attire.'

'I'm just saying, I *can* investigate.'

'She doesn't need you to investigate. She needs you to shut up.' Pearl's whisper is more like a very quiet shout.

'*You* shut up.'

Their exchange quickens. 'Nicholas, for goodness' sake.'

'It is for *her* sake! You wouldn't let me call a doctor!'

'Shh! And say what?' Her voice drips with sarcasm. 'Good evening, Dr Pomp. My cousin returned from the dead and led a group of bleeding ruffians to my door, after even more ruffians broke into her underground lair and kidnapped her former love...' She catches herself. 'Her former lovely domestic companion. Now that very companion has appeared again covered in lacerations. Do not report this to anyone, but please help?' Here, Delphine imagines Pearl punctuating her speech with a dramatic eye roll. 'Bela patched her up well enough.'

Bela? Delphine's face twitches, but they don't seem to notice.

'Not as well as a *doctor* would,' Nick retorts. 'Besides, I was thinking more along the lines of: *my assistant went missing; now she's back and injured.*

I needn't have mentioned any of your... your...' He gasps in frustration. 'See? I couldn't explain *your* antics of the past four years if I tried.'

Nick is rarely speechless – Delphine imagines Pearl takes this as a victory.

'Who even are you anyway?' Nick says eventually. 'Certainly not the cousin I used to know. She'd never break into my home. Threaten me! Bring me some shot-up Cornishman who eats through my entire pantry in a day! Actually, no, that's exactly what my old cousin would do.'

Delphine's eyes fly open to see a cream canopy above her. 'Colin survived?'

'You're awake!' Pearl shrieks and launches herself onto Delphine's bed. Delphine winces from the impact as Pearl reaches out to embrace her but then thinks better of it. She smells of cinnamon and home.

Delphine had guessed Pearl was faring well from the sound of her voice. But now Delphine sees her puffy eyelids and the red, raw skin around her eyes. It makes her think again.

'I'm awake.' She sits up slightly and sees that somebody has changed her clothes: she is wearing a clean, cotton nightgown.

Nick crouches down by the bed and takes Delphine's hand. Hers is stiff and swollen; his nails are chewed nubs.

'Did Nick wake you?' Pearl asks, frowning.

He scowls at her then redirects his attention towards the open chamber door. 'Hetty! Hetty! Delphine is awake. Bring up some tea!'

Delphine recalls a memory. 'I think whisky would be more appropriate.'

Nick pushes himself to his feet. 'I'll grab some. Move aside, Pearl.' They are exactly how she remembers them together as adolescents. In constant conflict. One pushing, one pulling. Both are stubborn to a fault.

As soon as Nick leaves, Pearl leans over and whispers, 'Maybe have some water first.'

'Water is a good idea,' Delphine croaks.

Pearl gets off the bed and hurries to pour Delphine a drink from a porcelain jug that matches the bluebells on the bedsheets.

Delphine thinks she'll only manage a sip, but before she's aware, she's gulped down the entire glass. She stifles a small burp and blushes. 'What happened to you all? To Colin?'

'All the intruders were killed or incapacitated, bar the two who took you. We managed to get almost everyone out. You don't know the two who didn't make it.'

Two. Delphine feels her unknowable guilt double in weight. 'Pearl, I—'

'Not now,' Pearl says, her face grim. 'First, you will rest. Then we will talk about them another time.'

Delphine lowers her gaze and nods. There is nothing she can say to Pearl now that will undo or atone for their murders. 'And the rest of you? How bad are the injuries? Where have you all been staying?'

'Jules fished a bullet out of his shoulder blade, and Bela sewed him up. With Colin it was more touch and go, but Bela managed to save him. You don't want to know how.' She grimaces. 'Afterwards, we rode to hide at a client's warehouse with the others. Then a few of us came here to persuade Nicholas to tell us where you'd been taken.'

That must have been the threats Nick was talking about.

'Only it wasn't Nick who sent those men after us,' Delphine says.

'It wasn't,' Pearl agrees. 'Once I realised this, we made amends as best we could, then I had to explain to him why I wasn't dead — you know how *that* goes — and I told him exactly what happened. It took some convincing, but he agreed Colin could come here to recuperate. But… Colin is not fond of *modern convenience*, and Jules was going mad without him. He left not long before you arrived three nights past.'

'Whisky.' Nick reappears in the door frame. He shakes an amber-filled decanter with one hand and three glasses in the other. Clearly, he's forgotten about the existence of trays, but how often does Nick serve anything himself? He nudges the water jug so it balances right on the lip of the bedside table and squishes the decanter and glasses on, too. 'I've asked Hetty to bring you the turtle soup from luncheon.'

Delphine grimaces. 'Anything but soup.'

Pearl smiles. 'Barberry macarons?'

Delphine's stomach grumbles in agreement, but her head says otherwise. Although it's a relief she wants to eat, she doubts she could handle something so sweet so soon. 'Maybe some green beans? Or radishes or cucumber.' She craves something fresh, something that tastes of life.

'Certainly,' Nick says. He takes the glass from Delphine's hand and replaces it with another. When he doesn't immediately let go, Delphine glances up. Worry is etched between his brows. 'What happened?'

Pearl takes a swig of her drink. 'She's just woken up. Give her a moment.'

'Or at least,' Nick pushes on, 'can you tell us who took you?'

There's no easy way to say it. So, she counts six pink and white marbles in a bowl on the bureau opposite the bed, two large swan feather quills, an inkwell and some parchment. She breathes out. If there's no easy way, she may as well say it. Shock them with the truth, then they can struggle, process and move on together. Or at least, that is what Delphine would like to do.

'Marion. Marion told Lord Harvey where to find me.'

'My... uncle?' Nick gasps. His face pales the same shade of white as his shirt. 'Working with the bawd?'

Pearl trembles and chews the side of her cheek. 'My father did this to you?'

A soup tray clatters to the floor. 'I'll kill the bastard,' Hetty says as the expensive turtle soup seeps into the floorboards. She balls her fists in anger. Then her fists shoot to cover her mouth in a little *x*. 'I'm sorry, missuses, Mister Lyons. About my language and the soup.'

'Never mind, Hetty,' Nick says. He's consumed by other thoughts but manages to add, 'Oh. Delphine didn't want soup anyway. Only vegetables.'

Hetty blinks three times in quick succession.

It makes Delphine smile, and she almost forgets the horror of what she's just said.

Hetty's hat bobs up and down as she nods. 'I'm glad you're up and with us, little D. Let me clear this up.' Her words come out shaky but heartfelt.

Once Hetty leaves, Nick spins out into a mania of questions. He paces furiously around the room. 'How did he know where to find you? How did he learn of the plot? Why didn't he inform the King? *He* did this to you? All of it? How did you escape? Thank God you escaped.'

The whisky is beginning to take effect, numbing the edges of Delphine's pain. But his pacing is making her tired.

As if Pearl senses this, she insists, 'Leave her be.' She turns to Delphine. 'Tomorrow, we'll talk if you're well enough. For now, you need more sleep.' She fluffs up the sides of Delphine's pillow and kisses her forehead.

Delphine is asleep before Pearl removes her lips.

When her eyes flutter open next, she remembers Vincent's letter.

Nick is reading a book by her side. The light of the early morning streams in behind him.

'Good morning,' she says.

He closes his book. 'Good morning.'

There are bags under his eyes, and Delphine wonders if he's given up his bedroom for her. Then she looks around again and reasons that this chamber is too well-ordered to be where Nick rests. 'Have you been sitting here all night?'

'No. Pearl did for some of it. I relieved her a few hours ago. Sleep seems to evade me of late. I was quite envious, really – you looked very peaceful.' He clamps his mouth shut. 'Well, no. I mean. Of course, I'm not envious…'

'I know what you mean, Nick. What day is it?'

'About eight in the morning on the thirtieth day in November.'

A frown settles over her face. She has lost a week of her life. 'Can you help me up?'

'Are you sure?' he asks, already on his feet.

'Quite sure.' The majority of the days when she was kidnapped, she was forced to lie flat on her back. Delphine would like to stand. Pulling off the covers, she sees the scabs that have formed over her limbs. Her wounds itch but no longer burn. As she puts her bare feet on the floor, the sensation of cold wood soothes her.

'Does it hurt terribly?' Nick says, taking her other arm.

'Not so much anymore.' She supposes she has had four or so days to start healing.

With a nod, Nick begins leading her aimlessly around the room.

'Where is the letter I arrived with?' she says. She doesn't yet have the energy to explain that it was from Vincent.

It takes Nick a moment to recall what she's talking about. Then he says, 'Ah. It's in the drawbrary. Do you think we can manage to retrieve it together? Or shall I bring it here?'

'Could you get it, please? I want to get ready.'

On the bureau, she spots a folded dress, underskirts, a corset, stays, a cloak, and new boots tucked beneath the chair.

'Ready for what?' His voice rises a little, emotional. 'Surely you can't mean to go out? It's not safe.'

'It's never safe,' Delphine says. 'But I need to. It's high time I visited Vincent's grave.'

It takes a fair amount of persuading before Nick agrees Delphine is well enough to leave the house. She knows that, in reality, she isn't. It'll take a long time for her body, heart and mind to heal from all she's been through. But she insists that going to see Vincent and reading his letter by his graveside will help her to heal. So, after she's washed, dressed and eaten a full breakfast, Nick finally stops arguing and calls the carriage, only on the condition that he will accompany her to the cemetery and bring a revolver along.

Pearl is still asleep when the carriage clops up to Cold Bath Street. A silent twenty minutes pass as they ride.

The sky is a clear azure when they step out of the carriage. They enter St Martin-in-the-Fields cemetery through its gated stone archway and wind along the gravel paths to Vincent's grave. Delphine is not sure she's ready to do this, but she's sure that she's almost ready.

Awe hits her when she sees it. It's the first time she's been here since the funeral, and the tomb is new – erected with the funds donated by signatories of Nick's petition. Nick had told her there was a new headstone, but this... it's the most spectacular resting place she has ever seen.

Nick shifts from foot to foot on the grass. 'You're certain you wish to be alone? It's no trouble, I can stay.'

'I'm certain.' She gives him a sincere smile before double-checking that her scarf is covering the scabs on her chest and neck.

Nick nods. 'I'll visit my mother, then wait at the carriage. Shout the instant anything seems out of sorts. Can you find your way back?'

She tells him she can, and after a moment's hesitation, Nick turns back up the path and disappears behind a crypt.

Alone at Vincent's resting place, Delphine feels a sense of finality settle over her. The tomb is made of yellow-gold stone and stretches higher than the grey cemetery walls. It's decorated like a mausoleum, but where the door would be an intricately carved apple tree rises, the fruits peeking out beneath the leaves.

Two pillars stand on either side of the tree, both engraved with epitaphs.

These words are inscribed on the left:

> VINCENT MOURIÈRE
> Departed this life
> The twenty-second day in October
> Year of our Lord 1770
> Aged Six and Twenty
> A Freed Man
> A Christian Soul
> Beloved brother
> Truest friend

Already, Delphine's lip quivers. She reads the engraving on the right.

> Here rests the body of
> THE FREEDOM FIGHTER
> Some men flee from hardship
> Some men accept their fate
> This fighter is owed this nation's debt
> For freeing England's slaves

This is no grave. It is a monument. The very least Vincent deserves.

'Hello, brother,' Delphine whispers, sitting beneath the columns. With the letter resting on her skirt, she lays a hand on the grass below. 'It's good to see you. I'm sorry it took me so long.'

She speaks to the ground as if he were just behind a wall in the next room.

Every time Delphine remembers that his body is lying cold and breathless beneath her, she swallows a bead of sadness. She tells him everything — how so many people pooled money together for her and this grave. How almost seven thousand people signed a petition demanding justice for his murder. About the vigil and how the protests haven't ceased since. About her plot. About how everything went wrong.

A breeze wraps around her and she imagines it's Vincent. The ghost of his touch brings her to the edge of tears.

'I miss you.' Of all the things she could say, it's the most obvious, the easiest. 'I'm sorry I couldn't protect you. You needed me, and I failed. You spent a lifetime saving me, but I couldn't save your life. I couldn't even save your memory.'

She pushes her head against the stone, and tears out a blade of grass from the ground. The air smells of disturbed earth. Delphine closes her eyes and pictures her brother.

Leaning coolly against a tree in St Lucia, picking sand from between his toes.

Handing her a little bird as they cross the ocean. Grinning as they gorge on lemon bonbons.

These memories are all she has left.

'I've been angry for a long time. I'm still angry. You did everything they asked, and it still wasn't enough. I wanted to bring the Empire to its knees for you. I wanted to force them to feel that same pain that I did. To feel your loss. All I did was make things worse.'

The weight of these last weeks descends on Delphine all at once. The sadness and pain threaten to burst her heart like water from a dam. For the first time, she allows her wall to crumble. She lets the sobs take her, wracking her body and shaking her torso until she crumples into a ball. She wants to reach down, pull Vincent up from where he rests, and beg him for one last shared moment. For one last hug. For one more happy memory. And she wonders what he would make of her now – this blubbering daft fool at his graveside.

While Delphine has been seeking revenge on ghosts, her brother has been here alone.

'But I'm here now. It may have taken me a while, but I'm here. And I'm so, so sorry. Whatever it is you wanted to tell me. I'm here. I'll listen.'

The breeze settles.

Delphine takes Vincent's letter out of her pocket and traces her fingers over his handwriting on the front of the envelope.

For Delphine

Chapter Thirty-Seven

> Make human nature thy study – wherever thou residest – whatever the religion – or the complexion – study their hearts.
>
> —IGNATIUS SANCHO

When Delphine returns to Cold Bath Street, she rushes straight to the drawbrary to re-read the last lines of Vincent's letter.

Above all else, sister, live a life you are proud of.

Do not let them force you into believing you do not deserve more. It is absurd. You do.

To say no is dangerous, but you must always have courage. Our parents had courage.

Do not spend any more of your life feeling ashamed.

Whether we be together or parted across counties or countries or oceans, I will be satisfied with my lot as long you promise me this:

Kontiné lèspiwasyon.

Protect yourself from the storm before it is in front of you.

You are all of my heart, Delphine. I know I don't say it enough. I love you.

Your daft fool of a brother,
Vincent

She reads the letter over and over until the words are etched into her mind like commandments into stone, until she has reshaped her thoughts around them. She hears his brother's voice in them, feels his wisdom in them. And they will help her come to terms with so much more than he knew: not only in her past, but in her future as well.

As she had suspected, he'd written of Pearl's visit to the prison, her confession to joining the smugglers, and her offer to help him. He'd also written things it will take her a long time to reckon with: shocking, heartbreaking things she never knew he'd thought, felt and experienced. Chief among them was why he had been so shaken by Lord Harvey's theft of the little wooden bird.

> *Thank you for bringing my bird back to me. I always thought it had been lost from our luggage when we were first taken to St James's Square. But knowing it was Lord Harvey who stole it has made me see certain memories of that time through new eyes.*
>
> *I'll hasten to my point: I suspect Lord Harvey was hurting my mother. Occasionally, I saw him smiling at her and stopping her to chat on the plantation. The day before Mama left, he noticed me playing with the bird, and he asked where I'd stolen it from. I think I said Mama made it for me, then he stormed away. I saw all this through a child's eyes and, at the time, thought nothing of it. But now, holding my beloved bird again in one hand as I write, I can't help but think the worst.*
>
> *If my suspicions are correct — for we shall never know — although the thought of Mama's pain hurts me deeply and makes me despise our master all the more, it also lightens another burden I have been carrying all my life. For perhaps, I think, that is why she left me — perhaps it was never my fault.*

Before reading this, Delphine had not thought it possible for her to hate Lord Harvey even more. In time, she will consider whether to share Vincent's dark theory with Nick and Pearl. But for now, she will keep Vincent's words as he intended, between brother and sister.

Inside the envelope, there had also been a short and simple note from Captain Grey.

Lord Harvey had me sweep Vincent's cell after he was killed. I kept this back in the hope I might return it to you — I am sorry it was in these circumstances. Please don't tell the boss.

She is wondering if the captain had read Vincent's letter when Pearl enters the drawbrary.

'Where did you disappear to?' Pearl says. She is dressed in her night shift and Nick's long silk banyan, and looks beautiful in the late-morning light. She wipes something from her eyes — either sleep or dried tears, Delphine isn't sure which — and plops herself on the velvet sopha next to her. 'Hetty said you took a carriage.'

'To see Vincent.'

Pearl frowns and tilts her head.

'His grave, I mean. I have not gone mad.'

Relieved, Pearl teases, '*Madder*, you mean. Thank goodness. I was worried.' She gives Delphine's knee a light squeeze — mercifully not the one that's still a patchwork of bruises, 'you seem much better today.'

'I do feel better,' Delphine says, and she means it. Although some of Vincent's words were hard to read, they have already impacted her more than she imagined they could. And with those final words of encouragement and affection, it's as if he has dusted some magical broom through her mind and swept aside the shame-filled thoughts that gather there.

You always make the worst decisions.

She will spend no more of her life undermining herself.

A beast like you has no right to love.

She is a person who is owed more love than she was given.

'I deserve to live a life I am proud of.' She didn't expect to say it out loud. The words taste odd on her tongue. It will take time until it feels like they belong there. Longer still, for the furious current that's flowed in her for so long to adjust to this new peace.

Nick appears in the doorframe, looking mystified. 'Yes. Well, of course you do,' he says.

He walks directly over to the globe between the two sophas where Delphine and Pearl are sitting, and gives it a spin. It's odd to see him not need to weave around clutter. Hetty truly does an excellent job here.

Which is convenient, considering what Delphine is about to ask him.

'It's very tidy in here, Nick,' she says.

'I know,' he chuckles as if he is just as impressed as she is. 'No more floor parchment or mountains of bookish doom.'

'Tidy enough to host a few guests, would you say?'

'If you're up to it. What did you have in mind?' Nick asks.

Delphine folds the letter shut and places it gently in her pocket. 'I'd like everyone to be here tomorrow for breakfast if they can.'

'Everyone?' Pearl asks.

'Jules, Colin and Bela. But promise me that when you speak to them, not another soul will hear that I am here. That any of us will be here.'

Nick nods. 'I promise.'

'Me too,' Pearl agrees.

The cousins exchange a worried glance.

Delphine paces around the drawbrary as they wait for the guests to arrive. 2nd December, nine o'clock, she'd requested. Will they all turn up? Or after everything she's put them through — endangering their lives, bringing death to their comrades, exposing the location of their den — will Colin, Jules and Bela never speak to her again?

She wishes there was something to do in the meantime. Some shelf to dust or table to tidy. This waiting. The dragging *tick... tock...* of Nick's pocket watch is driving her mad.

'What time is it now?' she sighs.

'About thirty seconds after you last asked,' Nick says. He leans his head back on the wall between the windows.

Delphine drums her fingers along the leather spines on the bookshelves, every book in the middle row receiving a few taps, then she starts to make her way back.

'Delphine, I implore you to sit down,' Nick pleads. 'You're setting me on edge.'

'Yes, do sit,' Pearl agrees. 'It's only a few minutes to nine. Don't worry, they'll be here.'

'Fine.' She folds her skirts beneath her to sit, but as soon as she does, her leg starts to bounce up and down so violently that both sopha cushions move with it, including the one Pearl sits on.

Pearl grits her teeth. 'Breathe.' She takes a big breath in and out.

Nick joins in, too. In... and out.

In...

The servant's bell rings, and Hetty's shoes tap down the hallway. 'Oh, thank goodness,' Nick says.

The trio resume holding their breath as they wait to see who has arrived.

'Ah,' says Hetty, 'the man of many stomachs returns.'

'Pleasure seeing you again, Miss,' a deep, Cornish voice replies.

Delphine jumps from her seat, and her bruises yawn in dull protest. 'Woman of the century. You made it!' Colin says as he reaches the drawbrary, throwing out the arm not being held up by a sling. Apparently, for Colin, all is forgiven.

'We all did,' Jules says beside him. His eyes are glassy as he quietly adds to Delphine, 'Thank you for getting him to safety.'

Bela is hanging back in the door frame. She says nothing, only lifts her chin in greeting as the others chatter away. 'Is there anything but coffee?' she asks at last, when Hetty returns with an urn, cups, saucers, and Nick's tin of lemon bonbons.

'Whisky, water or ale?' Nick says.

'Yes.'

'To which?'

'All of them.' She raises an eyebrow as if daring him to refuse her.

After a moment and three blinks from Hetty, Nick says, 'Good for you.'

When everyone is seated, with Hetty safely out of earshot, Bela swirls her cup of ale. 'On with it, then.'

Delphine takes a bonbon and swallows it with her nerves. *Let the sweets be a sign*, she thinks. She's not anxious about what she wants to tell them, but she's worried how they may respond.

'You must be wondering why I asked you all here,' she says.

'Not really,' Jules says.

'Not at all,' Pearl agrees.

'It's fairly obvious,' Nick concurs.

'As I said, on with it,' Bela insists.

'Right.' Delphine mentally cuts out the first part of the speech she'd prepared, aware that Bela has a tendency to storm out of rooms.

'When I asked you all to join me in this plot, I believed I was doing this for my brother. For Vincent. I thought any sacrifice would be worth it if I could avenge his death. If I could make the rest of the world feel my pain.' She breathes in. 'And that was wrong.'

She holds Pearl's gaze for a moment, then Nick's. He looks away.

'I should have realised that doing this won't change anything for my brother. He's gone.' She taps his letter in her pocket. 'But I don't regret what we were trying to do. The plot was the only way we could have changed things. For us, the people we love, and the people we don't know who also deserve better.'

Delphine closes her eyes momentarily and sees the thousands of people at the vigil. The hundreds who have protested outside Parliament since.

'More people in this country are dissatisfied than not. Jules, Nick, you've seen the people outside Parliament grow in number daily. Half the pieces in the newspapers talk about the need for a more liberated and fairer society. But nothing changes. Because the satisfied fear losing what they have, and the dissatisfied fear losing what they have left. No group was willing to take risks. Until we were.'

Delphine rises and crosses the rug in the middle of the drawbrary, to stand on the medallion at its centre. Now for the hard part. To lay her soul bare for everyone in this room, then see if they can accept her.

'The King knows nothing of the plot. The State Opening is still eight days away. I believe that if we are all in favour, it's still possible for us to go forward with it. But before you cast your vote, I want to tell you what happened to me when I was kidnapped and what I have learned since. I want to share my story, to show you why doing this is right for *me*. Then I want each of you to think about your life and decide three things. First: does this Empire do more harm than good?'

She pauses for a moment to let the question sink in.

'Second: if we are successful, will it make the world better than if we do nothing?'

Nick furrows his brows. Colin's smile grows wider.

'And, finally: do *you* believe this is the right thing to do?' Then, she tells them about Lord Harvey. For now, only the parts she can manage. Before she would have buried this experience deep among the thorns of her memories, let the worst shade of shame darken her life. But now she knows that there is no disgrace in showing her pain. That these people – this family – will not view her differently because of it.

No one interrupts her as she speaks – they are too sickened.

She has never seen Nick look so ashamed.

Then she tells them about Marion.

Bela's jaw tightens as she hears of the betrayal.

'The bawd has stepped far out of line,' Jules says. 'She's meant to sell us secrets. Not tell ours.'

'That's the last fucking coconut she's bought from me,' Colin says.

'I'll give her a coconut, all right,' Bela seethes. 'A coconut to the back of the head. She'll not get away with this.'

Marion did say she would only look out for herself, and Delphine cannot blame her. How could Delphine have expected anything else?

But in Bela, Delphine sees there is a new fire lit. She sees the makings of a rebellion.

Delphine takes a deep breath and looks at her friends – so many strands of society gathered in one place. These are the people who will decide what happens on the tenth of December. She can only go through with it if all of them agree.

'Now you have all the information, I beg you to consider, one last time, whether or not we should do this,' she says. 'I'm no longer afraid of what might happen to me if we are caught. I have been through too much to fear the Crown's punishment. But I do not expect the same of you. That is why, if you say yes to this, it cannot be for my sake. You cannot do it for me, or for Vincent. You cannot do it for revenge or to atone for past sins. The only reason to say yes is because you believe it's the right thing to do. Doing this would not be the end of a battle, but the beginning of a long war to improve things.'

After all that, Delphine is exhausted. But the exertion lacks the heaviness that has shadowed her since Vincent's death. She sits down on the sopha next to Bela and crosses her legs. She has said her piece. It's time for the others to decide.

It's Jules who speaks first. He walks to the spot on the rug where Delphine was standing, tugs on his ruffle collar and says, 'I have crossed a continent and seen much of the struggle you have seen. I was never doing this *for* you, but I have always been with you, Delphine. My thoughts have not changed. Vincent's struggle was my own. It is the struggle of my brothers and my sisters and yours. I was hesitant at first, but whether it was you or the next man asking, my answer would always have been yes.'

Delphine raises a hand to her heart. 'Thank you, Jules.'

He sits on the sopha's arm, and Pearl rises next.

'I don't know what the future will bring, but I know great injustice exists in this world. I have experienced some of it. I have had to hide from who I am or run away.' She half-smiles at Delphine. 'There is a struggle in my soul over what is good and right, but every time I think of this, no matter how loud a voice in my mind says *no*, I cannot help but feel that despite everything, it is both. My answer is yes.'

Colin remains seated but leans forward. He cups a hand beneath his chin and looks down at Delphine. 'I suppose wanting to see the explosion ain't reason enough?'

'No, Colin, afraid not.'

The Cornishman sighs. 'The night I decided I didn't want to be a miner no more was the night I pulled another kid's body from out the shafts. No one cares what happens to poor children. No one cares so long as the powers that be get their coal and coin. It's not right.' He thumbs the place where the lead struck him. 'The knaves who attacked us didn't find our powder. I said it'd take a week to get everything in place. Eight days is what we've got. It's a bit of a push, but I'll do it. I'm in.'

Three yeses. But Delphine is not getting her hopes up.

Bela shifts away from Delphine. She chews her cheek and scowls. 'I'm glad this is not about you anymore, Delphine, because if it were I would say no. You are a hurricane of disruption.'

Delphine can't deny it. She only nods.

Bela holds her gaze a little longer then drains her ale, and picks up her whisky. 'For a long while, I didnae understand where you were coming from. I ken you were angry, but angry people don't make good decisions. I respect what you've said today. And I respect you for having shown us your scars.' She clenches and unclenches her fist around her knee. 'You may have made a wrong turn, but you still saved my family in the end. If it is in my power to help, then I will. Aye, I'm in.'

'Truly?' Before today, Delphine could have sworn Bela would say no and that it would all be over. 'I'd say thank you, but you wouldn't accept it.'

'Try it anyway,' Bela smirks.

'Thank you, Bela.'

'What say you, cousin?' Pearl says quickly, before Bela can change her mind.

The room looks to Nick.

He lifts himself from the sopha and walks over to his globe, which stands between Jules and Colin's seats. He runs a hand through his hair. 'There's a quotation from Voltaire that comes to mind. He says, *faith consists in believing when it is beyond the power of reason to believe.* This year has certainly been a test of *my* faith.' He spins the globe beside him. 'I've been exposed to a way of viewing the world that has been at such odds with my own, and it has been difficult to make peace with that. I've learned now that sometimes, best intentions are not enough to help those who need it.'

Hope bubbles up in Delphine's chest.

'Voltaire also says that *every man is guilty of all the good he did not do.* You asked me to look into my heart, Delphine, and I have. It tells me that if I did not do this, I would be one of the guiltiest men alive.'

Silence falls as their choice settles over each of them. There's no great embrace, no clapping each other on the back and cheering. They have decided, all of them, that they are going to end an Empire.

Colin slaps his thighs and stands. 'If that's everything, I best be getting on. Lots to do.' He shares a smile with Jules, and the pair rise, followed by Bela.

There's a sombre air as Pearl leads them out. Delphine gets up to follow them but Nick touches her arm and says, 'Would you mind staying a moment longer?'

Chapter Thirty-Eight

The work of insurrection will go on.
—DENMARK VESEY

As soon as the others have left, doubt prickles at the base of Delphine's neck. Their decision was unanimous, but she knows that doesn't make it any less heinous. Scratching the doubt away, she wonders if the others are doing the same.

Nick looks surprisingly confident.

He hands her another cup of coffee and Delphine takes a lukewarm sip.

Another sip later, Nick says, 'Hewannora.'

Delphine wonders if he's about to quote another philosopher. 'Pardon?'

'Hewannora.' He says the word slowly. 'It's the name the Caribs gave St Lucia before it was called that.'

Hewannora. It's as though some stolen knowledge has been returned to her. She echoes the name aloud – a word that means both prison and home to her.

'When did you change your mind?' she asks.

'If you will permit me one more quotation,' he says, eyeing up the drawbrary shelves in search of something. 'This one, I promise, is a little different.'

'Go on.'

'Are you familiar with Descartes?'

Delphine shrugs.

Nick puts his coffee cup on the shelf without its saucer, setting Delphine's teeth on edge, and pulls out a very thin book. It's bound by a spiral wire instead of the usual leather. It's Nick's notebook. 'A brilliant philosopher, of course, but he is most famous for one phrase: *Cogito, ergo sum*. Or in his native French, *je pense, donc je suis*.'

Delphine translates. 'I think, therefore I am.' She doesn't quite understand his meaning.

'It means, yes, I must exist because I am able to think. But existence is a little more than that. I prefer my own slightly amended version.' He holds up the notebook and flicks through the pages, covered in a spidery scrawl. The pride on his face when he finds what he's looking for makes Delphine grin.

'I prefer, *je pense, donc je change*.'

Her grin widens. 'I think, therefore I change.'

'That is why I'll help you,' he says in a tone that conveys just how sure he is of the matter. 'But your plan is flawed. I've been thinking a lot about it and think I have a way to help.' He sits back down on the chair beside hers. 'The greatest problem is how we ensure the success of your plan...' He hesitates a moment. '*After* the explosion.'

Delphine and the gang have already begun to plan for this — her blackberry leaf concoction, some traffic mishaps, and a few discreet bribes will ensure the survival of the men who might help rebuild a fairer government. She has plenty of ideas for the future, but she waits to hear him out.

'It won't do to simply stop all radical MPs from attending the State Opening. That will look too suspicious and might weaken their influence in reshaping the government after the explosion. Instead, we'll need to make it look like I was there. When they find me among the rubble, we'll need to convince the world that it's a miracle I survived. Then, once all fires have been put out, I'll give a speech. Something emphatic, something epic. I'll say that it'll be a new day for Parliament, for the Empire. That from this tragedy we'll rebuild from the ashes and so on.'

Delphine's unsure if he's speaking to her now or practising the Prime Minister's speech he's always longed to give. That's not the plan she had in mind, but making a survivor of Nick might just win him the political backing he'll need to push their agenda.

'That might work. And here's what I think we should do after that...'

Nick's head lifts – this time, he's ready to listen.

'What if we create a temporary power structure?' she says. 'What if, where there is no automatic heir to a seat, the wives and sisters fill in while Westminster is being rebuilt? You'd argue it is a matter of urgency, that the women will be performing an exceptional duty to maintain continuity for the country. You know as well as I do that many women influence from behind closed doors. What if we open them?'

'Brilliant!' Nick agrees. He nods his head vigorously.

Encouraged, Delphine continues. 'And regarding emancipation. What if Jules returns to Parliament with the protestors after the explosion, to lead the clean-up effort? What if we become so visible that, were any of the Kings' Friends to survive, they daren't push their plans forward to overturn Vincent's ruling.'

Nick stands and paces the room. He smiles at his bookshelves as if they have prepared him for this moment. 'Yes. And when the new Commons sit for the first time, I'll make a big show of the protesters' services. How invaluable those communities are to the nation, how all our citizens – including the Negro – should be raised up in respect. I can also press the issue with the Foreign Trade Committee.'

Delphine brightens. 'Foreign Trade Committee? Does this mean you won the place?'

'Of course!' Nick beams. 'That pimple-nosed Lang boy was never going to beat me to it, was he?'

Delphine feels a glow of pride in her friend. Nick won this victory on his own merit – which means more than he'll ever know.

'That will be very helpful for our cause,' she says. 'You can use your influence there to reward those who've rebuilt the country, both on English soil and in the colonies. Every trade guild will be granted a voice. Every slave of the Empire will have their freedom restored.'

'And at last, the Bill of Rights Society can fulfil its purpose! We shall cite Mansfield's ruling as the start.' Nick's enthusiasm subsides. 'What of Mansfield? Is he one of the people you intend to save?'

The concern on Nick's face tugs at Delphine's heart. 'He is. The evening before the Opening, Colin will send a group of smugglers to pile up an apparent traffic accident outside his home in Hampstead. When Colin scoped out his estate he said there is only one exit. They'll make it impossible for him to leave through no fault of his own.'

'Right,' Nick says. 'Well. If that's all there is...' *All there is*, as if they've just decided who to invite for dinner. 'There is one more thing I wanted to say.'

Delphine doesn't like Nick's tone. She braces herself. 'Yes?'

Nick looks out at the scene below the window, at the frost settling on the cobblestones. 'I wanted to say thank you. For... putting up with me.'

'Nick...'

'I know I'm not the easiest man to get along with. I have very strong opinions and they often drive people away.' His lip quirks, and he turns his face away from her. 'When Vincent and I became friends – for arguably, he was my only friend besides my fellow reformers – I cherished it. And then, through Vincent's bravery and yours, one friend became two. But I have not always been a good friend to you, or a deserving one. Though I'm still trying to forgive you for keeping your plot from me, I think I understand why you did so. I shudder when I reflect on the person I was seven months ago. But I'm glad that you put up with me. I'm glad to be improving. To be the person I've become since knowing you.'

Mist coats Delphine's eyes. 'A true optimist, Mister Lyons.'

'I suppose so, yes.' He sniffs and wipes a knuckle under his nose. 'If that's the case, we'd better get back to discussing how to reconstruct the government.'

Chapter Thirty-Nine

> We are all full of weakness and errors; let us mutually pardon each other our follies – it is the first law of nature.
> —M. DE VOLTAIRE

Evening descends over Cold Bath Street and, as they are annotating one of Nick's maps of Westminster in the drawbrary, Pearl gives Delphine a wistful smile. 'Come on,' she says. 'There's something I want to show you on the roof, if you can manage?'

Bundled up in two of Nick's winter coats and a few extra shirts, they hurry out of the apartment and clamber up the stairs. By the third floor, Delphine's thighs burn, and the cuts on her ankles are close to splitting back open, but she walks through the pain. She's intrigued to see what Pearl has planned.

Pearl props open the door at the top of the stairs with a weight, and leads Delphine to the flattest part of the roof.

Stars peek out from behind the clouds over the city. Before the roof's iron railings, Pearl has laid out a wicker box on a thick rug, held down by six flickering hurricane lanterns. The winter chill turns Delphine's breath into fog, but she smiles as she shivers.

'You did all this?'

'I had the idea; Hetty made the wine, of course.' She curls her smallest finger around Delphine's own. Delphine squeezes it, surprised by how easily she and Pearl fit together now.

Once, when Pearl touched her, it felt like dark magic. A force so thrilling, so enchanting, that Delphine hardly cared she was in danger. Now, the power between them feels natural. And it flows both ways.

From the basket, Pearl reveals a hot jug of negus wine and pours some into two crystal goblets. With a flourish, she tops it with a slice of orange and a lump of cracked nutmeg, and they settle on the rug. In the light of the lanterns, Pearl's grey eyes shine like the moon. 'Hetty insisted. She says it'll settle your stomach.'

'God save Hetty,' Delphine says, inhaling the spices. They clink glasses and sip the hot wine. 'What's all this for?'

Pearl shifts closer so their arms are touching. 'I thought a picnic would be nice. But also, and only if you want to...' She reaches into the basket again to pull out two long table candles, a sheet of parchment and a length of charcoal. 'Bela once told me that when you've suffered a loss, this can help. You write down the thing or person you've lost, then you burn the paper. She said it makes it that little bit easier to accept what's happened, and that people often feel better afterwards. I wondered if you'd like to try it?'

Delphine's gaze softens. 'That's a nice idea. Give them here.'

Pearl's cheeks flush with relief, and she squeezes Delphine's hand before handing her the parchment and charcoal. Delphine puts her wine down, and takes a moment to remember. There are so many losses she could write down. The ones closest to her: her parents, Vincent. Those lost at the vigil, in the smugglers' den. Every soul lost in transit between the African and American coasts – one for every two who make it to the farther shore. The lives lost every day to wars and workhouses and empty bellies.

But she doesn't choose any of them, not at first. The first thing Delphine writes on her parchment is *moments*.

'Moments?' Pearl asks.

'Moments,' Delphine says, lifting the parchment to the flame. The ashes float out over the city, each fragment a reminder of every birthday she ever celebrated with Vincent, every long dinner she enjoyed with her parents, the silent togetherness she used to share with Pearl. The moments she has lost because she had been too busy fighting to enjoy them.

She relaxes as the end of the parchment burns, because though she has missed so much, though she can never reclaim those losses, there's less bitterness. As those last fragments disappear, what's left is acceptance and hope. 'For the moments I should have cherished.'

Pearl chews her bottom lip. 'My turn,' she says, taking the parchment and scribbling four letters: *love*. 'For the mistakes I've made. With us.'

The way she's looking into Delphine's eyes, with a quiet and kind sadness — a look that Delphine used to believe was pity — makes her want to look away.

She doesn't.

'Mistakes *we've* made,' Delphine counters.

'We all make mistakes,' Pearl agrees. 'With us, I made the biggest ones. But there were some problems we could never have worked through together, because we'd not solved them alone.'

'That's true. But when we were a couple...' Delphine pauses. It's the first time she's acknowledged out loud that they *were* a couple. 'I did always have my walls up.'

'Those walls kept you safe,' Pearl says. 'They still might need to sometimes—'

'I don't want to live behind a wall anymore,' Delphine interjects. 'I'd got so used to it being here, I forgot I can take it down, or even check if it's safe to look over the top.' Vincent's letter told her to live without shame, but they are only words. It's up to her to figure out how. 'I didn't know us loving each other was wrong until you told me it was a sin. It's like everything I am is the opposite of what I should be. Even though I can never be anything else.' She clears her throat. 'Try as I might.'

'I understand,' Pearl says. 'But Delphine, I didn't fall in love with you hoping you would become someone else. I fell in love with you because of who you are, everything that is you. When we planned to run away together, I wasn't ready to be the partner you needed. Two months ago, I wasn't ready to be the friend you needed, either. But these last weeks with you, seeing the woman you've become. The person I've become...'

Delphine looks to the stars as a well of emotion builds in her. Part of her mind is telling her not to allow the tears to fall. But it's a part she no longer needs.

'I can't change what has happened in our past,' Pearl continues. 'I can't replace what I took from you, but I will forever be sorry that I took it. For saying I loved you without seeing the consequences. For not hearing you when you tried to tell me. For covering up my shame by pushing you away. If you want to, and only if *you* want to, I'd like to try to be better.'

'You're already doing better,' Delphine says. For as long as the journey is that they'll need to go on before Pearl can win back her trust, before they can decide what they want to be to each other in the future, Pearl's already come so far without her — steps that she *had* to take without Delphine. 'I think who we are right now is the culmination of everything we needed to be to survive, but I don't think it's all we *can* be.'

Pearl sniffs. 'I need to learn that the decisions I make for myself impact other people, too.'

'That sounds hard,' Delphine says, wiping away one of Pearl's tears.

'It does, doesn't it?' Pearl agrees.

'And I need to learn that letting you in is a strength. When you ask me what I need, I should tell you.'

'Incredibly difficult.' Pearl laughs, in that husky way that is always inflected with mischief, even as the tears still glisten in her eyes and leans closer.

'I'm sure it will be.' Delphine takes Pearl's free hand. In the other, Pearl is still gripping the *love* piece of parchment. 'But I do vow this.'

'A vow?' Pearl smirks. 'How serious.'

'*Shush*. I *am* being serious.' She grins and shuffles closer to Pearl. 'I vow to trust you,' she says, setting the parchment alight.

'I vow to accept your choices,' Pearl replies, gripping her hand tighter.

Then, in half a heartbeat, Delphine closes the gap between them. Her lips are on Pearl's and she tastes like a memory; like cinnamon and stolen chances and spiced wine. For a moment, there's the same jolt in her stomach she had at sixteen, seventeen, eighteen. But this isn't a kiss of youth, all awkward angles and fumbling fingers. This kiss is urgent, assured, everything.

Delphine's heart swells with longing, with forgiveness.

It will be hard, wherever these feelings may take them. There's much that needs to be said, so much to learn and unlearn and learn again. But as Delphine kisses Pearl as her fingers trace the softness of her cheek, the mole-marked hollow of her collar bone, the full familiarity of her hips, Delphine decides that *this* — whatever this is — it is worth every difficult conversation, and the potential for heartbreak. Because as Delphine kisses Pearl, over and over, until their lips are swollen and their arms are covered in goosebumps, it feels vital, like breath, like connection.

As Delphine kisses Pearl, as the heat ripples from their bodies on this cold December night, as the last remnants of ash circle around them, Delphine chooses to try. Because here on this roof, for the first time in a very, very long time, she is *happy*.

Their love was unlikely, but not impossible. Delphine's favourite odds.

Chapter Forty

Great Preparations have been made by both the Friends of the Opposition and those of the Administration for the Opening of Parliament tomorrow; it is believed that the Popular Questions being debated across the nation will be included in the King's speech: the New Freedoms reported this year by the Press, the nature of English Slavery, the disputes in the Americas and His Majesty's proposed Marriage Act.

—IPSWICH JOURNAL

'Why have we stopped?' Delphine says, pulling Nick's watch from her pocket for the sixteenth time since leaving Cold Bath Street. *Forty-five minutes to go.*

Jules slides the carriage curtain open to pop his head into their compartment. 'More traffic, but it seems to be clearing.'

The carriage pulls off again, the horses blowing out impatient breaths as they resume clopping over the cobblestones. It seems they're as anxious to reach their destination as Delphine is. The traffic is Colin's fault, though, so she can't complain too much. To protect passers-by on the streets outside Westminster from the explosion, after smuggling the last barrel of gunpowder into Parliament, he sneaked into the yeoman's building dressed as a redcoat, and pinched the wooden blockades which now stand around Westminster, diverting carriages and pedestrians away from the blast zone. Still, she hadn't expected fourteen panels of wood to cause such significant delays. It's taken almost an hour to travel two miles.

An equally anxious Nick has spent the journey sitting opposite her, fiddling with his silk handkerchief, tying and untying knots and twisting it tightly around two fingers.

Bela sighs next to him. 'Is he always so...' She gestures vaguely in Nick's direction. 'Wriggly?'

'Always,' Pearl says, straightening her brunette wig. 'He never could sit still.' She leans over and rests a hand on her cousin's bobbing knee. 'Once more with the plan, go on...'

Nick grips the handkerchief, balls it up, then stretches it out as he speaks. 'Once we leave the carriage, Delphine and I enter Westminster through the Privy Garden with the rest of the Members and assistants. The King and his party should arrive a little later, around a quarter past eleven, fifteen minutes before his speech. The Master of Robes will take him to prepare for the ceremony while his brothers position themselves in the hall. We sneak up to my office.'

'No sneaking,' Pearl corrects, as soothingly as she can. 'It's *your* office. You can go there whenever you like.'

'Ha, yes, of course.' Nick forces a laugh and rubs his stomach.

'Is he well?' Bela says, arching an eyebrow at Delphine. 'He didn't...?'

'Nick, you didn't drink any of the port at dinner last night, did you?' Delphine re-fortified the wine with a healthy number of blackberry leaves before Bela served it to the unwitting nineteen MPs dining with Nick at last night's Beef Steak Club. MPs like Edmund Burke and George Savile. It's tradition that the club members toast with port *to beef and liberty* after every meal. Today, the only liberty they'll hope for is from the chamber pot.

Nick draws a hip flask from his pocket. 'I didn't.' He swigs. 'Nerves, only nerves.'

Delphine and Nick have spent hours every day this week reviewing the list of people they should save. They'd condemned a Bristol MP despite his advocacy to further worker's rights, because he was an even more vocal supporter of the slave trade. They questioned if having a plantation-owning relative could make someone guilty by association – not necessarily, because that would include Nick. Is abstaining from a vote on extending Catholic rights as bad as voting against them? Had they ever spoken against the state of relations in India? Or America? Were they a known abuser of power? Were they cruel or violent? Charity had helped with that one – plenty of MPs had been featured in her rebuff to Harris's annual prostitute review, which was published last week and has caused quite the stir in the newspapers. Some of the men named have committed the most heinous assaults on women.

But even after all this deliberation, the process has been draining.

It's impossible to know if they've made the right decisions.

But in the end they agreed on forty-five MPs, a dozen members of the Lords and thirty-seven members of the clergy.

They tried to lower the bar, but still couldn't find anyone else. 'While Delphine and I wait for the King's procession,' Nick continues, 'after Black Rod runs between the Houses—'

'I'll be making sure the waterman's docked the decoy ship in the right place,' Pearl cuts in.

The decoy ship – or *scapeboat*, as Nick's termed it – is the vessel they'll be pinning the explosion on. With England on the cusp of war with Spain over the Falklands, the army is already storing gunpowder in and around Parliament. It would surprise no one if a ship laden with powder (or barrels of something that *looked* like it) were on the Thames this morning.

And, if an unfortunate (non-existent) waterman were to drop his tobacco match into one of said barrels… And if Colin and Jules both happened to see the whole thing, because they were on Westminster Bridge at the time of the explosion, staging protests with the miners and abolitionists… That highly credible explanation would spread fast.

'And when you get out,' says Pearl, 'I'll be waiting for you both by the river. The getaway boat will be the—'

'Third on the right,' Delphine says, finishing the sentence in unison with Pearl. She glances at the watch – *thirty-nine minutes to go*.

'This is as far as I can take you,' Colin says from the driver's seat. 'They're not letting carriages go further. So either our barricades are still up, or they're trying to keep the square clean of horse shit before the King gets here.'

The Cornishman steps off the carriage and opens the passenger door with a flourish. 'Ladies, gentlemen and gemstone, your destination awaits.'

'Whatever has got you in such high spirits?' Pearl asks, rejecting Colin's hand as she jumps down to the pavement, landing unsteadily in her heels. She's still wearing her breeches under her cream cotton dress, but for her first task she needs to remain unnoticed.

'If all this goes to pot,' Colin continues, 'I reckon I'd make a good coachman.'

'I appreciate your confidence in us.' Delphine rolls her eyes but does accept the miner's hand. He guides her down to the freshly cleaned pavestones. They're almost as white as the sky, which is threatening to burst its snowy clouds above them. She shivers in the cold wind, which, thankfully, is blowing towards the river and not the town.

She's followed by Nick, who wanders a little down the road before Jules hops down from the footman's stand.

Colin swaps his coachman's hat and jacket for a threadbare waistcoat and battered tricorne before passing a similarly worn hat to Jules. Then he turns to Delphine, with a severe expression.

'Remember that while the fuse is attached to ye, your dress is highly flammable,' he says. Like she needed reminding. 'Good luck,' he adds.

'Have faith,' says Jules.

Delphine pulls them both into a hug. 'Thank you.'

'You're welcome. Now let's go,' Bela says, donning Colin's coach cap and sliding up to the driver's seat. Colin and Jules are joining the protestors now, and Bela is to wait with the carriage near Charing Cross. If things go well, she's to spread whispers encouraging a large spectrum of society to attend the clean-up effort. If things don't go well, she'll be aiding the surviving gang members to a swift getaway.

As the group makes to part ways, a terrible thought crosses Delphine's mind. This may be the last time she ever sees Pearl. She checks the pocket watch, decides they can spare fifteen seconds, and pulls Pearl closer.

'If I don't make it out,' she whispers, 'if this doesn't work...'

'It will work,' Pearl says.

'If it doesn't,' Delphine insists, 'stick to the plan. Get out of here. I want you to be safe. And I wanted to say—'

'I know,' Pearl smiles. 'I already know.'

But Pearl already knowing is not enough. In this last week, Delphine has been trying to give voice to her fears, to all her most frightening emotions. She still doesn't know quite how she feels about their night on the roof — whether it was the start of a different, new romance between them, or just a tender echo of the past. But she has had too many stolen goodbyes to let Pearl go without saying, 'I love you.'

Pearl flicks her cape out of the way to grab Delphine's hand. She squeezes. 'I love you too. And it's fine if you're feeling, you know. You've looked it for a while.'

Delphine squeezes back. 'Feeling what?'

'Powerful,' Pearl says. She bends down and kisses Delphine's wrist before letting it go. 'You look powerful.'

Delphine tilts her head and takes one second longer. One more second to see herself through Pearl's eyes, to push away the discomfort of hearing those words, to fight her natural desire to bat them away or dismiss them. For just one second Delphine allows herself to listen to Pearl's words and accept what she hears. *Powerful.*

Delphine agrees, 'We both do.'

Pearl disappears into the crowd. She takes half of Delphine's heart with her. Fortunately, Delphine retains all her strength.

Her heartbeat matches the ticking of the pocket watch — seventeen minutes to go before she lights the fuse.

They enter Westminster through the gardens. Pale irises have started to stick their heads up from the flower beds. But the grass has been trampled to mud by the visitors who are already inside.

They file into a room lit with oil sconces and swirling with pipe smoke. Nick points out a few notable individuals as they head deeper into the building.

'There's the First Admiral, Sir Charles Saunders,' he whispers in a breath so close to Delphine that he tickles her ear. 'He was why the English didn't starve to death at Abraham. Great tactician, sees the whole playing field before anyone else has set foot on it.'

The admiral waddles over. 'I didn't know we were bringing our Negroes!' he roars. 'I wish I'd brought mine to keep my coat. May I borrow yours? Promise I'll give her back.' He thumps Nick on the back as if they're old friends.

And Nick looks as though he's been slapped in the face with a wet fish.

'Unfortunately, Miss St Joseph has a full schedule.' Nick ushers them out of the room and away from the great tactician. 'Another time, Admiral!' he calls back, then whispers to Delphine, 'And that is why I said yes.'

Sixteen minutes left.

They continue through the inner door into the hum of Parliament. Excited chatter bounces off every wall. As they journey towards Nick's office, they turn onto a narrow corridor with stained glass windows, elegant arches and a tiled black and white floor. A few yards ahead, two scarlet uniformed yeomen emerge from one of the many doors to the cellars. They turn towards her, and the gold crowns embellished on their chests shine like a warning.

There's no way to avoid them as they walk past.

She bows her head, keeps her eyes down and focuses on the clip of her shoes against the tiles, hoping they don't question her presence like the first time she wandered Westminster's halls.

The shorter of the two, with cropped brown hair beneath a black cushioned cap, looks back twice as he passes them. Delphine stiffens and silently prays that the perfume Pearl gave her to mask the fuse's smell performs its trick. Even today, with everyone else dressed in their finery, she is the one who summons stares. The yeoman glances back, but thankfully, he does not stop.

'The cellar is the last place they search before the King's arrival,' she whispers to Nick. 'If they've not discovered the powder, they hopefully never will.'

Everything seems to be falling into place.

Delphine isn't sure whether to be worried or relieved.

As they head up the stairs to Nick's office, a chorus of trumpets and cheers rise — the King is arriving.

Delphine grips the banister, squinting to see the King's carriage through a mottled windowpane. There he is — though from how much his golden transport is shaking, she wagers he'd rather not be.

No one knows what ailment plagues the King, but in recent years his dismissive proclamations have far outnumbered his public appearances. Delphine has read each of his increasingly brief dismissals of the people's calls for change. Earlier this year, even the Lord Mayor decried His Majesty's reliance on self-serving advisors and his open displeasure towards his citizens.

He looks no bigger than a thimble from this distance, but she recognises the King's bright scarlet cloak as he stomps towards the Master of Robes.

With the King here, everything can be set in motion.

Twelve minutes to go.

Quickly, she and Nick rush inside his office. Delphine's hands go to her knees, and she hunches over while Nick loops his hands behind his head. 'If what we are doing wasn't so terrible, it would be exhilarating,' he says.

'It is terrible *and* exhilarating,' she agrees. 'Are you sure you want to do it?'

'More than sure,' Nick says.

With that, Delphine walks across the small office, pulls the desk out from the wall and clicks open the wooden panel. 'You should stay out here and keep watch while I lay the fuse. Can you hold up a candle behind me?'

After Nick has lit one of the candles, Delphine gets down on her hands and knees once more and squeezes into the darkened tunnel.

When her hand curls over the lip of the stairs, she stands up. It's only a few more paces and two corners to turn until she gets to the escape door. As she reaches the bottom, her shoe hits something hard — the first barrel of gunpowder. She traces her free hand over them: there are five in this area alone. She pictures the rest now, carefully dotted all the way around Westminster Palace.

The echo of the trumpets sounds again in the distance. Time is running out.

The watch ticks in her pocket, but it's too dark to see.

Delphine hoists her skirt up as she searches for the end of the fuse. In complete darkness, she must find it by touch, but if she rips it in the wrong place, she risks tearing the fuse in half and reducing their time to escape from ten minutes to five. It's another ten or twenty seconds until she finds the end, then she bites down on her petticoat and pulls and pulls to try and release it.

Bela had resewn the lining once they'd put the new fuse in. She's done the job too well. Delphine tears this way and that with her teeth, but it's no use. The fabric will not tear.

She curses herself for asking Pearl to shorten the fuse.

She stumbles over the steps, banging her knee on the barrels, and no matter how hard she tugs on the fabric, it still will not break.

Bela would not have done this on purpose, she tells herself. But it's infuriating all the same.

With no choices left and time falling away, Delphine runs back up the stairs and grabs the letter opener from Nick's desk.

'Everything well?' he asks, crouching under the table.

'Yes,' she says, prying the fuse free from its prison. 'I won't even ask what you're doing.'

She can't resist checking the watch.

Four minutes to go. Had she really been struggling so long in the dark?

There's no time to dwell. Once again, she descends and pulls the fuse from her dress, placing the end inside the farthest barrel. Then she carefully sets each of the other barrel tops ajar and unspools the fuse around them. Then she makes her way back towards the secret door, running the cotton thread as she goes. Her breath is heavy with stress and exertion, and even though there's very little chance someone will hear her rustling in the walls, worry still pricks at her.

It has been a tumultuous year for English politics, and a failed gunpowder plot is only a generation out of living memory. If there were ever a day for MPs to be suspicious, it would be today. With Vincent's ruling, the Falklands war brewing across the ocean, and the past twelve months' unrest in the North, it would be strange if they weren't on edge.

'It's done,' Delphine says when she's back in Nick's office. Taking a deep breath, she picks up the matchbox. With one last look at the clock she says, 'It's time.'

Then she shakes one match out of the box. And the office door swings open.

Chapter Forty-One

> I prefer liberty with danger than peace with slavery.
> —JEAN-JACQUES ROUSSEAU

Her muscles tighten as her body decides whether to freeze or flee from the boots that have appeared in the doorway. A red coat. White skin.

Things she has been taught to fear. Delphine wills her legs to stand firm, steady and strong as an oak. She smooths down her dress and looks directly at the intruder: he stands with his shoulders back, pug-topped cane in hand, a disdainful expression on his face.

Delphine glowers at the lord.

'Hello, *master*,' she spits, closing the distance between her and Lord Harvey in the cramped room. He returns her glare.

'I knew you would be here,' he says. 'You never learn.'

Her injured body aches in memory. She'll forever wear the scars he's given her, but Delphine will not let Lord Harvey cause her any more pain.

'It seems,' Delphine clucks her tongue, 'that neither do you.'

Below them, Westminster is silent, save for a loud knock of metal against a heavy door.

It's Black Rod, commencing the pomp and proceedings, but with this new challenge before her, Delphine suspects she may already be out of time.

'What are you doing here?' Nick says.

'My duty. The guards will be here any minute,' Lord Harvey snaps. He grips Nick by the lapel and spins him towards Delphine. In a frenzy, he says, 'Seize the Negress and I'll inform the Crown you had no part in her plans. She tricked you, used you, put you under her spell. There'll be shame, of course, but you can at least keep your life. Our legacy will endure.'

Once, Delphine may have believed Nick would betray her. But as she looks at him now, sees the defiance in his eyes, he'll be with her until the end. She's sure.

'You think I am concerned for our *legacy*, Uncle?' Nick twists his body, sending the lord's hand away. 'Maybe you and I thought the same once, but for me, now, there is much more at stake.'

Lord Harvey clenches his jaw. 'There is nothing that matters more.'

Parliament hums in excitement below as a thousand souls enter Westminster Hall.

Delphine retreats to the desk, puts down the matchbox, and slides her hand against the wood in search of the letter opener. She grips the handle tight.

Lord Harvey scowls. 'You have made a mockery of my family for the last time, girl. You think you're as clever as your mother, don't you, with your scheming and her witchcraft? You think I don't see what's been happening right under my nose? That I didn't then! I should have taken your life a decade ago, just to have seen the pain on your mother's face.'

Delphine swallows her shock. 'What?'

He smirks at her surprise. 'Before I present you to the King, let me tell you this. You know nothing of this world. Nothing of the hardships I have endured for my family. Of all I had planned for Vincent before he was set on ruining his life.'

He looks away from her, face drawn into a forlorn expression. 'I never wanted a plantation. I never wanted to sail the Atlantic to some inconsequential speck of sand. But *my* father left me no choice. He'd drunk and gambled away almost everything we had. So, it was up to me to gain back the money, power and influence our family had taken generations to build.' His hand balls into a fist.

Delphine remembers Hetty saying that each generation of Harveys is as cruel as the last.

'So I had no choice but to move away,' he continues. 'To seek a governorship somewhere across the sea where his stain couldn't reach. There was nothing good on that island. A god-forsaken cesspit of humidity and suffering. Nothing good but Abigail.'

Delphine feels sick. Was Vincent right in his letter? When she found the wooden bird in Lord Harvey's cabinet, she hadn't understood what it meant — and she's not sure she wants to now — but she'll never have this opportunity again. 'What of Vincent's mother?' *What of my own?*

'*My* Abigail,' the lord barks. Delphine shudders. 'Six years I had her, all of her, in ways you could not imagine.' His gaze darkens. 'She didn't love me, not at first, but then, ten years ago, she discovered she was with child. *Our* child. Something we had created together.'

A final fanfare trumpets, marking the royal procession to the Hall. 'Speak plainly, and speak quickly,' she says.

The seconds tick on.

'I'd just presented her with new accommodations beyond the waterfall. Somewhere more fitting to raise our son away from the rest of the plantation. I had business on another island and told her I'd be away for a few days. She promised to have moved in by my return. But when I got back, she was gone.' Harvey's voice catches, and he says through gritted teeth, 'The reed floor of her cabin was stained with her blood, and beside that stain were your mother's infernal tansy flowers.'

'Tansy?' Delphine gasps, mostly to herself. *Tansy is used as...*

'You think I wouldn't know what it was for?' Lord Harvey rages. 'That a shepherd wouldn't know the risks to his flock? Your mother murdered my child and killed the only woman I ever loved.'

Delphine catches Nick's distraught gaze. He too is clearly repulsed by this miserable tale of rape and consequence.

With her heart in her mouth, Delphine recalls the day she first met Vincent — a frightened boy who couldn't find his mother. Abigail had been missing for three days by then.

But if Delphine's mother *had* gone to see Abigail that first night, would it have been long enough for the flowers' effects to take hold?

To remove all traces of Lord Harvey from Abigail's body and for her to run? Abigail and Nneka knew using tansy to end a pregnancy is never safe – could it be that the fatal flower worked too well, claiming two lives instead of one? Delphine desperately tries to remember how her mother reacted to Abigail's disappearance: was she surprised, saddened or indifferent? But it's been almost a decade and the memory has faded.

Whatever happened, at least her mother had given Abigail a choice.

Let Lord Harvey call her a witch. For what Nneka did took great power.

'Vincent was all that was left of her. I would have claimed him for my own, had your murderess of a mother not taken him in. But then, I had a better idea.' Lord Harvey straightens. 'I let your mother keep him for a while, then I took you both to England.'

At this, Delphine's hands tremble on the table behind her. For ten years she believed she was taken to England as an afterthought, to serve her master's daughter. But this twists everything. To know that she was taken from her family not on a whim, but as an act of revenge.

Lord Harvey believes her mother took his child. So he resolved to take hers.

He let her mother love Vincent, let her teach Delphine everything she knew, let her instil in them the joy of little rebellions. Then he stole them both from her.

The malice of it is beyond imagining.

'I looked after her boy,' Lord Harvey says. 'And when we set our wager for his freedom, I intended to uphold it. He had the learning, he had the strength, and he was honest. All he needed was a little patience!' He throws his hands up in dismay. 'I would have freed him in the end. I just needed him to wait a little longer, to prove that he was loyal to *me*, and not to my coin. But he couldn't wait.'

He shifts his focus back to Delphine, casting her a look of pure disdain. 'I was never going to transport him! I only wanted to teach him a lesson. But you...' He curls his finger towards her. 'Just like your mother, you interfered and stole away my family. You are both to blame for everything that has happened.'

'You're a villain,' Nick spits.

'No,' Delphine says, 'he is the Devil.'

'And you are nothing.' Lord Harvey lunges for Delphine. Without thinking she swings the letter opener off the table, her heart thudding, and before she has time to realise what she's doing, Delphine plunges the blade into the lord's chest.

There's silence, save a hiss of air and the catch of metal between moving ribs.

Still, he does not see her. Still, he believes she is worth so little that when she ran away from him for a second time, he didn't bother pursuing her. Yet here Delphine stands, at the end of all his flawed contradictions. The daughter of a defiant heart, the sister of the boy he claimed to have saved, the woman in love with his errant child. Lord Harvey claims to have loved Abigail and cared for Vincent. But he does not know the difference between fear and love. He will take either, so long as he is in control.

'I was never nothing,' Delphine says as she stabs her master again. The motion is natural, without thought. She pushes the letter opener deeper this time, feeling no hint of regret. Then she pulls out the blade.

The lord croaks and gasps for Nicholas.

But his nephew steps out of the way.

They will never know the whole truth of Abigail's disappearance. They will never know what her child would have been to Lord Harvey, or to Delphine, Nick, Pearl, or Vincent. Men like Lord Harvey warp their past at will to satisfy their present vanities.

But she refuses to flatter those ever again.

Lord Harvey reaches for her, but all Delphine has to do is push him by the shoulders and the lord collapses, his hands trembling at his bloodied chest. The lord wheezes, and his face drains of colour as Delphine turns away, listening for the sound of Westminster below.

It's quiet. Everywhere is quiet.

She considers in these moments whether she should tell him that Pearl lives, that they are falling in love with each other. But there is justice and there is cruelty, and Delphine knows which she prefers.

Lord Harvey shudders out his final breath.

To dwell on the significance of his death is a waste of her time. She already has none to spare.

Shaking, she reaches for the matchbox.

'We can't, Delphine,' Nick says, his hand clutching his throat as if to hold in the nausea. 'He said guards are coming – they'll find us. There's not enough time.'

'There has to be,' she says, because she doesn't believe what the lord said. Vincent's death is not her fault. She cannot be blamed for Lord Harvey's actions. For the actions of the men who beat him to death. For the men who beat and enslave and murder and rape and kidnap and torture. *They* are to be blamed, and they must face the consequences. Just as she will face hers for the terrible thing she is about to do. 'If you're worried about the guards, lock the door.'

'They'll have a key!' Nick retorts.

'We just need time,' she says. Delphine crouches down before rolling the lord's heavy and lifeless form beneath the desk. As she does so, Delphine realises now there is no going back. 'Throw your cloak over the desk, then go.'

'Go?' Nick's eyes widen. 'What are you doing?'

The worst of her alternative plans is now the only one. 'We can still do this. But only if I cut the fuse. It'll leave us five minutes to get out and far enough away that we're not consumed as the building comes down.'

Nick's face is tinged green as he glances at the piles of law and philosophy books displaced by the corpse beneath his desk. He lays his cloak over them as Delphine asked – hiding his lost family member and all his former hopes for the future. Swallowing down what Delphine senses to be an unimaginable number of emotions, Nick says, 'Five minutes?'

'Five minutes.' Delphine nods, and with that, Nick rushes through the open panel into the escape tunnel. Delphine follows, bloody letter opener in hand, tracing the line of the fuse as she goes. It's too dark to tell how much of the fuse she's cutting off, so she gives it her best guess, her only guess — because what else can she do?

In the darkness, a rhyme plays in her head:

> Remember, remember the fifth of November;
> the gunpowder treason and plot.
> I know of no reason why the gunpowder treason should
> ever have been stopped.

Pushing open the matchbox, Delphine draws her weapon. She drags the match along the iron striker. A scratch, a hiss, then a flame. Within it, Delphine sees every rebellion, every moment that has led to this one.

She breathes in, and a man in Virginia sets a cotton field aflame. In Vermont, all a kitchen's pans have somehow been drilled with holes. In New York, six women lock up a building on fire, and burn their masters alive.

She breathes out.

In Barbados, a runaway takes his own life rather than face recapture. In Jamaica, a queen leads her maroons into the mountains, where they fight until they can call it their home. In Antigua, a mother kills her three children to save them from a life where no choice will be their own.

She breathes in.

In the jungles west of Bengal, five thousand villagers revolt to take back their land. On a cliffside of the Ivory Coast, a transportation cart's wheels are tossed into the ocean. Delphine's grandfather attempts to stop the departure of a slave ship, but is captured all the same.

She breathes out.

Outside Parliament there is shouting — thousands are crying for change.

And a woman with arms strong as roots strangles an enslaver with her chains.

In every corner of the Empire, a generation of women refuses to bring another into the world, in the hope that the next is born free.

She breathes in.

Rather than face transportation, Vincent changes the law. A free man is murdered, and London decides to march.

A vigil becomes a massacre, and Delphine makes a choice. And it will change *everything*.

She breathes out.

She breathes in.

Though she is frightened, Delphine smiles into the flame. Its warmth spreads up her hand, a comfort. She will never know all her fellow rebels' names. But she will make sure they are more than just a story.

They will be remembered.

Their sacrifice was more than enough.

The match crackles in her hand, the first spark of a secret revolution. One so small, so subversive, they never even noticed it.

Now, it is too late.

She breathes out.

And Delphine lights the fuse.

Epilogue

Custom House docks, West Ham
9th July 1773

Change comes quickly in a crisis.

The winter of 1770 was no exception.

Laws were passed, and money was found. Bodies were buried, and seats were filled by grieving brothers and widows. Time stretched in its suggestible curve, and denial became anger. Anger sought blame. And when no one could occupy the space left for the villain, blame shifted into acceptance. An accidental barge explosion claimed nearly twelve hundred lives, and left seventy-five injured.

It couldn't have been, became, *and yet it was.*

Now, three years later, soldiers swarm the docks, boarding ships with a single goal: quashing an American rebellion.

Crouched with Nick behind wooden crates and leather chests full of luggage, Delphine is preparing to join them.

'Oi, you pair,' a voice barks ahead, and Delphine stiffens at the sound.

'I fear our number's up,' Nick whispers, eyes dulled from a night of drinking. They both still have trouble sleeping, dreaming of gore and the lies they told at gravesides.

'It was worth a try,' Delphine mutters, grasping the handle of the trunk closest to her.

'Hold it!' the man demands, his voice carved by cliff tops and coarsened by coal mines. He lays a firm hand on Delphine's shoulder and says with an affronted glare, 'I know your game, and I'm having none of it.'

Nick laughs and straightens, holding his hands up. 'Where's that famed collier humour?' he teases. Half a dozen troops salute him as they tread by, their satchels bouncing against their scarlet uniforms. Though she no longer lives in fear of their attention, she is still unsettled by their presence.

'Lost somewhere between here and your arse, I'd say,' Colin says as he kneels and flicks open the trunk's brass latches. Delphine grins as he reveals the taxidermy ferret she and Nick had just hidden among his neatly folded clothes — a long-running joke about an ill-fated job.

'It weren't funny after the fifth time,' the Cornishman huffs, casting the stuffed creature into the Thames. Then, he turns to a chuckling Nick and says, 'You wipe that smirk off, Mister Foreign Secretary, or you'll be next in the river.'

'Not funny to you, maybe,' Jules chimes in, breaking away from his conversation with the dockmaster a few yards to their right. It's been a fortnight since he officially left his role at the Labourer's Protectorate, and even though he, Colin, Delphine and Bela are about to board a ship to America, it seems he's struggling to let the job go. Delphine understands that feeling.

The crew of the *Ann and Mary* lift the last of the crates, hauling them up the gangplank and onto the ship's deck. Delphine squints up at the helm and sees cropped blonde hair and brilliant white breeches glowing in the summer sun — Pearl is confirming orders with the vessel's new captain. After inheriting her father's property, she promptly relieved Captain Grey of his duties. Pearl laughs, and Delphine's heart tears. How can she miss someone she's not yet left behind?

Not everything they worked for has come to pass, but they're making progress. Last year, Parliament approved the ten-point Bill of Rights, ensuring fair compensation and labour conditions for all, including domestic, undocumented and indentured workers. The newly empowered women of Westminster and the trade guilds' creation of the Labourer's Protectorate played no small part, but it's also due to

Charity's list. Hers was the first of over three hundred documents published, outlining the abuse suffered by workers. Delphine only wishes Charity had been here to see the impact.

For someone who used to walk away from trouble, Charity certainly did the opposite. After rumours spread that she was behind the list's publication, Marion and a mob of London's brothel keepers sought revenge. The city was fast becoming unsafe for Delphine's friend, so Nick secured her a place as a teaching assistant at the Free Negro School in Philadelphia in the autumn of 1771.

'Captain says they're ready when you are,' Pearl calls from the top of the gangplank. Arms outstretched, she carefully places one foot in front of the other as she makes her way along the rickety wood. 'They've done a fine job furnishing your cabins,' Pearl says as she reaches them, though her eyes remain fixed on the flagstones. 'The journey should be more than comfortable now.'

The Bill of Rights changed a great many things, altering election and inheritance rules and abolishing excise taxes — much to the smugglers' elation. The American colony was content with their new representation in the Commons, but there was one new rule they could not abide: banning the sale and transportation of human beings. United against this latest strain of English oppression, the American Trading Charter was formed. Deals were offered, and reparations negotiated, but still the tensions spilled over into war.

And Delphine is sailing straight for it.

Once, she would have chosen the noose if it saved her from making this journey. Delphine swore she'd never see the Atlantic again.

But a single letter has compelled her to cross the ocean.

Nine words on torn parchment; postmarked three months ago with a Pennsylvania return address:

Delphine, come quick. Your mother's here. She needs you.

Since reading it, Delphine has imagined a thousand answers to a thousand questions. For now, the only one that brings comfort is knowing that her mother is alive. Whatever circumstances brought her to Charity, in the end, Delphine imagines Nneka could only be there for two reasons — freedom or family — because that is all there is.

All Delphine can hope for is that she's not too late, and that after so long apart they'll still recognise each other.

'I am taking the Captain's cabin,' Bela says, darting past them and the slack-jawed skipper.

'That's not how it works and you know it,' Pearl shouts after her, but Bela is already gone, disappearing into the belly of the ship. They've already said their goodbyes.

With freedom in reach, Jules has decided to return to Georgia and find his family — so of course Bela and Colin are going with him. But Pearl is staying here.

As a widow baroness, she has assumed her late husband's erstwhile position in the House of Lords, while Nick is in the cabinet as well as sitting in the House of Commons. If Pearl were to go with them, they'd lose their voice in that chamber. Then what would it all be worth?

The right choice is hardly ever the easiest one.

'See you later, *boss*,' Colin says, pulling Pearl into a great bear hug.

'Don't lose yourself,' Jules says, enveloping them both.

'We'll protect all that's been built here, don't worry,' Nick says, once the trio has broken away from each other. Then Colin and Jules head for the ship.

'Protect yourself too, Nick,' Delphine says, 'and be happy. You know the rules for happiness, don't you?'

Nick narrows his eyes. 'I do.'

'*Something to do, something to hope for and...*'

'*Someone to love*,' Nick finishes, arms folded. 'Immanuel Kant. But you know, although many scholars prefer Kant to the French philosophers, I—'

'Just *can't*,' they say in unison.

And from the bench overlooking the river in front of them comes a laugh. A light sound from a beautiful woman, ebony haired and olive skinned, hands clasped around a book. Her elderly chaperone is knitting beside her. The woman – whom Nick has been courting since spring – casts him a coquettish grin, and the Foreign Secretary blushes.

'Go on,' Delphine smiles, cocking her head towards the bench. 'Be. Happy.'

'Well, I...' Nick stammers, then gives Delphine a quick squeeze on the elbow. 'Farewell, my friend. Write soon.'

Then it is just two of them.

Delphine and Pearl. It has not always been easy these last three years, navigating a complex past, and a pressured present. But every day they remained together, and built something together: a choice. Pearl raises a hand to Delphine's cheek. It draws stares, but it doesn't matter. Delphine leans into it. With her eyes closed, she presses her lips to Pearl's wrist, tastes cinnamon, summer, hope.

'No one will ever know what happened here,' Pearl says; her words are a goodbye and a promise.

Letting go of Pearl for the final time, Delphine looks up at the ship and thinks of her brother. Of all they've achieved since his time on this vessel, and how different the world has become since his death. How all of this started with his mother's resistance, and now it continues with hers.

Reaching into her pocket, Delphine traces her fingers over Vincent's letter.

Hope is a very dangerous thing: it defies everything, beats unlikely odds.

Perhaps Pearl is right, and no one will ever know what they did.

But Delphine's reply is, 'Not yet.'

Acknowledgements

First of all, this is wild.

I always read the Author's Note and Acknowledgements section in books and the fact I have now written (and cried over), edited (and cried some more) and PUBLISHED (happy tears?) a novel with those things is... Well, it's just very, very cool.

During lockdown, the world felt like a big, scary mess and I didn't know how to process everything I was experiencing – so I started writing. A few months later a former colleague mentioned the HarperCollins Author & Design Academy. I applied, expecting a rejection (as is usually the way in publishing), but instead was met with my first yes. I likely wouldn't be writing these Acknowledgement without it. So, my very first thank you goes to Rose Sandy, who founded the Academy. You are an icon.

Thank you to everyone involved in the creation of the Academy and those helping it continue. Thanks to Anna Wilson for being such an inspiring tutor and to Pauline Gilbert for your insightful mentorship. Thank you to my writing cohort, who have encouraged me to persist with pages that I wanted to burn and for your love through every crisis of faith. May all your dreams come true, Mayowa Pamela Odunaiya, Zarah Alam, Sara di Fagandini, Felicia Drakes-Cunningham and Shana Byfield.

To all the HarperNorth team, especially to Genevieve Pegg, Taslima Khatun, Alice Murphy-Pyle, Megan Jones and Hilary Stein. Thank you for taking a chance on an unfinished manuscript from a first-time novelist and being such incredible champions. The work you do to diversify the publishing industry is vital, and I'm lucky to be published by such a game-changing imprint. From the wider HarperCollins team, thank you to HarperInsider and IndieThinking's El and Ben for working so hard to bring *Remember, Remember* to the attention of booksellers across the UK and to the team at Elevate for all your support. A big thanks to Micaela Alcaino for the gorgeous cover, to Idris Grey for sensitivity reading, to Theophina Gabriel for your copyedits, and to Morgan Dun-Campbell for proofreading.

To my editor, Daisy Watt, thank you for everything. For your incredible attention to detail, for your unwavering enthusiasm and vision for *Remember, Remember,* for every late-night response and every thoughtful note. You are an editor extraordinaire whose name should be lit up in Times Square in celebration of your skills and professionalism, but also because of your constant kindness, no matter how busy life gets.

To the team at Mushens Entertainment, thank you for seeing the potential in *Remember, Remember* and for the legendary summer parties! And a massive thank you to my agent, Rachel Neely, for every talk-Elle-down-from-the-ledge phone call and for putting your faith in my writing abilities. I'm very glad to hold the honour of being your first deal as an agent, and I can't wait to grow our careers together!

A special thanks to the teams at Mslexia for organising the 2021 Fiction Novel Award along with Marianne Tatepo, the late Dame Hilary Mantel and Jo Unwin for longlisting *Remember, Remember* when it was in its earliest form. To Molly, Megan, Bron, Hannah, L, Dhonielle, Sibyl, Germma, Amy, Dorothy and Gemma for being patient ears, early readers and good friends.

Historical fiction is nothing without research, so thank you to the many libraries that this novel was developed at. Libraries are sacred spaces that should be open and have growing collections forever more! Specifically, I'd like to thank the team at Birmingham Central Library for carting around the three (chunky) volumes of *The History of Parliament: the House of Commons, 1754-1790*. Being one of two people to have ever asked for them is a particular point of pride.

To the team at the London Library, especially Felicity Clark, thank you for including me in your magazine, for your ever-expanding online archive, for the book delivery service and… the lack of late fees. All things I will be forever thankful for. It is a privilege to have a membership and this book would truly not be as well-formed without it.

To the teams at Edinburgh Central Library and the National Library of Scotland, thank you for your offers of support, increasingly diverse book collections, distraction-free computers, and excellent soup. Thank you for your evening and Saturday opening hours, the inspiring exhibits, and the beautifully maintained spaces to write in.

Thank you to my nan, for your hugs and hot chocolates, and to my great-aunt Henrietta for your translations and pronunciations (and forgiving me for writing down a solely spoken language). To my mum and dad, I'm very sorry you spent so much money on those music and drama lessons over the years when you could've just bought a notebook and pen! Thank you for always encouraging my creativity. B and P, you are the best siblings in the universe, and I am so proud of the humans you are. Thank you for always being my co-stars/fellow directors/reviewers!

Thank you, J, for being such a wonderful partner. Thank you for listening to every word I wrote and telling me what you loved (and what you didn't). Thank you for every bunch of flowers and celebratory pizza, but most of all, thank you for carrying me through what has been the best and the most challenging period of my life. You deserve a hundred million LEGO Millennium Falcons.

Most importantly, thank you to every person who has witnessed or experienced injustice and found the courage to say no. This book would not have been possible without your bravery and resistance.

And finally, thank you, dear reader. Thanks for putting your faith in a debut author by choosing *Remember, Remember*, and whether you acquired this book at a well-loved chain, your local indie, from the library or through a friend, thank you for helping the bookish community to thrive.

You can follow Elle Machray on
TikTok and Instagram
@elle.andthebooks.

Harper North

Book Credits

would like to thank the following staff
and contributors for their involvement in making
this book a reality:

Micaela Alcaino
Fionnuala Barrett
Samuel Birkett
Peter Borcsok
Ciara Briggs
Sarah Burke
Alan Cracknell
Jonathan de Peyer
Anna Derkacz
Morgan Dun-Campbell
Tom Dunstan
Kate Elton
Sarah Emsley
Theophina Gabriel
Simon Gerratt
Monica Green
Idris Grey
Natassa Hadjinicolaou

Megan Jones
Jean-Marie Kelly
Taslima Khatun
Sammy Luton
Rachel McCarron
Molly McNevin
Ben McConnell
Petra Moll
Alice Murphy-Pyle
Adam Murray
Genevieve Pegg
Agnes Rigou
Florence Shepherd
Eleanor Slater
Hilary Stein
Emma Sullivan
Katrina Troy
Daisy Watt

For more unmissable reads,
sign up to the HarperNorth newsletter at
www.harpernorth.co.uk

or find us on Twitter at
@HarperNorthUK

Harper North